BEAUTIFUL SAVAGES

JULIE CAPULET

"Unique. Sexy. So much fun. Grabbed all my attention and refused to let go."

Five glamorous siblings. Five intertwined love stories. One shocking murder.

The five Savage siblings and heirs are American royalty. Ares the tycoon, Apollo the rock star, Athena the bestselling novelist, Eros the movie star and Artemis the supermodel have the world at their feet. But what few people know is that they'd trade all the money and fame for one thing.

What each of them wants is elusive: the same kind of true, real love their parents were famous for. But before the five of them will find their own happily-ever-afters—if they can get there at all—they'll leave a trail of broken hearts and obsessed fans along the way. And when someone turns up dead at the Wedding of the Year, it's not clear at first who the victim or killer is, or what the motive might turn out to be …

"If you loved the White Lotus you'll love this book. Just wow."

Note to readers

Most of my books are contemporary romances written in the first person narrative with dual POV. If you're arriving at this book because you've read my other books, please note:

This book is different to my other books!

Beautiful Savages is written in the third person narrative, it's longer than my dual POV romances and it contains five intertwined romances. It stars a fun cast of characters — and there's a murder mystery twist!

I hope you have as much fun reading it as I had writing it.

xoxo,
Julie

Dedication

Every summer, my family used to spend two weeks on Cape Cod. We always rented the same house, which was a quaint little saltbox only a few blocks from the beach. But the best part about that house was its overflowing bookshelves, which were crammed full of dog-eared paperback novels of every imaginable genre. It's where I discovered the fabulous old school blockbuster beach reads by authors like Jackie Collins, Sydney Sheldon and Jilly Cooper (honorable mention goes to the rollicking doorstoppers *Polo* and *Hollywood Wives*). It's also where I discovered the addictive, sweeping romances of Lisa Kleypas and Diana Gabaldon. And the contemporary blockbusters like *Bridget Jones's Diary* and *Big Little Lies*.

This book is my tribute to all the above. And it's dedicated to whoever it was who stocked those shelves.

Beautiful Savages

ARES SAVAGE

Heir to the Savage fortune and oldest sibling. CEO.
Ambitious to a fault.

APOLLO SAVAGE

Second-oldest Savage sibling. Rock star. Out of control.

ATHENA SAVAGE

Third Savage heir. Bestselling novelist and philanthropist.
Avoids the spotlight.

EROS SAVAGE

Fourth Savage heir. Movie star and cavalier social media
darling. Physically stunning.

ARTEMIS SAVAGE

Youngest Savage. Supermodel and artist.

JACK and CASSIE SAVAGE

Their rich, glamorous dead parents.

CEDRIK HUGO

British fashion photographer.

RAY GARMUSCH

Unattractive accountant.

TIFFANY CHAMBERLAIN

Gold-digging bitch from the Jersey Shore with several
secret identities.

BRUCE DAVIS

Sharkish head of the Savage legal team.

TAMAR TAKAHASHI

Control freak Editor-in-Chief of *City* magazine.

PERCY MERCY

Hot hipster film director. Last season's Oscar winner for
Best Director and Best Film.

MARLOWE MERCY

Drop-dead gorgeous up-and-coming starlet. Percy's sister.

SVETLANA EVANOVICHSKI

Percy's warhorse of a casting director.

ARLO ESTEVEZ

Artemis's promiscuous and flamboyant assistant. A public
relations genius.

COOPER SALAZAR

Acclaimed architect. A workaholic. Ridiculously sexy but completely unaware of it.

NICOLE WHITBY-SALAZAR

Cooper's cheating wife.

LEO PUCK

Winner of last season's Oscar for Best Actor, against the odds. Consensus around town is that his win was due purely to Percy's directorial talent.

LENORE QUATTRO

Eros's battle axe of an agent.

WYATT BOONE

Beautifully-built, rampantly-ambitious Texan billionaire with a heart and wallet of gold. A self-made man. Outrageously good in bed.

DAISY SULLIVAN

Irish-American girl-next-door. Saintly rehab nurse. A sweetheart.

ETIENNE DUMAS-MAGNUS

French-American designer and photographer. Considers France the pinnacle of sophistication and center of world.

JAZMIN DIAZ

Undocumented Cuban beauty. About to get deported.

VALENTINA DIAZ

Jazmin's equally-destitute 19-year-old sister.

ROSIE HARPER

Shy 7-year-old whose mother died of a drug overdose. Currently living in a homeless shelter.

DUDLEY HALFCOCK a.k.a. DUKE MANNING

Psychoanalyst graduate student.

CARL NELSON

Artemis's stalker.

J.T. LEE

Carl's techie cellmate.

NESTOR BEASLEY

Ares's perpetually-stoned neighbor.

LIAM SULLIVAN

Daisy's down-on-his-luck brother. Aspiring musician and boxer.

RUFUS ROSSI / BRUNO SUPERNOVA / GUS ERASMUS

Apollo's manager / Apollo's bass player / Apollo's drummer.

EARL WEATHERBY

Unscrupulous businessman on the verge of bankruptcy.

LENNY VANCE

An inexperienced security guard with, if one were to test it, a shockingly low IQ.

SENIOR DETECTIVE CLINT STATHAM

Jaded investigator.

NEWS UPDATES ONLINE @NewsUpdatesOnline
• 17m • BREAKING: Source: One of the Savage heirs has been involved in a HOMICIDE!! No word yet whether the Savage involved in the crime was the killer or the victim. Developing story. #exclusive #Savage #weddingoftheyear #SAVAGEMURDER

NEWS UPDATES ONLINE @NewsUpdatesOnline
• 11m • BREAKING: Confirmed: A Savage heir has been involved in a MURDER!! AT THE WEDDING OF THE YEAR!!! Still unclear which Savage it was or whether the heir/heiress was the murderer or the victim. A handgun was found at the scene and identified as the MURDER WEAPON! Developing story. #exclusive #Savage #weddingoftheyear #SAVAGEMURDER

NEWS UPDATES ONLINE @NewsUpdatesOnline
• 4m • BREAKING: Confirmed: THREE SHOTS WERE FIRED!! What we know: A Savage heir was involved in a homicide. Location: Wedding of the Year. What we don't know: which Savage it was or whether the heir/heiress was the KILLER or the VICTIM. Developing story. Updates soon. #exclusive #Savage #weddingoftheyear #SAVAVEMURDER

NEWS UPDATES ONLINE @NewsUpdatesOnline
• 1m • BREAKING: Source: A SAVAGE HAS BEEN SHOT!!! George and Amal are unhurt. Developing. Stay

tuned! #exclusive #Savage #SAVAGEMURDER #weddingoftheyear

Four
months
earlier

Prologue

SOUTHAMPTON, NEW YORK

CEDRIK HUGO WAS APOPLECTIC. Photographing beautiful people was his chosen profession and one he'd clawed his way up every conceivable rung of the brutal dog-eat-dog fashion photography ladder to achieve. You didn't reach the pinnacle of your game without being able to control a trying situation. And he had every intention of controlling *this* one, as uncooperative as his models might be.

He still had to pinch himself sometimes.

He was photographing arguably the five most glamorous people in the world, to be featured on the cover of *City*, the trendiest magazine in publication.

Cedrik congratulated himself on a daily basis and reminded himself now of his shitty beginnings as the youngest of eight in a squalid tenement row house in pre-trendy Hackney. He hadn't achieved his stellar success by kowtowing to a gaggle of overprivileged ego-maniacs like the Savage heirs.

Yet kowtow he must. Today, he would grovel, plead and beg on bended knee if he had to. Anything to get his million-dollar shot.

"Towards me, Athena," he crooned. "Give me approachability. Think less haughty and more *haute*."

Athena Savage glanced at Cedrik as though he was a

bug she would have enjoyed squashing under the heel of her diamond-encrusted Jimmy Choo.

Gently but firmly: "Apollo. Please. Take off the sunglasses. Show the world those to-die-for blue eyes."

Apollo made no move to take off his aviators. Instead, he flashed Cedrik—or more accurately, Cedrik's mousy assistant, Mira—a slow, cocky smile, causing her to giggle breathlessly. A vein in Cedrik's forehead visibly pulsated.

The magazine was scheduled to go to press in less than a week and the Savages simply weren't cooperating. They seemed more intent on sabotaging Cedrik's perfect cover than performing for him. Admittedly, *every* shot was very nearly perfect when it came to photographing the five Savage siblings, whose combined wealth exceeded the gross national product of several of the smaller European principalities. Possibly some of the bigger ones, too.

Cedrik didn't care. They would obey his direction if he had to wrestle them into place with his bare, small, sweaty hands. It was already being called the hottest cover of the year and damned if he wasn't going to nail this one. It would be the crowning glory of his already-illustrious career.

Agitatedly, he snapped his fingers at several of his underlings. One adjusted the drape of Athena's dress. Another fluttered around Eros, smoothing an errant curl into place. A third touched up Artemis's already-flawless lip gloss. Ares scowled as someone brushed a speck off his bespoke jacket.

Cedrik acrobatically maneuvered himself around the

grand porch of the Savages' Hamptons summer home, clicking maniacally.

It was one of five residences owned by the family, Cedrik knew. All of them had been inherited, he reminded himself. If he was going to earn *himself* a Hamptons "cottage"—which he fully intended on doing—he needed this shot to be fucking amazing.

The house was ridiculous. An enormous, rambling mansion full of generations' worth of heirloom furniture, first edition books and priceless paintings. Like the house itself, the furnishings were an eclectic mix of vintage charm and modern design. A Boca do Lobo sofa was flanked by mahogany end tables that had once belonged to the Queen. Several Picassos hung next to a Hirst, a Basquiat, a Kahlo, a Schnabel (overrated, in Cedrik's opinion) and a wonderfully lewd Haring, to name just a few. Knick-knacks and sculptures formerly owned by some Han dynasty emperor, Abraham Lincoln, Grace Kelly and Elvis sat side by side, quietly exuding a complex, bygone power that further illuminated the opulence of the Savages' luxurious lifestyle.

Damn them.

Cedrik was as in awe of the family as every other mere mortal. Secretly, he wanted to know them. Feverishly, he wished he *was* one of them. The Savages occupied that enviable stratosphere of society that kept the public riveted. And sold magazines like nobody's business.

The cover shot would be of the five Savage heirs, posing coolly on the stately patio of their dead grandmother's house, the Atlantic Ocean behind them a brilliant turquoise as though tinted specifically for the occasion.

At Cedrik's insistence, the five Savages wore white. He'd contacted all the top designers and invited them to send outfits custom-made for the shoot. Then he'd personally selected his favorites.

Ares was the oldest. Black-haired and regal, his white Armani suit was perfectly tailored to showcase his status as a billionaire businessman and one of the most eligible bachelors in the world. Ares had taken over as CEO of his father's companies. Hedge fund manager, internet entrepreneur, real estate mogul and Hollywood studio executive, all at the age of twenty-seven. He was deeply tanned, barefoot and had his hands in his pockets. His steel-gray eyes conveyed a look of arrogance and untouchable power.

Apollo, second-oldest, was the wild-child musician of the family. His albums were downloaded by the millions and his stadium shows sold out within hours. Now, he was seated astride his Ducati, wearing only a pair of off-white leather Balmain motorcycle pants (enhanced with divine ancient Greek-style suede detailing by the adorable Olivier Rousteing himself). His dark hair was lightly windblown. His chest and arms were gracefully muscular and artfully tattooed. His eyes, when he briefly slid his sunglasses up to pop a bottle of Moët—not his first of the day—matched the turquoise sea. Apollo's body was as buff and ideal as the classical god he was named for.

Then there was Athena. Privately, Cedrik thought she was the most exquisite of them all. Athena Savage was a bestselling novelist whose books, full of sex and fantasy, sold like hotcakes. They hit the sweet spot between literary credibility and mass-market gold. She got invited to all the events of the literati in-crowd, who marveled at her sales numbers and coveted her success. Her sideline *City* column, which chronicled some of the day-to-day highlights of her heiress lifestyle, had been moved to page three of the magazine due to its popularity.

Now, her hair spilled down her back in a river of expensively-enhanced honey-gold. A sequined goddess-style gown (Ralph, the genius) showed off her yoga-perfected body. Her slim, toned arms were decorated with curling, golden cuffs shaped like snakes with ruby eyes. Around her neck she wore one of the family heirlooms: a 40-carat diamond necklace that glinted in the summer sun.

She was ravishing.

The youngest of the brothers, Eros, was equally so. His Tom Ford soft-worked suede tennis shorts were tight, brief and left little to the imagination. It was clear that Eros Savage had lucked out in every conceivable category. Reclined on a chaise lounge, his long, lean body was spectacular. Eros had blond, cavalier curls and was one of the most physically beautiful human beings a person was ever likely to meet. On the strength of his name, connections and beauty alone, he got cast in a Steven Spielberg movie at the age of sixteen and was now one of the most bankable stars in Hollywood. He was mobbed wherever he went, from the red carpet events to the hot spots of the New York club scene.

He'd shown up late for the shoot—which had almost given Cedrik a coronary—arriving by helicopter from his cameo appearance in the latest Coen Brothers film, where he'd been paid six million dollars for three days of "work." Cedrik had seen all his films and personally felt Eros's acting was the tiniest bit amateur. Forgivable, perhaps, since the camera *loved* Eros Savage. Just like everyone else did.

Life was unfair, but Cedrik was determined to tip fate's scales in his own direction through sheer grit. Which was why he was going to get the perfect photograph or die trying.

Artemis Savage possessed a different kind of beauty. Raven-black hair and dark-rimmed green eyes gave her an edgy, aloof vibe. Her waifish frame made any outfit look good, especially one as perfectly tailored as the white Valentino silk jumpsuit she wore. Her angular shoulders were bare. Her hair was up, wound in a braid and styled like a crown.

It had been Cedrik's uncontestably brilliant idea, of course, to dress and style the Savages in Greek god and goddess revival regalia.

Artemis worked as a model and an artist. Her paintings, dubbed "pop culture meets reinvented Impressionism" had taken the art world by storm. Her insouciant glamour, her youth, her name, her effortless sense of style

—and now, the hype of this newest layer of fame, the one in which her paintings *of* celebrities *for* celebrities—had catapulted Artemis into the realm of the superstars. As if that wasn't enough, one of the city's hottest young designers, Luca Montevideo, had claimed her as his artistic muse and launched a line of streetwear that every man, woman and child was scrambling to get their hands on.

Everything these siblings touched turned to gold. It was being called "the Savage Effect."

Cedrik hyper-actively pirouetted around the porch, clicking madly.

It didn't hurt any of the Savages' careers that they were born famous. Luck, of course, had played a huge part in their success. The Savages were famous as much for their money as for their talent. This was more than obvious to Cedrik.

What Cedrik didn't know—few people did—was that each one of the Savages would have traded all the money and fame for one more hour with their dead parents.

They'd been born to this and were playing a role. Some days it was effortless. Others, it was a surprising kind of hell.

The siblings were selective with their publicity. This shoot, for *City*, a young magazine that one of the Savage companies owned—run at the highest level by Ares—was currently selling more copies per month than any other magazine publication in the world. The promised cover of the Chosen Five had already doubled those figures in pre-orders.

Cedrik tried again. "Apollo," he said, snapping his fingers at one of his dimwitted assistants. He would resort to groveling because there was literally nothing Cedrik Hugo wouldn't do to get this shot. Nothing. "Just one glimpse of those devil-blue eyes. Dazzle your fans. Give the girls and boys what they want. Here, Mira will take them off for you."

Mira, who'd recently accepted the marriage proposal of a pale-skinned real estate agent from Mineola, would have gladly tossed her minuscule diamond into the mirror-calm Atlantic if Apollo so much as winked at her. She blushed as she approached him. Tentatively, she removed Apollo's sunglasses and as soon as his azure gaze was unmasked, she swooned.

Cedrik shooed her away. He clicked several more frames and then, finally, allowed himself a rare smile. He could feel it in his bones: he'd done it. He had his cover.

The celebrations began. Apollo invited the magazine staff to come party with them. Apollo's groupies had to be blockaded by the long-suffering bodyguards, but that was nothing unusual. Apollo had been flocked by a harem since he was fourteen years old. Eros, too. And Ares, to a lesser extent, only because he was more intimidating than his brothers. It wasn't hard to figure out why. All three of them were stunning-looking men. A-list alphas with money and charisma to burn. Their pheromones were like crack to any woman who managed to get close enough.

Later, in a quieter moment once the larger party had

begun to wane, Cedrik lingered at several framed pictures displayed on a table near the grand piano. It was unmistakable: these were photos of the Savages' parents. In one, they were lounging on a Mediterranean beach, tanned, glowing, beyond glamorous. It was the kind of picture that made a photographer, like himself—and especially such a revered one—yearn. To get a shot like that one. Perfectly capturing the best of both its subjects. The father had been dark-haired, like Ares, Apollo and Artemis. The mother, blond and elegant, like Athena and Eros.

Killer DNA was what it was, mused Cedrik. He took another sip of his champagne and contemplated the ocean view. Maybe he'd try his luck with the blond goddess later. Or Eros, who definitely lived up to his name. You couldn't help but fall in love with him. Cedrik batted for both teams, so he was content to go with the flow. See how the evening played out.

It struck Cedrik that in all the photographs of the Savage parents, the mother, enchantingly golden, petite and green-eyed, wasn't smiling at the camera. In every picture, she was smiling at her handsome husband. Her shy adoration communicated pure happiness.

Even Cedrik, who was possibly the least romantic person on the planet—after his upbringing, which he preferred not to revisit, he simply didn't believe in it—this was proof: true love existed. Here it was, encapsulated beatifically in these timeless scenes.

Cedrik styled it in his shoots, or at least he tried to. He

would have stuck needles in his eyes before admitting it, but in his heart he knew he'd never quite hit the intensity he was going for. He blamed the vacant models who were infuriatingly difficult to direct. But here. *This* was the look he wanted to recreate on film. The magic of these sublime photographs.

He'd overheard people telling the story, of course. Of how the Savage parents had fallen madly in love at first sight and now their children were ruined for life. How could anyone follow in the footsteps of that kind of fairy-tale and not be disappointed by real life? No one would delude themselves into thinking it could happen again, not once … but five times.

It made him wonder idly about the Savage siblings. They often kept to themselves. They famously avoided long-term relationships. They worked like maniacs until their stars shone so brightly they were practically blinding. Cedrik, feeling unusually philosophical in the glittering late-afternoon sun, had a thought. Maybe these Savages imagined their bright stars would be visible all the way over there in the afterlife. Like a tribute. Maybe they hoped their parents would guide them from the great beyond, to their own versions of happiness of that magnitude.

And there, as though in answer, as he watched the five of them clink glasses against the backdrop of the sparkling water, it almost appeared that the rays of the sun *were* illuminating them, painting them in golden, star-crossed luck like the chosen ones they were. It was almost eerie, the strong sense that a force was at play that went beyond this moment in place and time.

But then, just as quickly as it had appeared, the sunlight faded under the haze of a passing cloud.

Cedrik chuckled to himself as a waiter approached him. He didn't usually have such deep thoughts. And he didn't intend to have any more of them, at least not tonight.

He tipped back his glass of champagne, grabbing another, and set out to find himself some action. Preferably with a Savage. He knew his odds were slim, but even that didn't dampen Cedrik's good mood. He'd nailed his cover, it was a glorious evening in the Hamptons and he was mellowly tipsy. If all else failed, he'd give the valet with the tight black pants who'd parked his Lexus rather more than a tip.

Senior Detective Statham: We'll be keeping the names of all individuals* involved in the incident confidential at this stage of the investigation. Let's begin with the shooting. When did you first hear the gunshots?

Individual 5 (~~Eros Savage~~ [redacted]): I thought it was fireworks at first. But then when people started screaming, we knew it was gunfire. Lady Baba—

SDS: Please refer to the list.

I5: Oh. Uh, [refers to list] … Individual 14 was rushed off-stage. People were panicking and screaming and running for cover. It was fucking mayhem.

1

———

Eros

SOUTHAMPTON, NEW YORK

Eros Savage zipped up his tennis shorts. Pleasantly high on endorphins after an almost (but not quite) offputtingly-expert blow job by two of the giggling photo shoot assistants, he reached for the bottle of Moët he'd wedged into a nearby sand dune and took a long sip. The sun was hanging, glowing just above the horizon, tinting the water, the girls and especially Eros's lean, bronzed body a rosy, idyllic gold.

He knew he should be counting his blessings. He had more luck than one human being was usually entitled to. And he *was* grateful. Being entirely irresistible to women did, of course, have its advantages. But he couldn't help himself. He didn't feel entirely happy. He wished that once—just once—he could find a woman that was more … on his wavelength. They literally drooled over him and jumped into bed at the click of his fingers. They ferociously fought over him like chimps fearing extinction. And as much as he enjoyed catfights, they weren't ideal at family gatherings. He'd finally relented by inviting them both into the dunes, where they'd proceeded to enthusiastically try to outdo each other.

He still felt dazed. A little drunk. As adrift as it was possible to feel when you were young, gorgeous and had spent the past three days getting paid six million bucks to pretend to be a hitman, spraying foam bullets all over four of the highest paid actors in Hollywood while meanwhile getting Jackson Pollocked with art-class red paint.

Poor you, asshole, Eros chided himself. *Life's tough.*

"Is it me or are there two shetting shuns over there?" slurred one of the girls.

"Oh my god, you are so *cute*," the one named Blair was saying, running her fingers over Eros's six pack. Or maybe it was the one named Neve. Eros couldn't remember and frankly didn't give a fuck either way.

"Not cute," corrected Neve. "*Hot.*" She was inebriated and was fingering Eros's glorious mop of disheveled hair.

He carefully extricated himself from the girls' clutches.

"Ladies, that was fun. Time to get back to the party."

"We can have our own party right here," whined Blair.

But Eros was already on his feet, heading up a dune. The girls scrambled after him.

"I read the interview you did for Gotham," Blair said,

linking her arm through his. "You were saying that you don't like relationships because they, like, make you feel smothered. I so respect that."

Eros looked down at the girl. His thoughts were elsewhere. He had an audition this week for a role he badly wanted. Percy Mercy was a new talent who'd directed three indie films over the space of eighteen months. Gritty, realistic and totally fresh, Percy's second film, Feral, had earned him the Mt. Everest trifecta of the industry: Oscar for best director, best film and best actor.

Through his connections, Eros had managed to get his hands on the script for Percy's next film, called Friction. It was pure genius. Eros's agent, the old Hollywood battle axe Lenore Quattro, had managed to score him an audition for the lead role but had told him there were "no guarantees."

What the hell?

He was *Eros Savage*. Of course there were guarantees.

The truth was, Eros hadn't auditioned in all the five years of his acting career. He didn't *need* to audition. People wanted him whether he could act or not.

It was true that his reviews weren't always glowing. A.O. Scott had called his acting "more robotic than Keanu Reeves." Which was hardly worth crying over, but it still irked him. He was in demand because of his looks, he knew that. Everyone knew that. Most of his reviews were almost humorously kind. *"Eros Savage, I'll forgive that performance if you'll marry me." "Eros Savage is so drop-dead gorgeous, you end up missing the plotline because you've spent the entire film fantasizing about going to bed with him. Wooden has never been sexier."* And so on. A gay film reviewer even coined the annoying tagline they were now captioning his film clips with: *Got wood?*

It was irritating.

It also didn't help that a couple of models he'd slept with (at the same time) had sold their story to Huffington Post. *"Yes, ladies—and gentlemen; we've heard he's not averse to a dash of experimentation—he's that good. It's huge, it's perpetually on call and it's the most outstanding O we've ever had! We want to have your babies, Eros Savage. Call us back, you sexy beast."* The girls, newly-minted models he'd met at a New York Fashion Week show—which he'd been paid a shitload to attend while wearing a paint-splattered fur coat—had since graced the cover of Vanity Fair (together, with the headline: *"We got wood!"*).

None of it interested him. He was so used to being talked about he barely noticed it anymore. The one thing he did notice was that they were talking about him for all the wrong reasons.

In his heart, Eros desperately wanted what every actor wants: an Oscar. In the grand scheme of things, life was good. He knew he should be thanking his glamorous dead parents and his goddamn lucky stars for all the breaks he'd been given. The problem was, it never felt like enough. He wanted to be known as more than a pretty face and a good fuck.

He wanted *validation.*

This, Percy Mercy could definitely provide. Percy was

one of those rare directing talents that *forced* good performances out of his actors. If Leo Puck could get Best Actor, then so could he. It was ludicrous. The guy was a total ham with a face only a mother could love. And he, Eros Savage, had to *audition*?

None of it made any sense.

He wanted that role.

Fine, he'd told Lenore. He'd audition his heart out. He'd wow those judges with his charm and his X-factor. Bring it on.

"Eros?"

One of the girls was talking to him. He'd forgotten about them. "Yeah?"

"So, as I was saying, I like totally understand where you're coming from. The last boyfriend I had was so jealous, he'd like go totally ape-shit every time I went out."

"That sucks." Eros yawned.

"I know! So I said no way, I'm not getting serious with anyone until I'm like at least nineteen. Who needs it."

"Right."

"So I was thinking maybe you and me could have like a non-relationship with absolutely *zero* strings attached. I mean, unless you like *wanted* strings. Which *I* wouldn't mind but I just thought, after reading that interview, that you might—"

"I'm not really doing a lot of dating right now," Eros said, his bottle-green eyes catching the glow of the setting sun.

He slid his arms from the girls' grasp, smiled gently,

and walked back into the house, leaving the girls, whose names were actually Barbara and Jolene, tearful, bereft and more than a little pissed off.

Senior Detective Statham: What do you see as the motive? Do you think there was one?

Individual 20 (~~Bruno Flynn a.k.a. Bruno Supernova~~ [redacted]): Oh, there were motives. Shitloads of the fuckers. All five of the Savages have pissed off dozens —probably *hundreds* of people. Everybody wants a piece and if they don't *get* a piece, then people feel like they've been snubbed. That's fame for you. Don't even get me started on all the jilted lovers.

2

———

𝓐res

MANHATTAN

ARES SAVAGE WAS in a foul mood. The chief financial officer of his largest investment company had just been caught with a prostitute who'd turned out to be underage. It didn't surprise Ares that Ray Garmusch had to pay women to have sex with him. He was about as attractive as a manatee in a bad suit. Ray was one of those people who never seemed to have relationships, friends or even family. He spent most of his time crunching numbers and as a result was extremely good at it. So good, in fact, that Ares had been talked into hiring him by several of his board members just over a year ago. Since then, company profits had increased by twelve and a half percent. Still, Ares was now severely regretting the decision.

It was late afternoon in August. From the plush air-conditioned cocoon of his limo, the city streets outside his tinted windows looked like they were melting in the shimmering heat. He didn't care. He rarely felt the urge to leave the mecca of New York City. He thrived on its energy and momentum. Ares's entire schedule revolved around his work so there wasn't much point leaving the island of Manhattan, aside from the occasional trip to L.A., where he co-owned a film studio. His brothers and sisters gave him a hard time about being such a workaholic but they were exactly the same. He didn't bother analyzing it but Ares knew why. They worked to forget.

Ares's limo pulled up outside the offices where his own overpaid brigade of lawyers was currently negotiating a deal that might—just—keep his colleague out of jail. He pushed through a small swarm of photographers and made his way inside, leaving his sunglasses on. *Shit.* The press were already onto the story.

Ares was ushered into a crowded conference room where the meeting was underway. Reluctantly sliding his sunglasses up, he saw Ray, a pack of lawyers and two men who could only have been detectives. They had the gray, seen-it-all pallor of people who had subsisted on coffee, nicotine and bad news for the past twenty years.

Ares sat in the only empty chair, unhappily. This was the last place on earth he wanted to be. He hadn't returned from the Hamptons until three a.m. this morning and was suffering from the worst hangover he'd had this decade. It had been worth it, though. It was the first time he and his siblings had all been together in over a year. Each one of their five homes was easily large enough to house the entire family, but the five Savages had unofficially claimed their own and spent most of their time in their chosen location. Ares lived in the three-story Park Avenue penthouse, Apollo in the Nashville mansion, Athena in the Hamptons cottage, Eros at the Malibu estate and Artemis at the Telluride ranch. And on the occasions when one of them had to travel for business or a getaway, they were always welcome wherever they chose to go.

Seeing them all together had been restorative in a way Ares hadn't expected. He hoped they could make a point of doing it more often.

"Mr. Savage, I'm Detective Hobbes, this is Detective Collins. I believe you know Mr. Garmusch and your lawyers. And this is Ms. Tiffany Chamberlain. She represents the underage defendant that was found tied to a bed at the Baccarat yesterday evening."

Tied to a bed? Hell. This day was getting worse by the second.

"In tears and begging to be set free," added Tiffany Chamberlain. She had dark hair that was pulled back into an austere-looking chignon. Aside from the ice-queen vibe, she was not an unattractive woman. Her low-cut black power suit revealed a lacy undergarment and a hint of bouncy cleavage. She crossed her legs, bringing attention to her toned calves and fuck-off stilettos. The steely look she gave Ray announced that she was planning to nail him to the wall and enjoy every minute of the process. As her glance slid to Ares, however, her aggression softened. She was admiring the cut of his Hugo Boss and, more specifically, the way it clung to his athletic body. "My client even refused to accept payment for her services. She was *that* upset."

She didn't look like a Tiffany, reflected Ares. More like an Alexa or a Veronica. She looked like the kind of woman who kept whips and leatherwear in her closet.

Damn it. His self-imposed workaholic lifestyle was taking its toll. He hadn't been laid in weeks. And now was the worst possible time to be feeling the effects of his monk-like existence.

"You can tell your client," said Ares, "that Mr. Garmusch's employment with Savage Enterprises is terminated, effective immediately." Ignoring Ray's pained grunt—a noise that again inspired comparisons to obese, flotational sea mammals—Ares continued. "I'm sure we can come up with a settlement she'll be happy with. We're hopeful we can expedite the process and do it quietly so she can get on with her life. I'm sure we'd all like to keep the publicity to a minimum."

"Two million dollars," said Tiffany Chamberlain, clicking one of her red talons against the glass surface of the table, suggestively, if he wasn't mistaken.

"Done," said Ares. "I'll have my lawyers here work through the particulars and we can all be on our way."

"Let's start the paperwork," said Bruce Davis, the shark who oversaw his legal team. Bruce could deal with the details. Ares needed air. His defenses were down. His hangover felt like a jackhammer had been implanted in his brain. Even worse, the way Tiffany Chamberlain was looking at him as she licked her full lips was hitting him hard and in a way that could soon become very awkward in a legal meeting.

Everyone murmured and began shuffling papers as Ares excused himself and stood up to leave. Thankfully, his exit from the meeting was relatively painless, as the lawyers' attention honed in on the documents like lions around a fresh kill. But as he was walking down the hallway toward the exterior door, he heard the clacking of high heels behind him. "Mr. Savage?"

Tiffany Chamberlain was following him.

Ares kept walking. She might have had a few womanly curves concealed under that tight outfit but she also had High Maintenance Bitch written all over her. Even so, as she placed her hand on his arm, he felt it all the way down to his cock, which had no problem with bitches.

"Could we discuss the particulars of the case over a cup of coffee?" she said, squeezing his bicep.

"We've already discussed the particulars. I'm paying your client two million dollars."

"Let me buy you a drink then, Ares. My team can wrap up the loose ends."

Tiffany Chamberlain was clearly a woman who, when she saw something she wanted, didn't hesitate to go after it. Ares couldn't have known that Tiffany Chamberlain had planned this encounter meticulously over the course of several months. Or that she'd generously paid the young "prostitute" to stage a very convincing—and incriminating—performance.

It might have been the hangover that clouded Ares's judgement. Or the way Tiffany Chamberlain had removed her hair clip and was now shaking out her long mane of deep auburn locks that hung almost to her waist. In a rare moment of weakness, he allowed her to link her arm through his and slide into his limo next to him. Before they'd even turned onto Lexington, she was straddling him, power suit discarded like a shed cobra skin (the stilettos stayed on), riding him ecstatically into a gilded sunset.

Senior Detective Statham: Did you have a physical relationship with Individual 2?

Individual 23 (~~Dawn-Marie Davidson a.k.a.~~ ~~Tiffany Chamberlain~~ [redacted]): [refers to list] Yes.

SDS: What happened?

I23: What *happened?* Where would you like me to start, Detective? With the phenomenally hot sex in the back of his limo?

SDS: Uh … sure.

I23: He didn't disappoint, let me put it that way.

3

Athena

MANHATTAN

AT 10 A.M. of the first Thursday of every month, Athena Savage had a standing appointment with the senior editorial team of *City*, which happened to include editor-in-chief Tamar Takahashi. Tamar was a walking cliché. Ninety-nine pounds of ball-breaking attitude, her wardrobe consisted almost entirely of animal-skin prints, as though she'd just flown in from an early morning big game hunt. She had no problem mixing leopard with cheetah, or zebra with giraffe, and always accessorized like it was literally going out of style. Today, as Athena walked into Tamar's palatial office with floor-to-ceiling views of the Empire State Building, she couldn't help but notice Tamar's *ensemble du jour* was a tiger wraparound cinched by a cow-print belt that, to Athena, seemed more Ben & Jerry's than Balenciaga. Thigh-high black boots and enough gold jewelry to plate the Taj Mahal completed the look.

"Darling," she greeted Athena, air-kissing her on both cheeks. Athena looked resplendent in a sea-green tunic and a pair of new-season blue silk Miu Miu heeled sandals Tamar happened to know weren't even available yet. All the Savages had naturally olive skin, and paired with Athena's flaxen hair and jewel-green eyes, she really was stunning. Tamar felt an unusual pang of envy. "Sit, sit."

Athena smiled at Tamar's executive editors, Selena Washington and Effie Fontaine.

The purpose of these meetings was to discuss ideas for Athena's column, which—although Athena was unaware of this detail—accounted for an increased readership of a ludicrous forty percent. They needed this column juicy and Tamar was fully up to the task.

Athena wasn't enjoying writing the column as much as she had at the beginning. The editors were always pushing for more and more intimate topics, like a minute-by-minute breakdown of an heiress's typical day or the top ten reasons why she'd dumped her last boyfriend. "Readers want to know," Tamar insisted. "They love you. They want to *be* you. Give them details."

Athena was, in actual fact, an intensely private person. She didn't want the world to know what she ate for breakfast. Or that she'd never actually had a satisfying "relationship" with any of the men she'd dated and at the advanced age of twenty-two was regrettably still a virgin.

Her social media presence was so brief that every time she posted a photo on Instagram, it would go instantly viral. *Rare glimpse of the heiress's cat!!!* Once when Athena had posted a photo of a serene water view from her yacht, speculation over the shade of her toenail polish had led to a new line with L'Oréal Paris for which Athena had been paid sixteen million dollars. Which she'd promptly donated to her own expanding charity foundation.

Like all the Savages, Athena was at heart a romantic. Foolishly, she'd been saving herself for The Real Thing. But she was getting tired of waiting for it.

Unbeknownst to the editors of *City*, Athena had made a decision that very morning. It was time to get real. She could save her fantasies for her books but when it came to actual men, she was going to have to lower her expectations or spend the rest of her life as a lonely recluse.

"So." Tamar was pacing. She was one of those people who could never sit still. Athena, who was the complete opposite and could sit for hours typing away on her laptop, reading a book or simply enjoying the color of the sky, always found this almost immediately annoying. "We've come up with the perfect idea for this month's column. You're going to love it!"

Last time Tamar had begun with that intro, she'd suggested Athena undergo the latest technique in colonic irrigation and chronicle how it affected her outlook on life. Athena had gracefully dodged that bullet but the glint in Tamar's eye today was particularly sadistic.

"There's a charity event," began Effie, on Tamar's signal. "It's an auction. For a weekend getaway."

"That sounds nice," said Athena, thinking she might have to donate her boat or house for the weekend. Easily done. She could go visit Artemis in Colorado for a few days. It would be nice to have a change of scenery. She'd been holed up in Southampton for three entire months, working day and night on her latest manuscript. She needed a break.

"It's like a date," said Selena.

"A date?" Athena was starting to guess where this was going and didn't like the sound of it.

"It's called the Matchmaker Charity Auction," explained Selena. "People bid for the date, and the winner gets to spend a weekend at an undisclosed exotic location with the celebrity they buy."

"Did you say ... *'buy'*?" asked Athena tentatively.

"All the hottest single stars have been nominated," said Effie. "Fans voted on their most-wanted celebrity and you were at the top of the list."

"No." Athena laughed lightly. "I would never do that."

"Our idea," continued Tamar, unfazed, "is that you spend the weekend with whatever eligible bachelor comes up with the highest bid, and you write about it in your column. Think of the *sales*, Athena. They might even rival this month's issue."

Athena's smile lingered. It was a ridiculous idea. "I'm sorry, but there's no way. I'm not for sale. Just say I'm unavailable and we can find a different topic for the column."

"*You* aren't for sale," Effie said. "Just your time. Two days."

"No one expects you to *sleep* with him, Athena," Selena generously pointed out. "You can sit back and sip your Mai Tais at whatever swanky resort he takes you to. There are very strict criteria about the bidders that can enter the competition. They need to fit certain financial requirements."

"In other words they need to be *filthy* bloody rich," giggled Effie, who'd been born and raised in Baltimore but ever since she'd found out through an Ancestry.com search that she was eight generations removed from British aristocracy, often broke into a train-wreck of some bastardized imitation of Kate Middleton. "Besides, it's only two days."

"Two days is long time." Four hours with the last loser she'd briefly dated had felt more like four lifetimes. Athena couldn't imagine being trapped on a remote island or in a faraway foreign city with some lecherous over-confident asshole for an entire weekend. "Get one of the Kardashians. I have a book deadline."

Selena looked at her guiltily. "Well, the thing is … we've already sort of accepted … on your behalf."

Athena couldn't believe what she was hearing. "Well, then you can *un*-accept on my behalf. Because I refuse to do it."

"All the proceeds go to a number of excellent charities." Tamar was circling like the tiger she was dressed as, easing into her carefully-planned rebuttal.

Tamar had predicted Athena's response. It wasn't like she could threaten to *fire* Athena; her family owned the magazine. And she certainly couldn't afford to bribe her. But she could appeal to Athena's overdeveloped sense of compassion. Tamar had worked with Athena long enough to know her few weaknesses. "Think of the children."

"What children?"

"The ones the charities support. Two days of your time could impact *hundreds* of lives." Athena wasn't easily manipulated but Tamar could sense her resolve wavering like a spider senses a fly has landed on its sticky web. "Maybe even thousands."

Athena considered this, and her unfairly green eyes blinked. Few people knew that Athena had donated half of her net worth to a major charity she had personally founded—under an alias. Like every other detail of her life, she preferred privacy. She wasn't donating for the publicity. She was donating because she was genuinely interested in doing good. "I'll give a million dollars each to three charities of your choice. That should more than cover the cost of my ... sale."

Tamar moved in for the kill. "There's one more thing. Four children get to meet you and your date at the end of the weekend. We've had thousands of letters from hopefuls, who would simply give *anything* to meet you. You could change someone's *life*, Athena. With very little effort on your part at all. It would be such a shame to let them all down."

Athena bit her lip. "Maybe I could just do that part of the weekend and skip the date."

"Then everyone would want to do that! If you pull out, next it'll be Bella and Kendall and then who? They'll all want the same treatment. It'll ruin the entire event!" Tamar twisted the knife and reached into her faux cheetah Hilde Palladino hold-all. "I have several letters here, hand-written by the children in one of the outreach programs …"

"Okay."

"Okay?" Tamar schooled her triumph.

"I'll do it," Athena said. "But after this, *I* get to pick the topics."

Senior Detective Statham: Do you own a handgun?

Individual 4 (~~Athena Savage~~ [redacted]): My brother bought me one because I live alone. I keep it locked in the drawer of my bedside table.

SDS: Have you ever fired it?

I4: No. I've never even unlocked the drawer. I carry pepper spray, which I've used only once.

SDS: Does the guest you brought to the wedding—I'll refer to him as Individual 11—does he own a gun?

I4: Yes. A revolver. He has a … holster, I guess you would call it, attached to his belt. To be honest, I was a little shocked the first time I saw it.

4
———

Eros

LOS ANGELES

Eros took a seat between two no-names, slouching into his ergonomically-incorrect plastic chair. Didn't these people know who he *was*? It was infuriating, having to wait his turn alongside amateurs who no doubt moonlighted as waiters or gigolos.

Mildly placated by the lingering glances of a casting pleb with an ass that rivaled JLo's, he entertained himself by winking at her and watching her blush as he considered Instagramming his own face. *Getting ready to audition for #Friction.* But then he thought better of it. What if the unthinkable happened and he didn't get the part? Documenting his own humiliation would only amplify it.

Percy Mercy was known for casting culturally diverse unknowns. He'd been lauded as a visionary in filmmaking who thrived on turning racial stereotypes on their head.

His films were full of fresh, multi-ethnic talent and plenty of it. In three humming but low-budget movies, Percy had already launched at least ten new careers.

The cute JLo doppelganger's iPad chirped. "Eros Savage."

She blushed again as Eros stood to his full 6'2" of chiseled glory and sauntered past her, letting himself in to the audition room. Inside, Percy Mercy was sitting behind a table, flanked by six po-faced casting directors.

Judgement Day had arrived.

Eros, who hadn't felt nervous so far this millennium, suddenly wished he'd fortified his courage with a shot or five of Grey Goose.

Percy Mercy was a hot, Black, built hipster whose bad-attitude genius gleamed out of his eyes like laser beams.

Percy leaned back in his chair and folded his muscular arms, staring at Eros like he was something the cat dragged in. Eros wasn't used to being harshly judged. He was used to being fawned over and adored. He felt his palms getting clammy.

It didn't help when Percy drawled in a voice that could have come from Samuel L. Jackson himself, "You better be Marlon fuckin' Brando, man. You've got a very persistent agent who I happen to owe a favor, otherwise you wouldn't be standing here. You better convince the hell out of me this wasn't a bad motherfuckin' idea."

"Yes, sir," said Eros, who'd never called anyone "sir" in his life.

"Do you need a script?" asked the woman to Percy's right, disdainfully. He recognized her as Svetlana Evanovichski, one of the most sought-after casting directors in town. She was old and ugly enough to be immune to Eros's charms. He knew from experience this was because she had no chance with him; it made women vengeful.

"No." He'd practiced the scene in his head for weeks. Memorized every line. Considered how much heart and soul to pour into every word, down to the syllable. "Thank you," he added, because if Svetlana had been able to shoot anything more deadly than metaphorical daggers out of her beady eyes, right now he'd be a bloody pulp on the floor. The entire panel was equally unimpressed, glaring stonily.

And so he began. Four minutes and twenty seconds of —he could only hope and pray—the best acting of his goddamn life.

By the time he was finished, Eros was sweating from the heat of the spotlights and the exertion of emoting his balls off. Luckily for him, the sheen only added to the golden glow of his tanned skin and catwalk-worthy features.

Percy's burly arms were still folded but his expression had changed to one of measured surprise. *Maybe there's more to this pretty-boy than surface good looks*, Eros imagined that look was saying.

Percy and Svetlana had a quick, murmured discussion. Then Svetlana turned to Eros. "We're going to get you to do one more scene. With the actor who will be playing Dazleen."

Eros had read somewhere that Percy cast his own sister in the role of Dazleen, the central character of the film. The plot was a series of intricately-woven threads that explored threesomes, racial divides, neighborhood gun fights and tense dinner parties, set here in Los Angeles. Percy himself had written the script, as he did for all his movies.

Eros turned when he heard the door open.

In walked the most striking girl Eros had ever seen. She was tall, with the kind of curves that could—and did—make grown men cry. She was pixie-cute, with cat-like eyes, full lips and flawless skin the color of butterscotch. Her eyes were a rich shade of dark, impossible green. Her hair was reminiscent of a 70s afro but each strand was a shiny little blond-tipped ringlet that stood out from her head as though she was a young, gorgeous version of Medusa.

Stunned by the vision of her, Eros felt like he *had* been changed. Not to stone but to a mess of hot, squirming infatuation.

"Eros Savage," drawled Svetlana, mildly entertained by Eros's reaction, "meet Marlowe Mercy."

Marlowe looked briefly at Eros—and was weirdly blasé about it, like she'd never heard of him, or hadn't seen him properly—holding up a piece of paper for them to read their lines from. "Let's make this quick. I've got a photo shoot in Venice at two."

She was sassy and disinterested. Nirvana in heels.

"I'll give you a ride," offered Eros, "I'm heading that way."

She stared at him like he *wasn't* Eros Savage, A-list actor, Calvin Klein underwear model, heir to unimaginable wealth and daily-trending social media superstar with more than eight hundred million Instagram followers. She stared at him like he was a mere mortal, an average Joe. A nobody. "I don't think so."

She was … *dismissing* him?

That had never happened to Eros before.

Weirdly, he found this intriguing. Did she not know who he *was*?

Marlowe started reading her lines, and her tone was one of boredom. She'd already landed the role, after all. From her own brother, who wouldn't care if she mouthed her lines backwards.

Eros was the one with everything to lose. And suddenly, what he had to lose expanded to include everything in this room.

He wanted this co-star. She was gorgeous, in a way that was making him feel hot and starstruck. And there was something kind of beguiling about the challenge. He so rarely had to work to get people's attention. The thrill of conquest dug into him in a way that was new, like she'd already succeeded in getting under his skin.

He wanted this director, with his smug, bad-ass charisma, to direct him straight to the Oscar podium.

He wanted this role.

So Eros acted his heart out for another six minutes and eighteen seconds, at which point Marlowe handed him the piece of paper, sashayed over to kiss her brother on the cheek, and walked out.

"We'll call your people if we're interested," said Svetlana. Then, into the microphone of her headpiece, "Next."

Senior Detective Statham: You left the scene expeditiously.

Individual 16 (~~George Mooney~~ [redacted]: I wanted to get my wife the hell out of there as quickly as possible. I hate weddings. I don't know why I keep getting invited to so many of them.

5

Artemis

TELLURIDE, COLORADO

ARTEMIS SAVAGE STOOD BACK to look at the painting she was working on. Her long hair was piled up in a messy bun, she wore no make-up and she was dressed in loose, paint-flecked vintage 501s and a worn t-shirt. It was a far cry from her usual high-fashion, jet-setting lifestyle and she couldn't have been more content.

Telluride, and more specifically this house, was her haven. Her favorite place on earth. Outside the massive windows, the late summer sun painted the landscape in a riotous blaze of greens, blues, purples and golds.

The colors, the lines and the feel of this place: these were her inspiration.

Her finished painting mirrored the trees and mountains beyond the glass almost identically. She didn't usually do landscapes, but today she was in a ridiculously good mood.

Mostly she was known for painting abstract, interpretive portraits, which she did of rich people and celebrities. Ever since she'd painted Saskia McCabe and Leo Puck at Leo's Oscars after-after-party at his Hollywood Hills mansion last year, people couldn't get enough. The painting had gone viral and spurred a bidding frenzy that made international news. Leo and Saskia were two of the trendiest stars in Hollywood and also an on-again, off-again couple who reunited during a particularly realistic sex scene in the movie Feral, which had earned Saskia a Best Female Supporting Actress nomination and Leo the coveted golden crown: Best Actor. Leo had ended up buying the painting himself—for two million dollars. Partly because the painting was an interestingly-lit and very flattering rendition of Leo.

Since then, requests for commissioned portraits had been pouring in. Everyone from Saudi Arabian sheiks to Ryan Gosling wanted to be immortalized by Artemis Savage's magic paintbrushes.

Her paintings sold well, but reviews were mixed. Maybe because Artemis was kind to her subjects, and painted the best of them. One pop culture magazine editor had called Artemis's work "the artistic voice of a generation," which Artemis found slightly cringe-worthy. So did the real critics.

Freya Bosworth was the founder of the revered and loftily-titled *Art That Matters* blog. Freya had art history degrees from Oxford, the Sorbonne and Stanford. She was an honorary curator of the Uffizi and MoMA and was an art editor-at-large for The New Yorker. In other words, she knew her shit. She was the reigning queen of art criticism whose opinion was taken as gospel.

Freya routinely and colorfully slammed Artemis's work. The last portrait Artemis had painted, of Miley Cyrus, Freya had called "Velveeta on canvas." About the portrait of Leo and Saskia, Freya had written, "I could bag my dog's deposits and sell them for two million dollars, but it doesn't mean they're actually worth that much." Which had seemed excessively harsh to Artemis. If someone's willing to pay two million dollars for something, then it's worth two million dollars, isn't it? Artemis noticed that she often used her platform to slam young female artists, as though she had a personal vendetta against them. She gushed over Reggie Slater and his derivative paint splatters, but then Reggie was handsome and regularly kissed Freya's ass at art events and across his social media platforms. Regardless, Artemis wasn't a fool. She knew her name and her connections had as much to do with her success—or much more—than her talent did.

There were worse problems to have, of course.

Artemis put her brush into one of the water-filled jars on her studio table. She might not be the real deal in the eyes of Freya Bosworth, but this was one of the best she'd ever done.

Artemis heard her phone ringing from the next room.

She walked along the raised glass bridge that separated her studio from the master bedroom.

God, how she adored this house. An architectural masterpiece, it was built almost entirely of stone, wood and glass. A sleek hybrid of ski lodge charm and a state-of-the-art modernism. Everything from the chef's kitchen to the swanky home theater to the third floor master bathroom was fitted with advanced, touch-screen technology. It was the newest of all the Savage homes. Her parents had spent only a few months in it after the building was finally completed, the winter before her father drowned.

Artemis's parents had known the architect, whose name was Cooper Salazar. It had been his very first job out of Cornell and he'd since gone on to become a young rock star of an architect. Once this house had been featured in several national magazines, Cooper Salazar was in hot demand. Montauk getaways to Big Sur cliff homes were being designed in the "Savage style." But none of them came close to capturing the magic of this house, not to Artemis.

Taking full advantage of its stunning setting, every expansive window was a living snapshot of jagged mountains, pristine rivers and idyllic fields with grazing horses. And each view changed by the hour as the sun highlighted silver trees or etched indigo shadows across the rocky hills.

It was paradise.

Artemis picked up the phone.

"Hi, Arlo." Arlo Estevez was her assistant, who, over the past two years had also become her closest friend. After a full month of traveling with Artemis for seven back-to-back photo shoots, he'd taken a couple of days off, in Denver.

"Hey, honey."

"I hope you don't have plans tonight," she said. "I'm about to make you an offer you can't refuse."

"I do have plans, actually. A hot date." Arlo was as flamingly gay as a person could get. He was lanky and gorgeous and possessed a mischievous charm that slayed any conquest he happened to blink his long, tinted lashes at. "With Maverick the dancer. Talk about *flexible*, oy. The boy has *skills*."

"Can you reschedule?"

Arlo laughed. "For you, anything. But at least tell me what the offer is."

"Backstage VIP passes at my brother's concert. At Mile High. He's sending a helicopter to pick us up."

"Holy fuck. Count me *in*, girlfriend. I'll tell Mav he's shit out of luck."

"Apollo's going to be staying with me for a few days. He needs a break." Artemis didn't mention that she was worried about Apollo. When she'd seen him in the Hamptons, he'd been completely out of control. Drinking as soon as he rolled out of bed, snorting enough coke to get an elephant high and popping pills like they were Skittles, Apollo spent the entire weekend either stoned out of his mind or the drunken life of the party.

The behavior wasn't anything particularly new. Apollo had been slowly spiraling closer to the brink for years. Two years, to be precise. Since that horrific night when he'd found their mother floating in the pool of the Hamptons house. More and more, he seemed to have a death wish of his own. He'd been in and out of rehab several times. He'd crashed cars and been arrested. He'd left behind him a string of ruined relationships and furious, heartbroken women a mile long. All of which enamored him to social media trends and the paparazzi to no end. Who didn't love a good scandal? And Apollo was always providing scandals.

It was becoming clear that Apollo was walking a fine line. He could pull off the bloodshot eyes—which only made the blue of his irises even more striking. And the bruise-like shadows under his eyes somehow laced his bad-boy appeal with a vulnerability that drove his fans wilder than ever.

But it was easy to see where he was headed. He was taking it too far. There was only so long a person could last on a diet of codeine, Xanax and Jack Daniels before things started to badly implode. Artemis hoped it was just the pressures of a world tour taking their toll. His "Hellfire" tour ended with a show in Denver tonight. Then he could take some much-needed time out. He could hike a few trails, ride the horses, swim in the river and generally clear his head. She could talk to him, and coax him into getting whatever kind of help he needed.

You better come, he'd texted her, and sent two tickets

with back stage passes. *Helicopter will pick you up at 5:30. See you at 7. We'll share a bottle of Moet before the show.*

Or, more accurately, thought Artemis bitterly, five bottles of Moët, half a bottle of Jack and enough pharmaceuticals to get Robert Downey, Jr. higher than he'd ever been.

"In that case," Arlo said, "let's think of some on-site assisting I can do this week. I'll stock the fridge. And some of those picture windows probably need polishing."

"He's a hundred percent hetero, Arlo. Don't overexcite yourself."

"I know," Arlo sighed. "But a boy can always dream."

"Maverick would never forgive you."

"Mav is hot, but he's definitely not the sharpest knife in the drawer. I overlook his flaws only because he can do the most amazing things with his—"

"*Arlo*. Please. Spare me the details."

"Oh, fine. I'm on my way over there now. Has that architect shown up yet?"

"What architect?"

"The one who built your house, sweetie. I told you he was coming to show some super-rich clients around, remember? You agreed to it."

"That's today?"

"At one o'clock. He'll be there any minute."

As though on cue, the security gate buzzed. "Oh, shit. He's here. I'm covered in paint."

"And no doubt looking as adorable as always. See you soon."

Artemis ended the call and opened the app on her phone that controlled all the settings in her house. Ares had beefed up the security systems to rival Fort Knox after a stalker had broken in about a year ago. Luckily, Artemis had been in Milan at the time. The police had taken the guy away and put a restraining order on him after he proposed to Artemis on camera during his arrest. The incident had upset her but she refused to let some crazed lunatic ruin her sense of well-being whenever she was at home. She could admit, though, that it was nice to know that the walls and gates surrounding her property were wired and impenetrable.

Her screen showed a shiny black Range Rover at the gate with tinted windows. One of the windows rolled down to reveal a dark-haired man wearing sunglasses. "Cooper Salazar," he said into the intercom.

Artemis knew his name, of course, and had idolized the man from afar for years. For his vision and for creating the most sublime spaces she could ever have imagined.

She buzzed the gate open, quickly changed out of her paint-spattered clothes, throwing on a white silk sundress her designer friend Luca had recently sent her, and went down to greet her guests.

When she opened the door, Cooper Salazar stood on the slate front step, flanked by a blond woman with a pinched, overly-Botoxed face and a man she could only have described as insufferably bland. But then, *any* man would have looked insufferably bland next to Cooper Salazar.

He was dazzling.

And very tan. His dark hair was well cut in efficient layers but a fraction too long. His eyes glinted with intense, grounded intelligence and a spark of humor.

Cooper Salazar held out his hand. "You must be Artemis."

Artemis shook his hand. His grip was strong. Warm. Oddly … reassuring. "Yes. Nice to meet you, Mr. Salazar."

"Please. Call me Cooper. This is Mr. and Mrs. Sloane. Your assistant said you'd be expecting us."

"Yes, come in." She could have invited them to help themselves, to view the house on their own, to take their time while she started another painting or cleaned up or got ready for her night out. But she didn't. "I'll show you around."

"That's very kind of you." Cooper smiled, holding her in his unwavering gaze. "You're definitely your father's daughter. The family resemblance is remarkable."

Artemis was horrified to feel her eyes sting as soon as he made the comment. She refused to let herself cry over such a benign, well-meaning remark, but Cooper noticed. His smile faded and he placed his hand on her shoulder. "I'm sorry," he said, "for your loss. Your parents were good friends. They took a chance on me when I was very young and they played a big part in launching my career. I'll always be indebted to them. You know, many of the ideas behind the design of this house were your father's. And your mother's."

"Really? I never knew that." She felt … needy. For information and for his time. He'd known her parents. He had stories to tell about them Artemis desperately craved to hear.

Artemis had no idea why she was reacting so strongly—and bizarrely—to Cooper Salazar. Maybe it was exhaustion after the insanely busy month she'd had. Or the fact that she missed her brothers and sister terribly and only realized how much after spending the weekend with them—the first in far too long. Despite the glamour of her job, she sometimes felt so intensely lonely, she felt overwhelmed by it, and didn't understand why. Actually, she knew exactly why. Artemis had been sixteen years old when her father died. They'd lost both their parents that day, although the loss of their mother had been a slow, agonizing one. Cassie Savage had checked out the exact minute she was told about her husband's death, never recovering from her grief.

But all that was water under the bridge at this point.

Even so, suddenly being confronted by this person—*this absurdly good-looking person*—who knew them in their heyday of hope and designing houses and having friends … it was unsettling.

"Your father was the one who discovered me, I guess you could say," Cooper said. "I'd won a competition with a drawing I did for my thesis. I hadn't even graduated yet. He saw the design—it had been published in a magazine

—and he contacted me. They'd just bought this ranch in Telluride, he said, and he loved my concept. But your mother wanted more glass and more light. It was all about the views, she said. I told them I could do whatever they wanted. They flew me out here and we spent three days working through all the details."

Artemis felt disoriented by this information. And its delivery. Cooper Salazar seemed to be practically glowing with the bond he had once shared with her beautiful, beloved dead parents.

As they walked through the house and Cooper explained the concepts behind each room to the Sloanes, who oohed and aahed at the beauty and grandeur of it all, Artemis listened to the deep, confident tones of Cooper's voice, how his eyes shone when he described his inspiration, which was often. His laugh was infectious, and genuine. As his fingers slid across the smooth wood of the minimalist hearth, she felt strangely wistful. His hands were tan and strong-looking. Capable and sure. There was something almost achingly appealing about them. She found herself wondering what their touch might … *feel* like.

She noticed it then: the faint circle around a particular finger, where the skin was paler, as though he'd very recently taken off a wedding ring.

Artemis had no idea what that meant, or why she was so curious to find out.

"It's certainly impressive, Cooper," said Mrs. Sloane, who was practically drooling over him despite the fact that her husband was following close behind her like an obedient, red-faced bulldog. "We'd like one exactly like this in Aspen. But double the size."

Senior Detective Statham: Is it true that you'd been shot at just days before the incident at the same location?

Individual 10 (~~Cooper Salazar~~ [redacted]): It was a case of mistaken identity.

SDS: In that instance, it was Individual 6 who fired the gun. Is that correct?

I10: [refers to list] Yes.

SDS: Had Individual 6 ever shot at you before?

I10: No. Of course not. I'm not in the habit of being shot at, Detective. It was my first time, believe it or not.

6

𝒜pollo

TELLURIDE

Apollo Savage opened his eyes. This took a colossal amount of effort—much more than his throbbing head could handle—and he closed them again, groaning a low oath.

With his eyes still closed, he attempted to pinpoint where exactly he was. On his tour bus? No, there was too much light, he could tell that even with his eyes closed. His bus had tinted, reflective windows specifically designed to keep sunlight and prying eyes decidedly out.

Had he been *run over* by his tour bus? Unlikely, although he couldn't rule it out.

The whole night was hazy as fuck. He could barely remember performing for the sold-out crowd of more than 75,000. Vague memories surfaced, of the screaming fans, lovingly belting out every word, almost drowning him out. Which was probably a good thing, since he'd basically been too drunk to sing. There'd been a breach through the beefy security guards in the front row. A scantily-clad girl, climbing onto the stage, had thrown herself at him. He'd been holding onto the microphone for support and had fallen over, with her on top of him. She'd kissed him and he'd let her, until the thugs dragged her away. He recalled the last note of the last song of his final encore, *Love Kills*. His most lucrative song ever. The crowd erupted and security had swarmed him and whisked him away before all hell could break loose.

That's right about the time when he must have blacked out.

He tried opening his eyes again. Slightly easier this time, until he could blurrily make out some blue sky and tree tops.

Oh, yeah. Telluride. The helicopter. Somehow they'd carried him into it and brought him here, then put him to bed. He could remember Artemis's worried little face.

He managed to roll over and slide his phone out of his back pocket.

It was dead, *damn it.*

He felt that small lurch of panic. *Did he bring his stash?* Or was it still on the bus back in Denver? He needed a hit, and pronto. He could already sense that awful wall of feeling that started to claw behind his brain whenever he went more than a few hours without something that would numb it and keep the wolves at bay.

He checked his pockets. Empty aside from two rolled-up hundred dollar bills. He unrolled one of them and licked the powdery residue off of it. Pathetic and possibly grossly cliché, but he didn't give a damn either way. The only thing he cared about in that moment was relief.

None came, and he crumpled the money in his fist.

There was a soft knock at the door. Artemis didn't wait for him to answer before opening it and walking quietly into the room. The sight of her held his attention. When had she become so willowy and put together? He still forgot sometimes that she was no longer a skinny little girl in her favorite purple unicorn t-shirt with two missing front teeth.

Artemis set a tray on the bedside table and sat down next to him. She was so slight her weight hardly made an impression. She brushed a strand of his hair out of his eyes. There was that same worried expression, but then it gave way to a tender smile. "I brought you some Tylenol. And water. And coffee."

"I'm going to need something a little stronger than that, darlin'." It was an endearment he'd picked up in Nashville. It sounded out of place, even to him, here in Telluride.

"Have some coffee first," Artemis suggested.

Apollo tried to sit up. The room swirled violently but that was par for the course. He gave it a minute and the horizon tilted a few times before settling more or less into place. Artemis put some pillows behind his back for him to lean into and, once she was sure he was upright, handed him the mug of creamy, sweet coffee.

"That was some show."

He couldn't tell if she meant this in a wow-your-success-is-so-deserved kind of way or a you're-a-mess-and-everyone-knows-it kind of way. He didn't want to think about it, or try to decipher it. He didn't want to think about anything. His brain was pounding like it was attempting to bust out of his skull. He needed a drink. To push the flood of feeling back down into its quiet corner where it belonged.

"What time is it?" His voice was husky from the excesses, of singing his guts out to a sold out stadium for three hours before collapsing into a drug-addled coma.

"Around seven."

No wonder he was feeling like a corpse that had been dug up. "Do we really need to be such early risers?"

"Seven at *night*, Apollo. Your concert was two days ago. You've been asleep for a while."

That explained why he was jonesing so fucking badly. He took a sip of his coffee, desperately hoping it was laced with something stronger. It wasn't.

Artemis wasn't going to judge him. She was as caring as a person could get, and she also knew about most of the army of demons that resided in his closet. He knew what she wanted of him, but he also knew *she* knew it was completely unrealistic. "I can't go cold turkey, honey." He could tell by her expression she understood. He loved her for that, but he also wasn't willing to compromise. He was too far gone to compromise.

"I know. At least eat something, Apollo. Okay? We can have some dinner, and sit outside, and we can talk."

"We can do all that." He wished he couldn't hear the distraction in his own voice. "What've you got?"

Artemis pulled a small silver flask out of her back pocket.

So that was how she was going to try to play this. Ration him. Try to keep him under control.

He could tell it wasn't full. A couple of shots at most. He wasn't proud of himself but he tipped it back and drank the whole thing. Artemis's eyes were round and sad and green as hell. But it helped. It fortified that fuzzy barrier that held back thoughts, memories, shards of his life that hurt too much to allow.

Apollo could play this game. Pretend it was enough for now. And he was, now that he thought about it, starving. His equilibrium at least partially restored, he jumped up and picked up his sister in a bear hug, twirling her around like he used to do when she was little. "This'll be fun. Two whole days of rest and relaxation, just you and me."

"You said a *week*, Apollo." Artemis squirmed away from him. "Stay for a week. Or longer."

"Can't. Got songs to write."

"Write them here. This is the perfect place to write."

"I'm supposed to be meeting up with a few people in New Orleans in a couple days. I'll see."

She could sense his distraction and its cause. "Let's eat before we make any plans."

Artemis would take that small reassurance from him for now, knowing that fighting him would only drive him away. They went downstairs to the pool area, where the cedar and glass folding doors had been left wide open to bring the outdoors in.

"I always forget how beautiful this place is," he said.

Apollo stripped down to his boxers and dove headfirst into the deep end, staying under just long enough to remind Artemis of the family curse.

But then Apollo's head popped up and he climbed out and wrapped a towel around his waist and sat next to her as she cooked up some steaks. He noticed a single bottle of champagne chilling in the small fridge of the outdoor kitchen and popped it, filling two glasses.

He clinked his glass against hers. "To my little sister." He took a huge swig. "The artistic voice of a generation."

"Don't," she chided, flipping the steaks.

"Seriously. I see your face everywhere. Your art. Your name. I didn't get much of a chance to talk to you last weekend. Tell me everything."

Neither of them mentioned the reason *why* he hadn't had a chance to talk to her. He'd been too out of it and was now pouring himself a second glass. She was determined to be patient and do her best to get through to him. Apollo would never listen to her if she tried to lecture him.

"I was at Leo Puck's. That's when the art took off."

"Never met him. But I've met Saskia." Artemis knew this probably meant Apollo had slept with Saskia. Most girls who met Apollo fell for him on the spot, and Apollo was never shy about living for the moment. And she could see, here and now—not that she'd ever wondered —why they loved him. Despite everything, he looked so … *exceptional* stretched out by the pool, relaxed and at ease. Everything about him was somehow larger than life. The glittering water lit his long body and jeweled his skin. His jet-black hair fell in silky ribbons across his forehead and his eyes were a blazing, startling shade of blue. He was waiting for her to continue and she could feel the depth of her brother's interest—and genuine kindness— like warmth. Like a sun that was too often obscured in clouds. *Don't destroy yourself,* she almost said. *It would be such a waste.*

"We stayed up all night," she said. "There were some blank canvases because Leo paints sometimes. We were all hanging out, swimming in his pool, which has this amazing view out over downtown, and everyone was buzzing because Leo had just won the Oscar. The whole night had this glow to it, it's hard to describe. I've painted at home for years but I never thought much of it. It was just something I did when I was alone. But that night, I started painting them. It all sort of took off after that."

"I'll say." He was smiling, watching her. "And the modeling? I saw you on the cover of *Vogue*, for Chrissakes, Artemie. That's huge." He hadn't called her that in a long time. They'd been close all those years ago, before Apollo unhinged. He was the brother she'd always gone to when she'd skinned a knee or fallen off her bike. But once their world shattered and Apollo disappeared, all that had changed.

"So's a sold out show at Mile High."

He gave her a humble smile that made Artemis's heart ache, for some reason. She so badly wanted to save him. To help him fix what was broken.

They ate the steaks and talked for a while but it wasn't long before Apollo was pouring the last of the champagne into their glasses. "Where do you keep the rest of this stuff?"

Artemis didn't usually drink, and she didn't fully understand Apollo's addiction. Surely he could go without for a few days, couldn't he? If she kept the house empty of booze, maybe he could overlook it and just stay clean for a few days because they were enjoying their time together. Before Artemis could gently break it to him, Arlo walked in.

"Hey, gang."

He'd been busy getting her schedule organized. They were leaving in a week for Paris, where Artemis had shoots for both Chanel and Givenchy. She would have willingly cancelled them both if Apollo would only agree to stay longer.

Apollo stood up. "I might take a walk down to the river and commune with Mother Nature for a while. It's been too long."

"Great idea." Artemis knew it: these few days would do him a world of good. Fresh air and mountain views could perform miracles, maybe even for Apollo.

Apollo picked up his jeans and walked off, disappearing through a squared cedar walkway that led toward the back of the house, in search of something—anything—to calm his nerves. Despite the few drinks he'd chugged, he was starting to feel very strung out indeed. It wasn't enough.

Checking his pockets again, he found two tiny pills.

He held them up. They were small and pink and he had no idea what they were. Probably nothing that would cure what ailed him.

He took them anyway.

Apollo ran his hand over the rough bark of a silver birch tree as he walked past it and had a moment of clarity. Maybe he *could* do it. Maybe a walk down to the river actually would clear his head. It wouldn't kill him to try it. He could swim in the icy-fresh water and dry himself in the warmth of the late summer sun. He could actually allow himself to feel something that wasn't pharmaceutically enhanced. For the first time in a long time, the thought didn't completely terrify him.

So he headed toward the trail, to follow the path through the trees and down to the river's edge.

But then he saw Arlo's car. A rental hatchback with the back door wide open. He'd done a food run. In the back of Arlo's car, along with ten or so bags of groceries, were two bottles of Bollinger. *Now there's an even better option.* Grabbing both bottles, Apollo continued down the path. He popped one of the corks and took a long sip. It took him about ten minutes to reach the giant slabs of rock that tilted like giant prehistoric steps looking over the serene view of the crystal-clear river.

Finally. He was completely alone. When was the last time he didn't have his manager or groupies or bodyguards hovering around him 24/7? He'd almost forgotten what this felt like. Peace. Privacy.

The chirping of the birds. The sun, a glowing orb hanging low in the sky, tinting the clouds across the horizon a surreal-looking orange that only grew in intensity with each passing minute.

This was good. Everything was going to be okay.

The rays of the sun shone down like they were reaching for him. He thought idly about his parents. His father. A shining star. A charismatic genius. A Harvard man, who wore his honor and honesty like a badge. Apollo didn't think the guy had ever had a single fault. It had been a hard example to live up to. Ares had taken up that mantle, anyway. Thank God.

Not that *he* could have, even if he'd wanted to. Apollo had always felt like the disappointment in the family. The second son. The lesser son. He couldn't have built a business to save his goddamn life. He didn't have a corporate bone in his body.

A musician? his father had questioned, when Apollo got his first recording contract, a dream he'd pursued in secret until he could finally announce that—yes—he'd landed a major deal because he was good at it.

It's a hard thing to sustain, Daddy-o had predictably criticized. *No job security. No guarantees.*

I don't need guarantees, Apollo had wanted to say. We come from old Pennsylvania steel money, for fuck's sake, which you've managed to triple, at the very least. Why does job security even matter? Can't you just be proud of *this*? Of the four million bucks I made last month touring the world and playing back-to-back sold out shows to stadiums full of screaming fans? Not good enough? Dang, and here I was thinking I was doing something right for a change.

They'd been difficult conversations, and ones Apollo would prefer to forget.

Luckily, the champagne was helping him do exactly that.

The sky was wide open, swirling with new possibilities and psychedelic magnificence. Apollo pushed those old thoughts aside and allowed the alcohol to numb his pain and inadequacies. Maybe those little pills had some kick to them after all. He felt better. Close to invincible, in fact … and it was the best feeling he'd had in a long time.

He tipped back the last of the bottle. "Cheers to you, universe. Mom, Dad, sorry I couldn't live up, but, hey, every family needs its black sheep. Luckily you've got four perfect children and only one fuck-up."

Shit. He'd finished the second bottle. The sun was dipping just below the tree line and a light rain was starting to fall.

His darker thoughts were back in their cage, mostly. Still, it would've been nice to have one more bottle.

He stumbled back up the path. By the time he reached Arlo's car, the light rain had stopped. Arlo's car was empty now, the hatchback closed.

Apollo let himself into the four-car garage.

Damn. Not what he needed right now: reminders, in the form of a few of his father's cars. There was his father's convertible Ferrari 458 Italia, the one he'd bought just so he could drive with their mother along the winding Colorado roads. They used to love doing that. She used to wear a scarf over her hair so it wouldn't get windblown, like a movie star.

The old yellow Jeep, Artemis's ride.

Three snowmobiles.

And his father's custom Harley XL 1200, which gave him an idea.

Apollo straddled the motorcycle's seat and curled his fingers around the handlebars. This thing was a goddamn work of art. Daddy had good taste, of course. Yet another thing he was perfect at.

It took some coaxing, but after a few tries, the Harley revved to smoky, gutsy life.

Apollo eased it out of the garage, flicking on the headlights.

He'd just go find a liquor store or a bar and stock up. He'd be back before Artemis even noticed he was gone.

The Harley drove like a dream. The roads were shiny with rain and moonlight.

It almost felt like he was flying.

Maybe he was.

Even when the road disappeared from under him and the tops of the trees seemed to rise up from below, he couldn't summon the panic. All he could comprehend was that everything was just so unbearably beautiful.

Senior Detective Statham: What was your role at the wedding?

Individual 12 (~~Arlo Estevez~~ [redacted]): I was the wedding planner. I couldn't *believe* we were able to get Baba—

SDS: Please refer to the list.

I12: Oh. Right. [refers to list] So, I couldn't *believe* we were able to get Individual 14 at such short notice. I mean, at first they didn't want a big wedding because it was so last minute but I talked, uh … Individual 6 onto making an event out of it and I told her I'd handle every-thing. So she agreed to let me put together something small, which sort of gained momentum, as these things tend to do. And Individual 14 was *a-may-zing*, of course. Until the shooting started, that is. She didn't even get to finish her set—which was a tragedy in itself. By the time I finally got her calmed down, the helicopters had already left. It was *so* awful. We didn't even get to release the lanterns and butterflies.

7

———

𝒜res

MANHATTAN

"Come back to bed, love."

It wasn't just the pinched tone of her delivery but the sting of that last word that irked Ares most of all. *"Love,"* my ass, he thought. *If this is love then someone hand me a goddamn loaded gun, so I can put myself out of my misery. My Smith and Wesson 500 is right there in the top drawer. Give it here.*

Ares still wasn't sure exactly why he hadn't kicked Tiffany out of his bed. They'd been "together," if you could call it that, for three weeks. The entire affair hadn't brought him even a milli-second of real happiness. Maybe he wasn't capable of happiness. The thought had crossed his mind more than once. Maybe he was a cold-hearted son of a bitch who thrived only on power and angst. Maybe he'd even been a little bit lonely—something he would never have admitted to Tiffany. The sex was okay, if not mind-blowing. Then again, when "okay" was the best adjective you could think of to describe sex, it basically meant that the sex was pretty damn unspectacular. It was tolerable to have her around mainly because she was so very *into* him, even if he couldn't quite return the favor.

Ares knew in his heart that the real reason Tiffany was still in his apartment had more to do with that first time they'd done it in the limo than anything else. The whole thing had been so completely unexpected, he hadn't even had time to put on a condom. He wanted to stick around long enough to make sure she wasn't …

Goddamn it.

He really hoped she wasn't. He'd been extra careful ever since then, which at times had been challenging because Tiffany seemed hellbent on repeating her free-spirited performance. But the possibility rattled at the back of his mind, like a ball and chain was already forming.

He hadn't told Tiffany he'd gone to get himself checked out. Ares was a type-A control freak. He'd never had unprotected sex before in his life. The thought of catching something or knocking someone up *accidentally*, especially someone he knew for certain he did *not* want to be linked with for the rest of his life, went against the grain of his entire personality.

The results of the tests came back clear. Once he knew for sure about the second concern, he would—

politely and with as much sensitivity as he was capable of
—tell her it was over.

It made him uneasy the way she'd practically moved
in with him and was already throwing the L word around
like they were in a committed relationship. The only thing
Ares was committed to was seeing out the rest of the
week, dealing with the situation at hand and spending as
much time as possible at work. "I have a meeting."

"Cancel it."

"I can't cancel it. It's with the managing director of
MGM."

Tiffany rose from the bed, clad in a see-through
negligee and nothing else. She sauntered over to him
suggestively as he tied his tie. He barely looked up except
to check his tie in the mirror.

"I guess that means the managing director of MGM
is more important than little old me?" The sing-song
playfulness of her comment wasn't playful at all. It was
petulant. Catty and mean. But then, he could only blame
himself for that. He'd known she was a bitch from the
first minute he met her. Yet still, somehow, they'd ended
up here.

You're an idiot who deserves whatever he gets.

Ares sighed. "No, it means we have more than a
hundred million dollars invested in collaborating on a film
with them, and I don't really want to fuck that up."

Tiffany scowled. At first he'd found her attractive, in a
severe sort of way. Now, at best, he could say she had …

an energy to her that was … feisty. An energy that was going to get *exceedingly* fucking feisty when he told her he wanted her out of his apartment and out of his life. She'd even moved some clothes into his closet, he'd noticed. And helped herself to a shelf in the bathroom and one of his drawers.

By now she knew her tactics of trying to manipulate Ares grated on him. He was too smart for that. Too impenetrable. So she changed tack. She licked her lips and slid her fingers across his chest. She smiled but it looked staged. "I want you," she whispered.

Ares felt nothing. "Maybe we can do a late dinner. I'll call you."

"'*Maybe*'?"

"Don't you have work?" She was a lawyer, for fuck's sake. Didn't she have cases to argue and people to prosecute? She seemed to spend more and more of her time in his goddamn apartment.

Ares had no way of knowing that Tiffany had neglected to tell him she wasn't actually a lawyer. Not anymore. She had been once, but she'd been disbarred for misconduct and fraud. That was before she'd changed her name. Now, she considered herself more of an actor. She was exceptionally skilled at impersonating a lawyer and creating admirably authentic-looking legal documents. "I'm working from home today." Her voice became softer. "And there's this thing I've been meaning to … well, to talk to you about."

Ares froze. This time, she got his full attention. "What thing?"

Just like that, the playful petulance was gone. Now, her tone was one of vulnerability, like she was struggling to come to terms with the lost innocence he'd cruelly stolen from her. She brushed away an actual tear. "I'm … well, I'm late."

Ares's blood went cold. His life literally flashed before his eyes. But he remained calm. "How late?"

"Only a few days." She exhaled a small sob, another tear painting a shiny line down her flushed cheek. "I wanted to spend the day with you, Ares. This is such a big deal and I *need* you but you never have time for me."

His phone rang. Ares pulled it out of his pocket, fully expecting it to be Harry Spears, wondering why he wasn't on time for their eight o'clock meeting downstairs. But the screen read *Artemis*. Some sixth sense jolted him with alarm.

"Artemis? Are you all right?"

His face looked stricken as he listened.

"Oh, that's just great," huffed Tiffany, placing her fisted hands on her hips. "Excuse me for thinking we were talking about something *important*. But I guess nothing to do with me or *our baby* is important enough for you."

Ares backed away from Tiffany, holding up his hand to silence her as he listened to Artemis.

"Jesus," he said. "Is he alive?"

Tiffany could barely hear Artemis's voice through the phone. She sounded like she was crying.

"I'm on my way," said Ares to Artemis. To Tiffany: "Apollo's been in an accident. I have to go. I'll call you when I can." Then he walked out, leaving Tiffany, her scowl and her hidden pregnancy test—which very clearly indicated negative—behind.

Senior Detective Statham: So let me get this straight. You *pretended* to be pregnant.

Individual 23 (~~Dawn-Marie Davidson aka Tiffany Chamberlain~~ [redacted]: That's not what's being investigated here, Detective.

SDS: Let me remind you that you're under oath and we're conducting a murder investigation, for which you are a possible suspect. Answer the question, please.

I23: I had my reasons.

SDS: Is that a yes?

I23: No, it's not a yes. Women aren't machines, Detective. Innocent mistakes sometimes get made. [Noted: polygraph sensors indicated that this response had a 98.4% probability of being untruthful.]

8

Athena

DENVER

ATHENA SAT by Apollo's bed, quietly typing on her laptop by the window of his private room. Athena, Ares, Eros and Artemis were all staying at a hotel in Denver, close to the hospital where Apollo was getting treatment. For the past five days, they'd been holed up, keeping vigil. Ares cancelled meetings, Artemis delayed work trips, Athena worked in stolen moments, and Eros, who was between movies, paced.

Miraculously, despite having driven his motorcycle off a thirty-foot cliff, Apollo's injuries weren't life-threatening. He had three broken ribs, a concussion, a broken arm and a variety of bruises and scrapes. Most critical was a severe case of withdrawal from the drugs and alcohol he'd been imbibing like a lunatic day and night for two solid years.

The doctors were keeping him sedated. When he'd briefly woken up, he'd become so agitated the doctors feared he would injure himself further. So they kept him doped up to the eyeballs—a medically-assisted detox strategy that was clearly necessary—until he could begin to heal and recover.

The past few days had been terrible, and the four of them had bonded in new ways. Apollo's near-death experience had had all the effect of an intense group therapy session. They'd spent most of the time sleepless, talking through the long nights and, in the process, learning details of each other's lives that none of them had ever shared before.

Apollo's doctors had announced that, after performing every test modern medicine offered, they expected him to make a full recovery. He might even be better off for the induced two weeks of rest and sobriety. As soon as he was stable, he would be transferred to a private hospital in the Hamptons that was located next to one of the most exclusive rehab facilities in the country.

Artemis walked in, carrying a cardboard tray with four cups of coffee she'd bought at their new favorite café on the corner. Ares was sleeping in an armchair. Eros was checking his phone for messages. Again.

They'd all noticed this near-manic obsession. Artemis couldn't resist. "Any news yet from your agent?"

Eros had told them he'd auditioned for Percy Mercy's new film. But he hadn't told them about the other call he was hoping for. "I met a girl at the audition. Marlowe

Mercy. I was hoping she might get in touch, but so far: crickets."

Athena wore no makeup and her hair was tied back in a simple ponytail. She looked even more stunning than usual. Eros wondered why his sister never seemed to have any romantic relationships. "I'm sure I've heard that name somewhere recently," she said.

Eros glanced at his phone again, tempted to throw it out the window. He hadn't even checked his Instagram since Apollo's accident. Unprecedented. And strangely … nice. To take a break for a few days from the scrutiny, the likes, the followers. He'd never thought about it before, but it occurred to him how invasive it all was. The attention-seeking. The *look at me, I have fans, I'm popular, people love me.* An extreme form of self-validation that, come to think of it, meant very little. It was a nice change of pace to just disappear for a while. For the first time in a long time, Eros felt steady and self-possessed. What mattered most to him was the people in this room and it was grounding to spend time with them, even in such stressful circumstances.

"Now that I think about it," Athena said, "I'm sure she was on the list of that charity event I'm supposed to go to in New York tomorrow. Which reminds me, I'll have to call and tell them I can't make it."

"What charity event?" Artemis was typing a reply to Arlo's message. He'd somehow talked both Chanel and Givenchy into rescheduling the shoots she'd had to cancel. The man was a P.R. genius.

Athena told them about the auction. "I wouldn't have agreed to it, but … well, I would have liked to meet the kids." Somewhere around 3 a.m. of the second night after Apollo's surgery, Athena told them all about the foundation she'd started under an alias, something she'd never told anyone. In fact they'd talked for hours about her plans and ideas for the charities.

Ares had woken up and was taking a sip of his coffee. "You might as well go and enjoy yourself instead of sitting around here watching Apollo sleep."

Athena closed her laptop. "Spending two days in the company of some twit and his over-inflated ego can't really be classified as 'enjoying myself'. I'd rather stay here. It'll spare me the agony."

Artemis added another praying hands emoji to Arlo's message and pressed "Send." "You have to go. They need you there." When Athena told them about her work with the foundation, Artemis had seen a very different side to her sister. Instead of being reserved and quiet like she often was, Athena had been so incredibly *into it* as she described the projects she'd help design.

The circumstances surrounding their parents' deaths had affected each of them differently. Ares became a workaholic, as though he could somehow reverse their curse by making money. Apollo had gone off the rails completely and Athena had withdrawn. And now she seemed intent on trying to save the world. She hadn't been able to save her parents, but at least she might make a difference to someone else.

"You heard the doctors," Artemis said. "Apollo's going to be fine. We'll call you if anything changes."

Athena looked unsure. "You really think I should go?"

"Yes," Ares confirmed. "Those kids are expecting you. Apollo would want you to."

Athena thought Ares looked much more handsome like this, dressed in a t-shirt and jeans, his hair messed up. It had been a long time since he'd stepped out of his stern CEO persona to take a few days off. Despite the worry, he looked more relaxed than she'd seen him in a long time.

"Of course he would." For some reason, Eros had perked up. He smiled at Athena. "And I've just had a brilliant idea about how I can start contributing to your foundation."

"How?"

Eros shoved his phone into his pocket. "I'm coming with you. I'm going to bid on the auction."

Ares laughed, for the first time in a week. "Let me guess. Marlowe Mercy."

Eros made an attempt to smooth his hair into place, as though already preparing. "It might be the only way I can get her to spend time with me. Because she'll have no choice."

"Don't they usually chase *you*?"

"Usually," Eros admitted, without a hint of arrogance. It was true, for better or worse. "Not this time."

Eros touched his palm to the bandage that was wrapped around Apollo's head. Apollo didn't stir. The bruises on his face were starting to take on shades of purple and yellow, but he looked peaceful. "See you soon, brother. Be good."

MANHATTAN

LESS THAN THREE HOURS LATER, Athena and Eros boarded their flight to New York. They both slept the entire way. At JFK, Effie was waiting with a car for Athena. Eros declined the offer of a ride from a blushing Effie, saying he had to go find a tuxedo and would catch up with them later. From there, Athena was rushed to a dressing room at Tribeca Rooftop, where the entire *City* fashion editorial team was waiting to prepare her for the "sale." Tamar was there, of course. She'd appointed herself the event's master of ceremonies.

"There are so many shag-worthy bachelors out there tonight," Effie said excitedly. "Plus loads of famous people. I even saw Harry and Meghan!"

The last thing Athena felt like doing tonight was being pimped and groomed like some prize poodle. She was hardly looking forward to the humiliation of being stared at like a piece of meat by a bunch of possibly-very-twisted trust fund assholes. But it was worth it. Athena knew she could do genuine good with the charity contributions at stake here. So she smiled, squared her shoulders, and sucked it up.

Her dress was Versace, sequined gold silk that clung to her curves like a second skin, with cut-out stripes around her stomach and hips, a plunging V neckline and thigh-high slits. It was far more revealing than she usually wore. "All the better to get those wolves bidding, my dear," Tamar joked, as she barked orders to the make-up artistry team. "More smoky kohl around the eyes. Even more. No, we want a siren-red lipstick, not that insipid pink. More glitter. And make sure she's showing as much skin as possible."

Athena's hair was smoothed into silky, butter-colored waves that spilled over her bare shoulders. "Men prefer women's hair worn long and loose," Tamar proclaimed," so they can fantasize about grabbing handfuls of it. And tonight is all about fantasy."

Gross, thought Athena. She wanted nothing to do with a bunch of loaded desperados' fantasies. What she really felt like doing was going home, curling up with a good book, sipping a glass of Pinot Noir as she watched the moonlit waves, and being alone. After the tension of the past week, she was exhausted.

Once satisfied, Tamar checked the schedule. "Time to mingle. Lay it on as thick as you can—to as many as you can—before the auction starts. Whip them into a frenzy, Athena. And don't forget to take notes. We want the whole weekend written about in glorious, gratuitous detail."

Athena sighed, psyching herself into her role as charming seductress—or whatever it was she was supposed to be doing—and made a beeline for the bar. Champagne would help.

The evening was mild and the moon hung full beside the skyscrapers like it had been specifically placed there for the occasion. The open-air terrace was swarming with celebrities, models, movie stars, singers—and billionaires. They prowled like jungle cats, their eyes bright with dollar signs and conquest. One of them sidled up to Athena. She recognized him as a young tech whiz who'd made his money on an app that helped people invest in the stock market by playing a game on their phones. Athena had recently seen him on a Forbes list.

He may have been newly-minted, but he was about as suave as a thirteen-year-old and sported a similarly—and regrettably—boyish physique. His eager eyes were level with her practically-spilling cleavage. "Hi, Athena," he said, nervously adjusting his bowtie. "I'm Ari Loxley. I s-saw you on the magazine cover. And, wow, um, the photo doesn't even come close to capturing how, uh, how b-b-beautiful you are."

"Thank you, Ari." She smiled at him, as she'd been instructed to do. This could be a good option, actually. At least she wouldn't have to spend the entire weekend fighting him off. He'd be too meek to proposition her, she could only hope. "Are you bidding on someone special tonight?"

"Y-y-yes. Y-you, Athena. I'm here to bid on you."

"How sweet." *Stay strong. You can do this. You can survive two days. Forty hours. Two thousand, four hundred minutes.* It suddenly felt like an excruciatingly long time.

"I've read all your b-b-books."

She'd gotten used to it, after four bestsellers, but it was still odd to meet strangers who had traveled the roads of her innermost thoughts and secret desires. She'd poured her heart and soul into those books. They'd been written in quiet, perfect privacy … and they included some very steamy scenes. There was something mildly invasive about publishing your heartfelt words. Especially when you came across someone like Ari, who seemed to be replaying those intimate scenes in his mind as he stared up at her.

"I enjoyed them." He winked. "A *lot*."

This was getting creepy. "Well, nice meeting you, Ari. Have fun tonight."

"Hopefully I'll s-see you later."

"Sure." It might not have even been the right response, she didn't care at this point. She was now desperately hoping Ari wouldn't win.

In her hurry to distance herself from the awkward encounter, she bumped right into another man. A very large, solid, *built* man, whose shirt was now wet from her spilled drink.

"I'm so sorry," she murmured, looking up into a pair of blue eyes, rimmed by dense lashes. He was ridiculously good-looking. And clearly very aware of it. Athena could read this as easily as if ARROGANT BASTARD had been tattooed across his forehead. He was dressed in a beautifully-cut suit but didn't look entirely at ease in it, like it was restricting the wild, outdoorsy freedom he was used to. He had thick hair the color of mink fur, and just as shiny. It had the slightest windblown wave to it, which was almost comically sexy. She could immediately sense he wasn't from New York. He was too beefed-up and swarthy-looking for an office worker. He looked more like a hero who might have stepped straight out of the pages of an erotic romance novel after spending the afternoon wrangling bucking broncos in the hot sun.

"Wyatt." He smiled as he held out his hand for her to shake. There was a twang to his accent. "Wyatt Boone."

Seriously? Had he ridden his stagecoach in from the frontier after a poker game at the saloon? Athena couldn't help laughing.

He laughed too, as though tuning into their private joke and finding it just as funny. His large hand completely enveloped her small one in its strong, warm, slightly-rough grip. Something about that handshake gave her a little thrill of awareness. He was so freaking … *strong*.

She wondered if maybe Ari Loxley would be a better option than someone like this man. She knew for certain there would be nothing meek or boyish about *this* bachelor.

"Wyatt Boone," she repeated. Now that she thought about it, the name was vaguely familiar. She'd read something about him. Oil, maybe. Texas, if she recalled correctly. Possibly from one of those old-money tycoon families with politicians in their pockets who stopped eco-progress in its tracks and caused all the world's problems. He looked like one of those types.

"The one and only."

"Well, if you'll excuse me, Wyatt Boone, I'm in need of a top-up. If you'd like to send your dry cleaning bill to the magazine, I'll make sure it's taken care of. A million apologies."

A million apologies? What the hell? Details of him were messing with her head. So she forced herself to decidedly *not* focus on the perceptive glimmer currently spangling in those devil-blue eyes, or the dimples, which he could tweak into existence without even smiling, or the chiseled jaw that already looked like it could use another shave. She concentrated only on the metaphorical tattoo across his forehead, which had been joined by several others: COCKY JERK, BACKWOODS REDNECK and TOTALLY UP-HIMSELF MEATHEAD.

He took a bottle of Dom Perignon from a passing waiter. "Allow me."

Damn, she thought. *Now what excuse can I use?* Then again, she'd been instructed to flirt with these smug bastards. To "whip them into a frenzy." For the money.

He filled her glass. Then he filled his own and clinked his flute against hers, with exaggerated care, as though she might spill her drink on him again. "To Athena Savage."

She wasn't surprised he knew her name. A lot of people did. Athena took a sip of her drink. "Thank you."

"The pleasure's all mine, sweetheart." He was teasing her. Fortunately, she could see straight through his alpha-male schtick. She'd never been the type of girl to swoon every time a remotely handsome ego-monger flicked her a loaded glance, and she didn't intend on starting now. "Did you say a *million* apologies?" he purred.

"I don't know why I said that."

Wyatt leaned in closer to her ear. "One for each dollar I'm about to spend on you," he said softly. Then he drained half his glass in one sip.

Athena's eyes widened.

"Unless it takes more, of course. I don't plan to be outbid." His accent reminded her of summer nights. Of sunshine and leather and green grass and the sugary-sweet taste of molasses. She had no idea why.

"Mr. Boone—"

"Wyatt."

"Wyatt. That's far too—"

"Ladies and gentlemen," Tamar's strident introduction began, cutting through all other noise in the room with all the subtlety of a foghorn. "City Magazine would like to wish all of our esteemed guests a very warm welcome indeed, and I'm pleased to see such a fabulous turnout tonight for our first annual Matchmaker Charity Auction! To our volunteers who have so generously offered their time for such a worthy cause, we salute you. To our bidders, we simply can't thank you enough for your outstanding generosity, which we look forward to putting to excellent use ..."

"Hey," said a familiar voice at her ear. "You look fucking gorgeous."

Eros.

She turned to greet him, glad for his moral support. She was suddenly feeling nervous. Two whole days in the company of Wyatt Boone? The prospect of being alone with him was daunting, to say the least.

Eros was dressed in a tux. His hair was combed into place but even so, a renegade curl fell across his forehead. Despite not sleeping much for past few days, he looked every inch the movie star he was. "So do you," she told him, noticing then that Wyatt was still watching her like a dog that had been denied its meat for several weeks—yet still managing to pull this off with a good-natured grin. She felt obliged. "Eros, this is Wyatt Boone. Wyatt, my brother Eros."

They shook hands. Wyatt was an inch or so taller than Eros, and burlier. Eros was usually one of the tallest people in any room, so Athena couldn't help but notice once again that Wyatt really was … *big* and very impressively … *put together.* Not that she was interested in him. But she could appreciate an exceptional specimen of beefcake, sex on a stick masculinity when it was literally staring her in the face.

Thankfully, Eros was, at least for now, diverting Wyatt's attention. "I didn't miss anything, did I?"

"No, it's just starting."

Tamar was basking in her limelight, her heavy make-up and floor-length jaguar gown making her look almost predatory, as though any minute she might pounce on one of the passing willowy, gazelle-esque models. Behind her, the moon glowed white, like it too was on the payroll and doing its best to please her. "We'll start the festivities with the new girl in town. She has the starring role in one of the most highly-anticipated films of next year. She's featured on the newest issue of *Vogue* and will grace next month's cover of *City*. Please get your bidding paddles ready, folks, as we welcome the lovely … Marlowe Mercy!"

Eros let out a strangled gasp. There, standing on the raised, spot-lit platform next to Tamar, stood Marlowe. She wore a green strapless dress that accentuated every to-die-for curve. Her jewel-like irises, even from this distance, glowed a deep jade green. Her skin gleamed and her hair was a wonder to behold, those gold-tipped ringlets taunting everyone in the room with their cute, sassy gorgeousness. She'd already started a new fashion revolution. Women all over the world were storming into salons and demanding "The Marlowe," and her movie wasn't even due to release until next spring.

"Let's start the bidding at a hundred thousand dollars, shall we?" trilled Tamar.

Still stunned from the sight of her, Eros didn't react as quickly as another man who stood to the left, whose paddle was already raised. "One hundred thousand."

Eros muttered a low oath.

Tamar was loving this. "Do I hear two hundred thousand?" She scanned the crowd, who seemed to want to perform for her.

"Two hundred thousand," came a voice from the other side of the room.

"Three."

"Four."

"Four fifty."

Eros raised his paddle. "One million dollars."

The crowd murmured and everyone turned to look at Eros. Including Marlowe Mercy.

Eros felt like his heart was about to thump right out of his chest and up onto the podium.

Tamar was practically singing. "Anyone? One million one hundred thousand? Anyone?"

Eros waited, evil-eyeing the crowd, ready to bid again.

"Going once." Tamar could hardly contain her adrenaline buzz. "Going twice … SOLD! To Mr. Eros Savage! Sir, you may make your way toward the booth in the foyer with Marlowe where the details will be attended to. What a *wonderful* start to the evening, ladies and gentlemen! Tonight, the sky's the limit." She gestured behind her with a thin, fluttery arm, to the full moon, which had obediently doubled in size.

Eros kissed Athena's cheek. "See you on Sunday night, honey." Then he shook Wyatt's hand. Athena wasn't sure how he knew that Wyatt had threatened to "buy" her. Maybe he could read it in Wyatt's expression, like some obscure man thing she didn't fully understand. Either way, he said, "Treat her right or I'll hunt you down and kick your Texan ass." It was good-natured in tone—a joke, no doubt—but both Athena and Wyatt stared after him as he disappeared into the crowd, which parted for him like he was Moses traversing the Red Sea.

What a generous donation!

You lucky bastard.

Don't turn into stone, man!

Accolades, taunts and congratulations wafted dimly through the air before being spliced decisively by Tamar's newfound sideline as a budding auctioneer. You couldn't help but wonder if she'd found her true calling.

"Next up … one of our own! Not only is she a best-selling author, a sometimes-model and a socialite of the highest order, she's also a columnist at our very own magazine, *City*—which I might add currently has the largest circulation of any fashion magazine in the country. Before I introduce her—and of course she needs no intro-duction—let me point out that this particular prize will be *writing* about her weekend … and in *very* revealing detail. What exotic location will the winner of the auction take her to? Find out in the October issue! Will sparks fly? Will he win her heart? Or will she shun him, like she does to all the men who try to woo her? *All* will be revealed! Everyone should be absolutely sure to get their own copy. Without further ado, let me introduce the one and only, beautiful inside and out, star columnist and acclaimed, bestselling author … Athena Savage!"

Jesus, thought Athena as she made her way onto the stage. She was fuming. *For the record, I don't "shun" all the men who try to woo me. I wouldn't need to shun them if they were fun or handsome or the tiniest bit appealing. On a human level. On the kind of level you need to be on with someone before you suggest a second date.*

"Just *look* at her, ladies and gentlemen. Who *wouldn't* want to spend two days with a real live goddess? Me, for one!" Athena glanced briefly at Tamar. It was a slightly odd thing to say but Tamar was already on to the auction. "I think we can all agree we should start the bidding at a generous sum. How about five hundred thousand? Surely we'll have plenty of takers at *that* bargain price. Give me five hundred thousand … anyone? … anyone?"

It was just as humiliating as Athena imagined it would be. Out in the crowd, a blue paddle was raised. It was Ari Loxley. "Five hundred thousand," his small voice called out.

"One million," another bidder said.

"One one," said Ari.

"Two."

"Three.

"One million five hundred thousand."

And so it went … until the bid was at two million dollars.

Athena couldn't believe this. *Two million dollars.*

She couldn't help but notice that Wyatt hadn't made a bid. Maybe she'd misread him. Maybe his teasing about the million thanks had just been a way to break the ice. Maybe he'd never intended to bid for her at all. Athena was relieved. *At least Ari will be harmless.*

But then, just as the bidding began to slow—they might have been up to two million, seven hundred, she couldn't remember—she heard that voice. That rich, Texan drawl.

"Four million."

The night took on a surreal glow.

Anyone? … anyone? … SOLD! To Mr. Wyatt Boone for four million dollars.

Senior Detective Statham: How well did you know Individual 7?

Individual 11 (Wyatt Boone [redacted]): Not well at all. We met the day of the wedding.

SDS: Would you have thought this individual capable of homicide?

I11: I think anyone is capable of homicide under the right circumstances, Detective. Myself included.

9

Tiffany, Chamberlain

MANHATTAN

TIFFANY CHAMBERLAIN WENT SHOPPING. She picked out a cute little black dress that would do nicely. She got a spray tan. Then she went back to Ares's apartment and prepared herself. For the occasion, she wore a very realistic-looking blond wig. She carefully covered the small butterfly tattoo on her shoulder with concealer, almost nostalgically. She remembered the summer she got that tattoo, down at the Jersey Shore with Santino, who'd taken her virginity and broken her heart. God, how she'd loved that loser. But those days were over. *Look at me now,* she thought. *In a penthouse apartment, as good as knocked up by a Savage. You're probably still flipping burgers and writing bad songs on your beat-up old guitar. Not me. That was never me.*

Once she arrived, she booked a room. Then she

settled in at the bar, making sure she was conspicuous enough to be seen. She had a good view of the people coming and going, and most of the tables. She sipped her gin, assessing her choices. He had to be black-haired, of course. Tall. As regal-looking as possible.

For a brief moment, she was almost overcome with tears. But she held them back. The bastard hadn't even *called* her. *Asshole!* His damn family always came first. She knew that. She *allowed* that. She could live with that, if only he would notice her when his family wasn't even around. Was that really too much to ask?

God, it wasn't like she was a bad person or anything. If he'd only let her in, she would treat him *so well.* She only wanted the chance to try.

She'd put so much effort into hooking him. And for what? He barely noticed her existence.

She should have gone for the ugly banker from Goldman Sachs. At least he might have appreciated her. But of course she hadn't been able to resist the conquest. Ares was so much better, in every possible way. He was gorgeous. Successful. Rich. And damaged. Cold. After spending almost a month with him, she wondered if he was even *capable* of loving a woman. She'd researched him so thoroughly she felt she must know everything there was to know about Ares Savage. His tragic family history had scarred him, she'd expected that. His father had drowned. His mother had committed suicide by drug overdose and was found floating in the pool by the brother that was now fighting for his life after some kind of accident. No wonder.

She'd realized, in fact, that she knew very little about Ares Savage. He was impossible to comfort. And he was as layered as anyone she'd ever met. As much as she tried, she simply hadn't been able to break through those layers. He'd barely even reacted when she told him she was pregnant with his baby.

Which she wasn't. Damn him.

Once, she'd succeeded.

Once, she'd caught him off-guard.

And she'd never been able to do it again. Not by crying or seducing or offering herself to him in the most genuine way she'd ever offered herself to anyone … since Santino.

Her plan had failed.

But Tiffany Chamberlain (or, more accurately, Dawn-Marie Davidson) was no quitter.

That's what tonight's mission was all about. There was still one thing she could do to make this plan work. All she needed was *one thing*. One tiny thing that would make this story as convincing as it could possibly be.

She saw him as soon as he walked in with his date. Similar height, slightly skinnier. His hair wasn't quite as dark, but neither was hers! Her mother had been blond, for fuck's sake. Babies weren't always the spitting image of their fathers. There was room for error here.

The couple sat down at a nearby table.

Tiffany watched them nonchalantly for a while, keeping her options open. They were positioned well. He was facing her and the girl's back was to her. So she ordered another gin and began to make eye contact.

He was cute. Young. Probably a good five years younger than Ares, but that hardly mattered. He'd be easier to seduce.

The guy noticed her, that was obvious. He was trying to be attentive to his date but Tiffany licked her lips, glancing at him occasionally. Smiling. Sending all the necessary signals. The girl even glanced over her shoulder at one point, noticing that his attention was diverted. And when his date excused herself to the ladies' room, Tiffany motioned with her finger. *Come here.* He did.

"I have a room upstairs," she said sultrily. "214. After you've taken her home, come see me." She could tell by his eyes that he would.

By midnight, it was mission accomplished.

Individual 23 (~~Dawn-Marie Davidson aka Tiffany Chamberlain~~ [redacted]): It doesn't surprise me at all. I could have predicted something like this would happen, if anyone had bothered to ask me—which of course no one did. I'm telling you, Detective, I feared for my *own* life and I, for one, would make sure … [refers to list] Individual 7 is put away for a very long time.

10

Apollo

SOUTHAMPTON

APOLLO KNEW the exact second his wheels left the road—which was exactly one second after he realized he'd miscalculated the curve. The treetops were below him, rising up to meet the American-made missile he was still sitting astride. The only times Apollo had ever been to church since his childhood were for a couple of weddings and the funerals of his parents—by far, the worst two days of his life. Right now, though, seemed like the perfect time to take up religion. *I'll stop*, he prayed to whatever god might be sitting up there and judging him while sipping cocktails at the tiki bar on Cloud 9 (which is where he always pictured the kind of deity he might worship). *I'll clean up. I'll never drink again if only you'll let me live.* Then again, what was the point? What had life given him except a whole string of tragedies and a full-blown addiction that held him firmly in its vice-grip? *You idiot,* raged his subconscious. *You're rich, you're hot, you're young and you've even got a small amount of actual musical talent. If you didn't insist on getting so thoroughly fucked up 24/7, you might even be able to write something good. Something better than those horribly cliché three-chord stadium anthems.*

Maybe his subconscious was right. Maybe, if he got a second chance at life, he could do better. And then, just as he was making contact with the cold, hard ground at incredible speed, which hurt like fuck, he realized: he really, really wanted to live.

Time passed, from somewhere inside a deep tunnel. He heard sirens. Someone crying. From time to time, he recognized the voices of his family, but he couldn't seem to reach them. There was pain. Sadness. Cravings that made him wish he were dead. Then, after what felt like several lifetimes, he suddenly surfaced.

Apollo's eyes opened. His first realization was that everything hurt. He thought he might be able to feel every individual cell in his body, and all of them ached on about ten different levels.

Where was he?

In a white room.

Confused, uneasy, he tried to get up. He couldn't. He was attached to something. Tubes were sticking out of his goddamn arms! He pulled at them, trying to free himself.

A lightly-placed hand touched his shoulder. "Apollo. Leave those in. Everything's all right."

He looked up and saw what could only have been an

angel. He must be … in heaven? Had he been good enough to get in? She was slim, dressed in white. He checked for wings but couldn't see any. She had red hair but it had lighter, yellow and white-gold tints in it, too, as though she was standing in an intense ray of sunshine instead of inside this sterile-looking room. Her eyes were a mesmerizing shade of amber, with little shards of gold that glinted as though she was lit from within.

Apollo calmed, only so he could feast his eyes some more on this … creature. He still wasn't sure if she was real, but he wished he could absorb some of that glowing inner light she was radiating. His psyche felt very, very dark. Like it had been harshly replaced by a big black hole.

"You were in a motorcycle accident." She adjusted something on one of the machines. "You've been unconscious for a while. But your prognosis is excellent. We expect you to make a full recovery." She held his hand, placing a little plastic clamp on one of his fingers. This light graze of her cool fingers felt indescribably good. "I need to let your doctor know you're awake."

"No," he managed to rasp.

"No yourself," she laughed softly. "We already know you're disagreeable. If you don't get your way, you thrash around and cause a lot of trouble. Lie back now, and be good."

He did, but only because he felt so fucking tired. How long had he been out?

"Your brothers and sisters wanted us to tell you you're

in good hands. You're stuck with me for the time being, but I promise to be nice to you."

"Who …?" Forming a question was surprisingly difficult.

"I'm one of your nurses. My name is Daisy Sullivan."

"Where …?" His vocabulary had been reduced to one-word segments of idiot-speak. Was he brain damaged? Apollo didn't feel brain damaged. His brain just felt scrambled, like it had been taken out, mixed around by a sinister lobotomist and hastily shoved back in.

"Long Island. You were flown here from Denver last night. You're in a rehabilitation facility called Southern Shores."

What the hell?

He was in rehab?

But he didn't need *to go to rehab!*

Before he could protest, she offered him a sip of water through a straw, like he was a goddamn invalid. He was so thirsty, he went along with it anyway and ended up drinking half of it.

The girl continued talking to him, rambling on softly about the weather, the traffic and some new restaurant she wanted to try. She checked the bandages on his head and his arms and the grazes underneath them, which were healing well, she assured him. There was a light sprinkling of golden freckles across her nose, like glitter from the wand of a passing, good-natured fairy.

She was overwhelmingly … cheerful.

It clashed with everything about this situation and was hard for him to handle.

He closed his eyes and could vaguely admit to himself that it was nice to have company. He didn't want to be alone in this cold white room.

She was telling him everything was going to be okay and he'd start to feel better and sometimes you have to go through the darkness to get to the dawn.

Seriously?

It must be nice to be so deluded and so … decent, was what he found himself thinking. Helping other people. Trying to make them see the light.

"I'm going to give you a little more of this sedative so you can sleep." She adjusted some tubes and he felt like saying, *Finally. Bring it on and don't be stingy.*

He could immediately feel that she wasn't.

Apollo had been fighting his own damages for a long time, mostly unsuccessfully. Dark demons haunted him like sticky shadows that never went away, no matter how sunny the day might have been. The words this girl was saying, weirdly, almost helped, here in this stark white cell. He could feel the drugs she was giving him swathing his sadness in a buffering layer. He was broken but he wasn't *bad.* He behaved like an asshole a lot of the time but he *wasn't actually an asshole.* He just *acted* like one, because he'd lost his way. There was a big difference. She was reminding him of that with her trite little monologue. It was ruffling some hidden corner of his soul he'd forgotten about, where calmness and happiness had once lived and thrived and peacefully co-existed.

It was so *elusive*, this place. So hard to find his way back to. It would be so nice to revisit it one day, was the last thought he held onto before unconsciousness dragged him under its dark, soothing tow.

Senior Detective Statham: Why did you reach for a loaded gun that was pointed directly at you?

Individual 3 (~~Apollo Savage~~ [redacted]): I thought he was going to shoot her. I didn't want that to happen. That's all I could think about. I couldn't let that happen.

11

Etienne Dumas-Magnus

PARIS, FRANCE

"Oh, for fuck's sake."

Etienne Dumas-Magnus was having a very bad day.

He was overseeing the fashion shoot that featured his latest collection, an exquisite (in his own opinion) selection of off-white garments made from silk, fur and leather. He'd recently hired several new seamstresses, two elderly spinster sisters fresh from the backwoods of the Romania who were absolute workhorses. With careful direction, they'd translated his ideas and sketches into high-fashion perfection. Seeing his masterpieces cling lovingly to the lithe models—and one in particular— made all the long hours and frustration of the past few months worth it. This was his best work ever. At long last, the snooty and brutally competitive Parisian fashion scene would finally sit up and take notice. They simply *had* to.

It was a perfect autumn day. The afternoon rays of sun gleamed like liquid gold over the stone façade of Notre Dame. It was the kind of light that could only be found in France. Paris, without a doubt, was the most beautiful city on earth. The product of a whirlwind summer romance twenty-seven years ago between a Parisian teenage "dancer" and a wealthy American property developer, Etienne was glad for the American passport. It meant he could work in New York when he needed to without the hassle of getting a visa. But, privately, he thought the place was overrated. And he couldn't stand the people. So utterly crass. French culture was so much more sophisticated.

At least it *used* to be, lamented Etienne, before the invention of fucking Twitter, which was directly responsible for the crowd that was currently in the process of sabotaging his entire photo shoot.

Of course Etienne knew that Artemis Savage was famous. Her face was everywhere and she even had a sideline as a mediocre (in Etienne's opinion—he was French, after all, and had a very refined artistic sensibility) painter. She was also one of those rare models who nailed every photograph. Your eye always went straight to her, over all others, no matter who they were. He was almost regretting hiring the two other girls. In every shot so far, Artemis had completely upstaged them.

Etienne was realizing he'd made a fatal mistake. He'd underestimated how voracious the public's appetite for Artemis Savage actually was.

He'd had the idea of photographing the shoot in the open air in front of Notre Dame. After all, what's more Parisian than Notre Dame? (Aside from the Eiffel Tower, of course, but as iconic as the tower was, Etienne also considered it somewhat twee and the damn thing had been done to death.) This had involved getting permission —neither an easy feat nor an inexpensive one—and roping off a large area in front of the building. Which meant that tourists were displaced and had now taken a zealous interest in the fashion shoot that was interfering with their sightseeing schedule.

Once the tourists recognized that one of the models was Artemis Savage, the crowds multiplied exponentially. And then the paparazzi had arrived and now all hell was breaking loose.

It was dawning on Etienne that ever since that American magazine had put Artemis and her brothers and sister on the cover, the public's interest in all things Savage had gone into overdrive. Before that, the siblings had been famous for staying *out* of the limelight; now, they were very much in it, whether they wanted to be there or not.

Etienne had bought a copy of the magazine on the sly, just like every other schmuck on the planet. He'd leafed through the pictures of their fabulous homes. He'd read the article that had included interviews with each of them, which had given the world a glimpse into exactly how glamorous and enviable their lifestyle really was.

People wanted more. They were fascinated by the

Savages' looks, their money and, most of all, their story. There was a vulnerability to each of the siblings that the public and the press couldn't get enough of. Speculations about their travel plans and their whereabouts trended hourly on social media. Headlines were inescapable, from The New York Times to French fashion blogs. This morning as he was sipping his way through four espressos, Etienne had seen a few.

One of Ares, getting out of a limo in Manhattan, looking grim like he always did. *His parents' tragic deaths still haunt him.*

Athena, radiant yet reflective at some glitterati event. *Her heart is still broken.*

And one of Artemis, here in Paris, wearing sunglasses and walking down the street, doing her best to unsuccessfully evade photographers. *Putting on a brave face.*

It wasn't just the tragedy the journalists and bloggers fixated on, but also the idea that each Savage was searching for true love. *Will they ever find that rare, one-of-a-kind love story their parents basked in——until it was tragically stolen from them by early, watery graves?*

Etienne cursed his luck. He should have seen this coming. He'd hired a few security thugs to stop the equipment from getting stolen, but they were no match for a thousand fanatical fans.

"Artemis!" Several teenage girls were shouting from behind a flimsy-looking barrier. The crowd was getting bolder.

Artemis watched them warily.

The gaggle of screaming girls broke through and ran up to her, fangirling hysterically. "Can we get a selfie with you, Artemis? OH MY GOD! I can't believe it's YOU! It's Artemis Savage! Eeeeeee!"

"*Merde*," muttered Etienne. The girls' high-pitched screams were a micro-decibel away from shattering the goddamned—and very expensive—camera lenses.

More people began closing in, stepping over ropes and pushing aside the untethered metal fencing. This was clearly escalating quickly into a dangerous situation. And their phone cameras were making those authentic-sounding clicks (he could admit this was an inspired design feature). But his garments! They would be seen without his permission or his control! It was unacceptable.

"Get them out of here!" screamed Etienne to his crew.

The van pulled up and Etienne quickly ushered the girls and several of his assistants into it and climbed in after them. They made their way through the crowd then sped from the scene. At least he'd had enough foresight to hire a van with tinted windows.

"Call the Louvre," Etienne barked at one of his assistants, the quirky one with the trendy little tortoiseshell glasses who seemed to have a knack for getting shit done. "We'll shoot there. At least we'll have some control over the space we're in." Brilliant. Etienne silently congratulated himself, visualizing his garments in front of the Mona Lisa, the Winged Victory and his personal favorite,

Delacroix. Now *there* was some drama. Give him a bare-breasted woman leading the French Revolution over a fucking landscape any day of the week.

Artemis

THE LOUVRE, PARIS

ARTEMIS DECIDED to take her opportunity and check out some art. They would be shooting late into the night. The equipment had to be back the following day and Etienne was manically determined to get the shots he wanted. Artemis didn't mind. Her plans for the evening included taking a bath, calling to see how Apollo was doing and going to bed early. It's not like she could go out in Paris, not without an entourage and a brigade of bodyguards.

There were downsides of fame.

The Louvre administrators had agreed—for a small fortune—to give Etienne three hours after the doors had closed to the public, under the supervision of four guards who would be paid overtime.

As she was waiting for the hair and make-up teams to set up, Artemis idly wandered through the grand halls of the museum, still dressed in a fur and leather skin-tight jumpsuit. She'd been to the Louvre before but never after hours. The place was ethereal at night. The paintings seemed to take on a realistic quality, like that movie where the statues and portraits come to life once all the people have gone home for the day.

Alone for the first time since early morning, Artemis stood in front of a painting of a beautiful, dark-haired man. He reminded her of that architect who'd designed her house.

Cooper Salazar.

After she'd given him and his guests a tour of her house, he'd shaken her hand. And then he'd driven away. Since then, she'd been too busy spending time with Apollo and working non-stop to revisit the effect he'd had on her. It had felt significant that day at the house, like a change in the weather.

As she stared at the painting, a thought came to her: she could commission him. She could build a recording studio for Apollo, down by the river, above those big rocks he always spent time sitting on whenever he visited her. Apollo had a state-of-the-art studio in Nashville, she knew, but this would be different. His life in Nashville was one perpetual party. Some of the members of his band practically lived with him. His house was constantly busy and full of hangers-on that only wanted the wild side of her brother. Which was probably part of the reason he'd spiraled so totally out of control. She could build him a getaway. A peaceful retreat where he could be alone to work on his music without interruptions. It might be exactly the kind of thing he needed at this point, once he'd recovered enough to check out of rehab.

She'd noticed the pale band around Cooper's finger.

Was he separated? Divorced? Or had he just forgotten to put his ring on that particular morning? She pictured him stopping in at the florist on his way home from a busy day of designing his newest masterpiece, buying his wife a dozen red roses to apologize for going out without that little symbol of their undying love on his finger, showing the world he was strictly off limits.

Or did he take it off for a different reason? On purpose? Was he sneaking around? If he was, he was doing a lousy job of it. The tell-tale paleness of that obvious circle against the tan of his hands gave it away all too easily. He seemed too perceptive to overlook a detail like that.

Either way, why was she even thinking about Cooper Salazar?

Artemis sat down on a giant forest-green velvet ottoman situated in the middle of the room. She googled him. There were articles about his work. A few photos. With clients. In his office. With his wife, at an awards ceremony. She was blonde and wore a lot of make-up. She wasn't smiling in either of the photographs.

There was another headline. A recent one, posted only a few days ago.

Acclaimed architect Cooper Salazar separates from wife of three years.

His home and office were in Boulder.

She keyed his listed cell phone number into her phone.

Senior Detective Statham: Can you describe what you recall of the scene?

Individual 6 (~~Artemis Savage~~ [redacted]): There was so much *blood*. I've never seen so much blood.

12

———

ᴬres

MANHATTAN

Aʀᴇs ᴡᴀs ʙᴀᴄᴋ in New York. He caught a cab from JFK to his building, desperately hoping Tiffany was at work. Most people would be; it was 4:45 on a rainy Tuesday afternoon. Unless she was "working from home" again.

He walked into his building, but before he could get to the elevator, the doorman approached him. "Mr. Savage, there's someone here who's been waiting to see you."

Ares looked over to the seating area in the lobby, which the doorman was pointing toward. There, a young woman sat on one of the couches, reading a magazine.

"She refuses to leave," the doorman said. "She's been here all day." Then, to the girl: "Miss?"

The girl looked up. "Oh. Is that him?" Her voice was soft but not hesitant. As she stood, Ares saw that she was tall and very slender. She had long dark hair and striking,

III

very-dark eyes. He wondered if she was a model. If she wasn't, she could have been. Despite her waif-like appearance, her expression was anything but fearful. She was clearly determined to get whatever it was she came for.

She walked over to Ares. The closer she got, the more fascinated he became. Ares was used to the company of beautiful women. And he was rarely lost for words. But this graceful, composed stranger had him momentarily speechless.

"You're Ares Savage?" She had an accent. Brazil, maybe.

"Yes," he finally said. "And you are?"

"My name is Jazmin Diaz. My sister is Valentina Diaz." She said the second name as though it should mean something to him.

"Should I know who that is?"

His ignorance appeared to irritate her. "I've been trying to reach Tiffany Chamberlain. She won't answer any of my calls."

Ares was tired. And strung-out for about ten different reasons. If it had been anyone else, he would have—possibly quite rudely—told them to fuck off. It wasn't that he was protecting Tiffany. He just had zero interest in hearing about her work issues.

But he'd already realized that Jazmin Diaz was not "anyone else." The look in her eyes was fiercely ... honest. Calm but heartfelt. This intrigued him. He was used to dealing with Tiffany and other women like her, who were manipulative and crafty and saw him only for his money.

"This nice man has been very kind. Thank you, Joe," she added, to the doorman, who smiled at her. Ares vaguely recognized the man. But he wasn't in the habit of chitchatting with the door people; he was too distracted for things like that.

"For confidentiality reasons," Jazmin continued, "Joe couldn't give out the kind of information I need, and I respect that. I googled Tiffany Chamberlain. I found out that she's been seen around town with you. So I figured she might be here. Joe couldn't confirm this, but he did accidentally hint at the fact that she's given him strict instructions not to be disturbed." To Joe: "Sorry, Joe, but you did."

Joe shrugged and gave Ares an apologetic look.

Ares still had no idea what this was about.

Jazmin pulled a manila envelope out of her bag. "There are some things I think you might want to hear about."

Ares couldn't help noticing the flawlessness of her sun-kissed skin, which was warm-looking and lightly bronzed, as though she'd spent the day on a Hawaiian beach instead of here in this cold, stark lobby. It wasn't something he would usually stop to consider, but he didn't think she was wearing any make-up. Make-up was invented so women could try their hardest to look like *this*. This flushed, healthy glow. Impossibly long eyelashes. Lips that were naturally full and plump and a shade of pink that made him feel strangely transfixed. She was achingly lovely.

"Could we go and talk somewhere for a few minutes, Mr. Savage? I don't want to sound rude, but I'm afraid I can't take no for an answer."

Ares almost smiled. He liked her attitude. She reminded him of himself. "In that case … yes."

"If we went to your apartment," Jazmin said, "we could include Tiffany in our conversation."

Ares didn't want to include Tiffany. He wanted to hear what this was about, without any interference. "You and I can talk first. There's a restaurant on the corner."

"Would you like me to look after your suitcase for you, Mr. Savage?" Joe offered.

"Yes," Ares answered abruptly. Then he realized what he sounded like. Did he always sound like that? Ares very rarely cared about what other people thought of him. In general, people fawned over, kissed up to and/or idolized him, which he found boring. So what if people thought he was arrogant? That wasn't his problem.

But for some reason, here and now, he cared. He wanted Jazmin's first impression of him to be something other than that of a total prick. "Thank you, Joe," he added. "And please don't bother Ms. Chamberlain with any of this."

"Yes, sir."

Ares opened the door for Jazmin, and walked with her, down to the corner, where a French bistro offered an excellent wine list and private, secluded tables.

"Order anything you want," Ares said. She looked like she could use a good meal. As beautiful as she was, it would have been easy to overlook the subtle signs that things weren't easy in her life, but Ares noticed. The shadows under her eyes that hinted at exhaustion. Her clothes, which were flattering but worn. Inexpensive. He felt an unfamiliar urge to find out what her worries were, and ease them.

Jazmin ordered a steak.

"Make that two," Ares said. "And a bottle of your 2009 Chateaux Margaux."

Jazmin happened to be reading the wine list. She shot Ares an incredulous look. "Actually," she said to the waiter, "please bring us a bottle of the Domaine Mercurey Rouge instead."

The waiter bowed slightly and hurried away.

Ares was watching her. She surprised him, which didn't often happen. "You prefer the lighter reds?"

"I just saved you thirteen hundred and fifty-two dollars. If you want to blow that much money, I can think of a better way to spend it."

He leaned back and folded his arms. "Which is … ?"

"Have you figured out who I am yet?"

"Not a clue."

Jazmin looked him in the eye, almost gently. She knew this might sting. "Tiffany Chamberlain paid my sister to pretend she was a prostitute so she could frame your CFO."

"What?" Ares couldn't believe this. Actually, he could.

He stopped himself from asking if she was bullshitting him, because he already knew the answer to that.

"She was our immigration lawyer. She was going to help us apply for green cards. But we didn't have enough money to file our documents, so she came up with a plan to stage … an incident."

"An incident."

"I'd just lost my waitressing job. The owner of the restaurant was paying me under the table. But it was too risky, he said. He was afraid he'd get busted. So Tiffany came up with this plan about how we could pay her. She said if we agreed to go through with it, she would cover all our expenses and we'd even have some money left over. Four grand, she said."

"*Four grand?*" Ares rubbed his hand roughly across his jaw. "So Tiffany asked your sister to sleep with Ray Garmusch. For four thousand dollars."

"She promised we wouldn't have to *actually* sleep with him. Just set the scene. She had hidden cameras so she knew when to … step in. Just as things got, you know, incriminating."

"*We?*" He had no idea why, but the thought of Ray Garmusch—or Tiffany for that matter—going anywhere near Jazmin made Ares's blood boil.

"The original plan was to both get caught in bed with him. But we needed another lookout. So we drew straws."

"You drew *straws?*" Ares had been reduced to repeating everything she said, like a fucking idiot.

"We drew straws because we both insisted on being

the one to do it. I didn't want her to be put in that position. She's nineteen years old."

As horrifying as this all was, something occurred to Ares. "My lawyer said she was underage."

"Tiffany made false paperwork. To up the stakes in the hope of getting a bigger pay-out."

"Jesus Christ," Ares muttered, having a hard time coming to terms with the fact that his now ex-girlfriend was *this* much of a manipulative, psychotic bitch. He'd had an inkling, of course, but had totally underestimated the extent of it.

Jazmin continued. "It doesn't make it any less horrific, though, does it? I mean, have you *seen* that guy? Of course you have, he was your CFO." Jazmin looked on the verge of tears for a split second, but then her expression changed, to one of anger. "That's how desperate we were. In the end, Tiffany insisted it be Valentina to be the one to do it, since the charges would be more damaging —and lucrative. But once Tiffany had the evidence and the money, she disappeared. Later we found out she didn't file our immigration papers at all. She'd moved offices. We couldn't find her. Which is why I've been waiting in your building all day."

The waiter brought the wine. He poured them each a glass, then discretely disappeared.

"I just wanted you to know what you're dealing with. Before my sister and I get deported."

"Deported?"

"Back to Cuba. We came over on a boat four years

ago with our brothers. One of them is now in a Mexican jail. The other one got sent back."

"My god. And your parents?"

"They're dead."

Ares stared at Jazmin, struggling to control his rage. He'd known Tiffany was capable of augmenting the truth, but this was taking things to a whole new level. This was crossing a line. This was trampling all over basic human compassion and common decency.

"And now we'll never be able to apply. Because my sister has a criminal record."

"What for?" But of course he knew what she was going to say.

"Prostitution. Your lawyers pressed charges."

Ares's brain was attempting to process the depth of how wrong this all was. He'd never aspired to becoming a shining pillar of morality, but people were being hurt here. People's lives were being destroyed. *Jazmin's* life was being destroyed. By him, his lawyers and his evil ex-girl-friend. And she'd come here to warn him.

"I can see why she wants you," Jazmin said. "You're the perfect target."

"What do you mean?"

"You're beautiful, you're wealthy, you're famous. And you're vulnerable. Like we were. Except with you, it's your emotional vulnerability she's honed in on. I read about you in that magazine."

Ares was rarely dumbfounded. He was a quick-thinking, high-functioning CEO of several Fortune 500 companies, who never let things get to him too deeply. Sure, he'd been handed a lot of wealth, but he'd also worked his ass off to keep that money. To grow it. Not for himself, especially, or even for his family, but because it was the only thing he knew how to do. It kept him from thinking too much or feeling too much. Now, he wondered if he'd been too blind. Too indifferent. Too selfish.

The waiter brought their steaks and Jazmin started eating, hungrily. Like she hadn't eaten in a while.

Ares took his phone out of his pocket. First, he dialed his lawyer. "Bruce … what? Yeah, Apollo's going to be fine, thanks. Listen, I need to meet with you first thing tomorrow morning. Bring everything you have on Valentina Diaz's case with you … Yes, that's the one. Eight o'clock. See you then." He ended the call. Jazmin was watching him. "You and Valentina will also want to come to that meeting," he added.

"You don't have to do that," she said quietly. Ares wondered if he'd ever met anyone with so much integrity before. Even now, she was thinking of him.

"I absolutely *do* have to do that. For both of us." He clinked his glass against hers and took a sip. "It's no Chateau Margaux, but it's not bad."

"I've never heard of anyone paying thirteen hundred and eighty-four dollars for a bottle of wine. You must have money growing on trees."

"Not quite." He scrolled through his contacts. "Where

do you live? I'll arrange for a driver pick you up at seven thirty."

At this, Jazmin hesitated. "Um, well, it's in Queens. It's more of a garden shed than anything. But it's big enough for a mattress. And it has a lock."

Ares's brow furrowed. He made another phone call. "I'd like to book a suite with two bedrooms … Yes, tonight. I have an account there. Ares Savage. My guests will be ordering room service, too, so please bill that to me … Right." He abruptly ended the call.

Jazmin was glaring at him. "Why are you … ?"

"It's right across the street from my offices. You and your sister can get a good night's sleep before the meeting. You look like you could use it."

"Mr. Savage—"

"Ares. The thing is, Miss Diaz—"

"You can call me Jazmin." She took a bite of a French fry and blinked.

"The thing is, Jazmin, I paid Tiffany—on behalf of her client, your sister—two million dollars."

Jazmin stopped chewing. Her eyes, which seemed to have more starry, glittery depth to them to any eyes Ares had ever seen, were wide.

"Yes," he confirmed. "So, by coming to me, you've saved me not only from allowing a lying fraudster to steal a shitload of money from me, but also from making a *huge* mistake. Oh, I had suspicions. But I didn't trust my own gut, even though I should have. So I want to thank you. I'm going to make things right. I'm going to make sure all charges against your sister are dropped and that you're not deported."

Jazmin, who was so pretty Ares was doing his best not to stare at her dreamily as she was eating her T-bone, had tears in her eyes. "Thank you, Ares. Really. I don't know what to say."

He squeezed her hand before realizing what he was doing. The smoothness of her skin had a strange effect on him. He felt … beguiled and spellbound.

Shit. This is not good, thought Ares, who'd been in a lot of relationships but had never been in love. Ever. He'd wondered once or twice along the way, but now he knew for sure. Because he suddenly understood. His heart might as well have taken a direct hit from a lightning bolt, it was that immediate and all-consuming. *I'm well on the way to falling head over heels for a total stranger I've known for ten minutes who rowed here in a boat and lives in a garden shed. And has more sweet sincerity than all of my staff put together.*

He wouldn't act on it, of course. But his heart was racing. Was he seriously considering—

No. He'd keep *her* best interests in mind, like she'd done for him.

Ares called Tiffany. Jazmin watched him, the spark in her eyes empathetic, like they were on the same team now. This link, inexplicably, made him happier than he could ever remember being. "Hi … I'm back in New York. I stopped in at the French restaurant on the corner, you know the one. Why don't you come down and join me … Good … Me too. See you soon."

Then he called the front desk of his building. "Is that you, Joe?" Jazmin watched him as she took another sip of her wine. She smiled at him and it took effort for him to focus on the phone call. "How's your night going? That's good to hear. Listen, I'd like you to do something for me. Once Miss Chamberlain has left—any minute now—I'd like you to have the locks on my door changed. Can you get someone to do that? Yes, tonight, immediately after she leaves … New key cards, that's right. And she should be prevented from returning to the apartment, once she's left. At all, yes. I'll make sure you're well compensated … What? Oh. You have a good night, too, Joe. Thank you."

MANHATTAN

TIFFANY HAD GIVEN up trying to reach Ares. He called her only when he needed something from her, which wasn't often. He'd called to remind her to water his goddamn plant, the bastard. She'd gotten over all that, though. She spent the week pampering herself, getting impregnated and pretending his fabulous apartment was hers. Soon, hopefully, it would be. Once her pregnancy was confirmed, most likely he'd ask her to marry him. She'd sign a pre-nup, if he insisted, which she knew he would. He was pedantic like that. She knew he didn't love her, but she would make it work, regardless. Love was secondary. She could do without love, but not money.

She fantasized about her life as Ares Savage's wife. Ski vacations. Dinner parties. A luxury baby shower with pink balloons and photo-worthy tiers of cupcakes at some upmarket venue. She'd never have to worry about money again. It would be such a relief. Yes, she'd gotten better at taking care of herself in the past few years, but the pressure was still crushing. Once she'd decided to be absolutely ruthless, things had become a little easier. That's what it took in this crazy city. You *had* to be ruthless. Or life was just hard. Always hard. She was tired of hard.

She was in the jacuzzi tub, taking a bath, sipping real French champagne. His wine collection was insane. She heard the buzz of her phone and almost ignored it.

It might be him.

So she stepped onto the marble floor and nimbly walked, naked, into his bedroom.

Ares.

"Hi, sweetie," she said.

"Hi."

"Where are you?"

"I'm back in New York."

"Oh. When did you get back?"

"I stopped in at the French restaurant on the corner, you know the one." She did. His voice sounded strained, she thought. Probably because of the nightmarish week he'd had. His alcoholic rock star brother had driven his motorcycle off a cliff or something. That kind of thing was bound to be stressful. "Why don't you come down and join me."

Odd how he wasn't asking. He was sort of telling. Then again, she had to humor him in every possible way until those wedding vows had been recited, witnessed and signed on the dotted line. "I'd love to, honey. I'm just getting out of the bath. I'll be there in ten."

"Good."

"I love you," she said. "I've missed you so much."

"Me too." The insincerity practically dripped off his words, but that was fine. *Keep your eye on the ball, Dawn-Marie.* "See you soon."

She dried off and put on a brand new Dolce and Gabbana jumpsuit she'd bought yesterday. Those little Cuban girls had been easy to dupe. She hadn't enjoyed doing it, but it was dog eat dog out there. Besides, Cuba was opening up now. That old Communist dictator had died, she was pretty sure. Things were probably improving. And she was only doing society a favor, after all. Giving jobs back to *actual* Americans. Posing as an immigration inspector at that restaurant the girl had worked in was a stroke of genius on her part. One of her better performances.

She quickly dried her hair, put on some mascara and lipstick and slid her feet into another new purchase: a pair of Stuart Weitzman heels. They'd been outrageously expensive, but she'd earned that money, fair and square. You simply don't do something you're asked to do without getting everything in writing first and making damn sure it's legally binding. Those girls would learn. They were still young. They had their whole lives in front of them, whereas she'd bypassed thirty two years ago. She hadn't told Ares that, of course. But she looked amazing for her age and could easily pass for twenty-six. And her new identity confirmed it. Driver's license, passport. Oh yes, she'd covered all her bases. It was what she was best at.

Checking her look in the mirror once more, she got into the elevator.

The doorman was at his desk and bumbled over to open the door for her. As he should.

He tipped his hat and smiled at her but she took little notice.

She always felt a little breathless when she was about to see Ares. He was *such* a catch. In some ways, she couldn't believe her luck. It had *worked*. She'd actually—almost—landed the hottest, richest, most perfect man in New York.

Tiffany walked into the restaurant. She couldn't see him.

"Madam," said the maître d'. She scowled. *God, she loathed when people called her Madam.* "Are you looking for Mr. Savage?"

"Yes."

"Right this way."

He led her deep into the restaurant, toward the back. She saw him. She waved. And smiled.

Until she got closer. He was with someone.

Holy shit. It was one of them. *Those little whores. The prettier one.*

"Tiffany." Ares stood up to greet her. "I'm glad you could make it."

MANHATTAN

DESPITE BEING YOUNG, Jazmin Diaz was not easily intimidated. Her childhood had been spent on the streets of Havana, playing cards, running wild and loving life despite the fact that her family lived in a one bedroom apartment in an overcrowded, crumbling tenement building. Her father had been a doctor with an overdeveloped sense of compassion and an intelligent mind. Too intelligent. He'd questioned the Communist regime one too many times and talked his wife, a feisty beauty who rolled cigars in one of Havana's many factories, into following his lead. They'd led a small insurgency movement that gained momentum. Until one evening, several armed guards burst through the door of their apartment and dragged them away. Jazmin had never seen her parents again.

It had been her older brother Diego's idea to steal a boat and go to Florida. He'd woken her, Valentina and Marlon in the middle of the night, thrust a bag in their hands containing food and several bottles of water, and led them to a small motorboat he'd tied up near the wharf. It had taken two days to get there. They'd hit sand on one of the Florida keys and slept in a boat shed for the first few weeks, stealing food. Diego had found a job as dishwasher. They'd been able to rent a room in a dilapidated hotel and had slowly dug out a small life for themselves. Every day, Jazmin pined for Cuba. But she could see the opportunity in their uprooted existence. And she was too smart and determined not to make the most of it. She'd taught herself and Valentina English so well they were now both fluent, and both girls had passed the high school equivalency test (off-record), even though they'd never been allowed to attend an actual school.

Once Diego got caught and sent back to Cuba, and Marlon got sucked into the drug ring that finally got him arrested, Jazmin decided that she and Valentina needed to go to New York. She'd read somewhere that the streets of New York were paved with gold. She knew they weren't *actually* gold, but she liked that thought. She'd booked two tickets on a Greyhound bus and they'd arrived in Queens with forty-two dollars in cash and the clothes on their backs. But she'd found a job as a waitress and made a surprising amount of money in tips. They found a small shed to rent—a palace compared to some of the accommodation they'd lived in over the past few years—and a lawyer who would help them get legalized.

Getting deported didn't scare Jazmin. In some ways, she yearned to go home. For her father's memory, though, she had a steely desire to conquer New York City. Other people overcame their challenges, why couldn't she? She had enough grit to do whatever it took. She'd get their green cards, maybe even apply for a scholarship to medical school one day. It would take a lot of work, but work didn't intimidate Jazmin. Work was life. She could become a doctor like her father. And earn the kind of money he'd never even dreamed of.

Getting fired from her under-the-table waitressing job had been a setback. But there were plenty of other waitressing jobs in New York. If only she could get her papers, it would be so much easier to get hired. When their lawyer had suggested blackmailing a wealthy accountant, she'd at first refused. But … *four thousand dollars* would go a very long way. And the lawyer—who'd immediately seemed *off* to Jazmin, but she'd had little choice but to trust her—said she could get their green cards within a few weeks with the extra money they would make. Paying extra would speed up the process, she'd promised.

It would be their first step toward a real life here. One they wouldn't have to hide. Valentina wouldn't have to worry so much and cry herself to sleep every night.

She hated that Valentina had seen so much hardship. Her sister had grown tougher over the years, but Jazmin still worried about her. The setbacks and difficulties were beginning to take their toll.

Valentina had always been a sensitive child. Things affected her deeply and she'd had more trouble adjusting to the loss of their parents and life on the run than either Jazmin or their brothers. Lately that sensitivity had begun to turn, to a quality in her sister that was hard to describe. Bitterness, maybe. Resentment. Jadedness. And all at the age of nineteen. It broke Jazmin's heart and she was driven to change things. To make them better.

So she'd agreed to Tiffany's suggestions.

It hadn't been particularly shocking to Jazmin when Tiffany Chamberlain stiffed them. Early this morning, Jazmin went to confront her, only to learn that Tiffany had moved offices with no forwarding address. For the first time in her life, Jazmin felt defeated. They had no money. They would return to Havana and get jobs in the cigar factory, maybe, or as cleaners for the new wave of tourists. She sat on a bench near a newsstand. And happened to pick up a magazine. With a photo on the cover of five famous siblings. She'd never heard of them, but she had to admit there was something striking about them. She read the interview with Ares. She'd been intrigued, enough to google him on her $29 smartphone. *He seems so sad*, is what she'd been thinking.

And then she saw the photograph of Ares walking out of a restaurant ... *with Tiffany Chamberlain*. They were dating, said the headline. There was another photograph, of Tiffany coming out of his building, wearing couture and Fendi sunglasses, the headline noted.

Jazmin had walked the sixteen blocks. The doorman could neither confirm nor deny but Jazmin got enough information out of him to guess that Tiffany was there. Jazmin made up her mind to wait until either Tiffany or Ares Savage walked through the lobby.

Now, she was glad it had been Ares. He wasn't at all what she would have expected. He was grateful. And under that hard exterior, he was kind. He reminded her, oddly, of herself.

"What's this *whore* doing here?" asked Tiffany Chamberlain, visibly ruffled.

"We didn't actually sleep with anyone for money," Jazmin pointed out. "Only you've done that. I just thought Mr. Savage should know the facts."

"How *dare* you, you meddling little bitch!" Tiffany seethed.

Jazmin stood up to face Tiffany. "How dare *you*, Ms. Chamberlain. You owe my sister four thousand dollars."

"And you owe me two million," said Ares.

Tiffany swirled, confronting Ares. "You believe *her* … over *me*?"

His response was cold. "As a matter of fact, yes."

"But Ares … I *love* you."

"You love my money, Tiffany. And my apartment. Which has new locks, by the way. Your key card will no longer let you in. Neither will Joe. I'll have your things couriered to wherever you'd like."

Hurt, and doing her best to summon tears: "But, *Ares.* What about our *baby?*"

"If there is a baby, and if it's mine—which will be determined incontestably with a DNA test as soon as it's safe to do so—we'll of course discuss how to handle that. I would like to have children one day, Tiffany. I just don't want to be tricked into it."

"I didn't *trick* you, Ares. You were as willing as I was in that limo."

Ares ran a hand through his hair and sighed, as though suddenly exhausted. "That was a mistake. And very well played, by you. Bruce will be contacting you tomorrow. I'll let you keep a hundred grand. That'll get you started on whatever path you decide to take next. I hope you choose one that's less ... evil."

"A hundred *grand?*" From Tiffany's tone it was pretty clear she'd already spent at least that much. Shifting gears from abject sorrow to all-out rage, she glared at Jazmin. "I'll kill you for this." Then she turned and strode out indignantly, leaving an ominous cloud of the newest (and most expensive) Chanel fragrance in her wake.

Senior Detective Statham: Do you feel that you were —possibly somewhat unfairly—taking out your frustrations over unrelated incidents when you threatened to kill Individual 8?

Individual 23 (~~Dawn-Marie Davidson a.k.a. Tiffany Chamberlain~~ [redacted]): No. She totally deserved it, that little man-stealing slut.

13

Athena

MANHATTAN

FOR THE SECOND time that evening, Athena Savage wished that she was heading back to her quiet, empty house. She wanted nothing more than to sit out and watch the moon's reflection over the waves and revel in solitude before climbing into bed for a solid nine hours.

But it was not to be.

Instead, she was in the back of a white stretch limousine with Wyatt Boone. It was typical of a playboy. The showing off. The smooth seduction. As if on cue: "Drink?" He reached into a tiny but well-stocked fridge.

"No, thank you. I'll have water."

His eyes crinkled at the edges and the blue of them sparked even in the dim interior of his limo. He handed her a small bottle of chilled water and poured himself a Jack Daniels, adding two ice cubes.

Athena watched him sip his drink as the lights of the city played across his face, gilding his features and his dark hair with tints of blue and gold as though with a genius's paintbrush. His head was beautifully shaped, his neck brown and strong-looking. She wondered why he'd bothered with any of this. He was clearly a man who could attract a date without paying for it.

"Why bother with the auction?" she asked. "Why not prowl the hot spots of the New York scene? It would have been a lot cheaper."

"'Cheap' isn't something I go out of my way to hunt down." He'd taken off his jacket and tie. The top buttons of his shirt were undone, hinting at a ridiculously powerful, hair-dusted chest. In fact, *everything* about him looked ridiculously powerful. Those guns, *Jesus*. And his thighs would've looked at home on an Australian rugby player. The sheer size of him was intimidating. Or at least it should have been. But she didn't feel afraid of him, even locked away with him in this oversized car. He seemed aware of that possibility and gave her plenty of space, moving slowly as though she were a frightened horse he'd lassoed on the range and was taking care not to spook. "Besides, I thought it might be fun."

Fun?

Okay, so he's hot. But to be bought like a prize pig at the county fair, it's so awkward. Once we get to wherever we're going, I'll politely excuse myself to bed. I'll sleep in tomorrow morning, then the rest of the day will go quickly. Then it'll already be Sunday and I can meet the kids and go home. Easy.

He was either the strong silent type or he was spellbound by her. Which was unlikely. They sat locked in this teasing, inscrutable staring contest. "So, you're from Texas?"

"Yep."

Wonderful. One of *those*. A man who gave one-word answers and squelched all attempts at meaningful conversation.

But then he surprised her. He continued, and when he spoke, his voice was deep and lightly husked, which for some reason made the tiny hairs on her arms lift. "Dallas. My parents were originally from a small town in West Texas. My father was a bricklayer, my mother a secretary. They died in a car crash when I was eighteen."

"I'm so sorry." She'd been eighteen, too, when her father died. Athena still remembered that awful day is if it were yesterday. The phone call. The shift behind her mother's eyes, of her sanity shattering beyond repair. The screaming. Nothing had ever been the same.

"It was years ago now."

Their eyes met, and something else occurred to Athena. A bricklayer? "I thought you said your family was in oil."

Wyatt took another sip of his Jack Daniels. "No. I started up a company when I was twenty that specialized in bypassed oil. The big companies take the easy extractions, but there are often leftover, smaller reservoirs that get overlooked. You can make some good money that way. We've also been diversifying into sustainable, non-fossil fuels over the past few years. It's a little less trendy in Texas, but getting death threats from the establishment adds a certain, I don't know, element of danger that makes the negotiations that much more exciting." Wyatt tipped back the rest of his drink.

"You get death threats?"

"Sometimes."

She wasn't sure how to reply to that, so she said, "Twenty is young, to be starting your own company."

"I was young but determined. It was either that or lay bricks. Which was never something I was going to do."

The car slowed to a stop. Athena looked out the tinted windows. They were at the airport. "Can I ask where we're going?"

"There are some people on board who are very excited to meet you. I'll explain everything once we get on the plane."

Wyatt opened the door for her and led her up the stairs to a private jet. Athena was surprised to see four children already buckled into their roomy seats and a woman serving them glasses of orange juice.

"Athena," said Wyatt. "This is Felicity Campbell, the children's chaperone from the Center. And this is—let me make sure I've got this right—Carlos, Ricky, Tia and Rosie."

"WHOA," said one of the boys when he saw Athena. They were gorgeous little boys with thick black hair and the kind of energy that filled a room, times two. They looked identical.

"*I'm* Carlos," said the other boy. "*He's* Ricky." With that, Carlos proceeded to poke his finger into Ricky's side, causing Ricky to giggle and spill his orange juice.

"*Boys*," said Tia pointedly, even though she was probably no more than eight. "Miss Campbell said to *behave*." Tia had little cornrowed braids all over her head in a style that was impossibly cute and wore a red t-shirt with *HUFFLEPUFF* written across it.

The little girl named Rosie said nothing. She had dark blond hair, pale skin and owlish, hazel eyes. She peered out at them through small round wire-rimmed glasses like a tiny, retro angel. She looked younger than the other three children, and much smaller. Athena didn't think she'd ever seen a more fragile-looking child.

"You brought the children?" Athena was overwhelmed. What an amazingly ... *kind* thing to do.

"Yes. We're taking them to Key West."

"KEY WEST!" said Ricky, his eyes bright with excitement. Then he turned to Tia, whispering. "Where's Key West?"

"It's in FLORIDA!" said Tia, clapping her hands together.

The boys wriggled in their seats as much as their tightened seatbelts would allow.

Rosie continued to stare at Athena.

Athena smiled at her. "I'm glad you're here, Rosie. We're going to have so much fun."

Rosie blinked but said nothing.

"She doesn't talk much," explained Miss Campbell.

The captain's voice crackled over the loudspeaker. "If you'd like to take your seats now, Mr. Boone, and guests, we'll be on our way. Flight time is three and a half hours."

After take-off, once the children's sugar highs spiked then wore off, they all fell sound asleep. So did Miss Campbell.

Wyatt and Athena were seated toward the front of the cabin, with a small table between them. The flight attendant asked if he could bring them a drink and some dinner.

"Don't make me drink alone," said Wyatt. "We're on vacation."

"Is that what this is?" Athena relented, accepting a glass of champagne. Between the mischievous blue eyes and that smile, he was absurdly charming, and he knew it. More than charming. She didn't want to admit it but he was … *nice*. It was there in the way he'd offered the kids a look inside the cockpit once they'd hit a cruising altitude. How he'd asked Rosie if she'd ever ridden a horse. He'd carried her back to her seat and explained that there were horse treks on the beach near the resort they were going to. Rosie just looked at him solemnly through her miniature John Lennon glasses and chewed on her finger. *I'll teach you how to ride, Rosie, would you like that? You can ride with me at first, if you want.* The little girl had nodded solemnly and even slid her thin arm around his neck. Seeing that, Athena had realized something: maybe Wyatt Boone hadn't bid all that money at the auction because he was a playboy. Maybe he'd done it because he knew what hardship felt like. He understood what those kids lacked. Maybe he genuinely wanted to help.

At the realization, Athena felt some little fissure in her judgment of him open a fraction.

Then again, maybe he was laying it all on just to get her into bed.

She wasn't sure. It wouldn't be the first time she'd misjudged someone, either way.

Athena's comfortable, idyllic life had literally shattered when she was seventeen, so profoundly it had changed her personality. From the outside looking in, strangers could only see the money, the lifestyle, the easy opportunities. But the reality had been much different.

Until her family had imploded, Athena had been a bubbly, outgoing, sunny-faced girl. The apple of her father's eye, partly because she looked so much like her mother, Athena had never really known sadness. Her parents were as much in love as the day they'd fallen head over heels at a college party in Boston. It had been love at first sight—Athena's favorite story, which her father used to tell her whenever she begged. They'd married six months later in a lavish Hamptons wedding. Her mother's family had old money from a Pennsylvanian steel magnate grandfather. Her father had a head for business and wide-ranging interests. He was so charismatic, people went out of their way to work with him and to fund his projects, which he dove into with the enthusiasm and energy of a man who'd never even considered failure. Their wealth grew. They bought more houses. They traveled extensively to fun, exotic locations with their five children, who were just as beautiful and destined-for-success as their parents.

Things hadn't always been perfect, of course. Especially at the end. There had been arguments, drinking, a feeling that her parents were experiencing some bumps in the road. But they never talked about it. To their children, they did their best to mask whatever it was they were dealing with behind closed doors.

And one fateful day, everything changed.

Jack Savage loved the water. He'd been on the rowing team at Harvard and swam competitively in high school. He spent most weekends on his beloved sailboat. He was equally at home in the ocean as he was on dry land. Fit and young-looking for his fifty-four years, no one thought anything of it when he went out one calm August afternoon for his daily swim.

In the end, the autopsy confirmed he'd drowned. No one knew of any "enemies." He had business rivals, sure, but what successful entrepreneur didn't? Mainly, Jack had had friends, colleagues and admirers.

Traces of sleeping pills had been found in his system, but it was a prescription he and his wife had both occasionally used. Alcohol, too, but it wasn't unusual for Jack to have had a gin and tonic with lunch every now and then. Multiple businesses, a long-term marriage with all the ups and downs that go along with it, and five busy, famous children … these things were stressful sometimes. A sleeping pill or a G&T were hardly grounds for a murder investigation.

It was the rumors of suicide that had dismantled his family as much as the loss. What reason would he have had to kill himself? A couple of his kids were on the wild side, but that was hardly unusual. His wife might have enjoyed a tiny bit more Chardonnay than the average housewife, but that was no reason to pull the plug on a life that appeared as perfect as a life could get.

But the rumors, as rumors tend to do, took on a life of their own. People wanted to speculate. Maybe their fabulous life wasn't quite as fabulous as the façade suggested. Maybe there were marriage troubles and secret vendettas.

The media and their bottom-feeding sidekick, the paparazzi, went into a frenzy. They hounded Jack's widow and children wherever they went, shouting questions, demanding answers. *Did your mother kill your father, Athena? I've heard she's a drunk and a psycho. There must be skeletons in your parents' closets. What are they? Give us some clues: what devastating truths could lead a man with a life like that to take his own life?*

The problem was: there *were* secrets. She remembered her parents' arguments. Her father's time out from their family life, enough to notice something was going on. Her mother's escalating drinking habit.

What had gone wrong?

The mystery only deepened as time passed. It never got easier, like everyone said it was supposed to do.

Why, Dad? You could have talked to me. Maybe I could have helped.

After her father's death, Athena had withdrawn almost completely. She dropped out of school, unable to bear the weight of both the grief and the scrutiny. The knowing glances and the whispered speculations. Both she and Artemis had finished high school with live-in tutors.

Security around the house was beefed up tenfold. And Cassie Savage had to be checked in to a mental institution, where she withered away into a wild-eyed husk of a person who mumbled and pointed at things over your shoulder when nothing was there. Eventually they'd brought her home. Apollo had insisted on it. Live-in help kept her stable and heavily medicated. Until one night, she'd been lucid enough to make her way down to the pool for an early evening swim and a dedicated mission to join her husband in the afterlife.

Apollo found her. And Athena found Apollo. Some tragedies don't ever get easier.

Ever since, Athena had kept to herself, avoiding the spotlight at all costs. She hated attention. And she understood heartbreak. So much so that she couldn't bear to get close to people outside of her own family. For the past four years, she'd created a bubble of her own design. She lived alone with her cat. She wrote her books—which she could immerse herself in to escape from her own thoughts—but shunned publicity that involved crowded rooms. And she visited with one of her brothers or her sister only every couple of months.

On the rare occasion when the solitude became too much, she'd relent and accept a dinner party invitation or a date with one of the overly-entitled trust-fund dweebs or self-impressed young bankers who lived nearby. Which were always disastrous. They were all so outrageously tight-assed. For such wealthy men, Athena marveled at their stinginess and greed. Their *meanness*. Their willingness to overlook corruption or complacence as long as their bank balances remained intact or, even better, fatter. No matter if others suffered as a result.

Wyatt Boone's compassion was refreshing.

And these children were about to have an experience that might make their difficulties feel a little less difficult.

For the first time in years, she resolved to spend the next day and a half living in the moment, without dwelling so tediously on the tragedies of the past—something she'd spent far too much time doing. She was in Key West with four excited children, their chaperone, and one … Texan. She could at least *try* to enjoy herself.

Individual 14 (~~Lady Baba~~ [redacted]): My life flashed before my eyes and I'm not taking any more chances. My design team is creating several bullet-proof catsuits for my next performance, made from a graphene composite that's stronger than Kevlar *and* spider silk. In sequined hot pink, a glittery gold lamé, and my favorite, nude.

14

Eros

PRIVATE JET
FLIGHT FROM NEW YORK CITY TO RURAL
TENNESSEE

Eros's weekend started somewhat more rockily. Eros had opted to take Marlowe to a luxury getaway in rural Tennessee. A friend had told him about the weekend she'd spent there, and how luxurious and serene the place was. Perfect, thought Eros. He had exactly thirty-six hours to convince his dream co-star that he was, if she'd only give him half a chance, full of depth and character—so much so, she'd be compelled to put in a good word for him to her brother (and also fall head over heels in love with him). The fact that Lenore hadn't called him back yet meant that they were still deliberating. Maybe they were on the fence. A nod from the lead actress might be just enough to get Eros over the line.

He'd thought it would be easy, like it usually was.

Usually, they fell at his feet and tripped over themselves to help him.

Not this time.

So far, Marlowe had glared at him once, when he'd paid the million dollars to spend the weekend with her. Then she'd dutifully but begrudgingly followed him to his waiting car, refused a drink, put her earbuds in and cranked up her music so loudly he spent the entire ride to the airport internalizing his concern for her eardrums and trying not to chug his vodka.

Once airborne, when the flight attendant had asked Marlowe if she could get her a drink—which Marlowe had to take her earbuds out in order to hear—Eros gently snagged his fingers through the thin cord connected to her phone. "Come on," he said softly. "Please. Just for a minute."

She shot him a look out of those green eyes that communicated, if not pure hatred, then something very close to it.

This was going to be harder than he first thought. But fuck it. He hadn't *done* anything, for Chrissakes. Except pay a shitload of money—to *charity*—to spend a couple hours in her majesty's company. It wouldn't kill her to make polite conversation for five minutes.

"I'll warn you now," she said, "I'm not into country music. Not in the slightest."

Oh, right: she'd noticed they were on their way to Tennessee. He stared at her, and tried not to be rendered agog by that cute-hot Medusa thing she had going on. Maybe she had a right to be resentful about giving up her time. Then again, she'd only done it so that others could benefit. At least she could *attempt* to appreciate the effort he was genuinely trying to make. Her holier-than-thou schtick was starting to piss him off. "I can hear that. And so can the pilot."

She fixed her emerald-bright eyes on him until he felt like he might be melting. Her pupils might as well have been forged from Kryptonite. He searched them for something that might be close to … adoration? Awe? The usual stuff. But there was none of anything in that neighborhood, or even close to it. She looked bored. And pissed off. "You can hear that?"

"Every dirty word." He glanced out the window to the twinkling lights far below. "And so can that guy down there in Philadelphia."

"So I happen to like music that has a brain and a message and isn't about bedding homecoming queens, getting drunk and driving around in a pick-up truck. I don't expect you to understand it. You *can't* understand it. Because you've never lived it."

Eros had been credited with co-writing one of Apollo's songs, as a matter of fact, and wasn't totally in the dark about the L.A. music scene. "I don't happen to think rap's message is all that different or necessarily more profound than one about drinking a beer with your girl and living your life down a dusty dirt road. Everyone's just trying to do the best they can with the hand they've been dealt. It doesn't make it better or worse. Just different."

They were practically arguing, but this time Marlowe's stony expression gave way to something else. There it was: the hint of a not-quite smile. "Damn," she said. "He's deeper than he looks."

If Eros thought Marlowe Mercy was stunning when she was shooting him angry glares, her smile had all the effect of a chorus of angels on steroids. Even if it was more of a laughing-*at*-you smile than laughing-*with*-you smile. But the ice was somehow breaking. So he forged ahead with his pick-axe. He had too much at stake here not to. "For someone so high and mighty about your music's message, isn't that a little hypocritical? You don't know the first thing about me. You've never even spoken to me yet you've already made up your mind about what I know and what I don't know. It seems to me, that attitude goes directly *against* the grain of your music's 'message'." He even used his fingers to make little air quotes.

"Not exactly," she said, entirely unimpressed by his philosophical outburst. "I'm judging you by the fact that you're using me to get to my brother. Admit it, the reason you paid to spend time with me is because you want me to put in a good word for you about the movie role."

Okay, so she was right. That had been part of the reason. The other part was that he was hoping she'd jump into bed with him.

He could lie and pretend neither of these details were true.

But then, Eros decided, if you're five minutes in to what you hope will turn into the most professionally meaningful relationship you've ever had—with the role of a lifetime that could possibly catapult your career into the award-winning stratosphere hanging in the balance—it was probably best to tell the truth. The more time he spent with her, the more she seemed to imprint him with a hot, sparked fascination that dug deeper than he was used to emotions digging. She disarmed him. None of the stuff that usually mattered to people mattered to her. The looks, the money, the name: these were strikes against him in her eyes and he wasn't sure how to overcome the details of who he was. The strength of his character was in play here and it wasn't a muscle he had to exercise very often.

Which was sort of problem, now that he thought about it.

He hoped he was up to the challenge.

Of course I'm up to it. Aren't I? Yes. I have to be. "It had crossed my mind," he admitted. "But it's not the only reason. I wanted to get to know you. And I knew you'd never give me the chance unless you were more or less forced into it."

She contemplated him, more gently this time. "You're right."

Eros smiled hopefully. "I promise I won't ask you to put in a good word for me. And I won't sing a single song about Chevys or Bud Light."

"Good." She accepted her cup of tea from the flight

attendant, thanked her, and unwound her headphones from Eros's fingers. "I appreciate that you've paid good money for a good cause. But I don't really respect the fact that you're trying to use that money to buy yourself a part in my brother's movie. Also, as far as what you 'know' and 'don't know'"—mimicking his air quotes—"I'll try to be as clear on that topic as I possibly can: I really don't care." Marlowe smiled sweetly before popping her earbuds back in and cranking up some Tupac.

Senior Detective Statham: How would you describe your relationship with Individual 5?

Individual 13 (~~Marlowe Mercy~~ [redacted]): [refers to list] Stormy … and all that implies.

15

———

𝒜pollo

SOUTHAMPTON

"WHAT EMOTIONS ARE you trying to hide from when you take drugs or drink to excess?"

Apollo was losing his mind. His family hadn't booked him into the kind of hospital that releases a person when their injuries are healed enough for them to go home. Oh, no. Those twisted sadists had booked him into a full-blown rehab. A "research rehabilitation facility," the staff kept reminding him, where doe-eyed medical students flanked the doctors like gaggles of intellectually-impaired ducklings.

He was pacing, as much as his hospital gown would allow. The bandaged wound on his side still hurt like hell, his head was wrapped and he had a full cast on one arm. If he could have climbed the walls, he would have.

"Gee, let me think about that," Apollo said, with exaggerated thoughtfulness. "Maybe it's the feelings of self-hatred that rise up whenever I think of how disappointing I would have been to my high-achieving hero of a father. Or maybe it's those pesky daggers of guilt that kill me a little more each time I think of my devastated, beautiful mother. It was me who insisted she was released from the mental hospital, did you know that? If the place was anything like *this* hellhole, I'm glad I did. Except for the part where she OD'ed with enough Xanax mixed with bourbon to kill her several times over before drowning herself. My late-night swim was especially eventful that evening, oh yeah."

"I think we're getting somewhere," the doctor declared, raising a small finger.

The shrink was strange-looking. Hairless except for a few wispy tufts, with a scrunched-up, wizened little face. If it wasn't for the ears, he could have been a distant relation of Yoda's. His sidekick was an earnest graduate student, so squeaky clean he was actually shiny. The whiteness of his teeth and the scribbling sound his pencil was making as he took notes were giving Apollo a crushing headache and the urge to kill, maim or jump out the nearest window.

"You say you feel guilty about your mother's death," said Yoda. "What do you mean by that?"

"I just *told* you what I fucking meant by that! Everyone else wanted her to stay in the mental hospital! But *I* kicked up such a fuss that they agreed to bring her home. Two months later, she was dead. See?: my fault." This was ridiculous. "She'd probably still be alive to this day if I hadn't loved her so much I couldn't stand to see quacks like you tampering with her fragile state of mind like a bunch of blood-sucking vampires."

"*You* didn't kill your mother, Apollo."

"I know *I* didn't kill her! But it was still my fault!" Apollo grabbed fistfuls of his hair before realizing he'd pulled off the bandage on his head. He threw it at the wall where it made a thwacking sound before hitting the floor.

"I think that's enough for today," said the Jedi master. The graduate student stood up and blinked at Apollo vacuously.

To Apollo, the only thing worse than spilling his guts to these psychoanalytical twits was returning to his empty room to stare at the ceiling for another twelve hours. Drug-free. To make matters even worse, that nurse, Daisy Sullivan, hadn't been back. It was hard to tell how much time was passing in this soulless insane asylum. He was starting to wonder if he'd dreamed her. And it was driving him almost as crazy as the lack of recreational painkillers he so desperately craved.

"Look," Apollo said. "I'll tell you anything you want to know. My demons aren't shy or difficult to understand. The reasons I self-medicate are so easy to interpret even this guy—" gesturing toward the doctor's round-eyed minion "—could identify them. At this point I'm out-patient material. We know why I'm fucked up. Let's diagnose me and send me on my merry way. I've had enough of this bullshit."

Instead of agreeing to Apollo's very reasonable suggestion, Yoda leafed through the papers in Apollo's hefty file. "It appears that you've been treated as an outpatient …" —more leafing— "… six times. You've been arrested for disorderly behavior and driving while intoxicated …" —leaf— "… seven times and four times, respectively. You've been admitted to the hospital for drug and alcohol-related issues including, in one case, a drug overdose …"

Another fucking leaf.

Apollo walked over to Yoda and—as gently as he was capable of—closed the file, keeping his hand on it. "Yes. I've got a sordid past, so what. It makes me an interesting conversationalist. You can't, however, hold me here against my will. I've already decided to get clean. I need to go home, take it easy for a while and get my life back on track. Message received, loud and clear. Now if you'll just sign my discharge papers, doc, I'll leave you all in peace and you can enjoy the rest of your self-important day."

Yoda leaned back in his chair and folded his tiny arms. If Apollo wasn't mistaken, there was a defiant gleam in his bulgy eyes. "I'm afraid I can't do that, Apollo. Your family has staged what we refer to as an intervention. This means that—"

"I know what a fucking intervention is!" Apollo

couldn't believe this. "I don't need an intervention! What I *need* is to get out of this prison and go home!"

"This 'prison'," said Yoda, unruffled, "is in fact the finest teaching hospital in the east. You'll be glad to know our success rate is among the highest in the nation."

Apollo took a deep breath. His headache was ballooning into a full-blown migraine, which didn't help his horrendous mood. "Let me call my brother."

"I'm afraid I can't do that, either. No contact with family is allowed for the first two weeks of rehabilitation treatment."

Apollo tried to remain calm. Surely he could reason with them. "This is all a big misunderstanding, doc. I'm fine now. I'll heal faster at home. I've got commitments. Please. Just let me call Ares."

Yoda, whose name in fact was Dr. August Finklestein —renowned expert in the fields of addiction and psycho-analysis, author of a number of teaching textbooks which included several chapters on this exact scenario and also the chief of staff of the hospital—had predicted Apollo's meltdown before it even began. He had three orderlies armed with sedatives stationed outside the door of his office, ready to barge in as soon as he pushed the small button located under his desk.

His finger hovered near its target.

"I can show you Ares's signature on the papers autho-rizing us to take the measures necessary for your full recovery, Apollo. If you'd like to see it."

Apollo eyeballed Dr. Finklestein. Then his gaze slid to the gormless graduate student, to assess his pockets for the telltale shape of a cell phone. Apollo sidled closer. "I *am* fully recovered. As good as. All I need is one phone call and—"

Dr. Finkelstein pushed the button.

Apollo almost had the student in a headlock before he was dragged off by two orderlies who'd obviously downloaded The Rock's motivational work-out app months ago. "This is illegal!" Apollo was yelling as they pinned him to the ground. "I'll call the police! I'll sue!" A third orderly injected a needle into Apollo's arm.

Almost immediately, Apollo felt the cool wash of the drugs numbing his system. It wasn't the outcome he'd been hoping for, but the tantrum had been worth it. At least he wasn't stone-cold sober anymore.

Apollo grasped at the memory of her. She'd told him her name. The one person in this hellish prison who might listen to him. The glowing angel with her golden eyes and her sunny face. Maybe *she* had a phone. "Let me see Daisy Sullivan." Apollo tried, unsuccessfully, to fight off the rising oblivion. "I need to talk to her. I need her. Please."

The graduate student, who had the unfortunate name of Dudley Halfcock, had so little pop culture exposure, he had no idea who Apollo was. He did, however, have several degrees and a theory. He also, possibly because he'd been ridiculed by his peers since the day he was born over his name (and, even worse, his nickname, Dud, which most people insisted on calling him, no matter how many times he corrected them), had an intense desire to prove himself by becoming the most successful rehab doctor the world had ever seen. He'd already begun the paperwork to change his name. He'd be Dr. Duke Manning by the end of the month. He'd eclipse the accomplishments of fucking Finklestein by the time he was thirty, he was determined.

Dud brushed himself off and grabbed his pencil from under the desk, where it had rolled during the scuffle, and scribbled the name Apollo had murmured onto his notepad.

Senior Detective Statham: Would you describe Individual 3 as unstable?

Individual 24 (~~Dudley Halfcock a.k.a. Duke Manning~~ [redacted]): Addiction is an illness, Detective. It's not necessarily a case of lacking moral principles, if that's what you're asking me.

16

Cooper Salazar

PARIS

"I WANT to thank you all for listening, and I wish you a very good evening."

Applause. Which Cooper Salazar barely noticed. He smiled, shook a few hands, made some banal small talk, politely excused himself and made his way out onto the street.

Cooper was feeling reckless. He'd just finished giving the keynote speech at the Innovations in Eco-Design conference in Paris. They'd flown him here and put him up in a luxury hotel. He even had a full day in Paris tomorrow with nothing to do before his flight back to Boulder the following morning.

Until then, he had one plan and one plan only: getting inebriated. What better place to do it, after all? He'd pull a Hemingway, wander around, sit in bars, people-watch and heavily imbibe his way through the afternoon. Instead of writing a book, he'd draw. He had an idea for a new building that had been bouncing around in his head for a while now. Ultra-modern. Glass. Not industrial-looking, but softened by the effects of wood and stone that mimicked its natural environment. He couldn't wait to get started. But first, wine and whiskey and plenty of it.

Cooper's thoughts returned again to the photographs his private investigator had sent him only hours ago. Of his wife. In bed with five different men on five different occasions. Occasions that had happened to take place *before* their separation.

He'd suspected it, of course. That had been part of the problem: he didn't particularly care.

Cooper had never felt that Nicole was the love of his life. Which was possibly the reason their marriage had been doomed from the start.

Even so, *five*? Jesus.

He could hardly blame her. He was away so much. If he wasn't sleeping, he was either at work or thinking about work. But that's what it took to get ahead in his game. Architects were a dime a dozen. Good architects, now they were a lot harder to find.

They'd met three and a half years ago. Nicole was five years older than Cooper and had been adamant they get married as soon as possible. She could feel her biological clock ticking, she'd said. Two years and no baby later, they'd gone to the fertility doctors. The problem wasn't with him, they reported, but with Nicole. It was some kind of woman's issue he hadn't wanted to hear about in too much detail. Once they told him everything in his department was fine, above average and in fact somewhat impressive as far as statistics like that went, he'd sort of tuned out.

In truth, he was more relieved than jilted, or angry. He hadn't been fully invested in the marriage in … well, for a long time, if ever. It was best if they went their separate ways, especially now. He'd file for divorce as soon as he got home.

Coop decided to walk back to his hotel. It was a beautiful night in Paris. The Eiffel Tower glowed gold. It was hard not to indulge your romantic tendencies in a place like this. Maybe he should have been a better husband. More attentive. More *into* it. The fact was, he'd never even wanted to get married, not really. He'd been young and hadn't felt entirely ready. His heart hadn't been in the whole baby-making drama either. He'd gone along with both, because it's what was expected. His upper middle class parents in Rye wanted a successful, stable family man for a son. Cooper was the only child of older, professional parents. His father, a lawyer, had wanted him to take over the firm. They hadn't spoken for a year when Cooper had changed majors his sophomore year at Cornell. Once he'd gained some recognition and started winning awards, his father begrudgingly forgave him. His mother, however, would never have forgiven him if he'd let Nicole get away. *Her family's from Scarsdale, how wonderful!*

And doctors! She's perfect. We'll put the announcement in the Times so everyone will see it. There's no point waiting. When are you buying a house? Are you thinking of having babies yet? You shouldn't put it off too long, she's nearly thirty. That had been two weeks into the relationship. They'd all been so excited about it, so insistent he and Nicole were the perfect match. He, however, had never been sure. But any reservations he might have had, as usual, were dismissed and swept aside.

Cooper had been doing what *other* people wanted him to do for far too long.

Tonight, in Paris, with the twinkling lights illuminating the city, he decided it was time to start doing what *he* wanted to do. Trying to make other people happy never worked anyway.

He took a detour so he could walk past the glass pyramid of the Louvre. Such an inspired addition to the museum, thought Cooper. The perfect balance of old world charm and innovative modernism.

As he stood there admiring it, he felt a light tap on his shoulder. "Mr. Salazar?"

He turned. Holy hell, it was *her*. The girl he'd tried—very unsuccessfully—to put out of his mind.

That day he'd first met Artemis at the Savage house in Telluride, he'd had the bizarre—and outrageously *intense*—urge to pick her up and carry her away and ride off with her into the sunset. It had been jarring, the sparks or the chemistry—*whatever* it was. He was so used to playing the professional, he'd managed to keep his cool and do, as he was so practiced at doing, exactly what was expected of him.

He'd told her that day she resembled her father. She had his dark hair. The more he'd watched her, though, the more he realized she was the spitting image of her mother, but even more stunning, if such a thing was possible. When he'd met the Savages, his first thought had been that Jack Savage was the luckiest man in the world. Cassie was gorgeous and smart and entirely smitten with her husband. Come to think of it, *that* was the detail that had held Cooper back when it came to his own marriage. He and Jack had intellectually clicked. They'd ended up having some intense conversations, and Cooper knew Jack's marriage to Cassie wasn't perfect. It was passionate and at times volatile but mostly it had been deep and very real. They loved each other and always would, you could just tell.

Cooper had witnessed whole-hearted love, and he'd wanted that kind of intensity for himself. As a young man just venturing into those waters, he'd hoped for something equally meaningful.

Things hadn't turned out that way.

She was dressed in a black, high-fashion outfit and, against the backdrop of the sparkling, moonlit glass pyramid, looked outrageously glamorous. "What are you doing here?"

"I just finished up a photo shoot inside the museum. We had to work late after a fiasco that didn't quite work out at Notre Dame. What about you? It's so strange to bump into you here, of all places. I've actually been thinking about calling you."

"You have?"

"I wanted to talk to you about a design, for a studio I'd like to build. In Telluride."

"I'd love to hear about it," Cooper said. "Would you … like to have a drink with me? My hotel is just over there. There's a bar that looks out over the river."

"I'd love to, Mr. Salazar."

"Cooper."

She smiled. "Cooper."

Artemis

PARIS

THEY WALKED TOGETHER along the Rue de Rivoli toward Cooper's hotel.

Artemis didn't really believe in fate or the alignment of the stars or whatever it was that explained wild coincidences like this one. Running into Cooper Salazar next to the Louvre's pyramid on a warm, late-summer Parisian night felt very random indeed. And just after she'd been thinking of him, only hours ago.

He looked striking, as he had at her house that day.

His thick hair was sort of swooshed back from his face offhandedly. He wore a navy blue suit, a striped business shirt and a dark blue tie with tiny white polka dots. A scarf with black and white stripes was loosely wrapped around his neck, giving him a cool, artsy vibe. He smiled at her, and it was a smile layered with disbelief, if she was reading him correctly. Exactly the same emotion she was feeling.

Before they could get far, two girls ran up to Artemis, overcome with excitement.

"Artemis Savage? Is it really you?" said one of the girls, out of breath.

Not again.

"I can't believe it!" squealed the other. "Can we get a photo with you?"

"Of course." But her heart sank. She didn't want to be mobbed tonight. How would she be able to have a quiet drink at the bar to discuss her plans for the studio with Cooper if word was already out?

By the time she'd taken several selfies with fans, a crowd was already forming. Which always made Artemis uneasy. Ever since that stalker had broken into her house, she felt wary of too much attention, especially out in the open, where she couldn't protect herself if she was surrounded. She carried a can of pepper spray in her bag, but she could hardly pull it out and threaten these girls with it.

Cooper noticed Artemis's anxiety. "Ladies," he said. "It's late. That's enough for tonight." He placed his hand reassuringly on Artemis's arm and began to lead her away.

"Who're *you*?" asked the girls. "Are you *together*? Oh my god, he's so *hot*! Who *is* he?" More squeals. A stream of hollered questions followed them, which Cooper ignored.

"Wow," he murmured.

Artemis had to walk quickly to keep up with his long strides, but she was glad he was here with her. Like a buffer against the craziness.

"I mean this entirely gentlemanly," Cooper said, "but it might be better if we have that drink in my hotel suite. I've got a balcony on the top floor with a great view, and a bottle of complimentary champagne I hadn't gotten around to drinking yet. Then I'll make sure you get back to wherever you're staying, safely."

"That sounds perfect." She tried to shield her face, but it was no use. People were taking pictures as she entered the hotel, and as they got into the elevator together. "I hope you don't mind being speculated about all over social media tonight," she added.

It was then that Artemis remembered: he was married.

They'd just been photographed together by at least twenty people, retreating into his hotel. Now, in the tiny, calm cocoon of the ancient elevator, she could see the beginnings of dark stubble on his square jaw. His eyes were the color of black coffee lit with glinting flecks of gold. "Your wife might not be too pleased," she pointed out.

"My wife and I just separated."

Artemis had seen the headline, but she was hardly going to ask him about it. They'd discuss the work project, then she'd make her way back to her hotel. "I'm sorry."

"We've been drifting apart for a while." Maybe running into an acquaintance next to the Louvre's glass pyramid on a perfect night in Paris meant you could share details of your life that you might have, under any other circumstance, kept to yourself. Cooper continued. "We'd already separated. But I just found out she's been cheating on me. With at least five different men."

Artemis's eyebrows lifted. "Five? Yikes."

Cooper shook his head and exhaled a single, defeated-sounding chuckle. "Yeah."

"No kids?"

"No kids."

They'd arrived at his floor and he led her down the hallway—which was mercifully empty—to his private suite. Now that they were here, Artemis wondered if this was such a good idea after all. She didn't know him, beyond the distant associations with her parents and her house, and this suddenly felt sort of … intimate.

But he was already popping the champagne and pouring it into two flutes. And he opened the doors onto his balcony, which was on the top floor and looked out over the rooftops of Paris, the low-hanging moon and the spire of the Eiffel Tower that insisted on infusing everything with its magical, romantic presence.

They sat next to each other on the cushioned bench to enjoy the view.

"Tell me about the building you want designed," Cooper said, "Is it an addition?"

"A studio. Down by the river. It's for Apollo. I think he might like a quiet place to work."

"I heard about what happened. How is he?"

"He'll be fine. He's in rehab."

"I'm sorry."

Artemis was sure Cooper was aware of all the gruesome details of her parents' deaths, and all the drama that had come before, including her mother's slow and alcohol-assisted descent into madness. He'd known them. There had also been no escaping the headlines, once the news broke. Her family's agony had provided a sadistically excitable feeding frenzy for the media. Like those weatherpeople that can't wait for the massive, incoming hurricane to wipe out as many communities as possible. It didn't make any sense to Artemis. "Anyway, I guess it runs in the family."

"Everyone has their demons," Cooper said.

Everyone? thought Artemis. She wanted to ask him what *his* demons were. Why had his wife cheated? Was the break-up his wife's fault ... or somehow his?

"Your parents had one of the most beautiful marriages I've ever seen," he said. "I used to envy them."

This was comforting to hear. And he was remarkably

easy to talk to. It felt *good* to talk about this dark secret—which wasn't really a secret at all but had always felt like one—with someone who'd known them. "I think they were happy. Aside from the arguments, which seemed to get worse toward the end."

"Marriages can be hard work. No one really know what's going on inside them except the two people trapped—well, it sometimes feels that way, at least—in there."

"How did you find out your wife was cheating?" She instantly regretted the question. Was it too personal? But Cooper didn't seem to mind. He seemed to be enjoying the openness of their conversation, just like she was.

"I hired a private investigator. But I already knew. It wasn't hard to figure out." Cooper tipped back the last of his champagne. He walked inside and brought out the bottle, refilling both their glasses. "I'm filing for divorce as soon as I get back."

"I'm sorry things didn't work out."

"Even if my marriage hadn't been very much on the rocks before that day when I met you in Telluride, it would definitely be over now."

"What do you mean?"

"You reminded me of what I want. Like what your parents had once, even if they hit a rough patch later. At least they'd known it. At least they experienced what the real thing actually felt like. I got married because my parents wanted me to." He chuckled morosely. "Which is a terrible reason to get married."

She smiled sympathetically. "Probably true."

"I also mean," he said slowly, "that I haven't been able to stop thinking about you."

She paused, but decided to be honest with him. "I've thought about you, too."

Cooper returned her smile, as though reading her thoughts. They were sitting close to each other now. Very close. His thigh was almost touching hers. "I'm very glad to hear that."

Artemis was a guarded yet very resilient person. Becoming an orphan in your teens will do that to a girl. Getting hounded by the paparazzi day and night ever since will do that even more.

Yet with Cooper, she didn't feel guarded. And she didn't feel the *need* to be resilient. Her usual desire to shield herself had entirely melted away.

She could see the golden glints in his eyes.

The champagne, the ridiculously romantic backdrop, the loneliness that had entirely disappeared somewhere between the Louvre's pyramid and right here ... it all converged in one forward direction.

She touched her fingertips to his face. Very gently, he kissed her lips. He made a low sound, almost like a sigh.

His kiss, his minted-whiskey taste and the smoky, manly scent of him infused Artemis with a frenzied bloom of lust. As they kissed, he lifted her easily and carried her inside, unzipping her jumpsuit, which fell to the floor. The only thing she wore underneath was a minuscule G-string. He kissed her hungrily, with an edge of desperation that was the sexiest thing that had ever happened to Artemis. She wanted his hands, his fingers, his mouth, with a fever she barely recognized. She couldn't get close enough fast enough.

He peeled off her panties, kneeling down to taste her. His mouth was there, enticing the heat with his tongue as he gripped her with strong hands—*those* hands that she'd once fantasized about. The violent bursts of beauty swelled in melting waves that were more than Artemis could bear, crashing through her in almost-unbearable surges of pleasure. She felt his hands catch her, hold her and lay her down on the bed. The slick head of his thick cock was sliding inside her, stretching her to receive him. He thrust himself all the way to the hilt, forcing the plea-sure deeper, and deeper, until the wild sensations Cooper Salazar impaled her with, relentlessly and with total, crazy passion, were the only things she knew or cared about.

Artemis
&
Cooper

PARIS

THE NEXT DAY and a half were, for both of them, a kind of fever dream. When it came to relationships, Artemis had led a sheltered but not uneventful life. She was neither reserved nor loose and she trusted her own judgment. She was a person who, once she'd made a decision, embraced ownership and ran with it. But she'd never experienced anything like *this*, swept up in the arms of a seasoned, exceptionally-virile beefcake in the prime of his life who was honed to perfection from the punishing lunchtime hour he spent every day at the gym. He was also—after three years of an unhappy marriage and more than six months of total abstinence—revved up and raring to go. All of the above conspired to make Cooper Salazar an exceptionally thorough lover.

Coop took his time—as much as he could with Artemis's passionate response to everything he did to her. He was careful yet stealthy, tender but insistent.

He was also sexy as fuck. Artemis couldn't believe how beautiful he was and how *good* he felt.

His heavy weight was on top of her, he was kissing her face, smoothing back a damp strand of her hair. Her arms and legs were wrapped around him. She could feel the slippery wetness of their bond, the huge bulk of him wedged deep, where the ripples of pleasure still lingered.

"I should have asked this earlier, of course," he murmured lazily, gazing down at her.

"Asked what?"

"You wouldn't happen to be on the pill, by any chance."

She blinked at him, mesmerized, once again, by his raw, masculine appeal. "I am, luckily."

A smile touched the corner of his perfect mouth. "That's good, I guess." He kissed her softly.

"I guess it is."

After an unhurried pause, he said, "It wouldn't have mattered. I wouldn't have cared either way."

It was sort of a heavy thing to say, especially considering they'd only just met a few hours ago.

But Artemis figured that sometimes things like this happened that you couldn't control or predict that felt so *right* you just had to go with it and not second guess it or overanalyze it. She'd gone on the pill to regulate her cycle and she was glad now. But he was right. They'd experienced one of those moments when the carnal cravings of animal lust had overridden common sense or the weighing up of consequences.

She and Cooper Salazar *clicked* and it was a bond that already felt important and magical, like he'd reached succulently into her body and soul and imprinted himself there with his vivid eyes and his gripping hands. She was already addicted to him. She didn't want him to disconnect from her body.

Or her life.

It was almost disconcerting that her reaction to him was *this* immediate and all-consuming.

But Artemis had already decided to go with it. He felt too good not to.

After several hours and, between the two of them,

seven profoundly intense climaxes later, they ordered room service. He wrapped the duvet around her and held her on his lap as they sat out on the balcony and looked out over the river and the lights of the city. Then he took her back to bed and made such sweet love to her again, she cried in his arms from the sheer overload of her emotions. Already, she couldn't imagine being without him.

They slept for a while, then spent the entire day in bed, entwined, telling each other their deepest, most sacred secrets.

They talked about lighter topics, too. Their favorite cities and movies and books. Artemis's thoughts for the studio she wanted to build. Cooper told her about the building he'd been thinking about—the one he'd planned to spend the day drawing. He was animated as he described the details of his design and Artemis loved the sound of it. His voice. His excitement. His passion for his work.

"I want you to build it exactly like that," she said, kissing his lips. "It sounds perfect."

He positioned her so he could thrust deeper inside her. The rhythm of her ecstasy set off Cooper's own.

They simply couldn't get enough.

The next morning came too soon. They both had flights back to Colorado. They showered together, as intimate as it was possible to be, then he helped her dress. As soon as he'd zipped up her little black jumpsuit, all he wanted to do was rip it off again. He'd never felt so desperate in his life. The thought of leaving her was physically painful.

"The photographers will be down there," she said, "waiting to pounce. They'll know we've been here together all this time. They'll know what hotel I was supposed to be staying at. And the pictures they took will already be all over the internet."

Coop had heard his phone vibrate with incoming messages but hadn't even considered answering it. "What do you want to tell them?"

A shadow of concern touched her expression.

"Artemis," he said gently, tucking a lock of her hair, wet from the shower, behind her ear. "We'll say whatever you want to say. We can go out separately. You can say you decided to stay in a different hotel, who's to know why? We'll give them a believable story. It's your call."

The thought of going down there alone was daunting. He'd handled those girls by the Louvre so deftly. And she'd given up worrying about the press's speculations about her love life a long time ago.

Then again, leaving together would confirm it. Maybe it was best not to. She had no idea what would happen next. If they would even see each other again. The thought brought tears to her eyes. "I'll go first."

Cooper kissed her lips for the thousandth time. "As long as I can see you again as soon as possible, I don't really care about the rest."

"What about … your wife?" Artemis believed the things he'd told her about his wife and his divorce.

Beyond that, she didn't know how to feel. She so badly wanted to take him home with her. *To keep him.* She felt disconcertingly connected to him already.

"My only concern about my wife is that she won't sign the divorce papers fast enough."

"Come to Telluride with me."

He wrapped her in his arms. "I'll tell my wife it's over and get the ball rolling with the divorce papers tonight. I have two client meetings in the morning. I can be in Telluride by late tomorrow afternoon. We'll figure it out from there."

Her life seemed to have jumped onto a completely different track than she'd ever expected. Now all she wanted to do was to keep it there.

"Everything will be okay," he said.

Would it? He was still, technically, very much married.

Cooper called and arranged for two separate taxis. Then he kissed her again, touching his tongue to her lips, addicted to everything about her, drawing away only to answer the call from the concierge. Artemis's taxi had arrived.

"Ready?"

Artemis took a deep breath. "Ready. But there's really no point getting separate taxis. Let's just go together."

"Are you sure?"

She nodded. The truth was, she couldn't bear the thought of facing all those cameras alone. She knew all about how vicious they could be when they smelled a story. What if *he* was there—the man who'd broken into her house—or someone equally as dangerous? It was terrifying, having people rabidly wanting a piece of you.

As soon as the elevator doors opened into the lobby of the hotel, the swarm rushed forward. Cooper's arm was firmly around Artemis and he led her through the throngs, pushing a few of the more insistent of the paparazzi aside. They were aggressive, shouting questions, snapping photos.

"Mr. Salazar!" So they'd figured out who he was. "Does your wife know you spent the last two nights with Artemis Savage?" *And* that he was married. It was easy enough to do with a quick Google search, of course.

"My wife and I are in the process of getting a divorce. Now if you'll excuse us, we're leaving."

Eventually, Cooper and Artemis made it into their taxi, which peeled out in a hasty getaway. A few cars followed them for a while, but the press had gotten the information and evidence they wanted.

They stopped by Artemis's hotel to get her luggage. At the airport, where Artemis was to be picked up and escorted to her private jet's waiting area—which was paid for by her modeling agency and was a necessity for her when she traveled—she couldn't help it: she broke down. As a person who barely ever cried (it never seemed to help), she suddenly felt overcome with emotion.

"I'll call you as soon as I get in," Cooper said, wiping her tears with his fingers. "I don't even have your number."

Once they'd attended to the details, he watched her

car driving her away from him. *Tomorrow night, Coop. Get a fucking grip.* He couldn't. He couldn't get any kind of grip at all. On his flight, he downed several small bottles of Scotch, still reeling from the intensity of what had just happened to him, fully realizing the next twenty-four hours would be the most painfully slow of his life.

Nicole Whitby-Salazar

BOULDER, COLORADO

NICOLE WHITBY-SALAZAR WAS SITTING in her multi-million dollar home in Boulder, sipping a glass of cool, crisp Pinot Grigio, watching the video, for the seventeenth time. Of Cooper … coming out of his Parisian hotel with that famous little whippet-thin hussy. Arrogant prick. He looked amazing, of course, but then Cooper always looked amazing.

Something about the way his arm was so protectively wrapped around her as he led her through the crowd of photographers … it was unbelievably infuriating. Had he *ever* been that protective of *her*, his own *wife*? Even *once*? No, was the answer to that question. He'd been a disinterested son of a bitch throughout their entire marriage. Even on their goddamn wedding night, he'd snuck off after the fact to watch a baseball game! *Bastard!*

Who the hell did he think he was, making some kind of pronouncement to the press about *their* divorce? When *she* didn't even know about it!

Like hell she would divorce him. She wouldn't give him the satisfaction. She'd cry to his parents, who adored her, and plead with them to help her. Cooper always caved when it came to his parents. He was a sissy-boy who did whatever mommy and daddy told him to. A bland and boring architect (*why* hadn't she taken her parents' advice and gone for Kip Stratton-Standish, who was now a surgeon based in Sagaponack????). Oh no, she'd wanted Cooper Salazar, who was just so cool and creative and handsome. She'd fallen for his looks, when she should have thought more about the big picture. He'd turned out to be an impotent jerk who hadn't even been able to give her a baby. Okay, so he wasn't *that* impotent. At all. Just so very distant. Sure, they'd said the problem was on *her* end. But she'd had it dealt with! She'd had two incredibly uncomfortable procedures (alone, of course) to solve the problem. Once the doctor gave her the thumbs up to try again, though, where was Cooper? Away on a business trip, of course. Then another. Then another. She'd had to take lovers on the side just to fill the empti-ness of her long, lonely days and nights.

It was true she'd taken a lover early in their marriage —very early, in fact. But she didn't think Cooper even knew about that one. She and Cooper's best friend Bradley had always been playfully flirtatious. She could admit that things the night of their wedding reception had gotten wildly out of control. Fucking the best man behind the patio hedge had not been her smartest move. She hadn't meant to do it. After three or four glasses of champagne, one thing had led to another and … well, at least he'd been quick. She'd sworn Bradley to secrecy and pretended like it had never happened. But, more than once, she wondered if somehow Cooper had found out anyway.

Regardless, it was Cooper she loved. It was Cooper she'd *married*. Which had to count for something.

All she'd ever wanted was a little bit of love and attention. But no. Not from Coop. Never from Coop.

And now there he was, gallivanting across Europe with a fucking supermodel! It was so unfair.

Nicole was livid, and she refilled her empty wine glass all the way to the brim. *Goddamn you, Cooper Salazar.* And goddamn your divorce papers!

Especially since she'd agreed to sign that airtight prenup (the bastard had insisted), which basically meant she'd be living in poverty if she agreed to divorce him. She'd have to go out and get a job! After more than three years of being out of the workforce, doing her best to be a good wife and—oh, how she'd hoped for it—a good mother.

Tears streamed down her face. She let them fall. At least Cooper and his new playmate were blurry now.

All her dreams were shattered. Meanwhile, Cooper got to live the jet-setting high life with rich, gorgeous, man-stealing bitches.

She picked up the phone and dialed Kitty Salazar, who she always called when Cooper was being mean to her.

Kitty picked up on the second ring and Nicole could only sob into the phone helplessly.

"Oh, honey, what's wrong this time?" Kitty gushed. "Is Cooper being distant again?"

Just try me, you bastard, Nicole thought bitterly, taking another large gulp of her wine before spilling all the gory details to her mother-in-law, whose fanatical desire for a grandbaby was at least as intense as Nicole's own longing for a child.

You'll get your divorce over my dead body.

Carl Nelson

LOS ANGELES

CARL NELSON WAS ALSO WATCHING the video of Cooper and Artemis.

It turned out that prison had come in handy. And he'd gotten out after only sixteen months for good behavior.

His cellmate had been jailed for illegally hacking into the security systems of several celebrity homes and high-profile offices. J.T. Lee was a little on the twisted side, but not a bad guy overall. They'd had nothing better to do, so J.T. had taught him how to hack. Explained it all with a pencil and paper, over and over, until he got it right. It was surprisingly straightforward, really. As long as you knew which pathways to take. How to add the coding in some places and alter it in others.

He'd done a couple of practice runs, at smaller houses, in case he made a mistake with his first few real-world tries. He'd tripped one alarm, but no harm done. He'd driven away before the cops showed up. He'd managed to disable the next three without a hitch.

Breaching the alarm system at Leo Puck's house had been slightly more challenging, but he knew he had time. Leo was shooting a movie in Spain and would be away for at least two weeks. These people were so clueless. Even his Artemis. She'd Instagrammed her schedule, for fuck's sake. *Three days in my favorite city ever! #IloveParis*

Once he got her alone, he'd have to tell her that kind of thing was dangerous. Never give your whereabouts until you're leaving or have already left. Anti-stalker behavior 101.

Artemis's house would be a real test of his skills. The place was fortified as fuck, with all the newest technology.

His fault.

It had been short-sighted of him, but these things happened. He knew better now. He'd make the next attempt count. He'd bide his time and make sure his plan was absolutely foolproof.

He studied some code, made a sandwich, googled her, to see what she was up to.

That's when he saw the video.

His Artemis.

With some other man.

Some architect. Good-looking guy, too.

But not as good-looking as he was. He'd win her, he had no doubt. It might take some convincing at first. But once she got used to the idea, he was sure of it: she'd look at *him* that way. Adoringly, like he was the one she'd been waiting for all along.

He would accept nothing less.

Senior Detective Statham: You're resentful.

Individual 26 (~~Nicole Whitby-Salazar~~ [redacted]): All I've ever done is tried my hardest to be there for him! [pause, as the speaker breaks down] I *so* don't deserve this.

SDS: According to the report here—and some fairly graphic photographs—you were unfaithful first.

I26: Oh, whatever. Are you married, Detective?

SDS: Divorced.

I26: No wonder.

17

Athena

KEY WEST, FLORIDA

ATHENA WOKE EARLY. She'd always wished she was one of those people who could sleep in, but every morning at dawn, as soon as the first over-eager bird started chirping, she'd wake. Her head would be so full of ideas and sentences, like a faucet turned on, she always ended up climbing out of bed and opening her laptop, letting the words spill out through her fingertips and onto the pages. It was relief to let it all pour out. If she ever tried to ignore the swirl of activity in her head, she'd start to feel crazy and off-kilter, as though her brain was getting too full and might burst like an overinflated balloon. Writing things down was how Athena stayed sane.

She hadn't slept well.

She'd woken at one point and, not being able to get back to sleep, she'd played around with a few ideas for the column Tamar wanted. *Texas billionaire playboy has a soft side*, she'd typed out, immediately deleting it. *The children, who have seen so much hardship in their short lives, are excited about the trip.* Delete.

It all felt far too personal, already. She didn't want to lay out Wyatt's foibles or good deeds or life in general for people's banal entertainment. And she certainly didn't want to describe Rosie's.

She already felt loyal to her little band of travel companions.

Finally dozing off at around three a.m., she'd fallen into a vivid dream … starring a certain blue-eyed, beefed-up Texan. She'd woken up tangled in her sheets, her hair damp with sweat.

Having an erotic dream about Wyatt Boone was ridiculous. Then again, he was basically the equivalent of waving a sirloin steak in front of a starving dog. Since meeting him, she'd begun to feel the effects of her late-blooming, commitment-phobic, hermit-like lifestyle choices much more acutely than usual. Most twenty-two-year-olds had already had experiences and relationships, three or four heartbreaks and many long nights of fabulous, meaningless sex. She felt wildly jealous of all those people who could casually *give* themselves like that, easily abandoning their baggage and their qualms—or at least letting them go for an hour or two. She'd kept her distance, to protect herself from … well, from a different kind of heartbreak she was suddenly no longer interested in thinking about, dwelling on or letting her life revolve around.

Being mired in the tragedies of the past was a waste of time, she was now fully realizing. Look where it had gotten Apollo. Almost killed and now trapped—she knew for a fact he was miserable as hell—in a rehab that was little more than a very expensive prison.

Sliding open the glass doors of the balcony, Athena breathed in the salty sea air. It was a gorgeous day in Florida. Her hotel room had views out over the pool and down to the beach, where jaunty blue and white striped umbrellas were being set up to shade neatly-placed loungers.

It felt like the kind of day to begin something. To get started.

She still felt flustered from the lingering effects of her dream. If Wyatt Boone was even one-tenth as good in bed as he'd been in her subconscious fantasies …

Not that she'd ever find out. They'd spend the day with the children, then they'd all be on their way back to their separate lives.

Athena brewed herself a strong cup of coffee and sat down to work on the next chapter of her newest book.

The hotel phone rang.

She walked over to answer it. "Hello?"

"Some of your fan club are already helping themselves to the buffet down here." Wyatt Boone's voice, over the phone, reminded her of hazy summer days. "I've booked us onto an all-day cruise that leaves at eight thirty.

Wear your bathing suit. There's a pool on the boat and we've got a couple of jet skis."

"Okay. Sure." She was glad he couldn't see her. She could feel her face getting hot as her mind kept revisiting her dream and the way his slow hands had ... and his—

"How'd you sleep?"

"Um … good. How about you?"

"Like a baby. I've got some plans for us tonight, by the way. It's a surprise."

"Oh. Great." What else could she say? He'd paid four million dollars to charity to spend the day—and evening—with her. She really didn't have a choice. "I'll see you soon."

Hanging up the phone, she took a quick shower, put on a pink retro-style bikini and a matching halter sundress. She grabbed her bag and a hat.

By the time she got down to the boat, Wyatt, the children and Miss Campbell were already on board.

The yacht had a pool surrounded by lounge chairs. There was an indoor cabin with a bar and catering service, and comfortable chairs and tables were set up with a variety of board games.

"Mister Wyatt," said Ricky, tugging on Wyatt's hand. "Can we ride the jet skis?"

"Once we get out into open water, I'll take you boys out and show you how to ride them. Until then, you can swim in the pool."

"COOL!" The boys immediately cannon-balled into the pool and began dunking each other happily.

The waiter served juice and Cokes for the kids and mimosas for the adults. Miss Campbell declined at first but Athena insisted. "It'll be a team effort today. You can enjoy the day as much as they are."

"Please," she said, "call me Felicity."

Once the boys had calmed down and were playing a game where they dove for weights in the deep end, Tia and Rosie sat in the shallow end. They had their new hats and sunglasses on and were sipping sodas out of bamboo straws.

Wyatt reappeared. He took off his shirt and tossed it onto one of the chairs.

"WHOA," said both the boys in unison.

Felicity slid her sunglasses down the tiniest bit to get a better view and both the little girls giggled. "You have BIG MUSCLES!" Tia observed, very accurately.

Yes, he did. Sculpted and burnished to bronze by the hot Texan sun, now wet and playfully tossing ecstatic, adorable children.

It was absurd.

Athena turned to Felicity, making a point of distracting herself. "Tell me about the children. Where are their families?"

Felicity took a sip of her drink. "They all live at the inner city shelter, where I work as a social worker. The boys live with their father but he lost his job last year so they've been at the shelter since then. We're hopeful something more permanent will happen for him soon. Tia and her grandmother have been at the shelter for almost a year. Her mother left when she was a baby and her father died a few years ago. They lived with Tia's grandmother in the Bronx, but the house was foreclosed after they had to pay Tia's father's medical bills. We think they'll be placed in a community housing situation within the next few months. It's looking hopeful."

Athena was almost hesitant to ask. She had a feeling it would be the saddest story. "And Rosie?"

"Rosie was born a heroin addict. She was on methadone for the first few months of her life. Her father was never in the picture and her mother overdosed about a year ago. Rosie's a kid that the system has really let down, unfortunately. She's had a couple of foster family placements that have ended … badly. So she's a ward of the state now, living at the shelter until we can find something better. We've put her name on the list for adoption, but most of the families want babies, of course."

Athena watched the little girl tentatively splashing in the pool. Her skin was noticeably pale and her new bathing suit, even though it was a size 6, was too big. A splash from Ricky and Carlos's exuberance sprayed the girls and Rosie wandered back to sit next to Athena. Tia joined the boys' diving game. Tia called Felicity over to watch them race Wyatt, who was clearly letting the children win, delighting them to no end.

Athena smiled at Rosie, and noticed that she was staring at her Goddess of the Sea toenail polish, the one L'Oréal Paris had designed for her. And paid her sixteen million dollars to promote. "I have some in my bag," she said to Rosie. "Would you like me to do your fingers and toes?"

Rosie stared at her like she'd just offered to fly her to the moon. The little girl nodded solemnly.

"Are you having fun, Rosie?"

Rosie's voice was so quiet, Athena had to lean closer to hear her. "I wish I could stay with you forever." Athena fell just a little more in love with this lost child.

Maybe it was because Athena had also lost her parents and had felt their absence like a black hole in the center of her life ever since. Maybe it was because she knew what sadness felt like. She knew about loss. But she was also fully aware she had no idea about sorrow and fear and abandonment of *this* magnitude. Maybe it was because she saw herself in these owlish little eyes and felt a connection she had no idea how to explain. Here was someone who needed her like no one had ever needed her before.

They spent the afternoon swimming, jet skiing and playing games. Tia picked up a small guitar, singing along as she strummed. She was remarkably good. When Athena asked her who had taught her, Tia said she taught herself. She liked making up her own songs. Athena recorded little videos of her so Tia could watch them, which she spent the rest of the afternoon recording and playing back.

Athena couldn't get enough of her new, tiny shadow. She felt as comforted by Rosie's presence as Rosie seemed to be by hers. Rosie, to Athena, felt almost immediately like a small extension of her own soul. The child's eyes were inky with sadness and hope. The thought of leaving her behind was unbearable.

It was unexpected.

Later, as the sun was just beginning to set, the cruise docked and they rode horses on the beach. Rosie, who'd spent the entire day holding Athena's hand, agreed to let Wyatt seat her on the quietest horse and walk her down the beach and back again. Then Felicity took the children back to the resort where they would have dinner and watch a movie before bed.

Rosie cried when she said goodnight to Athena, but Athena assured Rosie they'd see each other in the morning.

In that moment, Athena knew exactly what she was going to do. She was going to call Ares and ask him to help Ricky and Carlos's father find a job. She was going to buy an apartment for Tia and her grandmother. She was going to put college funds aside for all four of them. And she was going to adopt Rosie.

ATHENA HAD MADE ANOTHER DECISION, precisely at the moment Wyatt Boone took off his shirt. All the dizzying glory his tight-fitting clothing had previously only hinted at was suddenly on full display. The man was a specimen of hot, sweaty masculinity.

As she watched him, everything Athena had been

missing out on became painfully clear. She was tired of being lonely. She was tired of being a reclusive 22-year-old *virgin*, for fuck's sake, who'd turned down countless dates and several marriage proposals so she could spend even more time alone with her beloved laptop and her goddamn cat. Lulu was a sweetheart, but it was time for Athena to cowboy up—literally—and get real.

She was tired of being earnest and serious and overly precious about her painful past.

Athena wanted to have some *fun*.

More specifically, Athena wanted to have the kind of fun that involved one particular Texan hunk who happened to be making his way toward her, grinning, his blue eyes mimicking the color of the turquoise ocean water.

"Hey there, darlin'," he drawled, making things even worse. "You ready for that surprise?"

Yes, thought Athena. *I really think I*—finally—*am.*

Wyatt crooked his elbow and she took the invitation, linking her arm through his. The size and warmth of his body was beyond electrifying. He led her along a pathway, down to a private beach, where a canopy-like tent with tied-back flaps had been set up. There was a low table with colorful cushions placed around it, lit votive candles, plates of tapas-style food and a chilled bottle of vintage champagne. The sun hung low in the sky, almost touching the glass-like surface of the calm sea, tinting the sugar-sand beach and Wyatt's body with its golden glow.

Against all odds, the entire scene was quite literally … perfect.

The perfect setting and the perfect man to divest her of her ice maiden status and launch her into the realm of the carefree and sexually adventurous.

He led her into the warm water, circling her as he swam like a great white around a baby seal. But he kept his distance, those eyes twinkling, like they always seemed to be doing.

Athena had no idea how to seduce a man. It was pathetic, she knew that. She'd been told often enough that she looked like a goddess. She was *named* after a goddess. Yet she'd spent the past four years deliberately avoiding situations like this one.

It couldn't be *that* hard, she thought.

She swam closer. But every time she closed the distance, Wyatt swam away, laughing, splashing her like this was a game they were playing.

Fine. She'd wander onto dry land. If past experience was anything to go by—in jeans, a red carpet gown or anything else she happened to be wearing—a wet bikini that was barely more than a few strategically placed shreds of fabric would get his attention.

It did. Wyatt Boone was, in fact, in agony. The girl was like some kind of torturous fantasy come to life. He wrapped a towel around his waist and followed her up to the tent, fully aware his raging lust, which he'd been doing his best to keep under control (very unsuccessfully), was about as subtle as the Empire State Building.

He was starting to regret this whole thing. Damn his idiotic scruples.

Wyatt didn't trust himself to sit too close to her, so he popped the champagne and made a production out of pouring it.

But Athena had made her decision. And it was pretty obvious that Wyatt, or at least parts of Wyatt, were on the same page. She inched closer to him, her wet, pale pink bikini basically a formality at this point.

Her eyes were a pale, off-neon shade of green. Her hair, which was almost white-blond when dry, lay like strands of wet, silken-yellow straw against her skin.

After spending the last several hours thinking about this, Athena was done with ambiguity. There was a time and place for coyness and this wasn't it.

She kissed him.

Athena could immediately feel that Wyatt Boone was some kind of genius when it came to pleasing a woman. He gave her just a little more than she knew what to do with, at every turn. He was playing her like Yo-Yo Ma plays his cello. Even if she *hadn't* wanted to be putty in his hands, she already was. Since she very much *did* want to be putty in his hands—and was in fact enthusiastically squirming against him in a way that was coming very close to driving him insane—things got complicated.

"Darlin'," he said, breaking the kiss. "This can't happen."

It took her a few seconds to catch her breath. "What do you mean?" Wyatt Boone was six feet four inches—

plus ten, at a guestimation—of rock-hard muscle and virility. It was achingly clear he could have done any damn thing he wanted to do.

"What I *mean* is that I paid for this time with you. Which means I'll give you as much pleasure as you can handle, while taking none for myself. That's just the way it has to be."

His blue-on-blue eyes, his mussed-up hair and the flex of his outrageous deltoids, biceps and especially pectorals (she'd googled "male anatomy" for one of her books, had gone down a wormhole of detail and was by now fairly knowledgeable) were distracting her. What was he talking about? "You didn't pay for …" She could barely bring herself to say it, after all the time out she'd had—or, more accurately, all the waiting and missing out and never getting started so that now she was half-crazed with frustration. "… *me*. You paid for time. With the children."

"And you. Mainly you." Wyatt had grown up dirt poor, raised by his parents Bob and Eileen Boone, two intensely good, hard-working, down home, salt-of-the-earth people. There had been times in his life when Wyatt had tried to lie, cheat or deliberately do the wrong thing just to see what it would feel like. But every single time, he hadn't been able to follow through. He simply didn't have an amoral bone in his body. And he had no intention of cheapening *this*, no matter how much she wanted him to. Wyatt knew there was plenty he could do to placate her until their four million dollar date was officially over. "Don't worry, sugar. Tonight, I'm going to give you *almost* everything you want. But I'm in New York all week. For business. So tomorrow night I'm going to take you out and finish what we start right now."

Athena was about to protest. Or storm up the beach, back to her hotel room. She didn't appreciate being basically reduced to a puddle of primordial ooze then hung out to dry. She wanted him now.

But Wyatt Boone was no amateur. He was also well-aware of his own skills. So he gently, but with enough stealthy, well-placed force to keep her exactly where he wanted her, crouched over her, pinning her with the heavy, dizzying hardness of his spectacularly muscled, hair-roughened body.

She gasped as he pressed his colossal erection between her thighs, where the softness of her body cradled him intimately. "*Wyatt.*"

"Right here, darlin'." He kissed her, opening her mouth with his, stroking his tongue against hers.

Wyatt yanked roughly on the tie of her bikini top so it fell away. He kissed and nuzzled her breasts until they felt aching and heavy. Then he placed his hot mouth over her nipple and the vibrant pulls of his greedy mouth sent warm channels to her wet, tingling pussy.

Athena moaned as he took her other nipple, using the wetness of his mouth to swirl sensation, teasing in rough, pinching tugs.

She was writhing. She *needed* him to ease the aching emptiness and stoke her rising tide. "*Please, Wyatt.*"

He held her still, moving lower, forcing her legs wider.

Even though Athena had never done anything like this before and was usually modest and almost painfully shy, all she could do was practically sob with relief when he ripped the delicate fabric of her bikini to shreds and began feasting on her like a starving man on a juicy peach.

His hungry persuasion was the most intense thing that had ever happened to Athena in her life. Wyatt's mouth forced a hot pleasure that tumbled over an impossible peak, overwhelming her with luscious, clenching sensation.

She grabbed fistfuls of his thick-silk hair.

To keep him there.

But she didn't need to.

Gripping her with his iron-strong hands, he lazily teased her lingering rapture, taking her higher, and higher, until the lushly rippling waves shattered her again. And again. Until Athena was moaning, might have just seen God and could barely remember her own name.

Senior Detective Statham: Tell me about the death threats.

Individual 11 (~~Wyatt Boone~~ [redacted]): Business deals can sometimes get snarly, Detective. Lives are made and ruined with the flick of a pen. But all's fair in love and war, so they say.

SDS: So they say. Did you threaten to kill Individual 25?

I11: Only after Individual 25 threatened me—and more importantly, them.

18

Eros

RURAL TENNESSEE

Eros was losing his patience. And his mind.

Marlowe was completely impenetrable to his charms. He didn't get it. What was the point of the fame, the money, the lifestyle, the followers, if he couldn't break through to the one woman he actually *wanted* to spend some time with?

As soon as they'd arrived at their two-bedroom cottage, Marlowe retreated to her room without so much as a thank you for the luxury getaway or even a murmured goodnight, shut the door, locked it and hadn't shown her face since.

It was now noon on Saturday.

He'd tried calmly knocking. He'd tried asking her through several inches of solid oak if she'd like to visit the spa with him or go to the Michelin-starred restaurant.

No response.

Even begging hadn't worked. Neither had pleading or the promise of a massage by a Swedish guru who, in his spare time, doubled as a parkour instructor. Eros had read the brochure. Because he'd had nothing better to do.

Eros was bored. And lonely. He wasn't a person who liked to be alone. Luckily for him, there were always plenty of hangers-on who wanted to spend time with him. He had an entourage who lived with him in Malibu. Friends, groupies and staff who were basically at his beck and call night and day. Partly because they wanted to be seen with him, or post a photo of themselves in his house with the view of the ocean or drink their way through his plentiful supply of top-shelf vodka.

Why, then, had he paid a million bucks to stare at a door the entire weekend?

So he could secure a role in her brother's movie—and possibly, convince her he was the answer to all her sexual prayers.

Nice try, loser.

It was pissing him off. More accurately, it was making him feel depressed. It was highlighting the emptiness of large sections of his life: the ones where love and genuine friendship lived.

He wouldn't get the boost his career needed and he was obviously striking out on every level with his dream co-star. The divine and up-herself Marlowe Mercy wanted space. Fine. He'd give her all the damn space in Tennessee.

It was a drizzly fall day. One of those days where the fresh, misty air is like Evian spray on your face and you feel healthy and pink-cheeked. Eros decided to go out and check out the lake at the bottom of the hill he could see from the bedroom he was staying in (alone, so he'd regrettably had all the time in the world to notice the views out the window and the swirling grain of the wood in the repurposed Civil War-era beams above his bed [also in the brochure]). There was a dock with a little house on it, with windows and Adirondack chairs to sit on. And there was a rowboat tied to the dock. No one was down there.

Before he left, Eros knocked on Marlowe's door once more. "I'm going down to the lake to row a boat around for a while, since there's nothing better to do and no one to talk to—thank you for that. Then I'm going to go get some lunch. I'm hungry. Oh, it's fine, I'm content to sit there alone like a pariah, don't worry yourself over it. I might have a glass of wine, too, then a sauna or something. If you want to join me at any point, that would be wildly outstanding and would absolutely make my entire year and possibly even my decade. So maybe I'll see you later."

Eros put on a jacket and went outside.

He had to admit the place was beautiful. Rolling hills stretched far into the distance, hazy and romantic. Picturesque cottages dotted the landscape. The stone and wood buildings that were part of the resort were nestled cozily into the scene. Eros walked down to the dock and helped himself to the rowboat, unwinding the rope that moored it. He climbed in.

It was peaceful. He rowed out to the middle of the small lake and lay back for a while, watching the clouds overhead. This was such a different world to L.A., with all its glitz and energy. It was the first time in a long time he'd stopped to appreciate the beauty of nature. He used to love being out on his father's boat all those years ago.

A person could get used to this. A zone where hashtags and likes suddenly didn't feel as important as the graceful arc of a bird in flight, or the lapping of the water against the shore.

"Hey," he heard a voice say.

He looked up.

Marlowe was standing on the dock. She wore jeans, a white shirt and a fluffy faux-sheepskin white vest. She looked unfairly sexy. Eros was so shocked by her sudden appearance, he stood up.

The rowboat rocked. By the time Eros realized what he was doing, it was too late. The boat swayed again and tipped Eros into the frigid water.

Spluttering, he grabbed the rope and pulled it to shore, scrambling onto the sandy (trucked all the way from the Alabama shore* [*brochure]) beach.

Standing there like a wet dog, he looked up at Marlowe.

Who was—amazingly—laughing. A full-on, sidesplitting laughter that was entirely at his expense.

He didn't care. Her hair and her eyes and her little white teeth. He'd do it all over again. Her laughter was like musical soul food. It reminded him, weirdly, of his lost mother.

And the ice had finally broken. She'd not only emerged from her chambers but she looked almost … happy. Or at least entertained.

"If I'd known all I had to do was make an idiot of myself to get you to talk to me, I would have done it a lot sooner."

Marlowe laughed again, then grabbed a blanket from one of the chairs in the dock house. She walked over to him and draped it around his shoulders. "I'm glad you know how to swim. Because I don't. I wouldn't have been able to dive in and save you."

"It's only about three feet deep."

Her cheeks were flushed from the fresh air and her eyes were that crazy shade of green, like stolen jewels. "Your lips are blue. You should put on some dry clothes." She started walking up the hill. "Come on. You'll get hypothermia."

Eros bounded after her. He couldn't give a damn about hypothermia. "How'd you sleep?"

"Great. It's the first time I've had any time off for a while. It was nice to sleep in."

"I thought you were ignoring me."

"Not quite," she grinned at him. "I'm sorry if I was rude to you last night. I was really tired."

"You've been busy … " he thought about not saying

what he was about to say, but it tumbled out anyway, " …
with the movie, I bet."

"The movie won't start shooting until next month.
We've been busy with the auditions. My modelling
schedule is pretty hectic. I also work as a script editor for
my brother. And I'm writing my own script, too. Which
Percy is going to help me produce."

"What's it about?"

They were back at their cottage. "You get changed
and we'll talk at lunch. I'm starving."

Eros hastily put on some dry clothes and they walked
along a winding pathway to the restaurant. The host took
them to a table in the corner by a picture window looking
down over the lake, and Eros ordered a bottle of wine.

"So you're writing a script," he said.

"Yeah."

"Where's it set?"

"Percy said he never talks about a script until it's
done. He said it can jinx the muse. So, if you don't mind,
I'd prefer to wait and talk about that once it's finished."

"Yeah. Sure. I get that." Did this mean she might be
planning to see him again after this weekend? Eros was
quietly ecstatic. "Great. I'd love to talk about it when
you're ready to. Anytime."

"I'm co-writing it with my other brother who lives in
New York."

"That's cool. I have a brother who lives in New York,
too."

Marlowe took a sip of her drink. "I read about your brother Apollo. How's he doing?"

"He's in rehab."

"I read that, too. And that article about the five of you, in that magazine. About his past, and yours. I'm sorry."

Eros shrugged. His family's tragedies were hardly breaking news.

"I'm a fan of a couple of his songs."

This surprised him. "Not the one about drinking beer and driving in your pick-up, I'm guessing."

She smiled. "I'm not familiar with that one." A ray of sun passed over her, briefly highlighting the vibrant color of her eyes even more. *We'd have green-eyed babies*, Eros found himself thinking. "I like the one about Nashville. You can't help singing along."

It had been one of Apollo's recent hits. A love song to the city he adored.

Eros hoped Apollo was doing okay. They weren't allowed any contact with him for two weeks. He could only imagine what his brother was going through.

Marlowe might have picked up on his silence and the direction his thoughts had taken. She changed the subject. "We'll start filming Friction soon. Then it'll be day and night for three or four months."

Eros fought the raging urge to ask whether *his* part had been decided on, but he kept quiet.

Marlowe glanced down toward the lake. She smiled

again, as though fondly remembering his capsize. "They haven't decided yet on the part you auditioned for."

"Oh. Right."

She'd finally relaxed enough to talk to him and he didn't want to do or say anything that might transform her back into the steely ice queen version of herself who was only interested in giving him the silent treatment.

"I can put in a good word for you," she said. "But it's not my decision."

"It's okay. It should be more about whether or not they liked my audition." Eros's self-control wasn't one of his more developed skills and he fought—and won, barely —the urge to add, *But, if you really want to, that's fine, too.*

"The only reason I got the part is because of my brother, of course," Marlowe continued. "Everyone knows that. He's good to me. He said he wrote the script around that one character, just so I could play it."

Eros knew how it felt, to know that your luck and success was as much about your connections than anything else. Not that she cared, but he could relate. "He must have a lot of faith in you, to do that."

"Yeah, but what if I'm no good? I've never even acted before. I mean, I'm flattered, but what if I can't do the film justice? I've been having nightmares about screwing it up."

It never would have occurred to Eros that someone like Marlowe Mercy could be insecure about anything. "Well, you couldn't be working with a more talented director. Your brother seems to have a knack for getting good performances out of all his actors."

"With other people, sure. But who knows if it'll work for me? Maybe it's harder to direct your own sister."

"For what it's worth," Eros said, "I think you'll be a natural. And if you ever need someone to run lines with, just call me up. Anytime."

"Thanks, Eros. I'll keep that in mind."

He'd take that for now, and work on getting the rest later.

Eros

MALIBU, CALIFORNIA

Eros was back in Malibu. He was on his balcony, looking over the grassy bank that sloped down to his private beach, where the waves of the Pacific lapped gently against an arc of golden sand. The sun was starting to set, painting the landscape a warm, gilded shade of yellow. A vineyard worker was tending Eros's acres of vines. The laughter of friends and acquaintances (and a few total strangers) floated up from his pool and his hot tub.

Eros didn't join them. He was high on the still-fresh memories of his time with Marlowe. They'd talked all afternoon, wandering along a meandering nature trail through the woods. No paparazzi, no groupies, just them. The whole experience had felt strangely magical to Eros, like woodland fairies might emerge from little tree nooks and fly around their heads, casting spells.

He might have never been so *in the moment* as he'd been that day.

They'd had massages. Sven really knew his shit. They'd shared another bottle of wine over dinner.

Eros had even told her about his own script—something he'd been working on in private and had never told anyone about. It was about the four horsemen of the apocalypse. He was insecure about it. He knew people considered him a vacant airhead of a celebrity, all looks and no substance. Imagine their faces if he produced something outrageously *good*. He sometimes fantasized about winning an Oscar for best actor *and* one for best original screenplay. On the same night. Everyone would look at him differently. Like a shining talent instead of just a pretty face.

It was pure fantasy, of course, but Eros figured there was no crime in dreaming. Dreams were what L.A. was all about.

That Marlowe was insecure about her own writing and acting had made him feel like they shared something, like they were somehow on the same wavelength.

She'd thanked him and caught an early flight back to

L.A. on Sunday morning, where she had a photo shoot and a meeting with her brother and what sounded like an insanely hectic schedule in the coming weeks before the movie started shooting.

He found himself missing the color of her eyes and the soft, musical tones of her voice.

They would run into each other from time to time, probably, at events and around town.

Or maybe not.

Either way, it wasn't enough.

He didn't want to have to wait for a random encounter. If only he could *get that part*, he'd be able to see her every day and work with her on something meaningful to them both. Movies were bonding experiences, everyone knew that. You walked away feeling like you were forever entwined with everyone you'd performed with; it was that all-consuming.

He'd never wanted anything so badly as he wanted this role.

"Er-o-o-s-s," a girl's voice called.

"Come swim with us," said another.

Last week, he would've jumped over the balcony railing and splashed around with the hot tub full of girls before taking them leisurely to bed.

He'd changed. He missed the way she'd countered everything she didn't agree with, which was most of what he said. The jaunty gold-tipped ringlets of her hair. Her laughter when he'd fallen out of the boat.

His phone rang.

Lenore Quattro. His agent.

"Hey, Lenore," he said, his heart hammering in his chest. This was it. She had news.

"I got a call from Svetlana Evanovichski this morning," Lenore drawled in her two-pack-a-day rasp. Eros knew by now she adored torturing him.

This morning? It was fucking four o'clock in the afternoon. "And?"

"They've decided on the casting for Friction."

"And?"

"They said they found it a difficult decision."

Another excruciating pause. "… *and?*"

"In the end, it came down to the director's vision for the film."

He tried again, almost overcome with the clash of impending depths-of-despair disappointment on a scale he'd never experienced and life-changing, overblown joy. It would be one or the other. "Lenore. Please. Put me out of my misery over here."

He could hear her taking a puff of her cigarette, then slowly exhaling. "Percy wanted someone grittier, he said."

What? They'd turned him *down*? "*Grittier? I* can be gritty. I can be *very* gritty!"

"They went with Leo Puck."

"Leo *Puck?* He's not 'gritty'! I'm *way* grittier than Leo Puck!"

"Sorry, kid. I did my best. But, hey, I've got another script here for a Blue Lagoon remake. You interested?"

Eros had already ended the call. He found himself storming down the trail toward the jagged cliffs overlooking the ocean. He tore through the brambling blackberry bushes, which ripped his clothes and scratched his skin, but he didn't care. He couldn't feel any of it.

When he finally reached the edge, he threw his phone as far out as he could. It made a tiny splash and lit up as it descended into the waves. He contemplated jumping, dramatically throwing himself into the sea. But he wasn't high enough for the jump to kill him. He'd probably end up face-planting on the soft sand, with gentle waves lapping at his very-much-still-alive feet.

Goddamn it! He couldn't even *kill* himself convincingly. He was a vacant piece of shit with no substance. No wonder people wouldn't give him a role with any meat or meaning to it. Because *he* had no meat or meaning. He was Eros Savage, as wooden and dimwitted as it was possible to be.

He could swim out, like Dad. He *would* swim out. Until he was too tired to keep going. He'd sink into the murky depths, never to be seen again. Or maybe a shark would eventually fucking eat him.

He'd make the headlines. Everyone would mourn. *What a waste,* they'd say. But not: *What a waste of a talent.* Or: *What a waste of one of the most promising actors of his generation.* No. They'd marvel at his Instagram following and show a couple of his underwear modeling shots. *What a waste of a six pack and a social media platform.*

His entire legacy.

Was it enough?

No, was the answer to that question.

He gazed down into the gently crashing waves and pictured himself swimming as far out as he could go, where swarms of hungry sharks were probably circling.

Getting eaten by sharks sounded like a painful and gruesome way to go. Those empty, prehistoric-looking eyes rolling back as the razor-sharp teeth ripped your flesh apart and caused your severed limbs to get washed up on shore a couple days later, after the fish had already started eating them.

As miserable as he was, he didn't really want his severed limbs washing up on shore.

So he sat there for a long time, until the blazing sun got swallowed up by the horizon and the stars started twinkling overhead like little laughing, taunting reminders.

You suck.

You're a hack.

You'll never amount to anything real. Get used to it.

Senior Detective Statham: What made you decide to ignore Individual 13's pleas and repeated use of the words "no" and "stop"?

Individual 17 (~~Leo Puck~~ [redacted]): You know what chicks can be like sometimes, Detective. She said no but all her signals were saying yes.

19

Ares

MANHATTAN

ARES WAS SITTING in the smaller of his office's meeting rooms. Bruce Davis sat to his right. Valentina and Jazmin Diaz sat on the opposite side of the table.

"So, let me get this straight," said Bruce, holding up the high school ID card Tiffany Chamberlain had forged for Valentina and tilting it toward the light, as though admiring the handiwork. "You're not sixteen?"

"No," said Valentina. "I'm nineteen. And I've never attended a high school. We tried to sign up at twenty-two different Florida high schools. But none of them would let us in."

Bruce ruffled through a few more papers, not appearing to be particularly moved by Valentina's backstory. "Because you're undocumented?"

"Actually," Valentina added, "we could have gotten in at four of those schools. Under one condition."

Bruce looked up from the papers. "What condition?"

"Guess."

Bruce blinked at Valentina. Then he glanced at Ares before asking Valentina, "You mean ... sex?"

"Good guess." Valentina clearly wasn't particularly impressed by lawyers.

"They threatened to report us when we refused," Jazmin added. "We had to move each time. After the last one, that's when we decided to move to New York."

"So you can imagine," said Valentina, "that we were excited by the possibility of finally getting our green cards. And the option of *staging* sex with a sweaty, unattractive middle-aged man to achieve our goal instead of actually having to *have* sex with a sweaty, unattractive middle-aged man was appealing. Relatively speaking, of course."

"Uh ... of course," Bruce agreed awkwardly. For all his bullishness, he was clearly out of his depth here.

"Especially," Valentina said, "since we were offered four thousand dollars *and* our documents, which would mean we wouldn't have to move again."

Jazmin continued. "It also meant we'd be able to support ourselves without the threat of being caught and deported each time we worked a shift."

"Which meant we might even be able to get a real apartment," Valentina added. "With a solid door and sturdier locks. So we wouldn't have to listen to the pounding."

Bruce asked the question before Ares could form the words, which seemed stuck in his throat. "What pounding?"

"Oh," said Valentina, blasé. "The thugs who live in our neighborhood. So far we've been able to barricade them out. But we're never quite sure from day to day if they'll somehow be able to get in."

Each detail these sisters revealed about their hardships and fear was like another dagger piercing itself more deeply into Ares's chest. He tried not to feel the effects of Jazmin's downtrodden glamour or Valentina's older-than-her-years candor. But the combined onslaught of both was undermining the fortress of indifference he resided in with Spartan-like diligence.

"All charges against Valentina will be dropped," Ares said. "Obviously."

Bruce seemed relieved to launch into the more familiar territories of legalese and money. "Consider it done. I'll send a bill to Tiffany Chamberlain for 1.9 million to be deposited directly into the Savage Enterprises main account, and for four thousand to be paid by bank check to Valentina and Jazmin within five business days, or we'll threaten criminal charges of fraud."

Ares would box up all of Tiffany's belongings, which had accumulated exponentially in the past week, and leave them with Joe until she provided him with a forwarding address.

Done and dusted.

The only problem was, Ares couldn't bear to let Jazmin Diaz walk out of his life and back to her … shed. Possibly to be swallowed up by the unforgiving streets of New York or even deported back to Cuba and never seen or heard from again.

"File immediate immigration status for the girls," Ares instructed Bruce. "I'll pay whatever it takes to speed up the paperwork. And tell the officials I'll provide sponsorship or vouch for them or whatever they need."

Bruce gave Ares a look. But Ares was watching Jazmin, with an expression very similar to one a rescue puppy might give its new owner. This was highly unusual behavior from his boss, but Bruce wasn't about to question Ares's orders—or his love life, if that's what was going on here. Bruce's paycheck was too fucking fat for him to do anything that stupid. Ares was clearly either blinded by lust or besotted with the older of the sisters, but that wasn't Bruce's concern.

Bruce had known Ares a long time and had to admit this was a new look for his employer, who, at a stretch, might even be called a friend. He'd never seen Ares *this* far gone, not even close. Ares was usually cold, cuttingly direct and stone-faced, sometimes to such an extent that Bruce had wondered if the guy would ever find someone capable of thawing all that out. Apparently love—or mere lust; Bruce wasn't concerned about the technicalities —really *did* hit some people when they were least expecting it. Bruce had married his high school sweetheart straight out of college, who was now content to decorate her lavish Connecticut home, play tennis with the girls and drink gin on ice at the club all day in exchange for strategically ignoring Bruce's occasional wandering eye. He didn't overdo it and Marion was usually too toasted to either fuck or give a fuck, an arrangement that worked well for both of them. Bruce wasn't one to judge, especially considering the Danbury estate, the club fees, the pied-à terre on the Lower East Side and every detail of his life down to the Wilson Triad XP3s and the home-delivered cases of Beefeater were bankrolled by Ares. So Bruce diligently made a couple of phone calls and started the ball rolling.

Once the meeting ended, Ares walked out onto the street with Jazmin and Valentina.

Ares was feeling panicky and strange. He couldn't handle the thought of Jazmin walking away. What if something happened to her? What if he couldn't find her again?

"Can I buy you girls lunch?" he heard himself say.

"No, it's fine." Jazmin, after her night in decent accommodation, was looking even more ravishing than she had the day before. Ares had booked a room for himself in the hotel, too. He didn't even know why. His apartment was only four blocks away. He'd wanted to be close to her, that's all. In case she needed him for something.

"Please," he said. "Litigation always makes me

hungry. And I hate eating alone." Which wasn't actually true, but here he was saying it anyway.

"I'm still full from breakfast," said Valentina. She had that same air of level-headedness as her sister, but it was Jazmin alone who affected Ares with that straight-to-the-gut bedazzlement. "We ordered room service. The works. Thank you, Mr. Savage, for everything."

"Please," he said again. It wasn't a word he used often. "Bruce might have some news for us soon. We might hear back about your green card applications within the hour."

Jazmin tucked a strand of her hair behind one ear and Ares had to physically stop himself from reaching out to twirl his finger around the long, soft-looking lock, lifted by a passing breeze. What the hell was wrong him? He was going mad.

"Tiffany told us the applications can sometimes take weeks," Jazmin said.

"For Tiffany, maybe," Ares said, wishing she wouldn't mention that name. "We work faster."

So they agreed to have lunch with him, in a restaurant with big windows and lots of chrome, which only offset Jazmin's dewy complexion and shiny hair even more radiantly, sending Ares deeper into the depths of his own misery.

His phone rang and he excused himself from the table to take the call. It was Bruce, who launched straight into it. "They've been rejected."

"*Rejected?* How is that possible?"

"The rules are tougher now, Ares. The girls don't have skills, qualifications, financial resources or family. Even though the criminal conviction has been wiped, they don't have enough points to outweigh the fact that they're not considered 'culturally desirable.'"

"What does that mean?"

"It means they're not applying as creatives or graduates or as people who are able to make a cultural contribution, apparently. They're more likely to be a drain on the system than a contributor. So their applications have been denied."

Ares wasn't used to being denied anything. "Well, tell them we're not going to take no for a fucking answer."

"I already did," Bruce insisted. "They said we'll have to put our petition in writing and file it at the Alien Asylum Office, which takes longer and—"

"*Goddamn it*, Bruce, what am I paying you for? To get dismissed by some whiny, cubicle-dwelling bureaucrat? I said I want those applications dealt with! *Now.*"

"Ares," Bruce said patiently—and slightly desperately, as he pictured his wife's reaction if for some reason they could no longer afford the exorbitant country club membership. "I spoke to the most senior official in the city. I threatened legal action, I told him we were willing to pay whatever it took and then I offered to set the girls up with whatever kind of sponsorship is most desirable."

"What'd he say?"

"He said no. They're cracking down. It's policy now."

"I don't accept that! There must be a way."

"There's one way."

"What way?"

"Relatives or spouses of American citizens get special dispensations. If you want her to stay, Ares, you're going to have to marry her."

"EVERYTHING OKAY?" Jazmin said when Ares reappeared. Valentina was scrolling on her cheap phone in that pouty, oblivious way teenage girls had somehow perfected into an art form.

"Everything's fine." Ares did his best to arrange his expression into one that might convey calmness, even though he was anything but.

He was tempted to storm down to City Hall or wherever these matters were handled. But he knew Bruce was as hard-ball as they came. He also happened to know that Bruce had an entitled wife and a massive mortgage on an overpriced house and would do anything it took to wrangle a deal. If Bruce couldn't twist the senior official's arm, Ares probably couldn't either.

He sat down, leveling his gaze at Jazmin. "There's been a glitch with the documents. I know this might sound strange, but I have a five bedroom apartment and no one in it. Except for me, but you wouldn't even have to see me. Your living arrangements are … less than ideal. So I'd like you to come and stay with me. Just until we can push the paperwork through." Even to himself, he sounded odd. It was all he could do not to get down on his knees and beg.

A little furrow appeared between Jazmin's naturally-perfect eyebrows. "You want us to stay in your apartment? With *you*?"

"Just temporarily." *Or a little longer.* "I don't think it's safe for you to be living in a … shack."

"We do have a lock."

"Locks are actually very easy to pry open if you have the right kind of tools." It was something he'd learned a lot about when he'd been researching maximum security systems for Artemis's house. He'd since gone ahead and installed air-tight security systems in all the Savage houses. "You and Valentina could have your own floor. All to yourselves."

Jazmin blinked those gold-tipped eyelashes at him. "That's really not necessary, Mr. —"

"Ares."

"Ares. We've survived this long, and under much worse conditions. Even if we do get deported back to Cuba, it wouldn't be the worst thing. For better or worse, it's home to us. In some ways it would be a relief."

"I'll move out if it makes you uncomfortable having me there."

She shook her head a little. "Ares," she said softly. "I'm not sure why you're offering this. We're definitely not going to kick you out of your own apartment."

"I want to help."

"You've helped enough."

"I want to make things right. After you got screwed by Tiffany. I want you to be able to follow your dreams, whatever those might be."

"I can study medicine in Cuba if it comes to that. We have doctors there, too, you know."

"You want to study medicine?" *There! There's a skill she'll have one day. Those immigration officers were being short-sighted. One day she'd be making contributions to the system like crazy.*

"If I can. My father was a doctor."

"I can help."

She was staring at him, maybe registering a milli-degree of his despair. "I don't want you to think we're some kind of charity case. We're not."

"I don't think that. It's just one person wanting to help another person, that's all."

She studied his face. "You're very kind, Ares."

"Not usually."

She smiled. "I don't believe that."

He made a point of toning down his billowing hope. "Does that mean you'll stay with me?"

"Are you really sure you want us to?"

"Yes."

"Maybe we could stay for a couple of days. I'm sure you'll get tired of having us there. How long until we find out about the documents?"

As long as it takes to propose to you without sounding like a lunatic who just escaped from the maximum security ward of the nearest insane asylum.

It reminded him of something his father had told him and Apollo and Eros when they were young, out on the sailboat, his favorite place to give fatherly advice. *Boys, you might as well prepare yourselves. When a Savage falls in love, he falls hard, fast and irrevocably. Look at me, I was a hopeless wreck the minute I laid eyes on your mother. That's all it took. It's equal parts blessing and curse, because you'll fall so hard it'll feel like it's going to kill you.*

Jesus Christ. Was *that* what this was?

Holy hell.

He was in love with this beautiful almost-stranger. So much he felt like he might die if she disappeared.

ARES HELD the elevator door open and the sisters followed him in. He carried their small bags, which contained everything they owned. They'd spent the past two hours in the car. He'd had his driver take them to the east side of Ozone Park, where he'd been shocked to see the "garden shed" they'd lived in for the past six months. The thing was no more than a tin hut with a dingy double mattress on the floor, some rudimentary plumbing that could hardly be called a bathroom, and a small, dirty window with bars over it.

Every second of the journey had compounded his torment. Ares had never intended to save the world, but the thought of Jazmin and her sister living in that kind of squalor with no help, no protection and no money did something to his sense of control. Namely: obliterated it. He was now dedicated to making sure these girls were taken care of. He wasn't sure exactly how he was going to convince Jazmin that she needed him to be her savior from now on, but Ares had never been one to shy away from a challenge and he was more than up for this one.

Life had a sick sense of humor.

Less than a week ago, Tiffany had been begging him to do exactly that: bankroll her, love her and marry her. Now, Jazmin wasn't interested in any of the above. To Jazmin, he might have been nothing more than some benevolent stranger who was taking pity on her to make up for the actions of his twisted ex-girlfriend.

Standing there in her worn clothes and her long hair that had clearly been cut by Valentina, a five-year-old or herself—many months ago—Jazmin could not have looked lovelier. She also could not have been kinder, smarter or more unimpressed by whatever it was Ares was offering.

Ares had his work cut out for him.

His private elevator was being repaired so they had to take the main one.

Someone called out to hold the door. Ares had the urge to press the "Close Door" button instead, but fought it.

The man squeezed in just in time. Ares recognized him. It was his neighbor, Nestor Beasley, who lived a couple floors down. They'd met at a condo board meeting, which Ares was the chairman of. Nestor was an internet punk who'd made big money from a video editing app he'd developed and sold and was now living off his pile of cash and basically bumming around in his luxury apartment, playing his guitar, gaming and smoking copious amounts of good weed with a multitude of his loser friends. His eyes could not have been more blood-shot. Nestor couldn't have known this, but Ares had voted against allowing him to buy the apartment he now owned. The rest of the board had been more interested in his bank balance than his lifestyle. Nestor was one of those idiotic white men that grows his hair into dread-locks, which hung down his back like matted, dirty-blond ropes. Ares couldn't relate. The dreadlocks looked like they hadn't been washed in several years and could quite possibly have housed a metropolis of bugs. Why would someone like Nestor feel compelled to do this? Ares didn't know.

"Hey, Ares," said Nestor, assessing the girls. His thoughts played across his expression cartoonishly. *Nice! Two? Hookers, by any chance? Don't worry, dude, I won't tell the board!*

Dipshit. "Nestor."

"I'm having a few people around for drinks later. If you're not busy, stop in."

"We're busy. Thanks anyway."

Nestor grinned knowingly. *Right. I guess I know what you'll be busy with.*

Nestor then proceeded to check out Jazmin and it was a good thing they reached Nestor's floor before Ares completely lost his shit because the white-hot rage that flooded through his veins was anything but forgiving. For the first time in his life, Ares felt absolutely certain of one thing: he was capable of killing the very next person who looked at Jazmin the way Nestor just had.

Valentina Diaz

MANHATTAN

THE MINUTE VALENTINA got her payout, she told her sister she was going out for a while to do some shopping. Which was true. She knew exactly where she was going.

As interesting as it may have been that Jazmin was being drooled over by a rich businessman with a plush top-floor apartment, Valentina had no delusions. One whipped billionaire didn't assure them any happy endings. She may have only been nineteen, but Valentina was far from naïve.

The incident with the ugly accountant and that bitch of a lawyer was tame compared to some of the things Valentina had seen in her and her sister's never-ending struggle to find enough money to eat and to survive. The American streets were mean if you were young, alone, foreign, female and broke. She loathed bullies. She'd been chased, groped, threatened and put in danger more times than she could count, by creepy men with no scruples and no boundaries. She'd learned to defend herself. To hide. To fight back when necessary.

But there was only one way for a girl to reliably assure her own safety.

At the gun store, she picked out a small Beretta and a little holster that she could strap around her waist or her thigh, concealing it under her clothes. She loaded up the belt with ammo.

Then she went to the shooting range and got her first lesson. *Not bad*, her instructor told her. *You're a natural.*

On her way back to their new luxury digs, she bought herself an ice cream and allowed herself to feel the slightest bit relieved. She had a soft bed to sleep in tonight. A locked door. They wouldn't go hungry today or even this week. They had some money in their pockets and the possibility of getting their green cards. Time would tell.

Either way, no one would threaten Valentina or her sister again.

Not without consequences.

Senior Detective Statham: Have you ever had homicidal thoughts?

Individual 2 (~~Ares Savage~~ [redacted]): Yes.

SDS: How often?

I2: On practically an hourly basis, Detective. But it wasn't me who shot Individual 1.

20

Daisy
Sullivan

SOUTHAMPTON

DAISY SULLIVAN HAD HAD a long day. She'd finished her classes after daydreaming her way through three of them. Then she'd worked a nine-hour shift at the hospital. Mountains of homework meant she wouldn't get much sleep, and she had another full day tomorrow. She was finally getting ready to go home when her phone rang.

Daisy didn't recognize the number. "Hello?"

"Daisy Sullivan?"

"Yes."

"It's Dr. Duke Manning here. I work with the chief of staff of the hospital."

"Oh." She couldn't remember a doctor by that name. "Has there been a problem, Dr. Manning?"

"No problem. I'm calling to offer you a promotion."

"A promotion?"

"We'd like to offer you a full-time nursing position in the rehabilitation ward."

"But … I'm not qualified to do rehab nursing yet. I'm a nurse's aide. I'm working toward my certification, but I won't finish until next summer."

"We're aware of that, Ms. Sullivan, but we think you're the best person for this job. It's a patient you worked with briefly when he first arrived. His name is Apollo Savage."

"I remember him." Of course she remembered him. He would have been impossible to forget, even if he hadn't been a global phenomenon and the black sheep of one of the world's most famous families.

Dud—*no*, he had to keep reminding himself: Duke— had all but forced his idea down Finklestein's throat. Now that he was a Manning and no longer a Halfcock, his self-confidence had skyrocketed. He'd sold his theory so convincingly to his old coot of a boss, Finklestein had approved his request to let Daisy step into the role of primary care nurse for Apollo. He'd done his homework. He knew all the details. So much so that Finklestein had also asked Dud—*Duke*—to personally oversee Apollo's case.

"He requires a special kind of care that we feel matches your style and your experience. We're prepared to make an exception for you since your supervisors have spoken so highly of you."

"They have?" Daisy hadn't had any performance

reviews lately. But she was a hard worker. Maybe someone had noticed.

"Yes. You'll have help, of course, with the medical details, but we need you there in a … primary role. We're prepared to offer you a significant pay increase." Duke had convinced Finklestein that if they could send Apollo Savage home clean and keep him that way, the publicity for the Southern Shores Rehabilitation Institute would be outstanding. Every loaded celebrity with substance abuse issues in the country would be knocking on their door, demanding to pay astronomical amounts of money to be treated by him: *the* Dr. Duke Maximus Kingsley Manning (since he was legally changing his name, he hadn't been able to resist going whole hog). "We'd like you to start tomorrow."

"I have classes tomorrow. Until noon."

"That's fine. We're prepared to create a schedule around your classes that works for you—and for us. We need at least forty hours a week."

"I'm already working forty hours, so that's no problem," she said. "Will I only be treating the one patient?"

"Yes. We feel the continuity will be beneficial for Mr. Savage's rehabilitation."

"Sure."

"We're going to triple your hourly wage."

"Did you say … *triple*?"

"He's a very high-profile client, Ms. Sullivan. We're relying on you to be an integral and key part of his recovery."

"I hope I'm worthy of your confidence, Dr. ..."

"Manning. I'm sure you will be."

"Dr. Manning?"

"Yes?"

"Is there a reason you chose me, over all the nurses who specialize in rehab treatment?"

"Yes. He keeps asking for you. In fact, we have to keep him sedated because he becomes violent when we can't … produce you."

"What?"

"Apparently you made quite an impression, Ms. Sullivan. See you tomorrow."

It was late. Daisy turned the corner onto her street, toward her tiny cottage on the outskirts of Riverhead, New York. Even though her neighborhood was less than twenty miles from Southampton geographically, it was light years away in every other regard. But the location worked well for Daisy, since it was halfway between her job and the university. After her aunt had moved from Long Island to Denver to live with her sister, Daisy had rented a small and very-basic glorified shack, but at least it was her own.

Daisy had been raised by her aunt after her mother died soon after Daisy was born. Her father had been having financial difficulties at the time, and taking on the responsibilities of a new baby had been too much for him. Even so, the conditions of the custody arrangement had been that she spend two weekends a month with her father and older brother.

She'd dreaded those weekends with every fiber of her being.

Which is why, when she saw who was sitting on her dilapidated front porch, she turned off her car and sat there for a minute.

"C'mon, Daisy!" yelled Liam. "I've been waiting here for hours!"

At least her father had been a contemplative, pathetic drunk with only occasional outbursts of violence. There was nothing contemplative or occasional about Liam. He punched first and thought about it later, if he thought about it at all. When he was able to keep a job, he worked as a roofer. Mostly, he boxed down at the boxing gym with a bunch of tattooed apes Daisy would cross the street to avoid talking to. His nights were spent guzzling whatever adult beverages he could mooch, buy or steal. And now this. He'd figured out where she lived.

It was times like these that her regrets overflowed and felt like they were bigger than she was. She wasn't sure she could handle the next ten minutes. She wished her mother hadn't died all those years ago. She wished she'd had protection, a soothing, tempering force in her life. She wished her father hadn't been overwhelmed by grief to the point where it consumed him entirely. She wished she didn't feel guilty that she'd been the cause of both her parents' deaths, even though she'd told herself a million times that it couldn't have been her fault.

She wished her brother wasn't shaped by the collapse of a family.

And that he was a shitty human being regardless. Some people can overcome difficulties in their lives and rise to challenges because they have the strength of character to turn adversity into rocky roads that lead to better, more positive outcomes.

Liam wasn't one of them.

She wished she could help him.

But she couldn't help him. She'd tried talking to him, pleading with him, threatening him, hiding from him. Every attempt she'd made to lead her brother out of his twisted path of doom had failed.

Daisy had already made the decision that her own self-preservation was more important than trying again.

She was tempted to drive away. But she had homework to do and a new job to start tomorrow. And nowhere else to go.

Besides, she was done cowering from her loser brother.

Maybe she could bribe him to leave. She could get him a taxi and send him home.

Daisy got out of the car, approaching Liam as calmly as she was capable of. Her heart was hammering in her chest, but she refused to give him the satisfaction of being afraid. "Hi, Liam. How'd you find me?"

"I ran into that friend of yours. The one who works in

the coffee shop. She mentioned something about your new house on Jackson Street. The blue one. So I figured it out." He took a swig from the bottle of whiskey he was holding.

"Good for you. I'm going to get you a taxi and you can be on your way."

"Aw, don't be like that, Daisy. You're the only family I got left. I wanted to see you."

"Let me guess. You need money."

And just like that, the angry asshole side of Liam's personality—the one that lurked just under three units of alcohol—reared its ugly head. "Don't be such a bitch, Daisy. You can't even put your own brother up for one night?"

"Don't tell me you've been evicted."

"As a matter of fact, I have. And I need a place to stay."

"There's a perfectly good shelter down on 1ˢᵗ Street I'm sure would be glad to have you. Some of your kindred spirits spend time there, I hear."

She didn't know why she invited the abuse, but there it was. He slapped her hard across the face, with a closed fist, practically on cue.

There were pooling tears in her eyes when she looked up at him. Not from sadness. From pain and most of all from frustration. She was over this. She'd grown up dodging or taking these bullets most of her life. Just when she thought she was free of him, here he was. Again.

And he was more drunk than she first realized.

Stars danced in front of her eyes. She lowered herself to the ground and leaned up against the side of the house.

He was watching her. She felt numb, aside from the pain.

Liam almost looked remorseful at the sight of her reddened cheekbone that would most likely be a decent shiner by morning, and the glinting tears in her eyes. "Shit. Now look what you made me do."

She clutched her handbag, and she could feel the steely shape of the small gun she carried. "I have fifty dollars in my wallet. You can have it. I'll call you a cab."

He glared at her. Maybe he could see that she wasn't going to budge. "All right. Fuck. I'll go stay with Declan."

"Good idea."

"You sure I can't stay here just for tonight?"

"You can't ever stay here. Not ever. Please. Just leave."

It took some effort, with her cheek throbbing and her eyes watering, but she pulled her phone out of her bag and called a taxi. She held out the money and Liam took it.

By some miracle, the taxi came quickly. "Don't come here again," she said.

"Nice. Real nice," he said as he was walking away. "See you 'round, Daisy." Liam got into his cab and, as it pulled away from the curb, she felt a rush of relief.

Would she move again? Get a restraining order? Kill him?

After the last time Liam hit her, almost fracturing her

jaw, Daisy had bought herself a Ruger. She didn't want to be scared anymore, but she also wasn't sure she could bring herself to shoot her only brother. She was fairly sure that if she aimed just to injure him, as a warning, it would infuriate him. He'd want revenge. If she was going to use the handgun to protect herself from Liam, she'd have to kill him.

She didn't think she could do that, but she also wasn't prepared to be a victim.

Even though … here she was, yet again. Bruised. Beaten. Down on the ground. Feeling as defeated as ever, because this time she thought she'd escaped him, but he always seemed to figure out how to find her.

She'd move to a new city. Maybe she could change her name. Become invisible. Charleston had a nice ring to it. Or Savannah. Somewhere new and far away with no one who knew her.

She was too tired to think about any of those options tonight.

Daisy went into her house, triple-locked the door, put some ice on her cheek. She got into bed with her stack of books and, within reach, her loaded gun.

People were always commenting on her "sunny personality" and how relentlessly "upbeat" she was. If it wasn't for her childhood, maybe she would have thought those descriptions more accurate. Mostly, she was just trying keep as much distance between herself and her brother and to do the best she could to improve her life. She used optimism as a kind of shield. You can hit me but you can't break me, see? I'm still surviving and functioning and—even better—I'm still *happy*. You can't beat the happiness out of me because I won't let you.

But tonight she was tired in that way that felt bone-deep. Tonight she didn't feel sunny or optimistic at all.

By the third paragraph, she was sound asleep.

THE NEXT DAY, Daisy drove through Southampton, with its quaint buildings and sea views. She thought about where she'd go first, if she ever got the chance. She could start completely fresh, with no baggage and no history.

She might even see a palm tree. She might find a place that felt softer and kinder and full of opportunity. If such a place existed at all.

Daisy pulled into the hospital parking lot, her car sputtering to a stop. Now that she was getting a raise, maybe she'd be able to fix some of those things that needed fixing. Her car. Her house. Her life.

Dr. Manning (she could have sworn he'd had a different name last time she'd met him, but she was too distracted to worry about it) was there to greet her.

"We're easing him off his sedatives," Dr. Manning said.

Apollo Savage was unconscious and strapped to his bed. Even in this coma-like state, he looked … extraordinary. His lifeforce had obviously taken a hit but his hair was thick and unkempt and, even in this semi-vegetative state, his body looked solid and tanned and muscular and somehow at least ten times more magnificent than all the people who were awake and purposely bustling around him, checking his tubes and machines.

"Every time he wakes up he pulls out his IV, bangs on the door and when he finds it locked, he tries to smash the windows. So we've had no choice. We're hoping you'll be able to calm him down."

"I'm not sure why … *I* would make an impact like that. Maybe it's best to wait."

"On the contrary," said Dr. Manning, "the timing is perfect. In four days, he'll be able to contact his family. He'll be eligible for release and I have no doubt he'll plead his case to his insanely wealthy brother, who's not only very protective of Apollo but also expecting real results. It's imperative that we, and more importantly *you*, inspire some *remarkable* progress in the next four days, Ms. Sullivan. We're giving you license to use whatever means necessary to encourage Apollo Savage to choose to continue his treatment and to choose to get well."

It was completely unreasonable.

"Dr. Manning, it's not enough time. I'm not a miracle worker. It's unrealistic to expect Apollo to be cured of his addiction within *four days*. It sometimes takes—"

"Let me put it this way, Ms. Sullivan," interrupted Dr. Manning. "If you were to convince Apollo Savage to stay in our facility long enough to get clean, and if Ares Savage were therefore to find our services impressive enough to leave a glowing testimonial for us to post on our website, we'll pay you a bonus of ten thousand dollars."

"What?"

"Ten. Thousand. Dollars. We all have hopes and dreams, Ms. Sullivan. Mine include putting this rehab facility on the global map before eventually taking over as chief of staff. What are yours? Travel? Buying your own little house with a rambling country garden and views of a lake?"

How did he *know* that? Was her longing that obvious?

"He specifically asked for you," continued Dr. Manning. "Attachment can cure many forms of addiction. In fact, my theory is that it's the most effective incentive to recover from addiction."

"I ... I don't understand."

"He's been calling out your name. Even in his drug-induced coma, he murmurs to you. And when he wakes up, he looks around for you and when you're not here, he reacts badly. Nothing can calm him."

"I'm sure he's just hallucinating, doctor. That has nothing to do with me. I was in the room while he was being treated only twice, and one of those times he was unconscious."

"Regardless, it's worth a shot. I've got other patients to see, so I'll leave Apollo in your capable hands. There are two orderlies who will be in the room with you, at least to begin with, armed with emergency sedatives should they be required. If you have any problems, this beeper will alert me immediately, if you need anything at all."

Daisy almost protested.

She'd be *in charge* of him?

Apollo Savage was tall, and *big*. It was obvious he worked out a lot in his regular life, when he wasn't over-doing whatever it was he overdid. His tattooed arms were muscular and strong-looking.

It was comforting that orderlies would be on hand if she needed them, but she was still daunted by this whole arrangement.

Dr. Manning's suggestion that Apollo had become attached to her was most likely wrong, or overblown. He'd had some dream or vision that had affected his subconscious mind, temporarily. She'd read about cases like that; when the patients woke and recovered, they usually had no recollection.

Since she was here and had been given an assign-ment, Daisy decided she would do what she could to comfort Apollo Savage. She was a professional, after all, and good at her job. Her priority was to focus on healing her patient.

And ten thousand dollars was ten thousand dollars.

It would be enough to free her, or at least help her take the first step.

Dr. Manning opened the door to leave. "Good luck, Daisy. I'll be back later to see how things are going."

He left.

Daisy was alone with Apollo, aside from two stone-faced security guards.

And he was beginning to stir. As he battled to regain consciousness, he groaned and started to pull against his restraints.

Aware of the shiner from the night before—which hadn't darkened as much as she first feared, but was still noticeable enough for her to cover it with make-up this morning—Daisy felt her heart rate quicken. It was an unfortunate side effect of her upbringing: whenever she was this physically close to a man, she fought feelings of fear. But not all men lashed out like her brother. Some men were calm and kind and good-natured. She hadn't met many of those, but she was sure they were out there somewhere.

Daisy hadn't been able to cure her father or brother, but maybe she could cure her first rehab patient. It was the reason she was studying to be a rehab nurse in the first place. To try to succeed where, before, she'd always failed. She could cure Apollo, take the money and leave Long Island to start her new life. Everyone would get what they wanted.

She sat on the high stool next to Apollo's bed and held his hand. "Apollo. Everything's okay. You're safe."

Apollo calmed immediately. He stopped fighting. His breathing became more even. He seemed to be struggling to resurface. After a few minutes, his eyes slowly opened.

He blinked several times. Then he focused on Daisy. "It's you," he whispered huskily.

Daisy had been a nursing student long enough to know that patients sometimes did get attached to those who healed them. People who were lonely or alone. Once they got used to the attention, they didn't want to let go of it.

She couldn't imagine that Apollo Savage would be lonely. Or that he'd ever *been* lonely. If the headlines were anything to go by, all he had to do was click his fingers and every female within a hundred mile radius would drop everything to jump into bed with him. And he had brothers and sisters. Daisy had read the article about them. They'd described how they supported each other and made a point of seeing each other as often as they could.

"I'm going to take off these restraints now," she told him. "But you have to promise not to pull out your tubes. Okay?"

"Okay."

But when she tried to pull her hand away so she could unfasten his shackles, he held it tighter. As Apollo became more aware of his surroundings, his expression took on a darker edge. He recognized where he was and it was clearly a place he was entirely sure he did *not* want to be.

He seemed fully awake now. Calm. Unapologetic.

It was understandable. He'd been out for over a week. He was reacclimatizing to the real world and he needed someone to hold onto.

She smiled, to ease his tension. He looked so serious.

So lost. She smoothed a stray strand of his dark hair out of his eyes.

To describe Apollo Savage as handsome would have been a wild understatement. He was a damaged individual, he wouldn't be here if he wasn't. And those tendencies had taken their toll. But surprisingly light-handedly. She tried to find surface flaws. There were the bruises and bandages. The thick, black hair was a mess. She'd have to wash it for him. The denim-blue eyes were red-rimmed and underscored with purple shadows. She'd make sure he got plenty of good food and restorative sleep that wasn't infused with Ketamine dreams. Under his tan, he looked wrecked, tired. She would fix him and heal him.

It was her job, after all.

"I thought I'd dreamed you," Apollo said.

Gently, she slipped her fingers from his grip and began loosening the belted restraints. "The drugs can cause hallucinations that feel like dreams. You've still got plenty in your system. They can wreak havoc on your perceptions for hours. Days, even."

Daisy would tell him what he needed to hear. She would do everything in her power to make Apollo well again, to ease him into effective long-term counseling and place him firmly on the road to recovery.

Then she'd accept her bonus and get the hell out of Dodge.

Apollo

SOUTHAMPTON

FOUR DAYS LATER, Apollo was showing dramatic signs of improvement. Health-wise, at least. His mood had been consistently atrocious throughout and had only gotten markedly worse as the drugs continued to wear off. One arm was still in a cast but his head was no longer bandaged. He was, for the most part, calm and lucid.

Apollo had never lacked for energy or passion. He sometimes felt like he'd been born with more than his fair share of both, which was why he was so often compelled to go bat-shit crazy. Channeling some of the excesses into music, sex, booze and generally living life at maximum velocity was how he let off steam.

Now that the alcohol and pharmaceuticals were out of his system, he literally felt like he was in hell. He was too amped and unhappy to sit down and write anything. There were no available women around except a young, admittedly-cute yet relentlessly-chirpy version of Mother Theresa, who was currently putting fresh sheets on his bed as she hummed. When he'd first woken up, he'd been glad it was her who was here with him, the nurse he'd vaguely remembered. But whatever lightness she'd shone into the depths of his coma had worn off completely under the crushing agony of his detox.

Everything irritated him.

Who *hums*?

He was still dressed in a hospital gown that hung to the middle of his thighs with snaps holding it together—barely.

The only outlet he had for the hurricane of voraciousness currently residing in his soul was to pace. A lot.

But there was only so much pacing you could do in a sterile, twelve-by-twelve foot room full of blinking medical equipment and a large adjustable metal bed. Apollo leaned against a blank wall and folded his arms across his chest. "Can I at least put on some regular clothes? I'm sick to death of this rag you insist on dressing me in."

"Not quite the leather you're used to, no doubt."

It was annoying the way everything he said seemed to amuse her. Especially when so much of it was poking fun at *him*, or whatever this was. He was so far outside the realm of fun right now, all he could do was glare at her.

Which was always a bad idea. He hated how *glowy* she always was, when he meanwhile felt like he was residing inside his own personal black cloud.

"It's nice outside today," Daisy said. "There's a garden for residents with benches and a view of the ocean. I'm going to take you out. It'll be good for you to get some fresh air."

Apollo was surlier even than usual. "Ah, yes, the 'residents' a.k.a. the inmates such as myself can sit in a tiny, fenced cage like lobotomized zombies, admiring the outlook through tall metal bars. I can hardly wait."

None of that, of course, was Daisy Sullivan's fault, he could begrudgingly admit. She hadn't *forced* him to get wasted before driving his motorcycle off a thirty-foot cliff. And she seemed immune to his moods, plowing right on through them with her relentlessly brutal cheerfulness. "A dose of Vitamin D will help."

"As long as it's mainlined directly into my vein, count me in. Otherwise, I'll pass."

"No passing," she said in her annoyingly pure-of-all-evil-thoughts, bell-toned voice. "It's a well-known mood enhancer. And we both know that's something you desperately need."

"Ha ha."

She looked up from making the bed and smiled, which exasperated him even more. How could anyone be so entirely *upbeat*?

Look at her workplace, for fuck's sake. An insane asylum. You expected Nurse Ratched to terrorize you in a place like this. Not Daisy Sullivan, who—while the black cloud ruthlessly plagued *him*—seemed to exist inside an omnipresent and shining ray of sun, like a brightly-drawn cartoon character. What on earth had possessed someone like her to follow such a dismal and virtuous career path?

Apollo couldn't relate.

"I wasn't actually laughing," he muttered. "There was no need to laugh along."

She was still smiling. And still *humming*, as though thriving on the pleasure of tidying up his prison cell. "I wasn't laughing *with* you. I was laughing *at* you. Because you look so miserable."

"I can see why that would be hilarious to you."

She gave him an empathetic glance. "I know what you're going through is really hard, Apollo, but some of your recovery has to be about attitude. You can start by loosening up a little. Try to look at the bright side. You're alive and you're going to be fine."

This time his abrupt laugh was cutting. "Now you're *lecturing* me? On my *attitude*? Please. Spare me the lessons in how to have a better outlook on life. I'm beyond redemption."

That understanding smirk again. Like she found his asshole-style outbursts sweet and endearing. *Goddamn it,* she was infuriating.

"Some sun will do you a world of good." She went to his closet, unlocked it with a key from her keyring, and pulled out one of his t-shirts and a clean pair of jeans. Someone had brought some of his clothes. "I'll help you get dressed."

"I don't need help," he replied churlishly.

Daisy eyed his cast, then breezed past him. "Okay. I'll be back in three minutes to take you outside. Ring your bell if you need me."

"Are you going to make me wear a leash?"

"Only if you want me to." Another innocent smile as she closed the door behind her. He knew from experience the door locked automatically.

Damn her. *Only if you want me to?* What kind of come-back was that? A sassy one, that's what.

How was she able to rile him so easily?

The good news was, he had only three more hours in this hellish purgatory before he'd finally be allowed to speak to his family. At which point Apollo had every intention of calling Ares and demanding his brother get him the hell out of here.

It was basically impossible to pull his jeans on with a full cast on his arm and his ribs still sore, but after an agonizing few minutes grappling with them, he finally managed to do it one-handed. By the time Daisy returned, Apollo had his jeans on but he hadn't yet started with the t-shirt. He was sweating from the exertion. And his mood was even more vile than before.

"Apollo." She was standing too close to him, the light touch of her hand on his shoulder maddeningly cool against his blazing skin. "I'll be careful. Let me help you."

The effort of pulling on his jeans had seriously *hurt.* He'd wanted to prove that he could do it, but to what end? His ribs were throbbing and his broken arm felt hot. The room was spinning. He needed a stiff drink, which he clearly wasn't going to get. So he allowed her to thread the sleeve over his cast and his right arm before gently easing his shirt over his head.

Standing as close as she was, he couldn't help noticing her eyes were the color of cognac that had been warmed to a rich, swirling amber.

Or he was going mad with withdrawal.

The touch of her fingers and the scent of her—some maddeningly heady blend of sunshine, lemons and roses—dug up a deeply-buried memory. Of her. Chatting softly to him about a song of his she liked as she carefully tended to him and eased him back from the brink of death. Glowing, as usual. He remembered now: in his delirium, he'd mistaken her for a goddamn angel.

Apollo jerked away from her. He didn't *want* to be comforted by her peaceful presence or her seraphic face or the crazy-ass color of her hair. He couldn't deal with whatever garden variety of perfection she was. He couldn't handle perfection. It was part of the reason he was fucked up in the first place, because he was too far down toward the other end of the spectrum.

She hadn't noticed his reaction. She was putting some laundry into a cloth bag. Then she opened the door. "Let's go."

It was the first time he'd been outside since the night of the accident.

She was right, it was a beautiful day outside the four walls he'd now been cooped up inside of for too long. The caged area was bigger than it looked from his unbreakable window. There were benches spaced around a mowed lawn with a few trees dotted around it and, in one corner, a flower garden.

They walked toward one of the benches. Apollo shielded his eyes from the brazen sunlight, which only served to compound the dazzling colors of Daisy's hair and eyes, almost painfully.

It was then that Apollo noticed it. The brighter light revealed what the dimness of his room had not. Around her left eye was the lavender tint of a shiner.

He stopped walking. He reached to brush a strand of her hair off her face. As he did this, she flinched. Her reaction shocked Apollo.

She thought I was going to hit her.

She'd tried to cover it up. Indoors, it wasn't noticeable. Or at least he hadn't noticed it. Out here, she couldn't hide what was clearly a sign that all was not well in Daisy Sullivan's world.

"Who did this?" he demanded.

Daisy blushed and turned away. "Oh, that? I … bumped into the corner of a kitchen cupboard a few days ago. I'm always running into things." Her voice had all of its usual sparkle—but this time, Apollo could detect an edge to it. Some of this, he realized, was an act she was putting on. *She's pretending.* She's *not* perfect. And she's not immune. "It's nothing." She sounded almost convincing. Apollo couldn't have known that Daisy was very well-practiced at coming up with excuses. Or that she'd been doing it her whole life.

Except that he *could* read the lie. He could see it in the way her pupils swallowed up those golden irises, like she had something to hide.

Someone had hit her.

Apollo was completely unprepared for his own reaction. He'd been intensely irritated by her perkiness. Until it struck him that this little saint wasn't a saint at all, but a beautiful, battered girl who was protecting whoever it was who had done this to her.

The rage that boiled in Apollo's blood almost startled him.

"Mr. Savage?" It was an orderly, holding out a phone. "It's your brother."

It must be twelve o'clock. Ares had always been the punctual one in the family.

"I'll give you some privacy," Daisy said, wandering toward the nearby flower garden.

Apollo took the phone, but his gaze remained fixed on Daisy. He was reeling from his realization, and the clash of emotions that were so much more *forceful* without drugs. It was jarring and so very unfiltered. And it took a few seconds for Apollo to get his bearings enough to answer the phone. "Ares."

"How the hell are you, brother?"

"Still alive. Barely."

"Feeling better?"

"I will once I'm out of this place."

"They said you're making good progress," said Ares. "They're also recommending you give it another few weeks before you check out. They'd like you to stay another month."

"I'll agree to more treatment. On one condition."

"Name it."

"I want outpatient treatment."

Ares almost sounded like he'd predicted this request and rehearsed his reply. "Now, Apollo, remember we've tried that a couple of times and it might be best if we consider other options."

Apollo had no idea where this was coming from but the next thing he heard himself saying was this: "I want to bring my rehab nurse home with me."

There was a pause on the other end of the line. "I'm not sure they'll agree to that."

"They will. Tell that dink Manning I'll pay twenty thousand dollars each to Daisy Sullivan and to the hospital if I can have my nurse care for me for one month in the calming comfort of my own home. He's hungry enough to agree to anything."

"Apollo, do you really think that's a good idea? You might be better off—"

"I want a flight to Nashville this afternoon. A private jet. With her on it. Can you arrange it?"

Another doubtful pause. "If you're sure that's what you want."

"It is."

Ares sighed. "All right. I'll take care of it."

Individual 8 (~~Jazmin Diaz~~ [redacted]): I'm sure she saved his life. She seemed to know exactly what to do. She never left his side.

21

Cooper
&
Nicole

BOULDER

Cooper pulled into his driveway. The house was lit up like a Christmas tree, but that wasn't unusual. Nicole didn't consider things like energy consumption or carbon footprints, and she often claimed that she hated the dark, especially when Cooper was away—which was "basically 362 days a year," according to his wife. He happened to know the number was more like 338.

He was ready for the onslaught and Nicole was sure to bring it.

Cooper walked into the kitchen. His wife was there, and she could have been a stage actor with a team of stylists hidden behind a closed door somewhere who were dedicated to the archetypal portrayal of a devastated, jilted wife. Her hair was uncharacteristically messy, as though she'd slept on it several times in fits of sorrow, waking only to recharge her glass of Pinot Grigio and moan about her scoundrel of a husband over FaceTime to anyone who would listen. Which was, in actual fact, exactly what she'd been doing.

"How *dare* you?" she screeched, as soon as she saw him. "How dare you humiliate me in front of the *entire world*, you asshole!"

"I'm sorry." He'd already decided that in the interest of moving this along as quickly as possible, he would play contrite. He'd apologize, encourage the line that this-just-isn't-working-anymore-but-what-we-had-once-was-real in an attempt to placate her. And gently but firmly release her back into the wild.

But Nicole had no intention of being placated. Or released back into the wild.

"My feelings are obviously not a concern of yours," she wailed, her first tactic one that had always, in the past, worked like a charm. "But your *parents*! They're heartbroken! And mortified. You've not only humiliated yourself, Cooper, and me—but *them*! How could you do that? They haven't even been able to show their faces at the country club since the news broke! And so publicly, too. It's so *selfish* of you. So classically Cooper. Your ego could be assigned its own zip code!"

Even days ago, threatening him with his parents' disapproval would have made an impact. But things had changed. Cooper had tasted something so unexpectedly profound, he simply wasn't prepared to fake it any longer.

"Nicole," he said calmly. "I'll talk to my parents later

and tell them what's going on. But first I want to talk to you. I'm filing for divorce. I know about the many lovers you've slept with over the past year—beyond that I can only guess. And I know about Bradley." He pinned her with a scathing glare. "On our *wedding* night? Really? I mean, you've got to give me *some* credit for at least trying to overlook that. For not bringing it up or throwing it in your face. For genuinely trying to make it work, regardless."

"Trying? *Trying?* You *never* tried!"

"I *tried* to try. Maybe having my wife fuck my best friend at our wedding reception made it difficult, who knows? Either way, it's over."

She suddenly felt contrite, and full of regrets. "You knew about that?"

"Of course I knew about it! You disappeared and when you came back his shirt was untucked and your lipstick was gone. You both had leaves in your hair."

She stared up at her handsome husband and wished she could rewind time.

"What I should have done was to end it right then and there. You know why I didn't, Nicole? Because I didn't want to make a scene at the fucking country club." He laughed humorlessly. "Now I wish I had. I wish I'd walked away that night."

"But it didn't *mean* anything to me, Coop."

"Well, it meant something to me."

Cooper was being oddly unswayable tonight. What had gotten into him? Nicole didn't actually care that much about Cooper's affair. *She'd* had affairs. Lots of them. She knew they could be meaningless, that they didn't have to de-rail an entire marriage. "Coop, I forgive you. Neither of us are perfect. If you promise to end it immediately and to never see her again, we can pretend like it never happened and move forward. We'll begin a new chapter. A much happier one, you'll see. Your poor mother feels the same way."

"I have no intention of ending it, Nicole. And I don't *want* to pretend it never happened. What you and I had was … a very flawed marriage from day one. We tried, we failed, we can clock it up to experience, wish each other the best and move on."

Move on? This wasn't going at all how Nicole had imagined it.

"So you're leaving me for that little fashion slut whose house you designed? I thought you had more class than that, Cooper, I really did. You'll be the laughingstock of your beloved architecture conventions."

"Nicole, it's not 1952. People couldn't care less who I'm dating."

"Dating? Is *that* what you call it? Dating? *Fucking*, more like it!"

"Whatever. The semantics hardly matter at this point."

Having him confirm it like that hurt more than she was expecting. For all her own self-exploration, she was pretty sure this was the first time Cooper had ever strayed.

And she needed a new plan. Threatening him with a call from his mother wasn't working. Neither was rage. So Nicole tried a different strategy: heartbreak. Which wasn't hard to summon. She did feel heartbroken, very much so. For wanting something so badly. And for screwing it up, possibly beyond repair. Fat tears spilled down her flushed cheeks. "Cooper, *please*. Please don't leave me. I *need* you. We can work through this. We'll go to marriage counseling. We'll get help. We can still try for a family. The doctors have given me the all-clear. You'd like that, wouldn't you, Coop? A baby? A son? Little Cooper Junior? You can play baseball in the back yard and groom him to take over your business one day."

But her words seemed to bounce off him like laser bullets off a fully-functioning Death Star. He seemed different. Even colder than usual. As though he'd closed himself off from her completely.

"I don't want to go to counseling. I want a divorce. I've already asked my lawyer to draw up the paperwork. If I do have children one day, Nicole, it's not going to be with you." That one was quite possibly below the belt and he regretted the pain on her face. "I'm sorry. We gave it three years and it's just not working. I'll start moving my things out tonight. You can have the house. That way, if you decide to sell it and downsize, you'll have enough money to keep you going for a while."

For a *while*? He was heartless! "I'm not going to give you a divorce, you bastard! I won't sign."

"I have evidence that you've cheated on me with at

least *five* different men, Nicole. I don't need your signature."

She didn't want to be pathetic, she really didn't. But what choice did she have? Plus, her boundaries had been obliterated by her Pinot Grigio bender. She clutched at him and tried to hug him in a needy, desperate attempt to change his mind. "Coop. Please. We're meant to be together. Everyone thinks so."

He wouldn't even hug her. He placed his hands on her shoulders and held her in place, looking directly into her red, swollen eyes. "The problem is, *I* don't think so. You'll be okay, Nicole. You obviously have no problem finding men who are interested in being with you. I'll help you in any way I can, but it's over."

Since when had he grown a pair of balls? Since when was he so staunch and sure of himself? She hated him for it! She wanted *her* Cooper, the one who was easy to boss around and to keep in line.

But that Cooper had packed his bags and headed south, never to be heard from again.

"You'll never get away with this," she whined.

Cooper ran a hand through his hair, tousling it perfectly, of course, like a Nautica ad. He sighed. "There's nothing to get away with, Nicole. Please, just accept that this is happening. You'll be fine. Go back to school, re-energize your career. You might even be happier for it."

What was he talking about? She didn't want to go to

school or have a career! She wanted to live in her beautiful house and have babies with Cooper Salazar.

The very same Cooper Salazar who was now heading up the stairs to pack his things and begin his new life with a rich, underage bimbo—who Nicole begrudgingly discovered, after spending the past twenty-four hours googling like a maniac, was not only a talented artist but a savvy businesswoman. And not underage at all but fully legal, apparently consenting and also stunningly pretty in a fresh and sultry kind of way.

She'd lost her man. Her gorgeous, successful, kind-hearted-with-a-wry-and-quirky-sense-of-humor husband.

Something occurred to her then. A final lifeline to clutch at. If he had evidence that *she'd* cheated, well, so did she. "You *do* need my signature!" she screeched, hoping there might be some actual legal leverage to it. "Because I'm not the only one who committed adultery. The entire world saw you."

Cooper stopped near the top of the stairs and turned. She'd done it. She could see from the expression on his face that he knew she might be right. "I'm not sure why you'd want to, Nicole, but if you want to fight me in court on this, then it's game on."

Game on?

Did that mean he still wasn't going to back down?

Damn it all. How had things gone so utterly, terribly wrong?

Artemis

TELLURIDE

ARTEMIS PULLED INTO HER GARAGE. It was late, almost midnight, and she was exhausted. She hadn't had a full night's sleep … since before her life had transformed into something along the lines of an erotic fairy tale.

Cooper Salazar.

Her lover.

Of course she was wondering how Cooper's conversation with his wife was going, but she tried to put it out of her mind.

Artemis put her finger on the pad next to the door, so the security system could identify her. The lock beeped and clicked, letting her into the house. As it did, the lights came on and a song from her playlist crooned mellowly from her state-of-the-art sound system. The locks clicked back into place.

It was nice to know the place was secure, but every time the beeps and clicks did their thing, she was always reminded of the reason they were necessary.

Artemis was reminded, too, of how utterly alone she was, high up here in the mountains, miles from anywhere. Her nearest neighbors were four miles to the south.

But soon Cooper would arrive. Tomorrow. Would he want to move in with her? They hadn't had a chance to begin to discuss all the particulars. He could design Apollo's studio and … work here for a while. If he wanted to. Maybe they could both take a break from their busy travel schedules to concentrate on their new relationship. They could spend all day in bed, talking, laughing, making love, just like they had in Paris.

Her phone buzzed in her pocket. It was Arlo.

They were overdue for a phone call. He'd emailed her schedule for the next two weeks. She wanted to tell him to cancel a few of her appointments and appearances. Once Cooper arrived, well, they needed to figure a few things out. "Hi, honey."

"Artemis, is anyone with you?" Arlo's voice sounded odd, and panicky.

"What? No, I just got home."

"Get back in your car. Right now. You need to go stay in a hotel tonight."

"What? *Arlo.* Why would I—"

"Artemis, listen to me. Leo Puck said he's been trying to get a hold of you but you weren't answering your phone."

"I saw that he'd called. I haven't had a chance to call him back."

"Someone broke into his house."

Artemis went cold. But it could have been anyone, she reasoned. "Do they know who it was?"

"It was *him.* The stalker."

Artemis's blood iced with a prickly, horrible flood of intense fear. "He's out of jail?"

"Apparently they let him out early for good behavior."

"Good behav—"

"That's not even the worst of it, honey. Are you getting back in your car?"

"Arlo. Please. Tell me ... what *is* the worst of it?"

"They're not sure yet if he even took anything. He might have broken into Leo's house, they think, only to ... leave a message."

"What message?" But Artemis knew. She knew what the message was going to be.

"He vandalized the painting you did of Leo and Saskia. He wrote, 'If I can break into Leo's house I can break into yours. You know who you are. And I'm coming for you.'"

Senior Detective Statham: Were you working with Individual 1?

Individual 27 (~~Carl Nelson~~ [redacted]): Who?

SDS: Please refer to the list.

I27: Oh. [lengthy pause] Hell, no. I never even met Individual 1. Sounds like a real piece of work.

SDS: It says here in your file that you lied under oath during your arrest last November. Are you lying now?

I27: Me? No way, man. *Jeez*. Can't a guy reform without getting crucified around here?

22

———

ℰros

MALIBU

Eros woke up.

It was dark and he was cold, his clothes damp.

He'd fallen asleep, above the cliffs overlooking the water. The dark-purple sky was tinted along the horizon line with the earliest gold of dawn.

He wished his phone call with Lenore had been a nightmare. And the tantrum that had come directly after it. Apollo would be getting out of rehab today and he'd probably missed phone calls because he'd thrown his damn phone into the ocean.

Eros climbed down the narrow, winding trail along the rock face, making his way down toward the sandy beach.

What was wrong with him? It had been a major disappointment missing out on that part, to say the least.

But throwing his phone into the sea? Idiotic. Now, with the first rays of the morning painting the sky a surreal shade of pink, he looked for a bright side.

There wasn't one.

But it didn't mean he should be crying like a goddamn baby. He could deal with this. He'd audition his guts out all over town until he got a role as good. It wouldn't be easy. It would be practically impossible. No director was even close to as hot as Percy Mercy right now. No one was as gorgeous and up-and-coming as Marlowe. Not a single person in L.A. thought he could act his way out of a paper bag and the screenplay he'd told Marlowe he was writing so far consisted of exactly three paragraphs.

Eros stripped down to his boxers and waded into the water. It was cold. He waded further, diving into the waves, swimming deeper. Every swim, for the rest of eternity—whether he wanted it to or not—would remind him of his dead father.

Did you kill yourself, Dad? Or was it an accident? If you were such a strong swimmer, why did you drown thirty feet from the shore? What was going through your head that day?

Those long-ago halcyon days. Out on the yacht. Learning to sail. Their father's words of wise wisdom to his three sons.

You want things to happen to you, boys? Well, they won't. You have to go out there and make *them happen. No one's going to hand you anything. Ever. Nothing's perfect no matter how badly you want it to be, and you're going to make more mistakes than you know how to handle along the way. But it doesn't mean you shouldn't keep trying.*

What did that even mean? Eros didn't know, even if he fervently wished he did. There was no moral to the story, no meaning he could derive from the long-ago memories. Life was like that. It didn't always provide the answers you wanted from it. Then again, maybe it did. Maybe *that* was the answer: to make your own way and to figure things out for yourself.

Eros swam around for a while looking for his phone but couldn't find it. It didn't matter. He'd buy a new one. His stuff was backed up in the cloud, or wherever, he hoped. Some geek would help him figure it out.

If he stopped doing things like having temper tantrums and throwing perfectly good phones into the Pacific Ocean, maybe people would start to take him more seriously. If he followed his father's advice and stopped waiting for things to happen *to* him and instead made them happen for himself, maybe he'd get more of what he wanted in life.

Eros, for all the drama of the past twenty-four hours, was at heart an optimist. Sure, he had mood swings like the rest of humanity but something in his psyche wouldn't let him stay depressed for long. He could indulge himself from time to time when the situation called for it, but after a while he always had the urge to pick himself up, dust himself off and make the most of his day.

And so, at that moment, a new resolve clicked into place and Eros knew exactly what he was going to do.

Senior Detective Statham: Several of your house-guests said they saw you swimming at approximately 4:45 a.m. on the morning of September 29. Given your family history, they were concerned. What was your intention?

Individual 5: (~~Eros Savage~~ [redacted]): To find my damn phone.

SDS: Did you?

I5: No.

23

Athena

MANHATTAN

ATHENA SPENT most of Monday in meetings with the adoption agency people, filling out paperwork and writing checks. It was pissing her off that she wasn't allowed to see Rosie again until the shelter administrators were sure Athena would be approved; they didn't want to get Rosie's hopes up.

Athena was determined to take Rosie home as soon as possible. It killed Athena to be in the dark about where Rosie was and what she was doing. Was she okay? Was she scared or lonely or hungry or cold? The very possibility was completely unacceptable. Athena had connected with the little girl irrevocably, recognizing in her a lost, vulnerable, kindred soul. And she wasn't about to take no for an answer.

"I want her now."

"You can't have her *now*, Ms. Savage. There are legal protocols that need to be followed, which sometimes take weeks."

Weeks? Athena decided to take a page out of Ares's book. To hell with these bureaucrats. Rosie was as alone as it was possible to be in this world. And Athena, at least on paper, couldn't *be* a more model citizen, banker's dream client, homeowner with a clean record and so on. It really wasn't rocket science. "I want Rosie this week. Today. Now. I'm more than willing to pay extra to speed this up."

"I'm afraid today isn't possible," said the shelter's director, a sour-faced witch named Ursula Blitzkrieg, who'd clearly had a hard life and was hell-bent on making everyone else's equally unpleasant. "The paperwork can take a few days and then—"

"Fine. Wednesday it is."

"Ms. Savage. We still need to inspect the house and—"

"I'll fly you out personally. Right now."

"Now? To Southampton?"

"Yes. I'll have my driver take us to my brother's apartment building on Park Avenue. He keeps a helicopter on the roof. If I call now, I'm sure they can have it ready by the time we get there."

"Oh." Ms. Blitzkrieg blinked. "Well, I was supposed to go to a podiatry appointment at 4:30 to get my bunions checked. But I guess I could cancel it."

"I'm sure you could reschedule." *Jesus.* Athena was having a hard time keeping her cool. "That way, you'll see that Rosie will be well very cared for. She'll have her choice of any of the six spare bedrooms. We can paint it any color she wants—"

Ursula Blitzkrieg was one of those people who took a certain amount of glee in making things difficult for others. Because things had been difficult for her. Her father, Leopold Blitzkrieg III—whom she'd adored—had gone out to buy some ice cream one evening when Ursula was eleven years old, and the bastard had never come home or been heard from again. This had instilled little Ursula with a hatred of men in general, a distain for women (her mother had pathetically fallen apart, leaving poor Ursula to basically fend for herself from then on) and a twisted vendetta against anyone who happened to enjoy life or anything in it. But a ride in a helicopter? This was too good to pass up. She picked up the phone. "Cancel all my appointments for the rest of the day," she barked into it.

With all the budget restraints, Athena found it somewhat astonishing that Ms. Blitzkrieg had enough to hire an assistant, but then again, Athena's charity had donated significant amounts of money to this shelter and many others.

And Athena was prepared to play hardball. "Ms. Blitzkrieg. I know you'll do everything in your power to move this along. I can assure you that I'm the best option for Rosie and her future. Or at least better than having no family, living in a shelter and being passed around to unsatisfactory foster homes. If you can't see that, I'll be forced to reconsider how this facility is being run and how much money my charity is donating."

Ursula blinked her thin, pale eyelashes and glared at Athena frigidly. This was clearly a threat. Ursula liked having an assistant. It was fun to order her own personal Millennial minion around. And have Jennifer do all her work for her. Ursula was also secretly enjoying using the shelter's bank account to sneak extras into whatever items she happened to be buying. Like the leather office chair she'd added to the furniture list. And the modern marble-topped end tables she'd bought for her one-bedroom in Hoboken, where she lived with her carefully-tended collection of prickly cacti.

"Why don't you call your driver, then," Ursula replied. "And arrange the helicopter. Once I see the house, I can start to write up the recommendation."

"*Start*," *my ass*, thought Athena. But she knew riling Ms. Blitzkrieg would only slow this down. She needed to tread carefully. All she cared about was bringing Rosie home.

As she picked up her phone, it pinged.

Another message from Wyatt. *Have dinner with me tonight.*

They'd arranged to get together, but she'd been too busy to call him back and confirm. He was in New York all week for business.

Her stomach fluttered at the thought of seeing him

again in a few hours. She'd behaved … like a lust-crazed lunatic. And that was putting it mildly.

God. The things he'd done to her. The things she'd begged him to do.

She tried not to think about it, but the memories kept steamrolling through her brain with all the subtlety of a porn flick marathon. He'd basically done everything it was possible to do—except the one thing he promised to do to her … the very next time he saw her.

But now wasn't the time or place to think about Wyatt Boone—*or* what he intended to do to her. Especially in the company of Ursula Blitzkrieg. Who, after positively gushing over the helicopter ride, turned out to be more than satisfied by the living arrangements. Once she saw Athena's house and had toured the bedrooms, proclaiming the one with small balcony looking over the ocean the best, she helped herself to a chaise lounge by the pool and requested a glass of wine. "It's after five," she rationalized.

They sat and talked money and, with the help of several generous helpings of a 2012 Napa Chardonnay, it was agreed that Athena could adopt Rosie as soon as Wednesday afternoon.

Once Ursula was safely—and tipsily—aboard the helicopter to be delivered back to Manhattan, Athena called Wyatt.

He picked up on the first ring. "Hey, darlin'. What took you so long?"

That black-strap molasses drawl immediate found

Athena flashing back to a particularly orgasmic … *thing* he'd done … with his *tongue*, no less, that had not only been one of the most intense things that had ever happened to her but downright debauched. In a good way.

"I've been in meetings. The adoption's going to happen in a few days. I'll be able to bring Rosie home."

"That's wonderful news, honey. Looks like we've got some celebrating to do. Tell me you'll go out with me tonight." His voice was low. "So we can finish what we started."

Help, she thought. Athena felt equal parts excitement, hope—and also something close to terror. But she laid that third emotion to rest. This was the new Athena Savage. The one who threw all caution to the wind. By later tonight, she was pretty sure she'd no longer be a twenty-two year old virgin, thank God. She'd be a wanton sex goddess who could give as good as she could get (or at least give it a shot). The truth was, Athena had learned more about the actual *feel* of a man's body with Wyatt than she ever had in her life. She was embarrassingly inexperienced. Books gave you details, but they didn't come close to revealing the sweat and the surge and the heady effect of 100-proof pheromones. "Sounds fun," she managed.

"It's going to be more than fun, sweetheart. How's seven?"

"Seven's good. See you then."

She put on a light blue wrap dress that left little to the

imagination. There was no point playing coy, she reasoned. Hearing Wyatt Boone's voice had reminded her of the searing intimacy they'd shared. She opened another bottle of wine (Ursula had polished off the first one) and put on some music. The night was unseasonably warm and the sun hung low in the sky, painting the ocean water a brilliant shade of orange.

When her phone rang again she almost didn't pick it up. The name on the screen: Tamar Takahashi.

Athena braced herself. She'd sent Tamar an outline for her column article, knowing it wasn't at all what Tamar wanted. This conversation was never going to get easier, so she bit the bullet and answered the call. "Hi, Tamar."

"What the hell *is* this, Athena? Your assignment was to write about the *date* you were on with that scorching hunk of Texas prime beef! The hot and heavy make-out sessions over champagne! The sex at sunset! Not the goddamn day care schedule."

Athena hadn't been able to bring herself to describe … the hot and heavy make-out session over champagne. Or the almost-sex at sunset. "The kids were with us the whole time," Athena bluffed. "It was Wyatt's idea, Tamar, not mine. He thought they'd enjoy the experience."

"Which is admirable. But it won't sell magazines. And what's this about you adopting one of them? Have you lost your mind? Please tell me those kids weren't with you the *whole* time."

Athena made the mistake of hesitating. "Yes. They were."

Tamar was eerily astute. "Even at night?"

"Well, we were both tired from the flight and ... we really didn't have a lot of privacy."

"You didn't have dinner together or a drink or go for a walk on the beach alone even once? He paid *four million dollars* for you. And he's a Texan! I don't believe for a single second he didn't make some kind of move on you. And as hoity-toity as you might be, you'd have to be either certifiable or blind not to jump into bed with all that at your very first opportunity."

Damn it. It was none of this tyrannical bitch's business. What Athena shared with Wyatt was too raw at this stage to lay out for the public's banal entertainment. She just couldn't do it. But she needed to give Tamar something. Some tidbit to get her off Athena's case. "We did have a drink together. On the second night."

"Then use your imagination. Embellish. You're a *writer*, make something up. I want this segment re-outlined by the end of the day tomorrow. And make sure it's a hell of a lot more interesting than two solid days of babysitting." The call ended.

Technically, Athena was higher up the food chain at *City* magazine than Tamar was. She could pull the article altogether if she wanted to. She could pull the entire column. Maybe she would. Ares could get her out of whatever contract Tamar had bullied her into signing. But she saw an opportunity to do good here. If she was adopting Rosie, maybe other people would be inspired to adopt or foster some of the other kids who needed help.

She supposed she could describe non-specific details of her and Wyatt's "date." She could talk about his … abs. Or something. His charm. *His tongue and what he could do with it.*

Sure.

She typed a few ideas into her phone but couldn't quite get a feel for how much detail she wanted to give, so she gave up. She'd figure it out. In the meantime, she had Round Two to look forward to, and any minute. But when Athena glanced at the clock it read 7:41.

Wyatt was late.

He'd called her at least ten times earlier in the day so it seemed unlikely that he'd stand her up. If he was running late with meetings he would probably have called to let her know.

Had he been in some kind of accident?

Athena tried his number.

No answer.

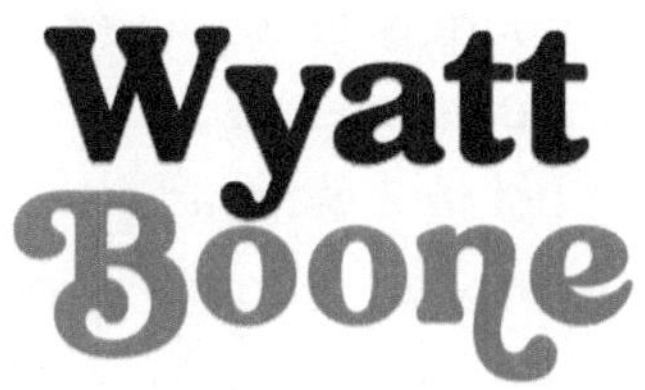

MANHATTAN

A HUNDRED AND twenty-two million dollars was at stake, so it wasn't surprising to Wyatt that they were after him. He was used to their death threats at this point and had purposely led them to believe he was taking a limo from the meeting, keeping his destination close to his chest. It wouldn't do for them to find out where he was headed.

The good ol' boy oilmen didn't like his biodiesel fuel deal, he knew that. Hell, he didn't blame them. He used to *be* one of them, even if it was in a new-kid-on-the-block kind of way. The old money cronies had never welcomed him into their fold, so he was used to being an outsider. He'd made his first hundred million in oil and appreciated it. But oil was finite. And dirty. There were interesting things going on in cleaner energy which he wanted a piece of. The Earth had enough to deal with on a daily basis and things were only getting worse. If he could do his part to slow down some of the damage that was being caused by air pollution and whatnot, Wyatt figured it was the right thing to do.

Not everyone agreed with him.

It started with the mail. Those single sheets of paper someone has painstakingly glued letters cut out of magazines to create blunt messages. *Halt the deal or else.*

That had been before he'd made the first deal.

But Wyatt Boone was nothing if not a Texan. And Texans didn't back down from bullies. They stood up and hit back. He considered himself as peaceful and law-abiding as they came. His favorite things were his horse, Blaze, and the old pick-up truck he'd bought when he was sixteen, a 1978 flat-bed Ford he'd saved up for over an entire summer of fencing. His hands still bore the scars of all the cuts he'd gotten before he'd been able to afford leather gloves. He had a fleet of newer trucks now, but something about the old Ford and the way she purred along the dirt roads made him feel free and happy and content.

His other favorite things: apple pie, his hunting rifles, country music and the literal goddess that was waiting for him out in her Hamptons mansion.

Wyatt gunned his speed to eighty-five and cranked up the sound system. He'd bought the car earlier in the week. He'd also bought an apartment. With the new deal he was working on, he knew he'd be spending more time in New York and he needed a place to stay.

Besides, he'd already decided he'd be spending a *lot* more time in New York. Once he'd tasted heaven, he was hooked. Now all he needed to do was show her such a good time she'd be as addicted to him as he already was to her. Easily done. He had no qualms about bringing out every weapon in his sexual arsenal. Wyatt just happened to be one of those men who could lay it on like few men could, a fact he was well aware of. He handed out orgasms like Santa did presents. And Athena Savage was about to get twelve dedicated hours of Christmas morning.

He was almost to her house. When Wyatt saw the

yellow arrows of an approaching curve, he tapped on the brake to slow down.

Nothing happened.

He slammed his foot down.

Nothing.

The car was only accelerating as he descended the hill he was barreling down at close to seventy-five.

Those fuckers. They'd tampered with his new Ferrari F60, goddamn them. He'd thought he'd covered his tracks, but someone must have found out about his new toy.

The car flew off the road, plowed down a sand dune and surged into the ocean at speed, creating a huge spray of water and activating both airbags, finally coming to a stop before the car was entirely submerged. He was glad now he'd decided on a convertible. Wyatt climbed out, waded to shore and made his way back up to the road. He pulled his phone out of his pocket but it was dead. So he stuck out his thumb and started walking.

It's going to take more than that to finish me off, boys, he thought, feeling remarkably unfazed by the accident.

Wyatt Boone was lucky. It's just the way things were. He was hot, tall, well-hung, outrageously good in bed and ridiculously rich. He *felt* lucky. They could do their best to de-rail his deal and even try to get away with murder, but Wyatt wasn't going to back down to anyone. If his number was up, there wasn't a lot he could do about it. He figured worrying about it was a waste of time. The truth was, his stars just had a way of aligning in a way that worked for him.

Like now. With his thumb out, he didn't have to wait more than a few minutes. A Mercedes pulled over. The window lowered to reveal a well-groomed, middle-aged woman. She ogled Wyatt for a few seconds, then smiled as coquettishly as a woman in her late forties who'd overdone the plastic surgery was capable of. "Where are you headed, cowboy?"

"The Savage house. On Seaview Road."

"I know the place. Jump in." Of course she knew the place. Everyone knew the place. The woman checked out the muscled shape of Wyatt's solid thighs, which were clearly outlined in his wet clothes. Her gaze slid a fraction higher, to his highly impressive package. "Lucky Athena," she commented brazenly in her smoker's voice.

Wyatt had rubbed shoulders with enough fat cats to know that their neglected wives were by far the most desperate and forward type of woman on the planet. This lady was probably the wife of a hedge fund manager who had a penchant for seventeen-year-olds. He'd seen it before, many times, and used his Texas charm to draw a line in the proverbial sand before she got too frisky. He wasn't about to tell this gargoyle in lipstick the details of his evening plans. "Lucky me, more accurately. Getting to have dinner with such a talented writer."

The woman cackled throatily. "Sure. No doubt you'll be doing a lot of reading once you get there. Could I interest you in a little … appetizer? My house is right up here on the left. And no one's home."

"As tempting as that offer may be, I'm already late. Had some car trouble back there."

"Aww," sulked the neglected housewife, lighting a cigarette. "You sure?"

Between the smoke and the wafting fumes of her perfume, Wyatt was doing his best not to choke. "'Fraid so, but I'm much obliged for the ride, ma'am."

"That accent is so adorable! I could eat you up."

Luckily, they were at Athena's gate. He opened the door and climbed out. "Thanks again for the lift."

"Anytime, sweetie. If you get bored of that damaged little heiress, come see me. It's number 1200. I'll show you the kind of good time she never could."

Doubtful. Wyatt winked at her. "Ya'll have a good night now." He shut the door and walked up to Athena's gate, pushing the buzzer. The woman, after staring longingly at his ass for close to a full minute, drove off.

The intercom crackled. "Wyatt? Is that you?"

"You want to let me in or do I have to climb over this thing?"

Athena & Wyatt

SOUTHAMPTON

WYATT MADE his way up the winding, cypress-lined driveway toward Athena's palatial home. When he arrived at the door, it was already open. Athena stood there, like a vision his lame imagination could never in a million years have dreamed up. She was *stunning*.

Noticing the state of him, she gasped. "What happened to you?"

He looked down at his clothes, like he'd forgotten they were still wet. "My brakes failed. Ended up in the drink."

"What? My god, Wyatt. Are you hurt?"

"Not a scratch." He shut the door behind him and snaked his arm around her waist, pulling her against him. He was too fired up to go slowly. "Remind me to call a tow truck in the morning, though, will you? If the damn thing doesn't get washed away before then, that is. But first, we've got something that needs attending to and I can't wait another second."

She touched his chest as though checking him for injuries, which only succeeded in driving him deeper into his barely-controlled frenzy. "But are you sure you're all right? Should I call a doctor?"

He scooped her into his arms and began carrying her up the grand, curving staircase. "Only you can cure what ails me, darlin'. Which room is yours?"

"The one at the end of the hallway. But why would your brakes have failed?"

Wyatt didn't want to get into the details of his death threats or the people who had a long list of vendettas against him. All he wanted to think about was finishing what he and Athena had started over the weekend. You don't put a horse away wet and you don't leave a man in the state of lust he'd been mired in since he'd left her. It was pure agony. He gently set her down on the bed and took off his jacket, tossing it onto a chair.

"*Wyatt*. What the——?" She reached for the revolver he had holstered into his belt. "You carry a *gun*?"

"Of course I do. I'm a Texan." As though it was the most reasonable thing in the world. He carefully took the loaded 629 Deluxe out of her hands and placed it on the bedside table. "And now that we're off the clock, you better get ready for your life to change."

He was arrogant, especially when it came to the subject of sex, she already knew that about him. What she would soon find out about in much more detail, however, was that he had outstanding reason to be.

Wyatt peeled off Athena's clothes, kissing every inch of her skin as he revealed it, reducing her to a puddle of hot, writhing desperation. He held her in place and licked her, eating into her like the starving man he was, making her come twice before he crawled up her body and laid himself over her. He bore her down, pinning her under his weight, holding her wrists in the manacle of his fist as he expertly, tenderly, lustily kissed her mouth. She could taste *herself*. She could smell the sea salt on his warm skin and the musky sheen of his rage-edged passion.

He spread her legs forcefully with his hair-roughened thigh as his monster—*Jesus!*—of an erection pressed rock-hard against her stomach.

His cock could have been classified as the eighth wonder of the world. He was built like a quarterback who moonlighted as a porn star.

Athena waited for his possession, breathing hard. She was too needy to be afraid of what he was about to do. She *liked* him rugged and riled. And hard. *And huge.* His gigantic cock was sliding itself devastatingly against her slippery, tender flesh and she was dizzy with desire for him. She wanted pleasure and pain. All of it. All of *him*.

"You ready for me, darlin'?" His deep voice was rasped with lust. "I want you like this. And that's how I'm going to have you, even though I've never in my life had sex without a condom before."

It was a bullyish thing to say. And somehow exactly what she wanted to hear. "I'm on the pill," she whispered. "Even though I've never in my life had sex before."

His blue gaze was vividly intense, his mink-brown hair sticking up in sexily unruly peaks. "I already thought you were perfect. You don't have to go breaking my heart now, baby." He tenderly traced the wing of her eyebrow with his thumb as he stared down at her like she was the answer to all his prayers and quite possibly the love of his life.

She weaved her fingers through the coarse silk of his hair and touched her lips softly to his, enticing him.

Wyatt slid the broad, slick head of his cock inside her, opening her with careful forcefulness. The stunning invasion rubbed against her still-rippling flesh and tipped her over another peak. They both gasped as her inner muscles spasmed invitingly around him. He drove deeper, using the rhythm of her pleasure to slide thickly into the nirvana of her body.

"You're so fucking beautiful, sugar pie," he growled.

Wyatt's hands moved down her body, exploring the curves of her breasts, her waist, her hips. He took her nipple in his mouth and sucked in greedy pulls before devouring her mouth with his.

Athena could sense that he was carnally *wild*. The intensity of his desire seemed to almost hum from his touch.

Wyatt thrust himself inch by excruciating inch deeper into her, gripping her with his hands, marking her flesh with painful strength that somehow only compounded her spiraling pleasure.

"That's my girl," he groaned, fully, deeply inside her tight, quivering body. "Let me in. Feel my obsession and my devotion, sweet girl. All of it. *Ah, hell,* you feel too good." Wyatt dropped his head, tickling her with his hair as he struggled to control himself. Then he gazed into her eyes and his voice was slurred with lust when he said, "When I saw your picture in that magazine, I knew right then that I wanted you. Just you. You're mine now, baby. I'm keeping you. I'm going to give you everything you need. I'm going to take care of you. Because you're the most beautiful thing I've ever seen in my goddamn life. I want everything, darlin'. Give me everything."

She was melting under the potency of his words and his sublime, perfect assault, perched on the edge of some looming physical abyss of rapture from which she might never recover. His effect was changing her life. Her fingernails dug into his skin as she tried to pull him closer, to become one with the insanely overwhelming craving to have of all him and all he was.

His measured, thrusting drives forced the aching beauty deeper, and higher. Until there it was, a bursting peak of excruciating pleasure that cascaded in jolting rushes throughout Athena's entire being. The rhythm of her bliss gripped him, tugging him deeper into her body. She could feel the gushing warmth of his own release mingling with her surging, rippling bliss. They were lost in their explosive bond, fierce and entangled, as connected as it was possible to be.

And that was just the beginning.

He didn't just take her virginity, he obliterated it.

All night long, the tidal waves of pleasure he delivered were so intense, Athena wondered if she'd survive the deluge. He was relentless, shattering her. The ecstasy went beyond physical into something closer to spiritual. She didn't know and didn't care about classifying it. All she knew was that she was in awe of Wyatt Boone's gifts.

By morning, all those million shattered pieces of her had somehow reassembled, but differently so, like they'd found a perfect, much more comfortable fit.

She stretched, feeling very sore and happy and alive. Outside the French doors that led to her balcony, the glittering Atlantic shone azure. But she had no desire to leave the paradise of her bed or the beefy magician in it.

Athena let her hands rest against his stomach. Then she slid them lower, grasping the hot, gargantuan length of him. Did the thing ever … go down? She hoped not.

Wyatt groaned softly. "You tryin' to kill me, darlin'?" His accent got stronger in bed.

She nodded, kissing his lips. "Yes."

So he laid her back and proceeded to outdo even last night's performance, until Athena wondered if she'd be able to live without this. Without him. And the things he could freaking *do*.

Senior Detective Statham: Have you ever aimed the firearm you carry at a human being?

Individual 11: (~~Wyatt Boone~~ [redacted]): Yes, sir.

SDS: Can you be more specific?

I11: [refers to list] I pointed it directly at Individual 25.

SDS: What was your intent? To threaten? To injure? Or to kill?

I11: To make a crystal clear point, Detective. I was hoping options two and three wouldn't be required. But I was prepared to do whatever needed to be done.

24

Tiffany Chamberlain

MANHATTAN

Tiffany Chamberlain was sitting, sunglasses on, blond wig carefully placed, at the upscale restaurant across the street from Ares's apartment, with an unobscured view of the front door. She watched the doorman open the door for Ares and his two guests.

She wasn't sure if she was more irate at Ares or those little Cuban sluts, who'd done nothing short of ruining her life.

Everything had been going *so* well. She'd worked so hard to get what she wanted! But then her dream lifestyle, man and apartment had slipped through her fingers just like that. All because those evil harlots had turned her in.

Well, she would be returning the favor, thank you very much.

She'd done everything in her power to please him.

But no. Nothing was ever good enough for Ares Savage, the self-absorbed prick.

Tiffany keyed in the phone number she'd googled. She was put on hold but busied herself by reapplying her lipstick and ordering herself another gin as she listened idly to the muzac, which ended abruptly.

"United States Immigration and Customs Enforcement," said the official. "How can I help you?"

"I'd like to report two illegal aliens and their whereabouts. They sailed here on a boat, they have no paperwork, they've been working here illegally and they're tricking their host into believing they're innocent and defenseless."

"What's their country of origin?"

"Cuba."

"And what's the address where they can be located?"

"Will you give them advance warning?" asked Tiffany. She was interested in the process of how this would all play out. "Do you deport them immediately?"

"No advance warning is given," explained the official. "We seize them, detain them until transportation can be arranged, then they'll be deported back to Cuba at the very first opportunity."

"Excellent," cooed Tiffany, pleased. "It's a Park Avenue address. Do you have a pen?"

Ares

MANHATTAN

ARES HAD NOT BEEN able to bring himself to go to work that day. A first. He'd answered a few emails from his laptop but had been too distracted to do much more than that.

One floor below him, in the guest suite of his apartment, was his brand new obsession. It was a situation he was not even remotely happy about. He, Ares Savage, simply wasn't the *type* to get attached, like some sentimental fool. Yet here he was, strutting around like he'd suddenly morphed into fucking Galahad.

The thing was, he knew Tiffany had an ace up her sleeve and wasn't going to be at all shy about playing it. He needed to stick around in case she made her phone call soon. His ex-girlfriend was clearly a bitch of the highest order and would be chomping at the bit to get her revenge. He only hoped they could push the paperwork through before Tiffany made her move. But the events of the past few days had him worried.

Ares wandered around, forgetting what he'd walked into the kitchen for.

How should he break the news to Jazmin and Valentina? And more importantly, how would he propose an alternative by … proposing?

Finally, by around six o'clock, he couldn't take it anymore. He called Jazmin's number, which he'd asked for so he could check on her to see if she needed anything while she was staying with him.

After a few rings, she answered. "Hi, Ares."

And least she was no longer calling him Mr. Savage. "How's the apartment? Everything okay?"

"It's amazing."

"I'm making some dinner. There's more than enough here for three. Would you like to come up?"

"The kitchen down here is stocked. You said we could help ourselves. I hope you don't mind. We've already eaten."

"Of course I don't mind." Damn it. Why hadn't he thought of that? "Well, then, how about a glass of wine? There's actually something I wanted to talk to you about."

"Is it about us being here? Because I don't want to impose on you like this for too long. We can make other arrangeme—"

"*No.*" Shit. He needed to calm down. He made a point of making his voice sound gentler, and less deranged. "No, no. It's nothing like that. I'm glad you're here."

She hesitated. "What did you want to talk about, then?"

"Would you like to come up? We can discuss it when you get here."

"Sure. We'll be up soon."

"Great."

We. At some point he was going to have to figure out how to get Jazmin alone. He was also going to have to figure out how to propose to her without sounding like a card-carrying maniac.

He opened a bottle of wine, making sure to choose something she might approve of. A bottle that didn't cost a thousand dollars. The only problem was, most of the ones in his cellar cost at least that much. So he chose a young Californian red from an obscure, relatively new vineyard. It might have cost him a hundred bucks. At least if she googled it, she couldn't accuse him of throwing money away.

Was he dressed? He couldn't remember what he'd done today. If he'd even bothered to put on something appropriate. He had, but barely. Worn jeans and a t-shirt.

He went into his room and put on a nicer shirt, but left the jeans on. He didn't want to come across as a try-hard. What would impress her more: a simple button down shirt or something more formal? Would she notice? Would she even care?

Christ, what was happening to him? It didn't usually even cross his mind what other people thought of him.

His feelings for Jazmin were a wild, open frontier he didn't know how to navigate. But he would *have* to figure out how to navigate it, and sooner rather than later. Her days were numbered. If he didn't find a solution soon, he'd lose her, before he'd even had the chance to get to know her and to tell her how he felt.

The elevator in the foyer of his lobby pinged, and the doors slid open.

It was her.

Just her.

Looking as ravishing as ever, in jeans and a fitted white sweater that was frayed at the cuffs. He wanted to give her everything she'd never had. But he had to keep his wits about him. If he let himself get too carried away, he'd waste time, which he couldn't afford.

Act normally, he commanded himself. *Don't fuck this up.*

He smiled at her, and poured two glasses of the wine. "Hi," he said, as casually as he was capable of. "Where's Valentina?"

"She's tired. She's been out all day. She decided to take a bath and go to bed."

"Wine?"

"Sure. Thanks."

They sat on the couch and looked out over the expansive views of the city.

"What was it you wanted to talk to me about?"

Ares took a large gulp of his wine. Then he set down his glass. "It has to do with the immigration papers."

She made a face, like it wasn't a topic she enjoyed. Not surprisingly.

"I'm sorry to bring it up. I just … I want to make sure you can stay."

"It's not looking very likely, is it?"

"My lawyers are exploring every possible avenue. But

if all else fails, there is one thing we could do. If we have to."

Before she could even ask him what that one thing might be, his intercom system buzzed. It was synced to his phone. Immediately, he knew exactly who it was.

Tiffany, damn you. You didn't waste any time at all, did you?

What the hell was he going to do now? He stared at his phone.

"Are you going to answer that?" Jazmin finally said, jolting him out of his panic.

He smiled at her uneasily, then accepted the call. "Hello?"

"Mr. Savage, it's Joe. There are several federal officers here at the front desk that demand I let them up to see you immediately."

Maybe he could stall them. Or ask them to come back tomorrow.

An officer took over the conversation. "Mr. Savage? It's Officer Anthony Briggs here. I'm with Immigration and Customs Enforcement. We have reason to believe you're harboring two undocumented aliens in your apartment. We have a warrant to search the premises. I suggest you cooperate fully with our requests or you're at risk of facing criminal charges."

Ares did his best to bluff. "Officer Briggs, I'm still waiting to hear back from my lawyer about—"

"According to our paperwork, your lawyer was already notified. The applications were rejected. Don't make this more difficult than it needs to be, Mr. Savage. We're on our way up."

Goddamn it. Why hadn't he thought this through more carefully?

He and Jazmin could run. They could take the back staircase. They could disappear until he'd had a chance to figure this out. But Ares already knew Jazmin would never leave Valentina behind. All he could do was face these officers head on and hope for the best. He wasn't completely unprepared, after all. He'd read the stacks of paperwork Bruce had sent him, cover to cover. And he'd memorized the clause he needed: *Spouses of American citizens are exempt from deportation in the majority of cases.*

Within minutes, the elevator pinged, slid open and four immigration officers entered Ares's apartment. Ares and Jazmin both stood up.

"Evening," said one of the men. "I'm Officer Briggs. This is Smith, Jones and Johnson. And you must be Ares Savage."

"Yes."

"And who might you be?" Briggs said to Jazmin, far too smugly. These guys *enjoyed* their job, you could just tell. "One of the girls who sailed on a rowboat from Cuba, by any chance?"

"I'm Jazmin Diaz," She couldn't have been completely immune to what was going on here, but she stared Briggs straight in the eye and appeared to be unintimidated by the four officers, who all had several large guns holstered to their belts. Through sheer composure and grit she seemed to be radiating some kind of loud cosmic message that made her practically glow with the kind of humanity Ares could only aspire to.

It wasn't the first time Ares found himself thinking about how utterly impressive she was. Already besotted, at that moment he fell cataclysmically in love with her.

There, in front of the officers, Ares got down on one knee. He took Jazmin's hand. "Jazmin, this may seem a little rushed, but … will you marry me?"

Jazmin stared at him. "Ares, you don't have to do this."

"I want to. Please, Jazmin, marry me."

Jazmin, round-eyed, blinked at Ares. Then she glanced at the officers. Briggs looked slightly bored, like this sort of thing happened all the time. Then Jazmin met Ares's gaze again. "I don't know what to say."

"Say yes," suggested Ares.

"If you're doing this so I won't get deported—"

"That's not why. I was going to ask you anyway. I've been trying to work up the courage. I know we haven't known each other very long, and I didn't want you to feel rushed. But I want to get to know you and give you everything you've ever wished for. We can have any kind of wedding you want. Here in the city, or at one of our other houses, in Nashville or Telluride or Malibu or the Hamptons. Anything you want."

Jazmin blinked again. She smiled a little, empathetically, as though detecting his angst and feeling for *him*, despite what was going on around them. "Are you sure?"

"A hundred thousand percent."

She hesitated, but her smile was heartfelt. "I've always wanted to see the Rocky Mountains."

Ares could barely bring himself to ask the question. "Does that mean you will?"

She laughed. "Yes. I guess we might as well."

Ares stood up and held Jazmin's face gently between his hands. "I know it's sudden and the circumstances are crazy. But I promise you won't regret it."

"Nice try, Casanova." Ares had almost forgotten he was there. Briggs rolled his eyes. "If I had a dollar for every marriage proposal, I could have retired to Palm Beach by now. As romantic as all this might be, a proposal isn't going to cut it. According to an anonymous source, this undocumented alien has been living in this country unlawfully for more than four years, evading authorities and even working under the table—which, of course, means we can add tax evasion to her long list of felonies."

"That's ridiculous," Ares began.

But Briggs was on a roll. "I'm afraid we have no choice but to take her into custody immediately and deport her as soon as possible." He gestured to Jazmin. "Come with me willingly please, or you'll just make things worse for yourself."

"*Wait.*" Ares held out his hands. His panic had reached critical levels. "We're getting *married*, for Chrissakes. You *saw* what just happened here. She said yes. Which means she'll be my *wife*. Which means, as the spouse of a citizen, she can fucking stay."

"*Language*, Mr. Savage," Briggs scolded. "As I just pointed out, she has in fact broken the law several times over. Even if you did marry her, she'd face jail time and possible deportation regardless."

"No!" Ares was losing his cool, a commodity that was already in short supply when it came to anything involving Jazmin. "I'll pay the bail. And the back-taxes. Whatever it takes. Those laws were broken out of desperation. She was *trying* to do the right thing, goddamn it! They'd hired an immigration lawyer to—"

"It doesn't matter," interrupted Briggs, getting bored with the entire argument. He wasn't proud of it, but after twelve years on the job he was basically immune to people's misery at this point. It was always the same: begging, pleading, threatening, bribing. All pointless. It wasn't *his* fault she'd rowed here on a boat. People had to suffer the consequences of their own actions, simple as that. Besides, he'd planned to finish work early and meet his buddies for a couple of cold ones and a game or two of darts (he was the reigning champion down at O'Flanagan's) and he was already running late. "The damage has already been done. Jones, Smith: seize the alien. Johnson: find the other one. She's around here somewhere."

Jazmin's expression changed to one of terror. "*No.*"

"No?" said Briggs, confused. "Isn't she here?"

Ares was used to getting his own way. His brain wasn't accepting that this time, he might not. He held Jazmin's hand, and recited the other part of the document he'd memorized. "'Siblings of the spouse of an American citizen may be sponsored by the American citizen if the citizen can prove financial resources are adequate for long-term support.'"

"Come again?" said Briggs, who'd not only neglected to memorize the rules it was his job to enforce, but hadn't even read them.

"I have enough money to provide bail and to support my fiancée and her sister indefinitely," Ares explained. "I'll sign the paperwork now."

Briggs was unswayable. "I'm afraid that's a matter you can take up with the supervisor at the detainment center." Again, to Jazmin, "Come with me, Ms. Diaz. Now."

Ares squeezed Jazmin's hand tighter and attempted to remain calm. "Let's be reasonable, Briggs. I'm more than happy to offer you a retainer. Right now. Just name your price and no one else has to—"

"Bribery would be an interesting option if we weren't wired, Mr. Savage. Stunts like that'll only be used against you later." Briggs would have been more than happy to take a bribe, but he'd been busted once, early in his career. And so had a lot of other officers. There'd been other kinds of incidents, too, like beatings and fights. The department heads had finally resorted to fitting the officers' uniforms with tiny cameras that were sewn into their collars and checked daily, in an attempt to crack down on the problems.

Briggs motioned to Jones, Smith and Johnson.

The three of them—Ares noticed now—were built like brick shithouses.

Ares had played football for a few years at his upscale private boarding school. Never one of the bulkiest guys on the field, he'd still been a pretty good tackler. And he worked out in his home gym at least five times a week and occasionally swam lengths in the Olympic-sized pool located on the fifth floor of his building.

When Johnson took a step toward Jazmin, Ares lunged. As it turned out, however, Officer Johnson spent much of his spare time honing his skills in mixed martial arts, and was making excellent progress. It was one of the reasons he'd been appointed for this job.

For Ares, high school had been a long time ago. Despite his all-out fury, he was no match for Johnson, Smith *or* Jones and especially not the three of them all at once.

Swearing at them didn't help either.

By the time he regained consciousness, Ares found himself bloody and handcuffed. And in the backseat of a police car on its way to the station.

"Where's Jazmin?" he demanded.

"She and her sister have been taken to the detainment center, as discussed," said Briggs, who was driving. "To be deported on the next flight out. Oh, and you're under arrest for assaulting three federal officers. You have the right to remain sile—"

The string of expletives were, in hindsight, a bad decision.

The on-duty sergeant at the police station played back the recording of the raid, the altercation and the arrest several times. Since each of the four I.C.E. officers agreed that Ares would likely head straight down to the detainment center and attempt to free Jazmin if they let him go, the sergeant made a decision. Ares would be kept in custody on the grounds that he was likely to commit further offenses if he was released on bail. It might have been the *I'll kill you! I'll kill all of you!*—which he'd yelled during his tirade and which he now severely regretted— or the *I'll fucking find her! I'll break them out of that detainment center before you can say illegal deportation, you fuckers!*

"No bail will be granted," said the sergeant, "until the girls are airborne. We'll do our best to speed up the process so you can be released as soon as possible."

Ares was allowed one phone call. He used his two-minute limit to rant at Bruce and desperately order his lawyer get him the hell out of jail and also find a way to rescue Jazmin and Valentina before it was too late. Ares's phone and wallet were then confiscated before he was thrown into a cell with an inebriated bum, who was snoring loudly from the only bed.

Ares curled his fingers around the prison bars and rested his head against the cold metal.

Please, he prayed, for the first time in a very long time. *I have to find her.*

Senior Detective Statham: Did you ever consider using the gun you had on your person to retaliate as you were taken into custody?

Individual 7: (~~Valentina Diaz~~ [redacted]): Of course not.

SDS: But you made every attempt to conceal the weapon?

I7: Yes. I knew I might need it.

SDS: So you were fully prepared to use it if and when you thought it necessary?

I7: I wouldn't have bought the gun if I wasn't prepared to use it, Detective.

25

Eros

HOLLYWOOD, CALIFORNIA

Eros raced his Maserati down to Universal Studios, parked it in a no parking zone and stormed onto the set of the Friction movie with his swimming-in-the-ocean-at-dawn-while-having-epiphanies-about-your-dead-father's-wise-beyond-the-grave-advice priorities firmly in place. Even though he wasn't on the cast list, the night guard let him through the gate when Eros agreed to give the guy an autograph and a shared selfie.

But now that he was here, Eros was feeling less sure about what he was intending to do.

It was probably a stupid idea.

It *was* a stupid idea.

But the motivational podcast he'd listened to was very clear about it: never hesitate. The less you hesitate in life the more successful you'll be. Hesitation is the space where doubt and fear live, the speaker had insisted. So Eros strode right up and knocked on Percy Mercy's trailer door.

No answer.

He knocked again.

"Who is it?" came the muffled, pissed-off reply.

"Mr. Mercy? It's Eros Savage. I wondered if I could have a couple minutes of your time."

After a lot of swearing and shuffling around inside, Percy opened the door. "What the hell do you want?" Percy greeted him.

"Nice to see you again, Mr. Mercy," Eros began. "I was hoping we could talk about something important."

"Dude, it's six o'clock in the motherfucking morning."

"Six thirty. Can I come in?"

Percy was shaking his head. But then, he stepped away from the door as though giving permission for Eros to enter. "I need to get up anyway. We start at seven."

Eros climbed up the steps into the trailer.

There were a few suitcases still packed and a single half-empty bottle of red wine on the table. Eros remembered that they'd only started shooting the movie yesterday. Percy clearly hadn't had time to settle in to his new digs.

Percy went to the espresso machine in his kitchenette. "You want coffee?"

"Sure. Thanks."

"What's this all about, then? And make it quick. You've got exactly five minutes."

"Thank you. I know I didn't get the part I auditioned for, but—"

"Oh, yeah," Percy said, glancing over at him and giving him a once-over. "Now I remember you."

"I auditioned for the part Leo got."

"That's right. You're the underwear model."

Damn you, Calvin Klein! The cool cats *always* zeroed in on that first. Always. "Well, yes, I have modeled underwear. But that's not the only thing I do. I've been in twelve movies now, including two indies and a couple of blockbusters."

Percy set two mugs of black coffee on the table. He didn't offer cream or sugar. "Uh huh," he said, sounding thoroughly unimpressed. He picked up a pair of sunglasses off the table and put them on, even though the sun was barely up.

"You must really like Leo's work, for you to hire him again," Eros commented. "I'd heard that you prefer to mix it up with the cast lists and—"

"I don't like a goddamn thing about Leo Puck. We cast him because the part calls for a misogynistic loser who sleeps around, fucks up a lot and deals bad drugs. You came across as too soft."

"Not gritty enough. I know. My agent mentioned it."

"You just didn't fit the part, man. It was nothing personal."

Eros had figured out by now that Percy Mercy was at heart a patient and open-minded person. Most people— especially directors at the top of their game—wouldn't have tolerated listening to this, it now occurred to him (and possibly should have when he was sitting on that cliff). Most people would have slammed the door in his face, or not opened it at all. "The thing about *acting*, Mr. Mercy—"

"Can you quit the 'Mr. Mercy' bullshit? Just call me Percy."

"Oh. Okay. So, Percy, the thing about acting is that I can do whatever it takes to *transform* myself into the character—"

"We didn't think you had it in you to make that big of a leap. You seemed too green for that kind of complexity."

This didn't shock Eros. He knew what he looked like. And Percy was basically putting it kindly. "I can see why you would think that. But I can assure you I'm not. I have it in me to do anything. Whatever it takes. I'll live on the streets if it helps me get into character. I'll starve myself or pump iron ten hours a day or do a Brokeback Mountain or shave my head or work for free or whatever. I want it that bad. I want to work with you. And I came here today because I wanted you to know that."

Percy eyed him through his sunglasses. Possibly. It was sort of hard to tell, but he was pretty sure he was being studied. "I'll keep that in mind."

Eros suspected that was a dismissal, and he didn't want to push Percy's patience further than he already had. "Thank you." He stood up to leave. "And thanks for the coffee."

"I might be able to place you as an extra in a couple scenes if you're interested."

"Really?"

"It's not much."

"I'll do it." Eros couldn't believe it. His plan had almost worked. He still had a mountain to climb but at least he'd been let into base camp.

"Stick around set and I'll see if I can hook you up."

Eros gushingly thanked Percy several more times and left his trailer.

So he'd just agreed to work for nothing as an extra. He wasn't sure why he felt so insanely happy about it.

Senior Detective Statham: Were the bruises on your face caused by the altercation that took place at 23:41 on the evening of October 17 at Universal Studios?

Individual 5: (~~Eros Savage~~ [redacted]): Sure were.

SDS: Are you prone to violent fistfights?

I5: Only when the situation calls for it, Detective.

26

SOUTHAMPTON

AT FIRST SHE REFUSED.

"It's a terrible idea," said Daisy.

Dr. Manning had called her into his office. She'd just returned Apollo to his room after their walk in the garden. The doctor explained the details of her new work assignment.

"I can't control Apollo Savage," Daisy protested. "Especially in his own home. I don't want that responsibility. He's not ready."

"I agree," said Dr. Manning. "But *he* doesn't. And you'd be paid very well to *make* him ready. Twenty thousand dollars for one month plus the ten grand we're already paying you. For one month."

Thirty thousand dollars?

It was more money than Daisy Sullivan had ever seen in her life.

But would it be worth it? To live with and babysit and act as the strict schoolmarm for a totally out-of-control hedonist who saw her as both an irritation and now, even worse, a victim? It would be unbearable.

"One month," Dr. Manning repeated, reading her hesitations. "Unless he chooses on-going treatment, but I doubt it'll come to that."

Dr. Manning could try to placate her as much as he wanted, but it didn't change the fact that he was asking her to move to Nashville for a minimum of four weeks and leave her entire life behind.

What's so bad about that? You've been desperate to leave Long Island for years.

Yes. On her own terms. Not those of a rich, infantile, arrogant addict. She was trying to escape addicts, not follow them around.

"Keep in mind, Daisy, if Apollo Savage does stay clean for a month—or longer, ideally—you'll have the option of any rehab nursing job you choose. I've even contacted the university and they're willing to let you continue your studies online while you're away, so you can graduate on time. This is a high-profile case and a once-in-a-lifetime opportunity. It'll give your career a real boost. I think you should take it."

He was right, of course.

There was also the fact that she was afraid to go home

tonight, like she'd been for the past three nights, ever since Liam had shown up at her house.

She could disappear for a while. And he'd have no idea where to find her.

"I'll do it," she said.

"Good," said Dr. Manning, pleased. "Your private jet leaves in two hours."

Daisy rushed home to pack, noticed her only plant was already dead from neglect so didn't bother calling her neighbor, and caught a taxi back to work.

When she arrived at the hospital, a stretch limo with tinted windows was parked out in front.

Let me guess. That must be our ride.

She was uneasy.

It was one thing to be locked in a hospital room with Apollo, where guards armed with sedatives were ready to come rushing to her aid at the push of a button. It was another thing altogether to be living in his house with him. Alone, as far as she knew.

Not that she was afraid of Apollo Savage.

He was surly. But most recovering addicts were. She'd seen glimpses of a different, softer side of his personality. He was smart, articulate and had a quick and perceptive sense of humor. After working with patients for the last year and a half, she was good at reading people. She didn't think Apollo was capable of violence, beyond the occasional temper tantrum. She'd seen him pull his own hair, yell into a pillow and do a lot of pacing. But she'd never felt threatened by him. If he was a threat to anyone, it was to himself.

Her biggest concern was … something else.

The fame, for one thing.

He was the entire world's manic obsession.

Apollo Savage was—she was only too aware—one of the planet's most sought-after men. He was not only a wildly successful rock star but, according to the headlines, the "hottest man alive" and "a sex god."

The thought of being not only alone with him but in charge of him was … a little intimidating.

She had a feeling she'd be earning every cent of that thirty thousand dollars.

"Ms. Sullivan," said one of the orderlies. "It's time to go."

She'd have to figure it out as she went.

They made their way into the limo, and the press had somehow figured out what was going on. The front of the hospital was crowded with reporters.

Bodyguards ushered her, then Apollo, into the back of the limo and slammed the doors. They sped away, only to be followed by a parade of traffic.

The airport was even worse. By the time they arrived in Nashville, thousands of people were awaiting Apollo's arrival, like he was the Beatles arriving in America for the first time or something. People were holding signs. *Welcome Home!*, *I love you, Apollo!* and *Marry me!* Swooning girls screamed at him from behind the row of guards, who had difficulty keeping the crowds from storming the boundaries.

They were ushered into another limo just in time. His rabid fans swarmed their car, pounding on the windows as they made their getaway, crying actual tears as they screamed Apollo's name.

It was terrifying. "How do you *live* like this?" She was thankful for the bullet-proof, tinted windows.

"You get used to it," Apollo seemed barely affected by all the hoopla. His unusual, sapphire-hued eyes watched her, like her reaction was mildly entertaining to him.

"I don't think I'd ever get used to it."

Apollo grinned. It might have been the first time she'd ever seen him smile. If that look could have been bottled and sold as an aphrodisiac, it would have tripled his income. Not that Daisy was affected by him in that kind of way, she made a point of reminding herself. He was her patient. She'd oversee his medications, make sure his healing broken bones weren't causing him too much pain, then she'd be on her merry way with thirty grand in her bank account and a real shot at making a new life for herself, as far from her past as she could get.

Apollo opened the mini bar. "I'd offer you a drink, but I guess that would be against the rules." He handed her a bottle of water and opened one for himself.

"Your rules are your own, Apollo. I'm only here to make sure you're on the mend."

Daisy didn't dislike Apollo, not at all. And she didn't *like* him, either. "Liking" Apollo Savage would be akin to putting yourself at the top of a 90-meter ski jump and promising yourself you'd go slow.

Besides, his life looked like hard work.

A different kind of hard work to her own.

A *harder* kind of hard work.

She looked out the window. They drove up to a massive gate, which opened for them. Daisy could only stare as they drove up Apollo's driveway. The place wasn't just a mansion, it was a *castle*.

Located outside the city, in Franklin, it was an older estate that had been completely renovated at some point, obviously with no expense spared.

They pulled up to the entrance, where an actual butler-type person took her single suitcase and showed her to the room she'd be sleeping in, which happened to be next to Apollo's master suite. The two rooms had their own wing.

Her room was like something out of a magazine spread. A king-sized bed with mountains of goose down and white linen. There was a sitting area with a cushioned window seat. And a little wrought-iron balcony that was possibly the most romantic thing Daisy had ever seen. Even the bathroom was marble and chrome and had its own jacuzzi and a walk-in shower that looked like a car wash.

Wow.

She opened the doors and stood out on the balcony, looking out over the manicured lawns and the lake with a fountain, over the treetops toward the city in the distance.

Imagine living like this, she thought. *Not having to worry about how you were going to pay for your next meal or whether you'd have enough money for both the rent and the electricity bill.*

Apollo walked in and sprawled himself onto the cushioned window seat in the sun, making himself at home. *Well, it is his home.*

"Is the room okay?" he said.

"Yes. It's a little more … luxurious than I'm used to."

Apollo already seemed much more relaxed, and he'd lost that cooped-up edge. "God, it's good to be out of that prison. I'm going to make a point of *not* driving my motorcycle off any more thirty-foot cliffs. If only so I don't have to get locked up again."

"I'm glad to hear that."

"Come downstairs with me." He stood up and headed toward the door.

It's what she was being paid to do, after all, so she could hardly refuse. But she would have liked to stay in her room and admire the view a little longer. She was almost glad now that she'd agreed to come. A whole month of sleeping in this room would make it that much more bearable.

Apollo gave her a tour of his house, which was unbelievable at every turn, and full of people. There were seven colossal bedrooms, each with its own bathroom; two kitchens; a dining room that looked more like a hip, busy restaurant; three living areas—each more expansive and luxurious than the last; a game room with a pool table and fully stocked bar (and bartender, who was currently mixing cocktails); an ultra-modern recording studio; a movie theater (showing a movie that hadn't even been released yet); a library; a gigantic stone and glass conservatory with vaulted wooden ceilings (occupied by a gang of glamorous, barely-dressed guests that could have starred in a music video, and given the location, probably had); an outdoor entertainment area complete with a pool, fountain, supersonic stereo system (currently cranked to what might have been full volume), TV area and hot tub (full of what appeared to be butt-naked young people chugging mixed drinks); gated picturesque rolling lawns dotted with trees, sculptures and statues; a pretty lake with a fountain and dock; and a guest house that was at least three times as big as Daisy's rental.

Apollo's band, who were hanging out by the pool, appeared to live with him. He introduced her to Bruno, his bass player, who had long dark hair and was holding a half-full whiskey bottle in one hand and a fat spliff in the other.

The drummer's name was Gus. He was blond and had a loose, laughing vibe that Daisy guessed made him popular and also one of the more eager in the crowd to party hard. From behind Apollo's back, Gus winked at her.

Apollo's manager, Rufus, wore yellow tinted

sunglasses and a cowboy hat. He followed Apollo around, wanting to talk about their schedule.

Groupies were swimming in the pool, calling out Apollo's name. Guests were helping themselves to his food and drinks. Some were clearly already wasted.

And everyone wanted a piece of Apollo.

Daisy felt out of place. What could she possibly give him that all these people couldn't give him? Stability? Hardly. Boundaries? As if.

Now that she was here, it was easy to see that the situation was a disaster waiting to happen. "No wonder you can't stop partying," she commented vaguely.

Apollo only shrugged, and led her to an outdoor seating area with plush, off-white couches, expensive-looking curtains that had been tied back against the stone pillars, and a large-screen TV, playing music videos. Daisy's mind reeled at the *expense* of everything. The TV alone probably cost several months' worth of rent on the house she'd left empty. She wondered if Liam had broken into it yet.

Bruno offered Apollo a beer.

"Uh … nope," he said, glancing at Daisy. "I'm sober now."

"*Sober*?" Like it might have been a dirty word he wasn't familiar with.

"He just got out of fucking rehab, you idiot," said Rufus.

Bruno crooked his thumb toward Daisy. "Who's she, the fun police?"

"This is Daisy Sullivan," said Apollo. "She's my …"

Please don't say rehab nurse. Please don't say rehab nurse. From the glares Bruno was giving her, she was pretty sure Apollo's entourage thought she was here to ruin everyone's good time.

"… assistant."

Thank you, Daisy thought silently. *I think.*

"Assistant?" repeated Bruno accusingly. "Don't you already have a brigade of those?"

"I needed another one."

Rufus slung his arm around Apollo's shoulders. "You've got a gig on Friday night, at the Troubadour. We're keeping it quiet. It'll be a small crowd. Something more intimate to get you back in the groove."

Daisy couldn't help herself. "That's a terrible idea."

They all stared at her.

"Apollo needs rest, not gigs and late nights and parties. He's still recovering. He just got home."

"Who died and put *her* in charge?" Bruno muttered scathingly, eyeballing her like she'd somehow morphed into Yoko.

I'm only here to keep an eye on his meds, she wanted to say.

Gus sidled up to Daisy. He wound an end strand of her hair around one of his fingers. "You're gorgeous."

Apollo's expression darkened. He carefully removed Daisy's curl from around Gus's finger. Then he shoved Gus into the pool.

Gus splashed around for a few seconds then swam to

the side. "What the fuck, Apollo? My phone's in my pocket!"

Apollo didn't appear to care about that. He'd changed since they'd left rehab. For some reason, he seemed almost protective of her. "If Daisy doesn't think I should play on Friday night, then I'm not going to."

"Jesus H. Christ," moaned Bruno, taking a puff off his joint indignantly.

But then someone cranked up the music and her decree was more or less absorbed into the conversation, and accepted.

So *this* was what she was being paid thirty thousand dollars to do? To follow Apollo Savage around, supervise his decisions and act as some kind of guardian/consultant?

Beers were distributed but she and Apollo were given Diet Cokes. He clinked his against hers as he laughed at something Rufus had said.

She sighed and sat back in her ridiculously plush chair, watching the scene. Gus had recovered from his outrage and was now frolicking happily in the water with some of the scantily-clad girls.

Look on the bright side, Daisy thought. *It could be worse.*

Senior Detective Statham: You had a clear view, then, of the moment the first shot was fired.

Individual 21 (~~Gus Erasmus~~ [redacted]): I was standing right behind him when the bullet hit. He took that bullet for her, that's what he did. And the thing was, we all understood why he would.

27

Artemis

TELLURIDE

ARTEMIS GOT into her yellow Jeep. She pushed the button that would open the garage door. After Arlo's panicked phone call, she was getting ready to drive down the mountain and check into one of the hotels in town.

But she couldn't bring herself to do it.

Being stalked made you paranoid—and terrified. It also made you angry.

Artemis didn't *want* to be bullied. Why should she let some random lunatic drive her away from her beloved house? It felt like giving in.

So she made a decision.

She wasn't going to run.

It's not like she was completely defenseless. After the first incident with the stalker, Ares had insisted she let him stock her house with several guns. He'd made a big production out of showing her how to use them, until he was satisfied she could protect herself whenever she was alone.

Artemis had never touched them. She didn't like the thought of the guns—or why they might be necessary. She preferred to get on with her life and pretend they didn't exist.

Until now.

There was one in the glove compartment of the Jeep she was sitting in.

One in the top drawer of her dresser.

One in the kitchen, locked above the fridge.

She opened the glove compartment and took out the small pistol. It was pink. A designer killing machine. Ares had chosen them specifically for her. At the time, he'd described why they'd be perfect for what she needed.

Perfect? she'd thought at the time. *What's perfect about shooting a man as he breaks into my house? Or killing him as he threatens to hurt me or kill me? I don't* want *to need this!*

She held it in her hands, clicking the safety catch to off.

She would wait for him.

No. Even better, she would let him in.

How dare he terrorize her? Especially now, when she suspected she might be closer to something resembling real happiness than anything she'd known before.

What was she going to do, move into a hotel room indefinitely? Hide and cower until the police eventually found him? Invite Cooper to come stay with her at the damn Marriott?

She took out her phone and turned off the master switch for the entire security system of her house.

Come on, then, you bastard. Come and get it. I refuse to be a victim. So don't fuck with me.

She sat there for a while, in the silence. Waiting for what, she wasn't sure.

Using her phone, she turned off all the lights in her house.

You won't be expecting me to fight back, will you? You'll be expecting me to run and hide.

But not this time.

She waited for her eyes to adjust. Then she opened the door of her Jeep and cautiously climbed out, holding her loaded gun in front of her, resting her finger against the trigger. Silently, she walked toward the door that led into her kitchen.

She opened it, peering into her house.

This is my sanctuary. I refuse to let you steal my peace of mind. I'm taking it back.

And there, as though on cue, on the far side of the open plan house, she saw movement. Outside the front entrance, where two glass panes framed the sturdy wooden door. Local spruce, she remembered. Now unlocked.

A man.

It's him.

She crept closer, making sure to move quietly, stealthily, remaining hidden.

The door began to slowly open.

He was dressed in dark clothing, she could see. Looking around, he stepped inside.

Should I kill him? So I never have to be afraid of him again?

No. She didn't want to live with his blood on her hands for the rest of eternity. It was yet another way he would win. By tainting her world forever with murder and death.

If I injure him, he won't be able to run after me. I can call the police and he'll be taken back to jail.

Not an ideal plan, but better than nothing.

So, as the intruder took another step closer, Artemis aimed the gun, just as Ares had taught her to do, and pulled the trigger. The blast of the gun going off rang through the house.

"Ow!" the man yelled, falling heavily to the ground. "Fuck!"

She kept her gun aimed directly at him, taking a step closer.

"*Artemis!* What the hell?"

Oh, shit.

It wasn't the stalker.

She'd just shot Cooper.

Senior Detective Statham: How well did you know Jack and Cassie Savage?

Individual 10 (~~Cooper Salazar~~ [redacted]): I worked closely with both of them during the design and build of their Telluride house.

SDS: How would you describe their relationship?

I10: I mean, it wasn't perfect, if that's what you're asking. It was just before my own wedding, which I was having reservations about. Their marriage had flaws, like all marriages do. He'd strayed once, he told me one night after we'd had a few drinks, but he regretted it. I think he was trying to reassure me, maybe. They'd had rough patches, is what he was trying to tell me. He'd fucked up once but their marriage survived it. They still loved each other. And she forgave him because she loved him too much to lose him, you could see that.

SDS: Do you think Jack Savage's death was accidental? Or suicide?

I10: There was no way it was suicide. I'd bet my life on that. He loved his family. He adored his wife. The Jack Savage I knew would never have left them on purpose. Never. His death was a terrible tragedy. A brutal hangover or a freak undertow, possibly. Tragedies happen all the time. But their legacy was all about the love they had for each other and for their children. It was a pronounced part of who they were. It gave them a kind of … I don't know, a *glow*. Of happiness. I've aspired to it ever since.

28

Eros

HOLLYWOOD

"Action!"

Eros did what he was supposed to do. He strolled along the sidewalk. Then he turned the corner of a realistic-looking recreated Compton city block, passing Marlowe and Leo, who were acting out a raging argument over a drug deal gone wrong.

That was Eros's entire part: walking twenty feet down the street, making eye contact with no one, wearing a dark wig and fake mustache, without a single line. But he kept reminding himself that a tiny part (as "Slightly Pimpish L.A. Guy Extra") in a Percy Mercy film was better than no part at all.

"Where's the *money*, Harley?" Marlowe fumed, fully in character. Her make-up was smeared and she was dressed in a cheap-looking, tight-fitting minidress that hugged every one of her eyewatering curves. "What'd you do with the *money*?"

Eros was seriously impressed. Marlowe could *act*. As he'd once predicted, she was a natural, so much so that she was making Leo, who Eros had never rated despite the Oscar, look like a bumbling amateur.

"I lent some to Spike," drawled Leo, unconvincingly. "Just a couple grand. He'll pay me back. Don't worry about it, babe."

"CUT!" yelled Percy. "Someone remind me why I hired this asshole, will you?" He yanked his headset off and stormed over to Leo. "Are you serious with that shit, man? Because I got fifty other actors lined up behind you who could've aced that scene in one take! We're up to twenty-fucking-*seven*, dude. Either pull some magic out of your fat ass or take a motherfuckin' hike."

Nice! thought Eros. Leo had been instructed to put on a few pounds for the part and was looking unappealingly bloated.

"I thought you wanted drugged-up and lethargic," fumbled Leo. "The guy's been high for three solid days."

"What I want is some *guilt*, some *remorse*, some *fear*, some *fire*!" Percy was on a roll. "What I want is some motherfucking *acting*! Harley knows he'll never see that money again. He knows he's fucked! Give me some goddamn *complexity*. Or you can fuck right back off to your Hills mansion and cry to your banker about forfeiting the next mortgage payment."

"I'll do it right this time," Leo insisted, contrite.

Percy headed back to his camera.

He had these outbursts every couple of takes, Eros was learning. He was demanding and extremely exacting, but Eros was watching the performances get better and better. That must be how Percy got results from his actors: by punishing them relentlessly until he got what he wanted.

It was getting dark by the time Percy was finally satisfied. "That's a wrap for today," he announced. "No partying. No staying up all night for any reason whatsoever. Get your beauty sleep and be back on set ready to deliver at seven o'clock sharp."

Everyone muttered their agreement and dispersed. Some headed back to their trailers, if they had one. Eros went to get some food with a few of the other extras. The nobodies, in other words. But it was cool. He was here. And Eros had already decided that once Marlowe had a chance to decompress for an hour or so, he was going to stop by her trailer. He hadn't really had a chance to talk to her since filming had started and, after all, they knew each other. They'd spent time together. They'd—sort of—connected. So she might not mind him stopping by to say hello.

"Eros Savage?"

It was a techie, dropping off his new phone. You had to love L.A., where the Apple store delivered. They'd been able to retrieve at least most of the stuff from his old phone and bring him the newest version, fired up and ready to go. Eros thanked the guy, paid him and gave him a huge tip. Almost immediately, his phone rang.

He answered it on the first ring. "Apollo. Are you out? How was rehab?"

"Mostly terrible. You're not going to believe this, but Ares is in jail. Where have you been, by the way? I've been trying to reach you for two days."

"I lost my phone." Ares was by far the most law-abiding of all his siblings, so the pronouncement had a surreal edge to it. An alarming one. "In *jail?* Hell. What did he do?"

"He assaulted three cops."

That definitely didn't sound like Ares. "*Shit.* Why?"

"He's engaged."

"What?" That also didn't sound like Ares. "What does that have to do with him getting arrested? And why didn't he mention that earlier?"

"Because it just happened."

"Who is she?"

"An undocumented Cuban who's right now in a detainment center awaiting deportation, according to his lawyer."

"What—when—...?" There were so many questions.

"He fought with the cops when they took her away."

"Jesus."

"They're keeping him in custody because the officers he assaulted all think he'd try to break her out of the detainment center. So they're holding him until they can deport her."

"Are you in New York?"

"I'm in Nashville. I'm waiting to hear back from Bruce. I just wanted to let you know."

"Is Ares okay?"

"He's fine. Pissed off, but fine."

"Are *you* okay?" Eros didn't bother with the *Are you still on drugs?* But his question was received loud and clear, even unspoken.

"I'm clean. I'm healing." Apollo laughed softly. "I'm miserable. But slowly adjusting."

"I'm glad to hear it, Apollo. I'm glad you're out."

"Thanks, brother. I'll call you back."

Shit. Ares in jail. He had no doubt Ares would be seething and climbing the walls.

Eros found himself walking toward the actors' trailers, at the far end of the compound. He felt like talking to someone. He found Marlowe's trailer easily, the small sticker name tag pinned on her door. He knocked. "Marlowe?"

No one answered, so he knocked again. He thought he heard voices coming from inside.

He found the door unlocked. He pushed it open a crack. "Hello?"

Eros could hear muffled voices, one that was unmistakably Marlowe's. She sounded upset.

He pushed the door open further. "Marlowe?"

Eros heard another voice. A man's voice. He should have left, of course, but the tone of their conversation, even though he couldn't hear exactly what they were saying, caused him to investigate further.

He could sense that something was wrong.

"Come on," the man was coaxing. "I know I can convince you if you'll just let me."

"*No.* I don't *want* you to convince me. Just get *off* me. *Get off me!*"

"But it'll be so *good* between us, baby." More aggressively: "Just let me *show* you how good—"

"*Please*, Leo." She was begging, maybe even crying. "Stop."

Leo?

Eros walked to the door of the trailer's single bedroom. There, on the bed, Marlowe was pinned under Leo.

"Leo?" said Eros. "What the fuck are you doing?"

Both Leo and Marlowe looked up at Eros. There were no lights on in the trailer, but the lights of the city outside were enough to reveal that Marlowe's face was shiny with tears. Her eyes were frantic—and in that moment, wildly relieved.

Leo looked furious. "Get out of here, man."

"Eros!" screamed Marlowe. "Get him off me! Please!"

Leo was probably around the same height as Eros, but stockier and much heavier.

Eros didn't even notice. He was so overcome with white-hot, electric rage, he pulled Leo off Marlowe easily.

Eros had always considered himself a lover not a fighter,

but you don't grow up with two older brothers without learning how to throw a decent right hook. Eros punched Leo in the face. Which turned out to be surprisingly painful.

Eros couldn't have known that Leo's second interest in high school back in Tulsa, after theater club, happened to be wrestling—where he'd ended up becoming captain of the varsity team. Or that he'd been an on-and-off member of the boxing club. He smashed his fist into Eros's jaw, following up with another punch to the stomach before clinching Eros and taking him to ground.

The two of them rolled on the floor then out the door, throwing punches, twisting and swearing in a blur of fists and blood until they ended up rolling down the metal stairs of the trailer onto the concrete. Leo's tactics were mean and the bastard was strong, but Eros was fueled on something more powerful than mere anger. He was fueled by a feral desire: to go after what he wanted. Which happened to be proving to Marlowe and Percy—and himself—that he was somehow worthy of them and of this and of being here at all.

He had never, however, been captain of any varsity wrestling teams.

Leo had him in a half nelson, possibly, or some equally-technical wrestling move, with Eros's face pressed painfully into the rough, hard pavement. Leo punched him again. And again. Until Eros was seeing stars.

And hearing voices.

"Pull him off," one of the voices was saying.

"Leo?" A deep voice turned incredulous. "*Eros?*"

Leo was dragged off and Eros, with effort, looked up at the faces. A crowd had gathered but it was hard to see. One of his eyes seemed to be swollen shut.

Leo was pinned to the ground by three or four very large people. And Marlowe was hugging Percy. She was still crying. She was explaining to her brother what had happened.

Percy was quiet for a few seconds. Then he said to the heavies who'd tackled Leo, "Rough him up a little, then evict him from the premises. Son," he said to Leo, "you can consider yourself out of a job and quite possibly arrested. Now get the fuck off my movie set. If I ever see your ugly face again I'll do some serious damage to it."

There was commotion as Leo was taken away.

Eros was dragged to his feet. His head swirled, his entire body felt like it had been run over by a truck and he felt a warm, liquid wetness on his face. He touched his palm to his head, then held out his hand to look at it. It was smeared with blood and dirt.

He tried to focus on a blurred Percy. "Is *this* gritty enough?"

Percy contemplated Eros. "Looks like I'm in need of a new lead actor ... what's your name again? *Eros?*" Like it was the stupidest name he'd ever heard. A couple members of Percy's ultra-cool entourage with names like Butch and Bulldog made noises that might have been muffled laughter.

"Yes."

"Well, *Eros*, this is provisional. I'm going to give you a

shot because of what you did for Marlowe tonight. You still have to prove you're up to it. Get that head looked at. Then get some sleep. See you at seven a.m. sharp. And be ready to work your ass off."

Individual 13 (~~Marlowe Mercy~~ [redacted]): I couldn't believe it when they started shooting at each other. I didn't even realize it was open carry.

29

Artemis
&
Cooper

TELLURIDE

ARTEMIS DROPPED the gun and ran over to where Cooper lay groaning on the floor. She kneeled beside him. "Cooper! You're hit!"

"*Christ*, honey!"

"I thought you were the stalker!"

"I *told* you I was coming tonight, remember? We talked about this."

"I know, but I got a phone call from Arlo—" Artemis searched inside his jacket for signs of blood. But there didn't seem to be any. Cooper was able to sit up. "Where are you hit?"

Despite traveling the entire length of his body with her patting hands, she couldn't find any wound.

"I thought you said you were hit."

"*You* said I was hit."

"You said 'ow' and fell to the ground," she pointed out.

"I thought I *might* be hit. I was trying to not *get* hit."

Behind him, she saw light glint against something. There, lodged into the solid wood of the doorframe, was the bullet.

"Thank God you're not a very good shot," Cooper said.

Artemis was wild with relief. "Jesus, Coop. I almost *killed* you."

"But you didn't kill me. You just embellished the architectural design of my house a little."

"Can you not joke about this, please? I almost *shot* you."

"Can you do me a favor and re-arm your security system? I drove right up to your front door and walked straight in."

Artemis pulled her phone out of her back pocket and reactivated the alarms and sensors. She could see on the screen that the only people inside the walls of her property were the two little moving, heat-outlined figures of her and Cooper. "He's not here yet."

"Good. And he won't be getting in tonight."

They helped each other to the couch, still shaken by what had almost happened.

"Are you sure you're okay?" Artemis asked him.

"I think I'll live. Even though I seem to be on a long

list of people's hit lists. Anyway, Annie Oakley, where's your champagne? We've got some celebrating to do."

"What are we celebrating?"

"That I'm still alive, for one thing. Also, my lawyer called as I was driving up here to tell me I have enough grounds for a divorce without Nicole's signature, even after the media circus in Paris. And I've cleared my schedule to design your new studio, starting tomorrow." He paused, searching her face. "If you want me to," he added.

Artemis kissed him. "Coop. Of course I want you to. But you won't be starting tomorrow. Or the day after. *Maybe* the day after that."

It turned out that a near brush with death could be an exceptionally powerful aphrodisiac. They spent the next two days in bed, making love in every conceivable position, in a slow, hot frenzy of desire, kissing, entwined and staring deep into each other's eyes like they couldn't believe they had found each other.

Individual 10 (~~Cooper Salazar~~ [redacted]): Individual 3 disappeared for a few minutes after the first set. Individual 9 recognized Individual 1 but no one else did. Individual 14 started singing, and then there was the altercation between Individual 3 and Individual 1—and Individual 9—and that's when Individual 7 stepped forward.

Senior Detective Statham: Wait, what?

30

———

Ares

MANHATTAN

ARES WAS asleep in his prison cell, curled up on the stained and dirty bare single bed under a thin blanket. He'd been given his own cell—the only small mercy in this sea of fury-inducing injustices—and was wearing a worn prison uniform. A banging sound from the next cell woke him.

In his dream, he'd been wandering through the streets of Havana. His subconscious had informed him of this unhappy fact: he didn't even have a photo of her. *Do you know the Diaz sisters?* he'd asked some guy on the street, who spoke English and offered him a cigarette, which he'd accepted even though he didn't smoke. But then the dream had morphed into a gloom-edged nightmare. *Sure, buddy, it's only one of the most common surnames in Cuba. You'll never find her. Not in a million years.*

Ares crawled into a sitting position and leaned back against the hard wall, scrubbing his hands across his face.

This was complete and utter bullshit.

Whatever happened to innocent until proven guilty? True, he'd been caught on tape assaulting and threatening to kill several officers of the law and refusing to comply—and would do it all over again if he could (except maybe the part about threatening to kill them and also giving them reason to incarcerate him without bail)—but he'd been *trying* to do the right thing! The *lawful* thing, according to the mandates outlined in the immigration documents. Just like Jazmin and Valentina had.

There was only so far a man could be pushed before he completely lost his cool.

And now he was trapped. Powerless to do the one thing in his life he'd ever really, truly wanted to do—for himself—and, most of all, for her. Not because he was duty-bound or obligated, like with every other thing he'd ever done in his goddamn life, but because—for reasons that were as sudden and unexpected as they were unfamiliar—he loved her.

He'd never even thought he was *capable* of love.

It wouldn't be perfect. It would be new and they'd have to go through the process of getting to know each other. It was crazy, but he didn't care. He wanted to try anyway. He wanted to do everything it took to win her trust and, maybe even eventually, her affection. Maybe, somewhere down the line, she'd even love him back.

But none of that was ever going to happen if he couldn't break out of this cell and go and find her.

And where was his fucking lawyer?

Why was it taking *days* for Bruce to deal with this? Ares had no idea how long he'd been in here. It could have been several days, or longer. There weren't even any barred windows to give clues about how much time was passing. He wasn't sure whether it was day or night.

He needed to get out of this godforsaken hellhole.

If that didn't happen soon, his overpaid lawyer was toast.

Jazmin
&
Valentina

THE BRONX I.C.E. DETAINMENT CENTER
BRONX, NEW YORK

IT WAS the misery that was the worst thing. The cruelty and blatant, outrageous inhumanity.

That, and the way the ugly guards were always staring at them, leering and winking and making lewd comments and dirty jokes. Jazmin and Valentina were only too aware they were completely at the mercy of these men.

345

It was far worse than their rickety shed, because they couldn't run. There was nowhere to hide.

The sisters were put into a cage with around twenty other women. The detainment center was huge. It might have been an old warehouse. The entire length of it was full of cage-like rooms, and each room was full of people. Twenty, fifty, sometimes more. There were mattresses on the floor and the inmates were given thin silver blankets that looked like tin foil. Jazmin and Valentina wrapped these around themselves, as everyone did. The warehouse was cold. Twice a day they were led single file to a make-shift cafeteria where they were given trays of unappetizing food. Five times a day they were allowed bathroom breaks. Once a day they were allowed out into a concrete exterior yard that was walled in by tall buildings. Guards accompanied them everywhere they went, watching. Always watching.

It was on the way back from the yard that it happened.

Valentina was the last person in line.

As they were led back to their cage, Valentina heard someone behind her. "Hey," the voice said. "Slow down."

She turned, and saw one of the more vile of the guards, a man who was maybe thirty, overweight and had an unnerving glint in his eye. And he was right behind her.

Before Valentina could react, his hands groped her, grabbing her in a terrifyingly intimate grasp. "Might have to find *you* a private room."

She jerked away from him, walking quickly to catch up with Jazmin. Valentina was wildly relieved when the door of the cage was securely locked, with the prisoners inside. The guards remained outside. They dispersed casually into the void, chatting and laughing like this was any other day.

Valentina's heart was racing. She sat next to Jazmin on a hard wooden bench and wrapped her tin foil blanket around herself. She rested her head on Jazmin's shoulder and allowed a tear to fall. She felt dirty. And scared.

Would he come back for her?

There were so many things to be terrified about.

What would happen to them, once they got back to Havana? Where would they live? Their parents were gone. They had no idea where their brothers were. They had a small amount of money that wouldn't last long.

She knew only too well that she and Jazmin were no longer the naïve young girls fresh off the boat, hopeful and optimistic despite their circumstances. They'd seen too much. They'd spent too many nights hungry.

They'd been threatened too many times.

Valentina brushed away the tear. She wouldn't cry any more. She let her fear harden into something else, as she'd gotten used to doing. She wasn't entirely defenseless, after all. And she'd already made her choice.

By some miracle, it had been a busy evening when they'd arrived at the detainment center. The officers hadn't done a thorough job of frisking her. Valentina's loaded gun was still strapped securely to her ankle, under her loose-fitting jeans. She didn't want Jazmin to know about it, in case she was questioned, or somehow incriminated for Valentina's crime of smuggling a weapon into a place like this. Things like that happened. She wouldn't put anything past these people, who treated them like they were less than human. What had they done that was so unforgivable? Want a better life for themselves and be willing to work for it?

Now they might die for it.

She wouldn't hesitate. She *would* rather die than allow herself or her sister be brutalized. She'd rather kill than be forced or even touched once more by an unscrupulous bully.

Valentina hoped it wouldn't come to that, but if it did, she was ready.

MANHATTAN

BRUCE KNEW ONLY TOO WELL that his ass and his assets—and quite possibly his marriage—were on the line here and knew exactly what he had to do. He called the number they had on file. What he needed at this moment in time was a manipulative bitch who was experienced with falsifying documents. And he knew of no one who fit that description better than Tiffany Chamberlain.

He was a little surprised when she answered on the second ring. He'd personally threatened her with criminal charges over the 1.9 mil, which she *had* repaid, almost. A hundred thousand—on top of the hundred grand Ares had already allowed for—was still outstanding. She'd claimed she'd spent it and was considering filing for bankruptcy. Maybe she thought Bruce was about to let her off the hook. Which he was. If she cooperated.

"Mr. Davis," she answered frigidly.

"Ms. Chamberlain. I wanted to personally thank you on Ares's behalf for returning most of the money you owed him."

"I've already explained that I can't afford to pay back the other hundred grand."

"We want you to keep it. On the condition that you'll help me with one small favor."

"What favor?"

There was no time for mincing words. "I need to send an email from a private, official, inaccessible email address. Do you have any experience with hacking?"

There was a pause on the other end of the line as Tiffany weighed up his question. "I have a guy who hacks for me," she finally said. "He's very good. And very discrete."

"Perfect. I want an email sent from the Bronx I.C.E. Detainment Center to the Midtown Police Station."

"Does this have anything to do with … those girls?"

"Yes. They've been deported," Bruce lied. "As of this morning. We want the letter to explain that in no uncertain terms. Officially. From an internal email server."

"They're back in Cuba?"

"They're on their way back to Cuba. So Ares can now be released from jail."

"He's in *jail*?"

"He assaulted several officers when the girls were taken away."

"Oh." Tiffany sounded almost emotional for a fraction of a second. But then her manner shifted, settling back into her more natural state of testy and ultra-composed. "God, he'll *hate* that. No wine cellar or billion dollar view."

Bruce ignored this. "He's being held because the cops suspected he would commit further offenses if he's released on bail."

"If the girls have already been deported," Tiffany said, "wouldn't that email already have been sent, or be in the process of being sent?"

The woman was shrewd.

But Bruce was also shrewd. So he bluffed. "The process can take longer than we'd like it to take. You know how slow all the red tape can be. And, obviously, we want Ares released as soon as possible. If you can get that email sent today, now, he'll waive the final hundred grand."

Another contemplative pause. "I'll do it. But it'll take longer than that. I'll need twenty-four hours, maybe longer. I want the hundred grand waived, plus an additional fifty grand."

She smelled a rat, possibly, and knew she had him by the balls. But there was too much at stake to refuse her offer. Bruce was also running the risk that she'd find out the girls hadn't *actually* been deported yet. But it was a risk he was willing to take. Maybe Tiffany would overlook that detail anyway, if she got the terms she wanted.

"Done," he agreed.

"And a drink."

"A drink?"

"You can give me the fifty grand in cash over gin on ice at Diva. It's on Fifth. You can meet me there at one p.m. the day after tomorrow. I'll make sure the email has gone through by then."

Bruce sighed. Thirty-six hours was longer than he wanted this to take. But what choice did he have? "Fine. I'll need evidence that the email was sent."

"Of course. See you then, Mr. Davis."

Senior Detective Statham: You chose to bribe a felon to commit a felony, and in the process you also committed adultery. Hardly ethical behavior, considering your profession.

Individual 18 (~~Bruce Davis~~ [redacted]): You obviously haven't met many lawyers, Detective.

31

Athena

SOUTHAMPTON

Rosie came home, and the exact second the little girl stepped foot into Athena's life, it doubled in size and became infused with something that felt uncannily like magic. The child was shy and soft-spoken, but she was also inquisitive and whip-smart and surprisingly talkative once she settled into her new home. The two of them became immediately inseparable.

Athena hadn't realized how intensely lonely she'd been for the past few years, until this tiny soulmate moved in and filled her days with the novelty of a new perspective.

Athena noticed views again. Things that had lately felt more like wallpaper—the color of the Atlantic at sunset, or the dramatic silver-lined billow of thunder-clouds—came back to life. Rosie got excited about these things. She asked questions and told stories. The Kahlo and the Matisse and all the other paintings that had hung on Athena's walls that she'd barely glanced at for a decade (she put away the Haring and several of the Picasso drawings), became the inspiration for elaborate, convoluted tales. Just when Athena thought she couldn't be more enchanted by her new daughter, it turned out that Rosie was a born storyteller, brimming with ideas about unicorns and lute bands that wandered the countryside and family units (something she'd fantasized about often) and cats who moonlighted as secret agents.

"If you could have your choice of a book with blank pages to write in," Athena said to her, "or a laptop to type onto, which would you choose?"

"Both," said Rosie. "Because I could draw pictures and be more freeform with my writing in a book, but on a laptop I could create polished final drafts and also surf the internet and listen to music."

Had she been that savvy as a seven-year-old? Athena was sure she hadn't been. "We'll get you one of each, then. And we can pick out the new colors for your room."

They baked cookies and made hand-squeezed lemonade. They talked about the things Rosie felt comfortable talking about, and left the rest for later.

As Athena looked through her Hermès Birkin bag (gifted, along with at least seven hundred other handbags she owned, which was causing her to question a few of her life choices), she pulled out the contents one by one. The thing was a bottomless pit. Rosie picked up a tube of lipstick. "Is this Goddess of the Sea?" She remembered, from the yacht in Florida.

"Yes. You can have it. Here's some nail polish, too."

"What's this?" Rosie asked, picking up a small canister.

"That's pepper spray."

"Is this for spraying bad guys in the eyes so they get blinded?" Rosie said.

"That's exactly what it's for. A girl should always carry some. Just in case." It was an unfortunate reality of the world they lived in. And Rosie was hardly unscathed when it came to reality.

They went through the rest of the bag until Athena finally found her keys, then Athena buckled Rosie into the backseat of her Porsche Cayenne Turbo.

As they drove out of her gated driveway and turned left, Athena noticed a car with tinted windows had been parked near her gate. When she pulled onto the road, it began following them.

It was keeping its distance, but it was still behind them when Athena pulled into a parking space on the main street of Southampton's small, quaint downtown.

Odd, she thought. Then again, it *is* the only road into town.

Athena helped Rosie climb out of the car.

She noticed that the man who'd been following them had parked right behind her and was now walking toward her and Rosie. She didn't know him. As he drew closer, until he was very close—too close—she could see him clearly. He was nondescript-looking, with brown hair, dark sunglasses, a black jacket and a blue shirt. One thing that did stand out was the little string tie he wore, clasped with a silver-edged stone. It was the kind of thing a Texan would wear. A New Yorker wouldn't be caught dead in one of those things, unless they were dressing up for Halloween or something. *As* a Texan.

The man opened his jacket a fraction. He was holding a gun. "Do exactly what I say," he said, "and no one will get hurt."

Seriously? On Main Street? "Are you crazy?"

"You live in a fortress," the man said. Definitely a Texas twang. "I had to take my chance. You're going to walk to my car. You're going to get into the back seat. Both of you. Now."

Athena stared at him and held Rosie securely behind her. "Why are you doing this?"

"Let's just say I need to get the attention of a mutual acquaintance."

"What mutual acquaintance? Who?"

"Get in the car," the man said again. "I'll explain everything on the way."

Possibly even last week, Athena's first reaction might have been fear. The thug was pointing what she assumed to be a loaded gun directly at her. But something feral and furious was happening to her. It might have been the maternal instinct, rearing its insanely protective head— and, *wow*, was it sure of itself. "If you think we're getting anywhere near that car, you're completely out of your mind."

Athena felt a small cylindrical object being placed into her right hand—the hand that was clutching Rosie. She knew immediately what it was. Rosie had reached into Athena's bag while the man was distracted.

Athena might get shot. More likely, though, her attempting kidnapper wouldn't be expecting this.

Athena sprayed him directly in the eyes with the pepper spray.

She vaguely heard him scream and the sound of a heavy metal object hitting pavement. She grabbed Rosie and carried her to the closest door, which happened to be to a day spa Athena often went to—they did the best Brazilians in town.

Athena got Rosie inside. She recognized one of the beauty therapists, Cecile. "Lock the doors! There's a man with a gun out there!"

Everyone had automated locking systems these days. Cecile pushed the button under the desk and the door's lock clicked into place.

They were ushered into a back waiting room, where there was a small fountain and plinking New Age music was playing. All the ladies were gathering in there, chattering, calling their husbands, lovers and 911.

Don't let me die, Giovanni! one woman was tearfully pleading into her phone. *And make sure you move your stuff out of the pool house before Morty gets back on Thursday.*

Athena held Rosie tightly, smoothing her hair and

adjusting her tiny round glasses back into place. "Are you all right, Rosie?" Athena said urgently. The thought of *what might have happened* was too devastating to consider. Somewhere between the time she'd stepped onto Wyatt's chartered jet for their getaway weekend in Key West and this exact moment, Athena's life had taken on a giant new purpose: keeping this little girl safe. Everything else felt wildly unimportant.

"I'm fine." Rosie wasn't particularly fazed. She had not led a sheltered life. She already knew that danger was something you had to deal with on a regular basis. Rosie seemed only too aware that you had a better chance of dodging it if you kept your wits about you. "Who was that man?"

"I don't know," said Athena. "But I think we might know someone who does."

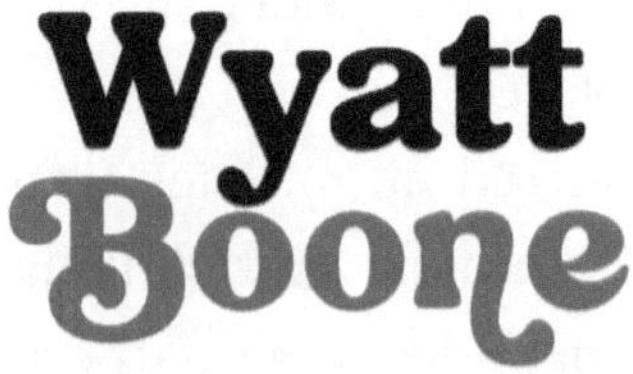

MANHATTAN

WYATT HADN'T SEEN Athena in almost a week. He'd wanted to give her some space, to get Rosie settled in and to let the two of them spend time together without interruptions.

They'd made plans to see each other tonight. After an entire week of non-stop work spliced with hourly fantasies retracing every detail of his nights with Athena, Wyatt was more than ready.

From the age of seventeen, when his parents had checked out early and left him destitute and alone in West Texas—a place known primarily for its dust, its desolation and its tendency to make anyone who hails from it as tough as guts out of sheer necessity—Wyatt Boone had barely looked up.

Seven years and approximately nine hundred and fifty million dollars later, he could admit it might be time to think about something other than money. He'd worked so hard and for so long, he'd forgotten how to do anything else. Aside from the very occasional weekend off, which he spent riding his horse west along the river at his ranch until he was as far away from civilization as he could get —and in West Texas, that was pretty far. The place was as devoid of humanity as Mars. Which suited Wyatt just fine.

Despite his overabundance of charm, Wyatt didn't actually *like* many of the people he met. In his business, most of the men he dealt with were single-mindedly greedy. The women were even worse. They wanted him for two things: his bank balance and his cock (and who could blame them?). But there comes a time when a man starts to crave something a little more meaningful.

Athena Savage had waltzed into his life at precisely the right moment, flooring him in every possible way.

She didn't need or want his money. And as far as his cock went, she didn't even have any basis for comparison. She might have thought he was *normal* in that department, bless her. Although he was fairly sure that somewhere in the middle of Round Two, she'd clicked that his talents in the sack were roughly equivalent to A-Rod's at third base. Either way, Wyatt was hooked. The fact that she was as strong and smart and self-reliant as she was genuine had hit him like a punch to the gut. That she happened to look like she'd just floated down from Mount Olympus or been born out of a seashell earlier that afternoon only compounded his problem.

He called her.

"Wyatt?" She sounded spooked.

"Everything okay, honey? Where are you?"

"*Wyatt*. Holy shit. The most terrifying thing just happened. A man just tried to get us into his car. With a *gun*."

A rush of cold rage iced through Wyatt's veins.

"We got away. And he fled the scene. But it was awful."

So much for proposing. Looked like his destiny, instead, was a life sentence for first degree murder.

"Wyatt?"

"Right here, darlin'."

"Do you have any idea who it was? He looked like he might be … Texan."

"I think I might have some idea."

"Could it be the same person that tampered with your brakes?"

Indeed it could.

Wyatt could hear sirens in the background of the call. But he knew the culprit would be long gone by now. "Honey, I'm going to go and take care of this. I might be a little late for dinner."

She was quiet for a few seconds. "Wyatt. We called the police. Please. Let them take care of it."

If she thought he was going to let the police "take care" of the man who'd threatened his future happiness, she might as well have accused him of being from goddamn Oklahoma.

"I'll see you as soon as I can, sugar. I'll make this up to you, I promise."

"Wyatt? Don't do anything crazy—"

But he'd already ended the call.

Earl Weatherby

MANHATTAN

EARL WEATHERBY HAD BEEN STEWING the entire drive back to Manhattan.

God, how he hated Manhattan. All he really wanted to do was to go home to Fort Worth and live out his days in the hot Texan sun, with his staunch, buxom wife by his side and a glass of scotch on ice in his hand, his horses grazing contentedly nearby in the shade of a Red Buckeye tree. But no. His retirement fund had been cashed in and he was in danger of defaulting on the extra mortgage he'd been forced to take out on his gentleman's ranch. And all because of Wyatt Boone.

The guy had a knack for undermining every deal he was on the cusp of clinching.

Every fucking time.

It was like the guy had a *radar* for it! Honing in on *his* payouts and somehow pre-empting them, siphoning them directly into his *own* bank accounts. It wasn't fair!

His eyes still stung like hell. Whatever they put in that pepper spray stuff was ridiculously effective. For several minutes after Athena Savage had pumped half the canister directly into his retinas, he'd writhed in pain on the sidewalk and thought he might be blinded for life. He'd forced himself to recover enough to climb into his stolen car and dangerously drive the three miles to the garage he'd chosen in an empty house that had been foreclosed on. He'd done his research. Then Earl had spent ten minutes splashing his face with cold water before driving his Cadillac back to Manhattan. So far, there was no sign the cops had picked up any whiff of his trail.

Still, it wasn't the outcome he'd hoped for.

At least he knew where she lived. He could try again after the hoopla died down—if the bastard continued to refuse to budge on his terms.

Earl parked his car in the underground garage, took the elevator up, and walked into his office, shutting the door behind him. He sat down in his leather office chair, leaned back and closed his eyes, still wondering if she'd done him permanent damage.

That's when he heard the sound of a Smith & Wesson safety catch clicking to the off position, right behind his left ear. He happened to own one himself and knew that sound intimately.

"*One* move and I'll empty all six of these puppies directly into that thick skull of yours, Weatherby."

Fuck.

He knew Wyatt Boone would try something but he'd obviously underestimated the man. It would not have been easy to break into his office undetected and without setting off any alarms.

Wyatt spun Earl's chair until Earl's red, swollen eyes were staring directly into the barrel of Wyatt's .44 Magnum 629.

"Come after *me*, and I can handle that shit," said Wyatt. "Go after *them* and you've got yourself some serious problems. A woman and a *child*, Weatherby? I knew you were a snake but I never knew you were a coward."

"I'm about to go bankrupt because of you, Boone.

I've *also* got a wife and daughter. I've got my own interests to look after and you're screwing them up."

Wyatt appeared to contemplate this. If Earl was reading the man correctly, something about the phrase "wife and daughter" had struck him right where he lived.

"If you so much as step within a hundred miles of either of those two girls ever again," Wyatt said, "I'll make it my mission in life—with manic dedication—to ensure your slow and extremely painful death. I don't care if I spend the rest of my days behind bars, Weatherby. I'll hunt you down like a—"

"I know you will."

Wyatt Boone glared at Earl for what felt like a long time. "*If* you agree to leave them alone for the rest of eternity—and to keep your hands off my goddamn car—I'll cut you in."

Earl wondered for a second if he'd heard him correctly. "You'll do what?"

"I'll cut you in on the biodiesel fuel deal."

Wyatt, despite everything, was offering Earl a lifeline. "You *will?*"

"You'll have to create the opportunities in your own directions, and give me a cut of whatever you make. What I'm saying is that I'll provide you with the platform. But it's up to you to make your own money out of it."

Earl was dumbstruck. "You'd *do* that?"

"I'll either do that, or I'll empty my revolver gleefully into your pea-sized brain. The choice is yours."

Earl stuck out his hand, offering it to Wyatt. "You've got yourself a deal."

They shook on it.

"Now," said Wyatt, who considered a handshake as good as etching the agreement into granite, "if you'll excuse me, I've got somewhere I need to be."

Senior Detective Statham: What compelled you to attempt the kidnapping?

Individual 25 (~~Earl Weatherby~~ [redacted]): Desperation, pure and simple.

32

Liam
Sullivan

LONG ISLAND

Liam Sullivan woke up on the floor of his friend Declan's house, surrounded by empty bottles and cans, pizza boxes, his beat-up guitar and several dogs. Someone else was already living on Declan's couch, so Liam was relegated to the floor. Noticing that there was an inch or two of whiskey left in one of the bottles, Liam crawled over to it and tipped back the dregs. Maybe it would ease his hangover a little.

It didn't.

Nor did it improve his mood, which had basically been dark for the past two and half decades. His life sucked. No matter how hard he tried to climb out of the rut he was in, he just couldn't seem to do it. He practiced his guitar day and night, but no one would hire him for gigs. He *knew* he was good enough. He *knew* he was destined for something greater than roofing or feather-weight boxing.

Declan's TV was on, but the volume was low. The channel was on some entertainment network. One of those ones that played back to back Kardashians with the occasional celebrity news report.

Breaking news! the headline said.

Apollo Savage was getting out of a plane.

Liam found the remote and turned up the volume. Liam happened to be a fan. He liked Apollo's music. He'd seen him in concert once, about two years ago. The guy was a legend. And totally out of control, which was something Liam could relate to.

But then—*what the hell?*—someone else was getting out of Apollo's private jet ... and it looked uncannily like ... his *sister*.

"Apollo Savage was seen landing in Nashville with an unidentified female companion. Who is this mystery girl? Fans want to know!" The report continued. "Apollo Savage appears to be almost fully recovered from his motorcycle accident and—reportedly—a brief stint in rehab. One source speculated that Apollo may have brought his medical staff home with him, because the young woman seen getting into his limo with him may or may not be a nurse employed by a rehab facility located in Southampton, which Apollo Savage reportedly checked out of earlier today. Our investigators are on the case. Any viewers with further information are urged to contact us at ..."

Holy shit. It *was* her.

Daisy was *Apollo Savage's* rehab nurse?

That little cow *always* got lucky, goddamn it! His whole life, she got *every* lucky score under the sun and all he got was shit.

He'd never forgiven her for killing his mother. Liam had adored his mother. The first six years of his life had been by far the best six years of his life. No contest. Until *she* came along. Little Miss Destruction. Some complication after Daisy's birth had killed their mother within weeks. Just like that, his pretty, happy, doting mommy was gone.

And it was all Daisy's fault.

Their father had been so grief-stricken he'd drowned his sorrows in a sea of Jim Beam. He'd never even been much of a drinker until he'd lost the love of his life. Once that happened, Pops had been determined to pickle himself into an early grave.

Again: Daisy's fault.

She'd stolen *both* his parents from him. She'd annihilated his family, ruining everything, like a little golden-eyed wrecking ball, from day one. Sure, she *looked* all innocent and harmless, but, oh, how he knew better.

What other choice did he have to dull the pain and the loss but drink himself into a haze, just like his father had?

And occasionally take out his frustrations on her.

She *deserved* what she got. All of it. In fact, he'd gone easy on her. He'd been downright *kind*, considering all the things she'd cost him in life. Just thinking about it made his blood run hotter. She couldn't even *see* all the pain she'd caused him. She acted like she was better than him and that he was the loser. *Bitch!* It always drove him crazy. He wanted to knock her off that high horse she loved to ride around on.

And now this. Now she was working for his favorite musician. His favorite outrageously *rich* musician. No doubt she was having the time of her life, as usual. Liam had seen pictures of Apollo's house and pool and tour bus and lifestyle. He'd read that article.

Had Daisy? Probably not. She didn't even like Apollo's music, as far as Liam knew. She wasn't even interested in music, boxing, beer or any of the good things in life.

There she was, being ushered into Apollo's limo by the rock star himself, like he wanted her there.

It wasn't fair.

She'd stolen his family, ruined his life and wouldn't even put him up for a few nights during his occasional times of need. And now she was hanging out in the lap of luxury with his idol. God, how he'd dreamed of a life like that.

Well, he figured, if Daisy was in Nashville with Apollo Savage, then her house was empty. And if she'd flown there on Apollo's private jet, then her car was available.

Liam's thoughts were interrupted by the TV. "More breaking news on the Savages! Ares Savage has been arrested and is currently in jail. For assaulting a police officer. But wait—this gets even better. He's also engaged to be *married*! Lucky girl, whoever you are. His lawyer's statement announced that the oldest Savage heir is engaged to a young woman who—according to our sources—is undocumented. The plot thickens, folks. According to the announcement, the altercation between Ares Savage and police happened when his beloved fiancée was being taken into custody by immigration officials. Will the two lovebirds be reunited? And if so, where will the wedding take place? And when? Surely this will be the wedding of the year—*if* it happens at all. Everyone who's anyone would kill to get their hands on one of those invitations, including me!—I'm available for publicity, Ares, just sayin'. Our investigators are working around the clock to find out more about these heart-breaking events ...'"

Apollo Savage would definitely attend his own brother's wedding. And, if it happened soon, his sister—of all people—might be going with him.

A plan was forming. Liam would do his research. He had time. He'd lost his job again. And he'd been banned from the gym for stealing a phone and pulverizing the dipshit who'd complained about it. His schedule was clear.

Liam remained pinned to the news reports. He checked out the Savages' social media accounts. Ares had no online presence, but the others did. Were they planning any trips? Had anyone seen them? They'd be secretive, but there was only so long five high-profile people could fly under the radar without being spotted.

He'd read the article, and he knew the general location of their five homes. Would they use one of those? Very possibly.

Liam would bide his time. And as soon as he got the information he needed, he would make his move.

Senior Detective Statham: Had the security system been breached?

Individual 28 (~~Steve Boyd~~ [redacted]): I've never in my sixteen years of owning and operating Boyd Security Services Incorporated had a breach, Detective. We're the premier security provider in San Miguel County and we pride ourselves on our watertight celebrity event security services. No one gets through us, and I mean *no one*. Whoever that murderer was, it had to have been one of the guests.

SDS: As much as I might admire your confidence, that is yet to be determined.

33

Apollo

NASHVILLE

FOR APOLLO, settling back into life at home in Nashville was proving to be more difficult than he'd expected.

He was worried about Ares.

Apollo had told Ares's lawyer that he was coming to New York to find out what the hell was going on. It shouldn't be taking this long to get Ares out of jail. But Bruce kept assuring Apollo that he was pulling every conceivable string to move things along as quickly as possible. Apollo had given him a deadline of one week to get the job done or he was coming to New York to do it himself.

Then there was the small matter of resisting the raging urges—which washed over Apollo like a tsunami at practically ten minute intervals—to have a drink.

It didn't help that there was a perpetual party going

on at his house, which had admittedly toned down once Daisy had politely but insistently asked some of the more raucous of the crowd to leave. They'd protested, of course, but Apollo had instructed his bodyguards to do whatever Daisy told them to do.

Maybe he was going overboard with the whole giving-Daisy-total-control-over-his-life thing.

After a few mere weeks in his house, *everyone* did what Daisy told them to do. She was like the newly-appointed CEO of his goddamn life. From his band to his groupies, if anyone wanted anything at all from Apollo, first it had to be cleared by his go-to "assistant." Whatever she decided was then accepted as gospel.

Apollo could begrudgingly admit that he trusted her opinion. She seemed to know what it took to keep him in line. And always, just like she had in rehab, she delivered her orders in that gentle, sparkly way she had. It irked him even more: that *"way"* she had was ten times more effective than any doctor's orders or threatened legal action had ever been.

That was the other problem.

He was feeling downright *reliant* on her. He hated to admit it, but he *needed* Daisy Sullivan. As much as he was second-guessing putting her in charge of his sobriety and his schedule, the thought of her month-long stay coming to an end filled him with a combined sense of terror, sorrow and dread.

Which pissed him off.

He was *Apollo Savage*. He didn't *rely* on other people.

He *inspired* people and stole every show. He broke sales records and sold out stadiums, working day and night to earn credibility and, while he was at it, made a ton of money. He was an extremely in-demand musician. An out-of-control one, sure, but a mega-successful one nonetheless.

For him to feel so desperately dependent on Daisy's presence and her belief in him was driving him slightly mad with frustration.

And now it was that time of day when she took him to his room and checked his blood pressure and made him do physical therapy so the mobility of his elbow wouldn't be affected by his injury for the long-term.

Daisy closed the door of his bedroom and opened her bag to take out the medical instruments she needed. "It's nice to have a few minutes of peace and quiet," she said. "Don't you ever get tired of all the people and the noise?"

"Not really."

She wound the blood pressure sleeve around his upper arm and started pumping it tighter until it sort of hurt.

"You seem to be getting used to all the people," Apollo commented. "You're dominating the entire household pretty comfortably for someone who doesn't like crowds."

He spent a lot of his time trying to gently rile her. Because she riled *him*. And because she seemed immune to his tactics. Predictably, instead of getting offended or ruffled by his almost-cutting remark, she smiled. "I'm just looking out for you, Apollo. It's what you're paying me to do, isn't it?"

This irked him even more. He barely stopped himself from blurting out something like: *Only* because I'm paying you?

What would he have even wanted her to say? *No, Apollo. Because I care about you. You've become important to me, like I obviously have to you.*

When it came to Daisy, his emotions were more difficult to navigate than usual. He often wondered if this was because of that dream he'd had, as he was resurfacing from his coma and was doped to the eyeballs, when he'd confused her for an angel. Something deep inside his psyche seemed to have attached itself to her, like a dark, deluded octopus who can't unstick its tentacles from a passing playful dolphin, as hard as it might try.

As he watched her record his blood pressure onto the chart, he noticed that her shiner was almost entirely gone, aside from one small mark that still remained, like whoever had hit her had been wearing a ring. He'd tried a few times to lightly question her, but she'd always gone a little bit pale before brushing off his questions altogether.

Daisy picked up his arm and carefully bent his elbow. It wasn't painful this time. And it moved more easily. "You're much better now, Apollo. Another week or so and I think we'll be able to give you the all-clear. You'll finally be able to get rid of me and get back to your life."

"*No.* I'm not ready for that yet."

She glanced at him, mildly surprised by his reaction.

"You will be soon. You're sober, you're healing and your vitals are all normal."

He tried to adjust his tone, so he didn't sound as desperate as he felt. "I want you to stay another month."

"Apollo, I'm not sure that's—"

"Please. I'll double your pay." She frowned when he said that and he instantly regretted it. He didn't want this to be about the money.

"It's not a good idea."

"Why not?"

"Part of your recovery is going to be about you doing this for yourself. You can do it without me. I know you can."

"I can't."

She eyed him. Understandingly, like always, but she *was* ruffled. Apollo wanted to unearth some *real* emotion in her, like she so easily did to him.

But when she spoke again, her tone was back to its breezy, I-don't-have-a-care-in-the-world default. "I think you can. Trust yourself. *I* trust you."

"You shouldn't."

"Besides, I have things I need to get back to. My job and school and a house that's probably been trash—" She caught herself just in time.

But not quite. Against his will, Apollo found himself fully invested in every little shred of information she gave him. "You were going to say 'trashed.' What did you mean? Why?"

"It's nothing."

He wasn't going to let her evade this subject yet again, so he took a more direct approach. "Is the person who's trashing your house the same person who gave you the black eye?"

She stared at him emotionlessly for several seconds. Then her eyes welled up.

Finally. Finally, he'd broken through. He didn't ask again. Her silence seemed to confirm what he suspected. Carefully, he pulled her to sit down beside him and he held her, smoothing her hair, which was softer even than it looked. It struck him how good it felt to finally *touch* her. The feather-soft textures of her and the flowery scent were wildly soothing to him, and it was disconcerting that her light contact made him feel like he'd been wandering adrift for all this time and was finally home. Her tears wet his shirt. Apollo knew all about angst and how it needed an outlet—sometimes through pathways you wished it wouldn't take.

"I'm sorry," she said, already beginning to make light of what had happened.

But he continued to hold her. "It's okay. You're okay."

Daisy smiled weakly, her huge amber eyes full of a sadness he'd only guessed at until now. He wanted to rip that sadness out of her, and ease it away. He wanted to hunt down whoever had done this and beat him to a bloody pulp. What monster could do such a thing—to *Daisy*, of all people?

"Tell me who it is."

"Forget it, Apollo. It's nothing."

"It's good to tell someone, Daisy. For a lot of reasons. Please. Tell me."

"It's … my brother."

"Your *brother*?"

"It's not really his fault, he's just—"

"Hitting you isn't his fault?" Apollo couldn't believe what he was hearing.

"He's going through some hard times. He's always been sort of … needy, and angry."

"Daisy. He shouldn't be taking any of that out on you. Ever, and especially not physically. He *hurt* you. That's not okay. You realize that, right? How long has this been going on?"

Apollo couldn't have known that he was the first person Daisy had ever told about this, or that she hadn't cried about it in a very long time. But now, she couldn't seem to stop. "It's always been like this." She wiped her tears and sat up a little straighter. "I'm sorry to be telling you. I shouldn't be."

"Of course you should. It's important to talk about it. I can help you."

"I don't need help, Apollo. I can handle it. I'm planning to move soon anyway. He won't have any idea where to find me."

Apollo was watching her. "Stay here. Not because I'm paying you. Stay until you figure things out. As long as you want."

"That's a kind offer. But I'll stay until my month is up, then I'll be on my way. It's best this way."

It didn't seem like the right time to push her on that point, but he was resolved to get his way. He still had time to convince her. The French-door-style windows were open to the view out over the grounds of his house, the fountain, and the twinkling lights of the city in the distance. "It's a nice place to watch the moon rise. I sometimes sit here and write songs."

They talked, about painful things and, later, things that made them laugh, until the moon was high in the sky.

"Thank you, Apollo," she said.

"Thank *you*, Daisy," he replied, meaning it. She had, in several ways, saved his life. She'd been there for him, despite his pain and gruffness and all the atrocious behavior he'd thrown in her direction. She'd taken it all, and somehow absorbed it, making his crosses that much easier to bear.

Apollo didn't want her to leave. Her face and hair and glittery eyes were blinding him again with that light she seemed to radiate, delivering jolts of realization that went deeper than lust. Deeper than greed or fun or selfishness or ego. He had this horrible feeling that if she disappeared from his life, he'd be plunged into darkness, like watching the sun spinning off into orbit to shine its light on some other faraway, happier solar system, leaving his own world joyless and cold and uninhabitable.

Apollo leaned closer. And closer. Until the anticipation became too much for him to bear. He kissed her, easing his mouth over hers, touching his tongue to her parted lips. And *here* was his brand new addiction. The taste of her made him dizzy with lust. It was a lust that had teeth and their bite was infusing him with a raw and vast kind of longing.

But, after several long seconds of the sweetest kiss of his entire life, Daisy pulled away from him. She stood up.

He didn't move, but he continued to watch her, feeling slayed but at the same time almost bemused. *So this is what this feels like.*

"You're my *patient*, Apollo," Daisy whispered.

"And?"

She stared at him.

"Oh. Right," he said gently. "You're too principled to cross that line. But I'm not."

"My father was an addict and so is my brother." She walked toward the door. It was enough of an explanation, of course. "Goodnight, Apollo. I'll see you in the morning."

"Goodnight, Daisy."

After she left, he sat at the window for a while. He was more fired up than he could ever remember being. There was no way in hell he'd be able to sleep.

Against his better judgment, he decided to go downstairs. He felt like writing a song.

When he passed the pool area on the way to his recording studio, he saw his band were sitting in the raised area near the pool. No one else was around, just them.

Bruno saw him and waved him over. Bruno, Gus and

Rufus were sharing a bottle of whiskey. Empty beer bottles and ash trays covered most of the surface of the table. "Come join us, man," said Rufus.

It had been a while since the four of them had hung out.

"Where's your supervisor?" asked Bruno.

Apollo didn't even mind the dig. "In bed."

Gus laughed and whistled a low note, getting entirely the wrong impression.

"Alone," Apollo clarified, even though he wasn't sure why he was bothering. He'd never been refused by a woman in his life, but that didn't matter either. Daisy was different, obviously. Better. And it was fucking with his mind. As though all his mistakes and shortcomings had compounded themselves and were now hovering around him in suffocating, excruciating detail.

"Want a beer?" asked Bruno.

"Don't offer him a *beer*," said Rufus. "He's trying not to fall off the wagon."

"One beer won't hurt," Apollo heard himself saying. "If I can't have *one beer* with my band, then what's the point?"

Clearly, none of them were going to argue with him and it was refreshing. To not have his babysitter watching his every move. He could finally just relax for a while, and be himself again.

Apollo drank the beer. It tasted ridiculously good.

Too good.

One more, that's it. Then he'd go down to his studio for a while.

The night took on a new clarity. He'd really missed his band. He'd been through so much with these guys. They always had his back.

"Bypass him," said Rufus, nodding at Apollo, as Bruno took a swig of the whiskey and started passing it around.

He'd already had two. One more hit was hardly a big deal.

Besides, it was beyond infuriating. He was irresistible to approximately fifty-seven percent of humankind. But *she* wouldn't treat him as anything other than a hapless wreck or a faceless, drug-addled patient. Fine. Then he'd live up to her expectations. Maybe *that* was the only way to get her to notice him. And to stay.

Apollo took the bottle and helped himself to a long sip.

NASHVILLE

Daisy also couldn't sleep.

She could admit she was letting her defenses down. He was getting harder and harder to resist, with that thick hair and those soulful eyes with their depth and their understanding that was starting to feel disconcertingly *safe*. A different kind of safety, one that was scarily appealing which she didn't allow herself to analyze.

He would be so devastatingly easy to fall in love with. And then he would proceed to squelch her soul like a slug on the sidewalk.

It was too dangerous. And too cliché, of course. Only the entire *world* was in love with Apollo Savage. That's what happened when you were drop-dead gorgeous and rich as sin. You got crowds of screaming girls pounding on your windows and chasing you through the streets. *Everyone* fell in love with you.

She'd put in her recommendation to Dr. Manning tomorrow. Apollo Savage was as recovered as he could be. Her services were no longer needed. She would finish out the next week and refuse to continue treating him. It wasn't worth the extra money at this point.

Her unsquelched soul was worth more to her than whatever amount he was paying her. She'd have enough, with what she'd made already, to start her new life.

It was a waste of time fantasizing about what might have been. How beautiful it would be to *try* if they could only meet each other halfway. But their worlds were too different and the obstacles too great. Any attempt at a relationship with Apollo Savage was obviously a disaster waiting to happen, that's all there was to it.

Why was she even thinking like this?

It would simply never happen.

She was hungry. She hadn't had much dinner and the house might be quieter now. It was late.

Making her way down the grand staircase of Apollo's house, she could hear loud music coming from out by the pool. People were still partying. She made her way into the kitchen and began to make herself a sandwich. But then she noticed, out the window. Apollo was out there. With his band.

Swaying on his feet, swigging from a bottle. Yelling and singing along with the others.

He was clearly very, very drunk.

Daisy didn't even bother making the sandwich. She suddenly felt sick.

She went back upstairs and packed her bag.

Then she made her way out the door and down the driveway where her ride was already waiting.

"Where to, miss?"

"The Greyhound Bus station. As fast as you can get me there."

Senior Detective Statham: Have you ever witnessed Individual 3 behaving irrationally?

Individual 9 (~~Daisy Sullivan~~ [redacted]): Yes.

SDS: How often?

I9: That's all I've ever seen him do.

34

―――――――

Eros

HOLLYWOOD

"I'LL GET it right this time," Eros assured Percy, after yet another tirade about Eros's long list of failures and inadequacies.

He *had* been studying his lines. Of course by now he knew this was Percy's M.O., to basically annihilate everyone's self-esteem before building them up again into an exact portrayal of the layered character he'd written.

The only problem was, Percy was about ten times more critical of *him* than he was of anyone else on set.

"Excuse me while I go rewrite the motherfucking script to make it easier for idiot-boy to remember a couple of one liners," Percy continued to vent unreservedly from behind his camera, for Eros's benefit alone. "Weren't you the one who showed up at my trailer spouting some bullshit about *acting?* Now's your chance, son. Now would be an excellent time to start."

"I'll try harder," Eros kowtowed.

There was also the small matter of his concentration being reduced to a puddle of mush every time he glanced in Marlowe's general direction. She was sitting half naked on the kitchen counter drinking a beer, as the scene called for.

Her body. Holy fuck.

How was he supposed to breathe, let alone remember a complicated series of lines … and *act* while he recited them?

The last thing he wanted to do was to fixate, or be yet another lecherous Leo. But not noticing was impossible. So he tried his best to absorb, respect and innocuously appreciate. This was difficult to do *while* he was trying to remember his lines and generally not make a total ass of himself.

To make matters even worse, despite their brief connection during their months-ago weekend getaway, Marlowe's manner now seemed to mirror Percy's, and everyone else's: that Eros was a weakling and a thoroughly dispensable hack whose last brain cell died in 2016.

There'd been one brief exchange on the morning he'd started in the lead role, when she'd thanked him for fighting for her, and for getting rid of Leo. "Of course," he'd said. "It was nothing."

"It was a lot more than nothing," she replied quietly, before walking away.

Since then, though, she'd been living and breathing in character, until he couldn't tell if she loathed him because she actually loathed him or because her character loathed his character.

Whatever.

His head hurt.

Don't give up. You can do this. Make things happen. Work harder. Eros was getting tired of reciting these self-help mantras. They never seemed to help as much as he hoped. But he sucked it up, steeled himself and tried again. "Do I look *that* fucking clueless, Dazleen?" he grumbled passionately (at least this was a line he could thoroughly relate to).

"You look even *more* clueless! And don't give me that shit about waiting up all night, Harley. I *know* you were at Spike's place." Marlowe emoted effortlessly, of course. In fact Eros was more impressed by her talent with each take. She had a natural ability that was beautiful to watch. He'd never worked with someone so instinctive and so incredibly *good* at this.

He, on the other hand, had to consider every nuance, every pause, every word, and he was second guessing himself. Eros could admit to himself that he was way out of his league—but he was determined that no one else realize this. Percy might have had an inkling, but at least he hadn't fired him yet, which was something.

"Cut!" yelled Percy. "Give me *more*, man! More! Your

girlfriend spent the night running drugs and very possibly having sex with strangers, she won't tell you either way. You want to punch your fist through a wall, dude, not barely *notice*."

"Right. Got it. Got it." When Percy put it like that, he *could* get pissed off. Eros let his turmoil rage through his lines—thankfully remembering what they were this time.

"That was better," encouraged Percy. "Do it again."

Thirty-four takes later, Eros was a mess. Exhausted, strung out and feeling like a train wreck who'd been yelled at by every cast member, stunt double and even the caterer, he made his way back to his trailer when Percy called a wrap for the day. His bruises from Leo's pummeling were starting to fade, but his headache wouldn't quit.

Eros climbed the steps into his trailer and closed the door behind him.

And halted in his tracks.

Two giggling girls sat on his couch. They were wearing as little as it was possible to wear and still technically be clothed. He recognized them as two of the bubble-gum-chewing extras. "Hi, Eros," one of them tittered. "Your trailer wasn't locked."

Ah, the good old days, pre-Marlowe and Percy and this annoying *drive* to prove himself, which involved more effort than Eros had ever given anything. He'd been carefree and aimless. Adored. He hadn't been punched or yelled at or constantly put down. Everyone had loved him.

For an indulgent moment, he felt nostalgic. This. *This* was the treatment of a movie star. Scantily-clad girls throwing themselves at him and giving him the kind of attention he deserved. *Here* was the natural order of his world. Not tyrannical and condescending rage-mongers who seemed to hate his guts for no reason.

"Want to hang out?" asked the second girl. They might have even been twins, they looked that alike. Cut-out wannabes from the same styling school as half of Hollywood.

He contemplated them for a few seconds, wishing he could forget the memory of Marlowe's ludicrously perfect curves, which had been seared into his brain after the marathon he'd just endured. And the seamless, emotion-drenched delivery of her lines. The soulful look in her inky eyes and the flawless shrug of her angular shoulders.

Damn it.

How was he supposed to *deal* with this shit without losing his mind? By having meaningless sex with a couple of bimbos?

Weirdly, he didn't want to.

He went to the small fridge in his trailer's kitchen and took out a beer. After watching Marlowe drink out of a Budweiser bottle filled with water for the past twelve hours, he was thirsty. "Want one?" he said to the girls.

"Sure," they said in unison.

He took the girls their beers and sat on a chair. At a safe distance. They eyed him and continued to titter and flick their hair.

Only a few short weeks ago, by now he would have been happily romping in bed with these chicks. They were cute. And willing, obviously. Hell, the weekend before his audition, he'd been doing exactly that.

Now, though—*goddamn it!*—he felt nothing.

That unforgiving, gorgeous, impenetrable fortress of one hated him. And had now ruined him for anyone else. He was about to explain this in a very condensed version to these girls, along the lines of *please leave*, when there was a knock on his door.

He stood up to open it.

Speak of the devil, there she was. Looking stunning, like she always did. But his mood was still dark. "To what do I owe this astounding pleasure?"

"Let me in, Eros," Marlowe said, pushing past him. "I need to talk to you." She stopped when she saw the girls. "Looks like you've already got company."

"Yes. They were here when I got here three minutes ago. Some people actually *want* to spend time with me, amazingly, and don't treat me like a lobotomized leper. Even so, I was about to ask them to leave."

Ignoring the girls, Marlowe pointed her finger into his chest. "What was *up* with you today? Every time you don't get your way you cry like a spoiled baby."

Eros glared at her. No, he didn't. Did he?

"I guess it makes sense," Marlowe continued. "You're so used to being fawned over that you can't handle a dose or two of constructive criticism, even when it comes from someone who just so happens to be trying to help you."

No, he wasn't. Was he? He chugged the second half of his beer and slammed the bottle onto the table.

"You need to toughen the fuck up," Marlowe said.

That was just great. She knew he wasn't unscathed. He'd had hard times just like everyone else. Maybe not *financially*, but there were plenty of skeletons in his closet, some of which he'd actually told her about, in a roundabout way. And he was sick of being stomped on. "You know what, Marlowe? Forgive me for not living up to your exacting standards of being either Lawrence Olivier or goddamn Ice-T! So I'm not as cool or as talented or as tough as you, so what? Not many people are."

Marlowe glared at him. But then her expression softened. She laughed. A real laugh. Goddamn her, he *loved* the sound of her laughter. He wished he could inspire it every day. "Since when am I cool or talented *or* tough?"

He threw his hands up and sat defeatedly onto the couch next to the nearly-topless girls. "You're all those things on steroids. And I'm a talentless hack who can only watch you in amazement and awe."

The girls cooed sympathetically.

Marlowe glanced at the girls. "If you don't mind leaving, Eros and I need to talk."

He was about to launch into another outburst, but held it. She wanted to be alone with him?

The girls tittered their way out the door.

Eros stood up to face her. "Why'd you come here, Marlowe? To laugh at me? To rub in how shitty my day has been?"

"No. I came here to tell you that Percy said you nailed that last scene. He said you improved a lot today. He thinks you might have serious potential."

"You mean I did something *right*? Incredible." But then it started sinking in. He'd done something *right*. Incredible.

She was standing very close to him. Those green eyes had him completely in their spell, but he could feel his own draw. She'd chosen to be here, after all. In his trailer, alone with him. "Careful, Savage," she whispered. "Don't fall in love with me."

"Too late," he whispered back.

She grabbed the front of his shirt with her fist and pulled him closer. Eros felt almost stricken with lust, anticipation and feverish heat. She occupied some higher, wiser, hipper plane than he'd ever reach. The sparks practically flew out of her eyes and off her warm skin, burning little scars of need into his body.

When she kissed him, he let her have anything she wanted of him, at first. Here was his real audition. *This* was where he could really shine. Because if there was one place Eros knew he could give as good as he could take, it was in bed.

Six hours later, after the most electric, grueling and orgasmic sex of their lives, they lay drenched in sweat, limbs tangled, breathing hard.

"*Damn*," she breathed.

Eros's back was covered in scratches. His hair was an unruly mess. With her body, her voice and the fire in her eyes, she'd tampered with his soul and somehow marked it with her seal of ownership. "Holy hell," he agreed.

Marlowe laughed lightly. Those green eyes had somehow become even more bejeweled in the pre-dawn half-light, as though she was a video game character that was fully charged with health. "That all you got, cowboy?" she teased him.

Luckily, Eros was in the prime of his youth and could spring back to life with all the consistency and enthusiasm of a Jack-in-the-box.

So he laid himself over her and gave her even more—all of himself—the best parts of everything he had, until she was crying out, clinging to him and moaning his name.

They lost themselves completely in the moment.

When he woke again, she was gone and his alarm was buzzing.

Back on set, Percy was already gearing up to take out his frustrations on his new favorite chew toy. "The motherfucker's *late*? Seriously? I got—"

"I know," Eros said. "Fifty other actors lining up. I'm not late. I'm one minute early. Let's do this."

Percy was probably shooting a few daggers out of his eyes at him from behind the sunglasses. Eros couldn't exactly tell, but it was an educated guess. Either way, it didn't matter.

What did matter was the way Marlowe was watching him. Like he'd surprised her in all the best ways. Like what they'd shared had been unexpected.

Like she might even have plans for him tonight.

Eros aced his next scene after only twenty-two takes.

Senior Detective Statham: You had reason to be angry.

Individual 17 (~~Leo Puck~~ [redacted]): I *was* angry. But not angry enough to *kill*. I'm no murderer, Detective. Hell. I'm an Academy Award winner, for Chrissakes. You realize no charges were ever even filed, right? Besides, I got offered another job the very next day on a Tom Ford movie about a slightly overweight sexual deviant who ends up getting shot. Not sure why he wanted to cast me in the role. Probably because it calls for a lot of complexity. So I agreed to do it.

35

Apollo

NASHVILLE

APOLLO WOKE with the mother of all hangovers.

Fuck.

Why had he slept in a chair by the pool? Why were Bruno and Gus also asleep in chairs by the pool?

Then he remembered. He'd drunk half a bottle of whiskey and at least a six-pack of beer last night.

Possibly more.

Definitely more.

His clothes were still damp from an impromptu swim into the pool. His throat was sore from singing and yelling obnoxiously to loud music. He'd not only fallen off the wagon, he'd run over it with a fleet of eighteen-wheeled Mack trucks.

He checked his pockets for his phone. Nothing. He spotted it on the table between an army of incriminatingly empty bottles, which he pushed out of the way. One fell off and smashed on the ground.

Shit. It was 11:04 a.m.

Daisy would be up by now, no doubt about it. She was an early riser. One of those people who whistled in the mornings and commented on how blue the sky was.

She would have seen him by now, he was sure of that.

Would she be mad? Disappointed?

Of course she'd be disappointed.

My father was an addict and so is my brother.

He'd just confirmed all the worst things about himself.

Apollo knew as well as anyone how addiction can ruin lives. *Her* life had been ruined. She was trying to climb out of its wreckage, and all he was doing was reminding her of that while simultaneously introducing yet more pain and more regret.

In that moment, something became achingly clear to Apollo. She'd become necessary. Her sunny, steady kindness had given him a reason to live.

What had he given her in return? Bad behavior, infantile churlishness and one hell of a relapse.

She didn't deserve it, is the epiphany that stampeded through his head like a herd of horned Pamplona bulls. He'd noticed the shadows under her eyes and the almost-spooked look about her. But he'd always been too wrapped up in his own problems to take much notice of hers.

As though his dark cloud had moved away from a suddenly-blinding sun, Apollo realized with certainty right then: what he wanted most in this world was to be good enough for Daisy Sullivan. He'd never be a saint, but he *could* be more than a totally self-indulgent prick. He wanted to prove to her that he was better than everything he'd so far shown her.

Ignoring his colossal hangover, he jumped up and walked into the house. People were milling around. But he couldn't see Daisy.

She'd be forgiving, like she always was.

She'd say something tireless and understanding.

It's okay, Apollo. These things happen. We'll try again. I'll help you. Everything will be okay, you'll see.

Wouldn't she?

She wasn't in the kitchen or the great room.

Or the game room.

Or the library, where she sometimes sat and read in the chair by the window.

Apollo ran up the stairs.

The door of her room was open. The bed had been made and the room was empty. He checked the closet and drawers.

She'd packed up her things.

Daisy was gone.

Apollo's stomach lurched in panic, like he'd just hit the summit of a roller coaster ride and now the only way to go was down. *How could she do this? How could she leave like this? I need her!*

It occurred to him that what *she* needed was to keep

her distance from drunken jerks. She'd told him that. She'd explained why.

And he'd gone ahead and done it anyway.

Apollo ran downstairs, where Bruno, Gus, Rufus and around twenty other people including friends, his staff and total strangers were either cleaning up after last night's excesses or gearing up for yet another day of hedonism and debauchery.

"Listen up, everyone," he announced.

They all gathered around.

"I need you to help me find Daisy. She's gone."

Apollo was almost surprised by how dismayed everyone was. Even Bruno, who'd never seemed to like her, was deeply concerned. "Why would she leave us?"

Daisy had charmed them all, it seemed, in that *way* she had, of genuinely caring about the people around her.

Everyone began talking and butting in at once, speculating on her exit route and possible destinations. One of Apollo's (actual) assistants found some security footage of Daisy unlocking a smaller gate next to his main gated entrance (for foot traffic, which Apollo had never even known was there) and walking through it. It showed a car pulling up to the curb. Daisy said something to the driver before getting into the back seat of the car. But there was no audio.

"She got an Uber!" someone deduced triumphantly.

"Maybe she went to the airport."

"She's probably headed back to New York."

"She's frugal, though. Would she fly … or maybe she'd take a bus."

It was true. She *was* frugal. Painfully so. And she would head back to New York, most likely. To find out whether her house was trashed. With her brother possibly still in it.

Apollo went cold.

He'd hurt her again. Or worse.

Apollo barked orders to several of his assistants. He recruited a team to go to the airport to see if she was there. "I'm going to the bus station."

"I'll come with you," said Bruno.

Twelve minutes later, Apollo's McLaren 720S Coupe screeched to a stop at the Nashville bus station and Apollo leapt out of it. He ran into the crowded station, searching for Daisy.

He couldn't see her.

Apollo had no entourage or bodyguards with him. People began to recognize him and take pictures. He didn't even notice. He ran to the ticket counter. "When's the next bus to Long Island? Or New York City. Have any gone within the past few hours?"

The man behind the bullet-proof glass stared at Apollo. It wasn't a starstruck stare—the guy was approximately seventy-five years old—more of a bored one. Excruciatingly slowly, he checked the printed timetable on the desk in front of him with a gnarled finger. "The next bus to New York leaves at 12:17. Gate four." He pointed vaguely. "Over there. It's boarding now. Do you want to buy a ticket?"

Apollo sprinted to the gate. She'd be easy to spot. No one else had her hair or that utterly unique Daisy-tinted glow.

People were lined up, waiting to get onto the bus.

There. Inside, at the very back of the bus, he thought he saw the glint of gold. A wavy halo. Yes. She was wearing her white jacket, the one with the fake fur. *It was her.*

Apollo pushed his way toward the front of the line. "I'm sorry," he said, when a guy swore at him. "But I need to get on that bus."

"Aren't you … *Apollo Savage?*" someone said.

He ignored the question and climbed onto the bus. "Excuse me." He weaved his way around people putting their bags into the overhead compartments and squeezing their over-sized bodies into too-compact seats.

She was preoccupied, pulling a book out of her backpack. He slid into the seat next to hers.

Vaguely, Daisy glanced at him, as you do to a random stranger when they sit down next to you. Then she did a double-take.

He smiled. *That* smile, the full-wattage one, but it wasn't an act; he was wildly happy.

She stared at him, stunned at first, but her expression took on layers. Anger—which he'd never seen on her face before and it was painfully adorable. Frustration. Resolve. "Apollo," she greeted him coldly.

"Daisy."

"I'm leaving."

"I can see that."

"Don't to try to talk me out of it, Apollo. I'll give back the money you've paid me. I can't stay and watch you damage yourself again. I just can't. I won't."

"I know. I'm sorry."

Her eyebrows furrowed, like she hadn't expected him to say that.

People were staring at them, murmuring, pointing, snapping photos. He didn't care. "I've been a complete asshole, totally self-involved and unforgivably stupid. For a long time. Because of you, I can see that now. I *want* to kick my habit. I want to prove to you—*you*—that I can. Please don't leave me, Daisy. I'm sorry. I know I fucked up last night. What I did is unforgivable. I'm not asking you to forgive me." A heartfelt pause, into which all of Apollo's emotions spilled. He took her hands in his. "Okay, I *am* asking you to forgive me. Because I'm in love with you, Daisy. I love you. I do. And I'm begging you to please give me another chance. Please stay so I can make it up to you a million times over and prove to you that I can be good enough for you. That's all I want to do. I need you. And I really, really want more than anything to show you how important you are to me. Please give me one more chance. Please. If you're still mad at me after that, you can leave and I won't try to stop you." Another emotion-drenched pause. "Okay, I will try to stop you. I'll always try to stop you. Because I'm completely one hundred percent head over heels in love with you, Daisy. I can't bear to live without your golden glow and your exquisite face and the way you make everything better than it's ever been. I want to take care of you, instead of you always taking care of me. So much. Please come home with me. I promise I'll make it up to you, sweetheart. Please. I'm sorry."

Daisy stared at him in round-eyed shock and he was *glad* he'd shocked her. He wanted her to feel as crazy and shocked and elated as he did.

She was disconcertingly quiet, but he thought he could detect the tiniest edge of that *understanding* she used to bask him with. He craved more of it so much it hurt. Maybe there was more to it, too. Maybe the glimmer in those golden eyes meant that—just a little and he would start with that, if only he could just have that—she loved him. Or liked him. Or would put up with him for a few days longer. "I don't know what to say."

"Say yes, Apollo, of course I'll give you a chance." His words felt more heartfelt than any he'd ever spoken. "I might fail, but I *really* don't want to fail. I want to prove to you that I can do it. Will you help me?"

He'd suspected her weakness by now, of course: that she wouldn't refuse a person in need. He could only hope that his confession would be enough. He'd *make* it enough. He'd follow her to the goddamn ends of the earth. Nothing else mattered anymore. He wanted her more than he wanted drugs or booze or the self-absorbed hedonism that never felt as good as you thought it would when you jumped head-first into it. Apollo had disappointed her once (okay, maybe more than once). But he would mine every ounce of his willpower now to make sure it never happened again. He could feel that vow solidifying, taking shape, because he *wanted* it to. It made him feel stronger than he had in a long time.

The loudspeaker of the bus crackled. "Please take your seats, ladies and gentlemen. The bus will depart as soon as all passengers are seated."

Apollo was still holding Daisy's hands. "If it takes me all the way to New York to convince you, then so be it."

Softly: "You're incorrigible, you know that."

He gazed at her hopefully. "In a good way?"

"In the worst way." She glanced out the window at the gathering crowds, who'd somehow already created *Marry Me, Apollo!* banners. "But how are we going to get out of this bus?"

Apollo eased his warm hand around the nape of her neck and kissed her. This time, Daisy let him, and as his mouth opened hers, she gasped at the intensity of him. The pure, brutal appeal. He tasted like dreams she'd never even thought to yearn for.

"Don't break my heart," he whispered.

"I won't break yours if you don't break mine," she whispered back.

"Deal."

Apollo slung Daisy's backpack over his shoulder and scooped her into his arms. Carefully, he carried her off the bus, where the crowd went quiet. At the sight of them, some of the women burst into tears.

"Does this mean he's taken?" one of them sobbed tearfully to her friend.

"Yes," Apollo said.

Senior Detective Statham: Was the relationship between Individual 3 and Individual 9 personal in nature?

Individual 19 (~~Rufus Rossi~~ [redacted]): He was head over heels. We'd never seen him fall like that. It was a new look for him but it turned out it was the best thing that could ever have happened to him. Except for the shooting, of course.

36

Bruce Davis

THE BRONX I.C.E. DETAINMENT CENTER
BRONX

Bruce Davis had almost gotten used to the stench of garbage after almost an hour of lurking behind the strategically-placed dumpster. The building was the size of an entire city block. He'd walked around it, and had determined that this was the janitors' door, so he was biding his time, hoping for a lone wolf. Someone he could bribe without witnesses.

While he waited, he lamented this afternoon's mistake. He'd debated how to try to piece together all the details of his plan. In the end Bruce decided he'd meet Tiffany, *then* rescue the Diaz girls, *then* get Ares out of jail before packing them all into Ares's helicopter and dispatching them to a small regional airport in New Jersey (which he hoped would be less likely to smell a rat or ask questions), where they'd get on a chartered private jet to fly directly to Telluride. Bruce wanted them out of New York State as quickly as possible. In Telluride, there were places to hide, if need be. Or at least that was the direction logic had steered him. He'd called Apollo and Artemis and told them the plan so they could organize the wedding logistics and get the two married as soon as they arrived.

Tiffany had delivered on her promise. Unfortunately, that wasn't *all* Tiffany had delivered. She'd worn some slinky little number that clearly announced her intent. Bruce was stressed out and he'd been an easy target, he could admit. Once he'd given her the fifty grand she'd demanded, she'd plied him with G&Ts until his judgment was impaired. She'd then proceeded to fondle him under the bar. They'd ended up getting a room and having a very intense quickie.

The woman was mildly terrifying, in hindsight. A dominatrix, of all things. He'd not only *slept* with the enemy but engaged in a number of activities that were probably illegal in several states.

He still felt dirty. Sort of in a good way, but mostly in a I've-been-used-and-enjoyed-it kind of way, and he wasn't sure how to feel about that. He desperately hoped Ares would never find out.

Regardless, the email had been sent to facilitate Ares's release and he had the papers in hand to prove it. That was the main thing.

Finally, after what felt like several eternities of waiting

behind the dumpster, during which time his mood had grown progressively worse, the door of the building opened.

The man was alone. Another janitor. He was wearing a one-piece coverall uniform with a badge pinned to it. His keys jingled from one hand and in the other hand he held a mop. Bruce watched as the guy made sure the door was locked behind him before heading down the street.

Bruce stepped forward. "Sir?" he said.

The man turned. He was an older guy, maybe in his mid-fifties, with graying hair. He looked at Bruce with confusion.

"Sir, I'll give you fifty thousand dollars for that uniform, badge and the key to this door."

The man stared at him for a long moment. "Did you just say *fifty thousand dollars?*"

"I did, yes. In cash."

"I'll lose my job if they catch you."

"I'll promise you I'll be very discrete. You can say your things were stolen. If you do lose your job—which I don't think you will—fifty grand should ease that blow. Actually, how about we make it a hundred grand." In fact Bruce had much more in the interior pockets of his zipped jacket, which he'd altered just for this purpose, rolled into neat wads. He'd been prepared to offer up to a million (of Ares's money), although he'd suspected it would take much less.

"A hunnert *grand?*"

"Yes, sir."

"Shit, man. You got yourself a deal." Right there on the sidewalk, the man stripped off his overalls and handed them to Bruce, along with the key to the door. "You want the mop, too?"

"Uh, yeah. Sure. Thank you." He handed the man the cash. "If you'd like to count it, I'm happy to wait."

But the guy appeared to be satisfied, and stuffed the wads into the pockets of his boxer shorts before wandering off, whistling.

Bruce put on the overalls and used the key to open the door.

Inside, the lighting was dim and artificial. Children were crying. People were moaning with despair. There was a strange smell.

Jesus Christ, what the hell was the world coming to? This place was awful. He desperately hoped he could make this quick so he could flee back to his plush Connecticut bubble, where despair could be muted with gin and money. But he was also well-aware that his Connecticut bubble would pop very decisively indeed if he didn't deliver on his promise.

He only hoped they were still in here.

Thankfully, the cages were mostly made with chicken wire, so he could see the outlines of the people inside them, and the few guards milling around the enormous warehouse.

He crept deeper into the facility, peering into the cages. "Jazmin?" he said cautiously. "Valentina?"

Bruce's heart almost leapt out of his chest when he

heard a guard approaching. He retreated into the shadows and pretended to do some mopping as the guard walked past him. *I'm so not cut out for this shit, goddamn it! I'm a lawyer, not fucking James Bond.*

He had no choice but to keep looking.

Thirty minutes of searching and no luck later, he heard the clang of a cage door being opened. A guard was leading some of the inmates along a corridor. Bruce followed at a safe distance to see where they were going. Bathroom breaks. The guard was leading them to the restrooms, which were located near the door he'd come in through.

Holy shit. This might actually work.

Bruce lurked as inconspicuously as he could, mopping, hiding, keeping to the dark corners, of which there were many.

He waited until … *there.* He thought saw Valentina. Were they together? Where was Jazmin? Could he pull this off?

He concentrated hard on the Aspen vacation he and Marion were planning over Christmas this year. They'd booked it ages ago and he'd been looking forward to getting away for a while. Work had been so all-consuming lately.

One thing was certain: *no Diaz girls, no Aspen.*

No more Friday nights at the club.

And no more Marion.

He'd long suspected his wife would trade up if he so much as hinted at the possibility of unemployment. She was still a good-looking woman and was regularly flirted with by the club's various loaded silver foxes whose wives had either left them or drunk themselves into a stint at Betty Ford or a Danbury Memorial plot.

Bruce crept out of the shadows, and let his mop fall against the concrete wall, where it made a soft thwacking sound.

Valentina looked up. Her eyes looked red, her expression one of undiluted terror.

But then she recognized him. He motioned subtly with his hand. *Follow me. Get Jazmin. Come now.*

Valentina's eyes were wide. She looked behind her and—by some miracle—Jazmin was with her.

They followed him quietly and quickly, fully understanding what was at stake here.

Bruce led the girls toward the exit.

He heard the voice of a guard, ordering the inmates to hurry up. Getting closer.

Fumbling with the key for several unbearable seconds, Bruce unlocked the door.

And, just like that, they were out.

THE BRONX I.C.E. DETAINMENT CENTER
BRONX

J AZMIN D IAZ WAS NOT a person easily intimidated or beaten down. But *this place* was quickly becoming impossible to bear. All their possessions had been confiscated except the clothes on their backs, they were all being treated like animals (in fact animal shelters were probably kinder places), and worst of all, her sister was being terrorized by one of the guards. Valentina would not leave Jazmin's side. Her fear had taken on an edge to it that frightened Jazmin. Valentina had become jittery and withdrawn. When Jazmin desperately asked for help from one of the female guards, the response was: "You should have thought of that before you rowed here on a boat."

Fuck you, was what Jazmin had been thinking. But it wouldn't pay to piss off the guards. She'd seen other inmates beaten, yelled at, put into solitary confinement and denied food. They had no power, no voice, no identity.

Jazmin would die before she'd allow her sister to be hurt. Both scenarios might happen, it was obvious, if the escalating threats of Valentina's pursuer were anything to go by. It would be far better to be sent back to Cuba—at least they'd be able to run and fend for themselves and do their best to piece their lives back together. But they were given no information about when that might happen, and the hours stretched into long, nightmarish days. Time became both sluggish and alarming. Every clang of the bars meant *he* might be back, with that cagey, hungry, calculating look in his eyes, waiting for his moment.

In quieter moments, she thought about Ares, of course, and his … proposal. Despite everything, it had been unexpected. And unexpectedly … *sincere*. He'd really sounded like he *meant* all that stuff he'd said. Jazmin didn't know how to feel or what to expect. His layers and his difficulties and his life were so incredibly removed from her own. He was striking to look at, wealthy beyond anything she had ever seen and he'd gone out of his way to help and protect them every chance he got.

Jazmin had learned long ago that when something seemed too good to be true, it usually was.

But when Ares had gotten down onto one knee with that beseeching, heartfelt look in his eyes, she'd wanted nothing more than to believe him.

But then … *where was he?* Had he changed his mind? Maybe he figured she and all her baggage were more trouble than they were worth. Maybe he'd retreated back into his luxury penthouse and breathed a sigh of relief.

It had been three days, at least. Maybe more.

Jazmin had almost given up on him.

Her attention was so thoroughly fixed on Valentina and her safety as she walked behind her sister down the dimly-lit hallway, Jazmin almost jumped out of her skin when the dark figure stepped out of the shadows.

She was ready to attack, to gauge his eyes and scream for help.

But then she recognized him.

That lawyer.

Ares's lawyer.

He was frantically motioning for them to follow him. Toward a door.

Jazmin hesitated for only a moment. Her fleeting thought was that she wished she could take more people with them. But it was too risky, of course. She grabbed Valentina's hand as they rushed through the door and into a car that had been parked nearby.

Through her haze of relief she struggled to understand what Bruce Davis was saying. *We're picking up Ares from the police station where he's still being held. You'll have to lay low while you wait so you're not seen. We'll go straight to Ares's building where a helicopter is waiting for us on the roof.*

After what they'd just endured, Jazmin felt like she was dreaming.

Valentina seemed mute, almost in shock. Jazmin just held her sister's hand tightly, trying her best to absorb some of her stress and terror, which had taken a turn in Valentina. Jazmin could see this. Something in her had either hardened or broken. Days of threats. And the numbing fear that violence was waiting around the very next corner.

When Ares finally slid into the passenger seat of the car, he looked as wide-eyed and bedraggled as they were. He reached for Jazmin's hand and squeezed it. "Are you all right?"

"Yes." They *would* be all right, she felt. He gave off that vibe: he'd make *sure* they were all right, or die trying.

"Valentina?" Ares said.

"Fine," she said, even though her eyes were still spooked.

In the helicopter, Ares made sure Valentina was strapped in before sitting next to Jazmin and tightening her seatbelt.

Ares held her hand as they took off.

The city below them looked deceptively scenic and serene from this vantage point, far above it. They crossed the river and landed at a small airport, where a private plane was waiting. Once they were airborne and on their way to Telluride, Ares shook Bruce's hand heartily. "Remind me to give you a raise," Ares said.

The landscape below grew vast and majestic as they traveled further west.

Valentina slept.

And Ares sat with Jazmin and held her face gently, wild relief making him playful, almost crazy. He kissed her slowly and she kissed him back.

"I'm going to spend every second of my life keeping you safe," he whispered, "and making all your dreams come true."

Jazmin wasn't sure if she was falling for him because he'd just saved their lives. Or if it was because he looked so *human*. With the same now-rumpled shirt and jeans he'd been wearing the night he'd proposed to her and with those dark shadows under his eyes, this wasn't the CEO who demanded total control. This was a man who'd spent many sleepless nights in prison because he'd fought for her, worrying about her, doing everything he could to get to her before it was too late.

Ares held her hand as they took off. "Please marry me," he whispered.

She smiled. "Yes, Ares."

Jazmin couldn't be sure *why* she was falling deeply for this complicated, intense, beautiful man.

Only that she was.

Individual 7 (~~Valentina Diaz~~ [redacted]): I only did what anyone would have done. It was the right thing to do.

37

Liam Sullivan

LONG ISLAND

LIAM HAD WALKED to Daisy's house. He'd broken in through the back window. Searching the entire house—and practically destroying the place in the process, which had felt satisfyingly cathartic—he still couldn't find what he was looking for.

Where would she hide them?

He needed to be more strategic. More thorough.

Back in Daisy's bedroom, Liam stood in front of her closet. He pulled the chair from her desk over, and stood on it. Reaching behind some clothes on the very top shelf, there, at the very back corner, he found a locked metal box.

Bingo.

The padlock was unbreakable, but he smashed the hinges of the box with a hammer, finally prying the thing open. In it, he found a hundred dollars in cash, the keys to her car, two credit cards and some jewelry of his mother's, which he could sell if he needed to. *He* didn't kill their mother: he should at least be entitled to her diamond engagement ring.

There was something else in the box, too, wrapped in cloth. He unwrapped it.

A Ruger. And a box of ammo.

Little Daisy packing heat—who would have thought? Maybe to protect herself from *him*. It was a possibility. He'd lost his cool a couple of times, but who didn't? He was a boxer, after all, and a good one. These things happened.

He tucked the gun into the waistband of his jeans and put the cash and credit cards in his pocket.

It was time for him to even the score a little. Liam was tired of watching Daisy get all the good things in life while all he got was shit.

If Daisy got to go to the Wedding of the Year, then so was he.

He was her *brother*, after all. And a smooth talker when he put his mind to it. If they wouldn't let him in, well, then this little Ruger was as good as an invitation.

Maybe he could play Apollo a couple of his songs. Yeah, that's would he would do. That could be his ticket. Maybe Apollo would be the one to finally recognize his genius. Who knew, Apollo might even ask him to join his band.

The more he thought about it, the more Liam felt it

was destiny. Why else would Daisy be Apollo Savage's nurse? It was fate. Leading him to where he was supposed to be. On stage. Part of one of the biggest acts on Earth.

Liam fantasized and it was the first inkling of happiness he'd felt in a long time.

He scrolled through Eros's Instagram. And Artemis's. No new posts.

So he tried Twitter, searching different names and hashtags.

Nothing.

He helped himself to Daisy's food. He slept in her bed. And he waited.

And there it was, finally: a clue. *#ErosSavage and #MarloweMercy seen leaving set of Mercy movie for a weekend getaway.* Then, a random fan's tweet: *On my way to Denver and #ErosSavage was on my plane!!!!!! In first class and wearing a hat and dark sunglasses but I'm almost sure it was him!!!!!! OMG!!!!!!!!!*

Denver.

One of their houses was in Telluride. That's where they'd be going, he was sure of it.

He bought a plane ticket with Daisy's credit card and booked a limo. It would be waiting for him upon his arrival.

He revved Daisy's car to life and backed out of her driveway, heading toward the airport. He might *finally* be able to catch a break in this cruel world.

Individual 15 (~~Amal Mooney~~ [redacted]): I'd like to offer legal representation to Individual 7 if there's a need for it. Here's my card. It's my direct line. Any time is fine, except for the hours between five and seven p.m. We prefer to do as much hands-on parenting as we can and the children are insane at that time of night.

38

Lenny Vance

TELLURIDE

LENNY VANCE WAS in a great mood. His new job was turning out to be awesome. He'd only been hired a few days ago. Some big-name celebrity was getting married and every security company in the state of Colorado had been maxed out. The celebrity's family needed to be guarded from all their fans, apparently, and also from some convict who was stalking one of them and was still on the loose. So Lenny had somehow managed to get posted at the entrance to the wedding. The actual door where all the guests would be arriving.

Lenny had heard that A-list movie stars would be there. Musicians, too. That guy called Apollo, whose songs were on the radio and who was always getting messed up. Lenny had even heard that some models were coming. Shit, he might even get lucky. Chicks always dug a guy in uniform, everyone knew that. It wasn't exactly a *uniform*, but he was wearing all black, and a tie, like all the other security people, so at least that counted for something.

He checked to see if anyone was watching, then made a quick call to his brother, who was at home in Centennial getting high and playing video games—exactly what he'd been doing only a week ago. Ever since he'd graduated from high school last year, that's pretty much all Lenny had done, until his mother threatened to take away his Xbox if he didn't go out and get a job. Working wasn't as bad as he was expecting, though, especially if he got to meet models.

"Guess where I am."

"Where?" said Randy. Lenny could hear the laser strikes of his gun as Randy blasted some Hell Eaters.

"I'm a door lord to the stars!" Lenny gushed.

"What are you talking about? Where are you?"

"I'm working security at this rich dude's wedding. In Telluride. Ares something."

"Ares *Savage*?"

"Yeah." Lenny was pretty sure he was right. "That one."

"Holy *shit*, man! George and Amal are going to that! A bunch of famous people are going, I saw it on Instagram. All the guests have to keep the location a secret."

Randy kept up with stuff like that. Lenny, for the most part, didn't. He was way more interested in blasting Hell Eaters. In fact he was ranked 7,112 in the world.

"Aw, *man*, how'd you find that?" Randy said. "Can you get me a job?"

"No, it's too late. People are already arriving. I better go."

"Say hi to Amal for me!"

Lenny hung up and put his phone back in his pocket. He didn't know who Amal was, but at least he'd made Randy jealous.

The guests had to go through a checkpoint at the gate where Lenny's boss made sure they were on the guest list. Then they drove up to the entrance of the house, where Lenny and two other guys opened the doors of the limos to let them out.

There was even a helicopter pad in the field where some of the people would be getting dropped off.

What a life these people led.

A couple of cars pulled up to the gate and were let through, one after the other. He'd been told not to talk to the people as he opened the doors for them. Rich people didn't like small talk, apparently. He was basically a robot to them, which was cool.

Their clothes looked super expensive. One guy looked vaguely familiar but Lenny couldn't remember where he'd seen him before. On TV, maybe. His wife was wearing a glittery dress and was pretty hot for her age.

Lenny's phone rang.

It was his boss, Mr. Boyd. "Lenny, I need you to cover the gate for a few minutes. There's been an incident at the southwest corner."

"An incident?"

"The stalker has been apprehended. He was trying to climb the fence."

"Oh. Wow. Sure, I'll be right there."

So they must have caught the convict. Lenny walked down to the gate. Mr. Boyd looked agitated. "Make absolutely sure you don't let anyone in who isn't on this list. You got that? I'll be back in fifteen minutes tops."

"Sure thing, Mr. Boyd." Lenny would show Mr. Boyd he was reliable and fully up to the task. How hard could checking a list be? This job was too easy.

Liam Sullivan

TELLURIDE

FOR THE FIRST time in his life, Liam Sullivan finally felt like things were starting to go his way. Daisy's credit cards each had a five thousand dollar limit, so he was treating himself. The limo had been a stroke of genius. He'd had the driver take him to the shopping area of Telluride, along the main street, where he'd fitted himself out in new clothes, a new leather jacket and a pair of Ray Bans. He bought himself a bottle of Johnny Walker Red that would fit into the pocket of his jacket, and he'd already made a nice dent in it. He was now approaching the gates of the Savages' Telluride ranch in style.

This was more like it.

He was positive Ares's wedding was taking place in Telluride. He'd seen as many as four different clues. A few helicopters were flying around the area, too, which all but confirmed it.

Liam had always known he was destined for greatness.

His driver pulled up to the gate. "Pull up a little further," Liam instructed. "I want to speak to the guard myself."

The driver obeyed.

The guard was surprisingly young. "Name, please."

"I'm not on the list," said Liam. "There's been a last-minute change. Apollo's playing at the wedding and he asked me to do a guitar solo during the wedding song. He called me this morning."

The guard looked unsure. "I'm … I'm not supposed to—"

"I'm in the *band*, man. *Look* at me, you think I could afford all this if I wasn't? They're not going to list each individual member, are they? We're a collective."

The guard looked puzzled, uselessly consulting the list once again.

Liam noticed a small tattoo on the kid's right hand.

He was a gamer, he knew what it meant. "What's your rank?" Liam asked. "I'm 5,208."

"No way! I'm hoping to break seven thousandth on the next day off I get."

"Good luck."

"Thanks. Listen, I better just call my—"

"What's your name?"

"Lenny."

"Well, Lenny, how about this: I'll get Apollo to send you two tickets to our next concert. Front row."

"That would be awesome!"

"*If* you let me get to this gig on time. I don't want to be late."

After a split second of further indecision, the kid shrugged and waved him through.

Individual 22 (~~Lenny Vance~~ [redacted]): It was like a freaking video game, man! That dude died how he lived. There's glory in that, bro.

39

Valentina Diaz

TELLURIDE

VALENTINA DIAZ WATCHED her sister walk down the aisle toward her waiting groom and felt, for the most part, happy. Jazmin was glowing, and her dress was divine: a fitted lace bodice with a full, floor-length skirt made of the softest white feathers. Her hair was up, with a few coiled strands spilling over her golden shoulders along with the veil, which was held in place by a tiara made of actual diamonds. Like something the royals would wear.

Valentina hoped Jazmin wasn't marrying him just to get them out of their dire situation. They'd talked about it. Valentina assured Jazmin she didn't *need* to do it. They could figure out another way. Really, she'd pointed out, it was no different than almost sleeping with that ugly old accountant—which, secretly, had been one of the creepiest experiences of Valentina's life. Trapped in a room with that bumbling fool, who'd stared at her like—anyway, she didn't want to think about it. It was over. At least the situation had led them to *this*. To her beloved sister's wedding to a handsome billionaire.

Jazmin insisted she liked the person he was. She wasn't just marrying Ares for the money and the green cards. *He's kind,* she'd said. *Yes, it would have been nice to get to know him better before marrying him, but desperate times call for desperate measures. If it turns out he's lying to me or somehow faking his devotion, I can always divorce him later. But I genuinely hope it won't happen that way, V. And in the meantime, we'll be safe.*

Valentina could admit that it would be nice not to have to worry so much. She thought about her parents. Would they be happy to see where their daughters had ended up? She didn't know. She'd been eleven years old when their apartment had been stormed by armed, angry men. They'd never seen them again. Gone, just like that.

That's precisely when the little kernel of fear had lodged itself in her chest, the one that never really went away. Fear of intruders. Fear of being taken away and disappearing forever. Fear of falling out of the boat. Fear of not having enough to eat. Fear of not having a place to live. Fear of having her brothers taken, just like they'd taken her parents. Fear of the cruelty in the faces of people they dealt with every day, who saw them as trash or as invisible. Most of all, fear of the men who followed them, banged on their flimsy doors, locked them up and threatened them with unspeakable violence.

She hoped Ares would be good to her sister. She hoped he would treat her like the beautiful person she was.

The first few times they'd met him, he'd seemed no better than all the other bullies, throwing his money around to get whatever he wanted.

If there was one thing Valentina hated more than anything, it was bullies.

But soon Valentina realized that Ares—even though the man clearly had more money than God—didn't *bully* them into doing what he wanted. He *asked*. Whatever they wanted, he'd provided it in spades.

At first she'd thought he felt guilty because his hideous ex-girlfriend had stiffed them. But it was clear that he was dazzled by Jazmin. He didn't look at her like all the other men did, like they wanted to own her. He looked at her like he wanted to *worship* her. And it was that detail alone that made Valentina wonder if maybe this marriage might last after all.

"Do you," the minister was saying, "Jazmin Liliana Diaz, take Ares John Savage to be your lawfully wedded husband."

"I do," came her sister's steady reply.

The look on Ares's face made Valentina smile, for the first time in a long while. He looked almost overwhelmed with his own joy. He took his vows, then he kissed Jazmin carefully, and whole-heartedly.

Maybe it *would* last. Something about that kiss made Valentina believe that it wouldn't just last, but would be spectacular. He slid a glittering ring onto Jazmin's finger.

The music started up and everyone watched as Ares and Jazmin danced. Valentina drank half a glass of champagne and talked to people at the reception. She'd met most of Ares's family over the past twelve hours as the wedding preparations had taken place, and liked them. She danced with Cooper, the architect, then Wyatt, the Texan, then with Eros, who had some fading bruises on his face but seemed high on life. She talked to Marlowe and Artemis, who already felt like friends.

The champagne was making her feel light-headed, so she walked past the dolphin ice sculpture and down to a lawn area behind a hedge row to admire the view.

That's when she heard it.

It sounded like softly-spoken arguing.

She could barely see Daisy, the shy, gorgeous friend of Apollo's, who didn't say much and had a calm and comforting presence that made you want to spend time with her. She was talking to someone. A man.

Valentina walked closer.

Daisy was upset. "What are you *doing* here, Liam? How did you even get in?"

"Call him," the man was saying. His tone was aggressive. Angry.

"*No.* I'm not calling him! You need to go now. Just leave. *Please.*"

"Why are you always trying to get me to leave, Daisy? I'm starting to think you don't even like me. Your own brother. Well, guess what? I'm not leaving. I'm staying right here. And you're going to do what I tell you to do for once."

Valentina heard a small sound of distress, like he might have grabbed her and was hurting her.

"I'm not doing it," Daisy said. "I'm not. Absolutely not."

"Call him. Tell him you want to see him. Tell him to come find you."

"No. I *won't.*"

The man slapped Daisy, hard across the face.

Valentina was closer now. She could see the man clearly. She could see that he was taking something out of the pocket of his jacket. "I didn't want to have to do this. But you give me no choice. Call him now. Call him or I'll fucking kill you both. Do you hear me? *Do it.*"

"*Liam.* Where did you get that? You—"

"Who were you planning to shoot with this, Daisy? Me? I'll tell you what you're going to do, you little bitch. You're going to call your loaded loverboy and tell him to come down here. He and I have some things to talk about. Do it now or I swear I'll pull the fucking trigger, Daisy. *Do it.*"

"No. You'll hurt him. I won't let you do that."

"I won't hurt him. I just want to talk to him. Then I'll leave, I promise. Five minutes, that's all. Then I'll go."

Daisy wiped her eyes with her hands. "You'll go?"

"Yes. I'll go. I promise."

She looked at him, unsure, and swiped at her tears.

"I just want to talk to him. That's all. Five minutes."

Valentina didn't know who the man was. But she did know a bully when she saw one.

"All right." Daisy was crying harder now. "But then you need to leave. Okay?"

"I will. I give you my word."

Daisy was fumbling with her phone, calling Apollo's number. "Hi," she said into it. "I'm down by the pool. On the lawn below it. Apollo, I'm sorry—"

The man—Liam—grabbed Daisy's phone, before she could change her mind.

And Valentina could see Apollo now. He was up by the pool, looking for Daisy. He saw her. He was walking toward her.

As he got closer, he could see that she'd been crying. "What's wrong? Are you okay?" Apollo's gaze slid to the man. "Who are you?"

"I'm Liam. I'm Daisy's brother."

Apollo looked at Daisy, then back at Liam. It was clear by the look on his face that he knew about Liam. He *knew*. This had happened before. Daisy had shared this secret with him, Valentina could see that. Liam could see it, too.

"What the fuck are you doing here?" Apollo said, his voice low. "You need to leave."

Liam held up the gun and pointed it at Daisy. To Apollo, he said, "You and I are going to talk for a minute."

"Jesus," Apollo said, stepping in front of Daisy, shielding her with his body.

"I want to join the band."

Apollo stared at Liam. And he stared at the gun. He raised his palms, as though to show he wasn't armed. It was obvious that Liam was severely unhinged. And very drunk. Apollo spoke calmly, trying his best to diffuse the situation. "Sure. Fine. Just put the gun down. We can talk. Give me the gun."

Liam laughed. "Not a chance."

"Daisy, you go back to the party. Liam and I will—"

"She's coming with us," Liam said.

"No. You don't need to do this. I know what it's like to be out of control but there's a way back from that. Just give me the gun. Daisy doesn't need to—"

"I said she comes with us."

Daisy stepped out from behind Apollo. She placed her hand lightly on his arm. "It's all right, Apollo. I'll come. Liam, put the gun down. Please."

The idea of Daisy being put in danger appeared to be more than Apollo could handle. He gently pushed her behind him. Then he grabbed for the gun.

The gun went off. The sound of it was impossibly loud, shattering the air.

Apollo fell to the ground. Daisy screamed. She kneeled down next to Apollo. Her hands were covered in blood.

Liam still held the smoking gun. "*Bitch*. Look what you did. You ruin everything! You always have." He pointed the loaded gun at Daisy, his finger on the trigger. "I'll kill you for this."

Valentina didn't hesitate. She lifted the hem of her bridesmaid dress. She pulled the loaded Beretta from its small holster strapped to her thigh. She took aim. Then she shot twice, in quick succession, just like the instructor at the shooting range had told her to do. *Better chance of felling your aggressor with two shots. Once might injure. Two is more likely to make sure the attacker stays down. If they're holding a gun, shoot to kill or there's every chance they'll kill you first.*

People were running toward them. A crowd was forming. Apollo's family was gathering around him.

Valentina was vaguely aware that Jazmin was there. Jazmin was hugging her and checking her for injuries.

Valentina felt surprisingly calm.

She walked over to where Liam lay, and where Apollo was being put onto a stretcher. Daisy was applying pressure to Apollo's gunshot wound, begging him to live. One of the helicopters on the lawn was starting up.

A security guard checked Liam's pulse. Then he shook his head, took off his jacket and draped it over Liam's face. "This guy didn't make it."

Senior Detective Statham: The doctor said the bullet missed all your major organs. Glad to hear it.

Individual 3 (~~Apollo Savage~~ [redacted]): Thanks. They say I'll make a full recovery. And Daisy was unhurt, which is all I cared about. He'd made her life a living hell for a long time. There was no way I was going to let him hurt her again. I mean, it's too bad that it had to end that way for him. We could have tried to help him. But I'm glad ~~Valentina~~ [redacted] [Individual 7] acted quickly, otherwise who knows what might have happened. He might have killed us all. I'm just glad it was me and not her. I'll take a bullet for ~~Daisy Sullivan~~ [redacted] [Individual 9] any day of the week.

SDS: That's a noble sentiment.

I3: There's nothing noble about it, Detective. We're all just doing the best we can with what we've got. She's the most beautiful thing that's ever happened to me and I wasn't about to lose her. When you find something as real the way I feel about the golden angel that brought me back from the brink of darkness, you tend to want to hold on to her with everything you've fucking got. That girl is my salvation. All I could see was her. All I cared about was her. I'd take a thousand bullets if it meant I could keep her safe. And spend the rest of my life with her in it.

SDS: [chokes up]

[end of interviews]

Senior Detective Clint Statham: A post-mortem is currently underway but according to the evidence presented to date, this appears to be an open-and-shut case and I will be submitting my recommendations accordingly.

*List of Individuals

Individual 1. Liam Sullivan

Individual 2: Ares Savage

Individual 3: Apollo Savage

Individual 4: Athena Savage

Individual 5: Eros Savage

Individual 6: Artemis Savage

Individual 7: Valentina Diaz

Individual 8: Jazmin Diaz

Individual 9: Daisy Sullivan

Individual 10: Cooper Salazar

Individual 11: Wyatt Boone

Individual 12: Arlo Estevez

Individual 13: Marlowe Mercy

Individual 14: Lady Baba

Individual 15: Amal Mooney

Individual 16: George Mooney

Individual 17: Leo Puck

Individual 18: Bruce Davis

Individual 19: Rufus Rossi

Individual 20: Bruno Supernova

Individual 21: Gus Erasmus

Individual 22: Lenny Vance

Individual 23: Tiffany Chamberlain

Individual 24: Duke Manning

Individual 25: Earl Weatherby

Individual 26: Nicole Whitby-Salazar

Individual 27: Carl Nelson

Individual 28: Steve Boyd, Boyd Security Ltd.

Individual 29: Percy Mercy

Individual 30: Officer Anthony Briggs, I.C.E.

**STATE OF COLORADO,
DEPT. OF PUBLIC SAFETY
OFFICIAL INVESTIGATION SUMMARY**

November 30

From: Senior Detective Clint Statham

**To: The Honorable High Court Judge Penelope E.
Chauncey**

INCIDENT: Wounding by gunshot of Apollo J. Savage
by Liam W. Sullivan; fatal shooting of Liam Sullivan by
Valentina R. Diaz, at approximately 18:45 hours on
Saturday, October 27 at 4567 Mountainview Road,
Telluride, Colorado (property owned by Savage Enter-
prises and Trust Inc.) at the "Wedding of the Year."

SUMMARY: After interviewing 211 persons of interest,
it is this officer's belief that the defendant, Valentina Diaz,
acted in the interest of public safety, specifically
protecting Apollo Savage and Daisy Sullivan against the
harmful intent of Liam Sullivan. Armed with a loaded
Ruger LCP II, Mr. Sullivan shot and wounded Mr.
Savage; medical reports indicate the bullet struck his
upper left chest, narrowly missing his heart. Liam Sullivan
vocalized his intent to fire his weapon with intent to inflict

fatal bodily harm to Daisy Sullivan. Ms. Diaz fired her Beretta Nano 9 mm specifically with the intent to prevent Liam Sullivan from inflicting what she believed to be intended grievous bodily harm to Daisy Sullivan and possibly other persons in the immediate vicinity. Ms. Diaz fired two shots at Mr. Sullivan, which both struck him directly in the heart, fatally wounding him.

Valentina Diaz, furthermore, demonstrated remorse, and this officer—who has served in the role of Senior Detective for twelve years and Detective for ten years before that—believes the defendant acted with genuine regard for public safety in mind. The defendant is clearly a person of conviction and integrity.

Additionally, it is this officer's opinion that Valentina Diaz's green card application should be granted. Ms. Diaz has the full financial sponsorship and support of Ares J. Savage, Chief Executive Officer of Savage Enterprises Inc. (supporting doc F-304), as well as letters of recommendation from the National Association of Architects' Chairman, Cooper D. Salazar (F-311); multi-Grammy Award winner, Lady Baba (F-316); two-time Academy Award winner, George Mooney (supporting doc F-314); and this officer (F-321).

Police Officer Name/ID: Senior Detective Clint Statham (#345092)

CStatham

High Court Judge Name: The Honorable Penelope E. Chauncey

P E Chauncey

Epilogue

Apollo and Daisy were inseparable from that moment onward. Daisy figured that if Apollo was willing to take a bullet for her, she should give him a chance. She allowed herself to admit that she'd loved him all along. They married at his home in Nashville and honeymooned in Italy, after Apollo healed from his gunshot wound, which missed all major organs. Daisy began working toward a PhD in psychology, specializing in addiction treatment. Apollo, after Athena played him the songs written and sung by Tia, flew Tia to Nashville, collaborated with her and paid her enough to set her and her grandmother (and her children and children's children) up for life. The album went multi-platinum. Daisy went with him on tour, which Apollo insisted on. He fell off the wagon twice, which she not only helped him through but tirelessly forgave. Apollo, recognizing that his wife was far more important to him than his addiction, finally got clean and stayed that way for the rest of his life. The two went on to have three children, Willie, Waylon and Emmylou, who all became musicians.

Liam Sullivan, as it turned out, was on parole for two counts of aggravated assault. He also, once new evidence came to light when his possessions were inspected by

Senior Detective Statham, was posthumously convicted of the murder of a woman who had disappeared near the boxing gym he regularly frequented. Daisy was devastated by this news but not surprised. She also found in his belongings an old photo of her mother she'd never seen before, which she wore in a locket to remind herself that sometimes things didn't work out the way you wished they had. And sometimes they did.

Eros and Marlowe were both nominated for Oscars, Eros for Best Actor and Marlowe for Best Actress in a Leading Role. Eros lost to Woody Harrelson but didn't care; he already felt like he'd won the jackpot. Watching Marlowe accept her award was the best thing that had ever happened to him. Their relationship was a stormy one and even though Marlowe tried to quit him several times, she couldn't. They married, divorced and married again. Marlowe gave birth to a baby girl they named Sadie, who had wild ringlet curls and bright green eyes and went on to become a highly successful actor, script writer and director and the first person to win an Oscar in all three categories on the same night.

Artemis and Cooper got married as soon as Cooper's divorce became final, in a small private ceremony on a beach on Maui. They coordinated their work schedules so they could travel together since they couldn't bear to be apart. Both their careers continued to skyrocket but they were happiest at home in Telluride and spent more and more time there, drawing, painting and raising their twin sons, Jack and Cooper Jr., who both went on to become professional baseball players and eventually architects.

Tiffany Chamberlain had not—thankfully, in retrospect—been knocked up by the young and unsuspecting conquest from the bar. She got distracted from her vendetta against Ares and Jazmin by a brief affair with Bruce Davis that involved whips, nipple clamps and leatherwear, but once it became painfully clear that Bruce would never in a million years leave his wife, Tiffany returned to the Jersey Shore to reunite with her hometown lover Santino Siciliano, who was and always would be the true love of her life. As Dawn-Marie Siciliano, she enjoyed a modestly successful second career as a real estate agent. Despite Santino's dogged and die-hard attempt to become the next Bruce Springsteen—a goal he never even came close to achieving—Dawn-Marie forgave him his flaws (which were many), loved him anyway and the pair went on to have three argumentative daughters and a reasonably happy if not financially satisfying life.

Arlo Estevez had found his true calling and started his own wedding planner business. He was so good at it, all the celebrities wanted him and he was flown around the world, taking on only the most exclusive, high-end events and earning himself an absolute fortune. He planned all five Savage weddings and he and Artemis remain close friends.

Athena and Wyatt moved in together the week after Athena adopted Rosie. Wyatt proposed to Athena the week after that. Rosie was the flower girl at their wedding, which they held on the patio of the Hamptons house. They divided their time between Southampton and Wyatt's ranch in Texas, where Wyatt gave Rosie a horse called Moonshine, a bull-headed yet lovable beast that bestowed the little girl with the kind of confidence and joy few other things could have. Cutting Earl Weatherby in on his biodiesel fuel deal turned out to be a lucrative decision; the two, in time, became lifelong friends. Wyatt and Athena went on to have two more children, a boy, Elias, and a girl, Amelia, who idolized Rosie. Athena continued her charity work and wrote ten more bestsellers. Rosie, following in her mother's footsteps, wrote her own novel, based loosely on her own life, which won her the Pulitzer prize for fiction at the age of twenty-four.

Tamar Takahashi never did get the juicy article from her prize columnist. Athena flat-out refused to write about her new romance. Lashings of hot sex with a Texan beefcake had clearly inspired some gumption in the girl, and Tamar was privately glad to see it, especially when Athena offered her an exclusive for three pictures of

Athena's adorable new family at their Texas ranch. Even better, Athena felt indebted to Tamar for leading her to both Wyatt and Rosie. Tamar was in glossy, editorial heaven when she was given exclusive magazine coverage of the heiress's to-die-for wedding to the outstandingly photogenic and bo-hunky cowboy (Tamar had a minor crush on both of them). The wedding issue broke all previous magazine sales records.

Bruce Davis got a fat raise and became an infinitesimally better person after his heroic detainment center rescue. His wife noticed the difference and decided not to leave him after all. Despite breaking his leg on the very first ski run in Aspen, the two re-bonded in the lodge over whiskey sours and backgammon and remained married for the rest of their lives.

Nicole Whitby-Rutherford (formerly Whitby-Salazar, among others) ran off with Cooper's ex best friend Bradley, who was also on the rebound. Between Brad's moderate trust fund and the capital gain from the sale of Nicole and Cooper's house, the two were able to buy a swanky condo in West Boulder, where they quickly grew mind-numbingly bored of each other. Both went on to marry several more times. Nicole never did have children but she did adopt a rescue puppy named Skippy with husband number five, Tripp Rutherford, who she adored (the dog more than the husband) and started her own line of dogwear called *Skippy Rutherford: Dog Extraordinaire*, which got picked up by several national chains, making her an instant multi-millionaire.

Duke Maximus Manning got promoted after Ares (following a barrage of email reminders) left a glowing testimonial. Duke eventually became chief of staff at the Southern Shores Rehabilitation Estate and married a graduate student named Xavier.

Carl Nelson, Artemis's stalker, went back to jail after his badly-timed and unsuccessful attempt to breach the Telluride property's walls, where he again shared a cell with J.T. Lee. Tired of incarceration—and disappointed by the fact that Artemis had actually married the good-looking architect, a detail that subdued Carl's enthusiasm for continuing to stalk her—while serving out their sentences, the two reformed felons decided to form a legitimate security systems company upon their release, called Stalker Busters. They opened a small office in Los Feliz, marketed their services to celebrities and became moderately successful. Carl met a waitress named Florence who taught him that respecting women was a lot more gratifying than stalking them (and also involved less time in jail).

Ray Garmusch deeply regretted the incident at the Baccarat and was determined to restore his good karma by doing at least one good deed a day. He got a job as a middle-management accountant, taking a massive pay cut, but was thankful he'd at least escaped jail time. On a whim he decided to join a gym, became obsessed, adopted a protein-rich diet and eventually pursued body building (to the unending amusement of the gym's young, buff team of personal trainers). He never won a competition but he did meet a plus-sized lingerie model named Avery, proposed after three dates, wrote a reasonably-successful cook book titled *Protein Will Change Your Life* and lived a contented life in suburban Detroit.

Ares and Jazmin got to know each other after their wedding. She found him to be as imperfectly perfect as a man could possibly be, complicated in all the best ways and utterly devoted to her. She worked to get into medical school and eventually became a renowned heart surgeon. For several years, Ares traveled with Jazmin to developing countries, donating money to build hospitals. He oversaw the Savage Enterprises empire from afar, hiring a number of vice presidents to run things while he followed his wife around the planet. They spent time in Cuba with Jazmin's brothers—who had no desire to ever leave Cuba again—before returning to Manhattan. They divided their time between the Park Avenue apartment and the small island Ares bought for Jazmin on their seventh wedding anniversary, located off the coast of south Florida. They went on to have five children, three boys and two girls, who all became CEOs of the family's various companies—except the youngest, Dante, who became an Olympic athlete, winning gold medals in snowboarding for both big air and halfpipe; during the off-season he surfed, played polo and was the highest paid male model in the world.

Valentina Diaz was all over the headlines for several months. The Honorable High Court Judge Penelope E. Chauncey granted the sisters immediate green cards, ordered Valentina to hand over the Beretta and serve six months of community service, during which time she was finally allowed to be visible in society. She made friends, found her true calling and used her social media platform to raise awareness of immigration issues. She aced law school, became a federal prosecutor and eventually a judge. In her thirties she met a Brazilian soccer player named Iago ten years her junior and had a son, Joaquin. At the age of fifty-two (after a law change initiated by Arnold Schwarzenegger), she became President of the United States.

Cedrik Hugo, after nailing the *City* cover starring the five Savage heirs, went on to enjoy a long and lucrative career in fashion photography. He satisfied his ambition of buying a Hamptons home, where he summers with his aging toy-boy, Silas (who was once a parking attendant). After reading in detail about the events of Ares's wedding, the ensuing drama and the seemingly star-crossed love lives of the Savage siblings, Cedrik occasionally mused about that long ago summer day when he took their photograph and wondered if their parents' spirits guided them from afar to find their own individual happily ever afters. The answer, it seemed, was yes.

Thank you for reading!

If you enjoyed this book, please consider leaving a quick review or rating on Amazon.

This book is a little different to the other books I write, which are steamy contemporary romance written in first person dual POV. To find out more, visit <u>my website</u> and my <u>Amazon page</u>.

Below I'm including the first two chapters of **Billionaire Boss**, a fun, sexy standalone billionaire romance and the first book in my **New York Billionaires** series.

xoxo,
Julie

Please come join my Facebook reader group, Julie

Capulet's Romantics, where I share cover reveals, insider info and we discuss all things romance!

Sign up for my newsletter to receive my free bonus content and get access to sneak peeks and exclusive giveaways!

Visit my website @ www.juliecapulet.com

Our deal was simple. One night. Fake names. No strings attached.

Until it turns out he's my new boss...

I couldn't believe my luck when I got sent to a work conference in Hawaii. Living the dream after years of pulling myself up by my bootstraps.

The sand, the palm trees and the blue water were straight out of a romantic fantasy. So was the guy at the beachfront bar, let's be honest. Blue eyes. Broad-shouldered in his business suit but with a rough-around-the-edges swagger and a filthy mouth.

We laughed and had a night of crazy passion that enlightened me in every possible way. I understood what dreams coming true might actually feel like.

And then I left without saying goodbye.

That was two months ago and I've mostly been able to put him out of my mind. I've been busy landing my dream job in New York City.

Imagine my surprise when my new boss turns out to be Mr. Dirty Talking Swagger.

He's been thinking about me too, he says, his blue eyes dancing. He's been searching for me since that night.

And he wants to see me in his office...

Billionaire Boss is a steamy billionaire romance and the first book in the New York Billionaires series, starring the four Maddox brothers. Each book in the series is a complete standalone with a sexy fairy tale HEA.

New York Billionaires

Chapter One

"This is your hotel here, Dusty." My Uber driver, Earl, who I've learned on the twelve minute ride in from the Honolulu airport has been married to his high school sweetheart Marion for twenty-seven years, retired to Hawaii three years ago after Marion decided she could no longer handle the brutal Pittsburgh winters, has five grandchildren who visit for two weeks every Christmas and, as much as he loves seeing them, is always relieved when it's time for them to go. I even know their names: Huck, Brodie, Cassandra, Milo and Imogen. "It's the best hotel in Waikiki. No contest."

We pull up outside an unbelievably luxurious hotel with tall columns and a welcoming row of stately palm trees. The scene is as picture perfect as…well, as a life-long fantasy of being sent to Hawaii for a fully paid-for work trip can be.

Travel brochures and marathon binges of Hawaii Life don't really capture the neon turquoise of the water. Or the ideal temperature of the balmy, sea-scented air.

This place is unreal.

"Just wait until you see the views once you get inside," Earl tells me. "You're in for a treat. This is the oldest hotel in Oahu. The two towers on either side of the main building are the new additions, but the original hotel is where the charm is. The whole place is pure luxury."

"It's right on the beach?"

"Sure is. Best waterfront bar in Waikiki, hands down. An absolute magnet for love birds. I'm always giving rides to couples who are coming back to celebrate the place they first met, at least once a week. They're on their honeymoons, or they're here to celebrate their fifth, tenth or twenty-fifth wedding anniversaries. I once had this older couple coming back for their fiftieth. It's as if this place is spiking its drinks with aphrodisiacs and love potions. And you have that look to you." He winks at me in the rear view mirror.

"What look?"

"The starstruck one. The one that tells me your life is about to change."

I laugh lightly. "Oh, no, I'm just here for a conference."

"That's what they all say." He grins at me, then gets out to retrieve my bags.

I wriggle myself out of the backseat of the cab, no mean feat in the tight pencil skirt I poured myself into ten grueling hours ago. It was clearly the wrong choice for a hellish day of travel, but this is my first ever work trip and I was hoping to give the first impression of a put-together professional—a slightly crumpled one at this point, after a commuter flight from Austin to Houston, then eight and a half hours to Honolulu. I couldn't really rock up to the business class lounge in my usual jeans and cowboy boots, as tempting as that might have been. If I want to be taken seriously as a newly-minted financial advisor, straight out of college and fighting her way to the top of a dog-eat-dog, heavily male-dominated scene, I at least need to look the part.

I thank Earl, giving my best to Marion, Huck, Brodie, Cassandra, Milo and especially Imogen (who suffers from stage fright and has a piano recital next Thursday), immediately rate him five stars and give him a huge tip. "Bye, Earl."

"See you on your honeymoon," he winks.

I smile and wave as he drives away. Good old Earl.

As much as Earl might think of himself as an oracle, I laugh off his prediction. For better or worse, the circumstances of my life have made me a die-hard realist. Any romantic tendencies I might have been born with got trampled by ambition and circumstance a long time ago.

I heave my gigantic suitcase—because I've never been on a work trip *or* to Hawaii and you never know what you might need—up the ramp. God bless the genius who invented wheeled suitcases, is all I can say.

Walking into the lobby of the hotel, I have to stop for a minute just to take in the breath-taking view.

Woah.

There's a giant banyan tree (thank you, three a.m. googling sessions) in the middle of a scenic, wide-open courtyard. A glittering pool sits to its right and there's a restaurant with a colorfully-lit stage, even in broad daylight, where a musician is singing a Hawaiian classic I recognize.

Somewhere Over the Rainbow.

You can say that again.

It's so beautiful I feel like I'm hallucinating.

The bar is perfectly positioned under the majestic tree. Beyond that, the golden sand of Waikiki Beach and the twinkling blue water are as idyllic as a fantasy.

"Pretty spectacular, huh?"

A man is standing next to me. He's dressed in a suit and has reddish, thinning hair and eyes so pale blue he almost looks see-through. He checks me out before his gaze lands once again on my face.

Um, no.

"Are you here for the conference? I'm Brad Channing. I'm with Rothwell and Dodd Financials."

"Oh. That's…nice."

I'm beyond grateful when two of his colleagues walk over and hand him his key card. "Ogilvie wants to meet with us pronto," one of them says to him.

I take that as my cue to flee. "I better check in. Enjoy your stay." I make a beeline for the check-in desk before Brad can corner me with more chitchat. He glances back at me as he follows his colleagues outside.

Not a chance in hell, Brad. I'm definitely not here to get picked up by a junior assistant in a bad suit. My ambitions are on overdrive. Besides, I have way too much to achieve to get bogged down by a relationship, no matter what Earl might have joked about.

I wait in the check-in line. The hotel is busy with happy, relaxed people. Some are obviously here for the conference and are dressed in now-wrinkled business clothes, but most of the guests are wearing bathing suits and tropical prints. The more suntanned they are, the more relaxed they seem to be.

As I wait, I gaze out past the row of rocking chairs that line the deck, where people are reading books and sipping cocktails, to the beach and the cluster of surfers in the distance, catching wave after perfect wave. I'm already counting down the minutes until I can slip into my bikini and immerse myself blissfully into that blue, blue water.

I still can't believe this is *real.* I've flown business class to one of the most beautiful places in the world without having to pay a cent for any of it. In fact I'm being *paid* to be here.

Until a few hours ago, I'd only been out of the state of Texas once in my life.

The truth is, the struggles I watched my mother deal with my entire life have been implanted in my brain by now, and they motivate me to work like nothing else could, until the universe has no choice but to hoist me out of the rut my family seems to have been mired in for a long time. After my dad went AWOL when I was four years old, my mom and my older sister Skylar and I moved into our tiny bungalow in a lower-rent neighborhood (at the time, at least) of central Austin where my mother has lived ever since. She spent my childhood working day and night to meet our very basic needs. Both Sky and I started working as soon as we were old enough to help her.

And she did meet our basic needs. After searching for my dad but always coming up empty, she finally gave up. We later found out he'd changed his name—what a hero —then died in a drunk driving accident two years later.

So we made it work on our own, because we had no choice.

It was a struggle. We never had any extras. My mom used to make light of it and call it our no-frills lifestyle. We ate what we could afford, we had one pair of shoes each and we bought our clothes from thrift stores. When my friends took trips to Europe and vacationed in the Bahamas, I stayed at home with my paper route. When my classmates bought all the latest gadgets, I watched them play with them. And as I did, I set goals.

I read somewhere that you're 43% more likely to achieve your goals if you write them down. The room I shared with my sister was so decorated with Post-it notes, she complained. I started a dog-walking business when I was seven. I got a paper route when I was ten. I got a job in a coffee shop when I was twelve, working under the table until I turned fourteen. When I wasn't working, I was studying.

UT was within walking distance to our house, so I started going to the library there when I was in sixth grade, skimming my fingers along the rows of books, watching the college students with their stuffed-full tote bags, their shiny MacBooks and their colorful Longhorns merch. I vowed I would not only get accepted into UT, but also put myself through college, graduate near the top of my class, and land myself a job that would pay me enough money to help my family and make sure we no longer had to struggle so damn hard every single day of our lives.

And I've *done* it.

The way the sunlight is sparkling on the white-capped

blue waves is reminding me that all my hard work has finally paid off.

My new job might not be perfect but it's one step closer to the security I've always craved. My next goal: to land my dream job in New York City.

I visited my roommate from college in New York the summer after my freshman year and completely fell in love with the energy and the buzz of the place. I was enchanted by the look of it and the glamour. The opportunities to build something incredible out of your life had me hooked—that feeling that you're in the center of the world, where anything can happen. You could *feel* every lyric to all the songs that have been written about New York City. *Concrete jungle where dreams are made of. There's nothing you can't do. It's up to you, New York New York.* I wanted to be a part of it so badly I could taste it.

So I've been working my heart out every day since to get there.

"Next." The woman behind the desk smiles.

I step forward. "I have a reservation under Rose. Dusty Rose. I'm here for the Emerging Into Investments conference."

The receptionist types in my information. "You're here with Stellar Investments?"

"Yes, that's right."

"I'll just need your ID. The room is fully pre-paid."

She types in my info, sliding two plastic cards into an envelope. "Welcome to Hawaii, Ms. Rose. Your room is on the fourth floor. Number 417. Courtyard view, which is the best view, in my opinion. Here's your key and this card is a towel voucher. Swap it for a towel at the desk next to the pool and when you return it they'll give you a new card. Here's the finalized agenda for the conference, which is being held right across the street. And here's some information about the excursions and activities we offer if you have some downtime. Wi-Fi is complimentary and the elevator is right over there. Enjoy your stay."

"Thank you." My heart feels so full it might burst.

I find my way to the elevator, pressing the button for the fourth floor, charmed all over again by the surreal scene outside the open doors of the foyer, which leads to a bar area where a grand piano sits.

As the elevator takes me up, I scan the conference agenda. It's a two-day event with a jam-packed line-up of speakers, starting first thing tomorrow morning. At four-thirty each afternoon, the conference winds down, replaced by a cocktail hour.

My room is as beautiful as the rest of the hotel. There's a king-sized bed and tropical-themed art on the walls. Open French doors are framed by plantation-style shutters, leading out to a tiny Juliet-style balcony that looks out over the courtyard and beach. I can hear the live music.

After all the hours of studying, the exhausting internships, the working two jobs to pay my way through college: all of it—right here and right now—finally feels worth it.

For a second I just take it all in, wondering what it

would feel like to come back here on your one-year anniversary, or your twenty-fifth. To revisit this magical place and reminisce about that one weekend where it all began.

You've got that look to you.

I laugh to myself.

Sure I do.

Putting on my bikini, I tie a pink hibiscus-print wrap dress over it and head for the beach.

Chapter Two

Bzzzzz. Bzzzzz. Bzzzzz.

Reaching blindly for my phone alarm from under mountains of plush duvet, I turn it off, stretching luxuriously. *Wow,* this bed is comfortable. Note to self: as soon as you can afford to, invest in good bedding.

From my pile of goose feather pillows, I grab the day's agenda and scan through the schedule I chose.

- 7:30: Tropical Buffet
- 8:30: The Magic of Compounding Interest
- 10:00: Index Funds and Why You Need Them
- 11:30: Diversify Like a Pro
- 1:00: Tropical Buffet
- 2:00: Keynote Speaker Ty Dyson: Managing Stockholder Expectations [Please note that Mr. Dyson will be taking a few questions at 3:40 but will be unavailable after 4 pm]
- 4:30: Cocktail Hour Meet & Greet

The perfect day. Rung by bullet-pointed rung, I'm climbing my ladder. All the way to the freaking top.

I take a shower and put on the outfit I laid out.

I'm excited to see the keynote speaker, Ty Dyson. He's the CFO of a Seattle investment fund that was recently bought by one of my top three dream companies to work for in New York City. Invested Enterprises is run by three or four brothers who are investment geniuses.

My plan was to stick it out at my new job for at least a year before applying to New York companies, but now that I'm ready for my day, standing here on my little balcony with my view of the tropical blue sky and the ocean waves, I change my mind. Today, anything seems possible.

Why not apply now? If I could land a job in New York in six months instead of a year, I'll streamline my goals.

I decide to start applying as soon as I get back to Austin.

Checking my look in the mirror before I head downstairs, I pause for a few seconds. My two hours on the beach yesterday afternoon have already given me a sun-kissed glow.

Damn, girl, you look different in Hawaii than you do in Austin. You actually look like a confident professional. A CEO on the rise. A ball-breaker.

Which is good, except maybe for that last one. It's true that I have to be more than just self-assured in the industry I've chosen. A lot of my peers still see finance as a man's game, which in this day and age seems sort of ridiculous, but it's true. Today I'm going to need every ounce of confidence I can get.

I'm wearing an off-white skirt and a white silk top. It's professional-looking but also feminine. My curves aren't exactly being advertised but they're also not disguised. I can pretend I'm one of the guys or I can be exactly who I am: female, in a very man-heavy scene. I'm determined to make that a strength, not a weakness—which I've already learned plenty of men seem to think it is.

But I'll prove them wrong. I know I have enough grit to make it to the top or die trying.

By the time I get down to the restaurant, it's busy.

A buffet and allocated tables have been set up for the conference attendees. I help myself to some fruit and coffee at the buffet and find a small table at the far end of the terrace. The area is overrun by men in suits, laughing loudly.

There's barely a woman among them.

I missed the meet-and-greet drinks in one of the hotel's conference rooms last night, deciding to stay on the beach instead. After a life-transforming swim in the clear blue water, I laid on my beach towel for a while, just appreciating the sand on my skin, two slushy guava cock-tails from the bar (to die for) and my book. I was so blissed-out I couldn't tear myself away.

But now, I realize it might have been a mistake to not spend at least some of my evening with the rest of the delegates.

I'm not easily intimidated, but the testosterone level on this patio is as thick as my Kona double espresso.

Being a recent graduate in a new job is never easy, but one of the hardest things has been being treated like a naïve, mindless girl who knows nothing about the compli-cated, old-school mechanics of finance, or—worst of all —like a clueless piece of ass.

A couple of guys get up from the table next to mine, glancing over at me, checking me out. "I heard the Victo-ria's Secret conference is being held at the hotel down the street," one jokes.

I smile sweetly. "Which is why I'm wearing my edible thong and diamond-studded wonder bra under my power suit." Jerk.

The other men roar with laughter and the pack of them wander away.

Whatever.

I eat my (amazingly delicious) papaya in silence, giving myself a silent pep talk. Not everyone is that rude. I'm used to being underestimated, which I can handle. I'm young. And I know what I look like. Give me a couple of years and I'll be paying that guy's wages and deciding which one of his friends deserves a bonus or not.

To my relief, the day's workshops go better, only because everyone takes them seriously.

Each room I go into is full of people who are in fully-focused business mode. Ties have been straightened and new friendships put to one side as the sea of young and hungry attendees hang on every word of the speakers.

It feels good to be in a place where everyone has the same goals. I don't have to pretend to be unambitious or change my personality like I sometimes had to do in college. I can be the cool, corporate version of Dusty Rose, without worrying about being "likable" or "smiling more." I can focus on absorbing the kind of knowledge that will take me all the way to New York.

By the time I've sat through three back-to-back seminars and a keynote speech, my head is bursting with new information.

With the workshops done for the day, everyone heads to the beach bar. I'm about to join them when I see Brad and his friends. They're talking to the three guys who were sitting next to me at breakfast.

Wonderful.

And so I decide to pass on social hour. I've already

done my research. The only New York companies with delegates here at the conference have sent their lower-level employees. Like me. This conference is for people on the rise, not the ones who have already made it.

I *want* to be social. But I can't quite face the brigade of loud-mouthed macho men dominating the bar right now who are already well on their way to getting inebriated on the company credit card.

So, instead of joining them, I head back up to my room and put on the bikini I splurged on when I found out I was coming to Hawaii. I bought a plain black one-piece that I thought would be more professional if I hit the beach with any new acquaintances, but I couldn't help myself when I saw the tiny leopard print.

It may as well be Victoria's Secret, for all the coverage it gives me. It shows off every curve I own and then some. But I'm in *Hawaii*. I want to make the most of it. My olive skin tans easily and I'm looking forward to a few more hours of baking myself happily in the late afternoon sun.

I throw a pink cotton sundress over the top for the elevator ride, grab a hat, slip on my flip-flops and head down to the beach.

My bikini is definitely too risqué for the hotel's pool, where I might run into Brad and Co. So I wander a little further down the beach to find a place to swim. I park my towel and pull out my book.

I can still hear the hum of conversation from the beach bar, laughter and the sound of glasses clinking. A guy with dirty-blond dreadlocks is giving a surfing lesson to two kids nearby while their parents watch.

I take off my dress and wander into the water, which is the exact same temperature as the tropical air. I float there for a while, feeling like the luckiest person in the world. Maybe one day, after I've conquered New York City, I'll come back here. Maybe I'll buy a little condo near the beach.

Maybe I'll come back with my lover to celebrate at the beach bar where we first met.

Sure. Earl has lot to answer for, planting romantic ideas in my head when I'm the least romantic person on the planet. After my father left, I watched my mother not-quite-date a series of losers throughout my childhood. She was always wary of bringing men into our lives and I was grateful for that. Not one of them seemed like someone I hoped would stick around. And they never did. They left my mother just a little more disappointed, jaded and broken-hearted each time, and I watched her motivation to conquer life slowly leak away. They killed her dreams and, little by little, she allowed it.

So it was up to me to figure out my own dreams. I always knew that only one thing would get me where I needed to go: my own hard work. And there's only one person I can rely on to get me there: myself. So there's not much point daydreaming about things that will never happen. If Brad is the caliber of guys on offer at the beach bar, I'll pass.

I wander back onto dry land and lay on my towel, letting the sun dry my skin.

A shadow darkens the page I'm reading.

"Hey."

Shading my eyes, I look up to see the surf instructor grinning at me. His eyes are green and his skin is deeply tanned. He looks like the ocean is his one and only source of bathwater—not that he looks especially dirty. Just… salty. Earthy. He's probably around my age. "Hey."

"You want a free surf lesson?"

"Um. No thanks."

I try to go back to my book, but he sits, reclining next to me like we're old friends, not caring that he's getting covered in sand. "You ever surfed before?"

I don't reply right away, half hoping he'll take the hint. The one in which I'm not interested in being ogled by an admittedly cute surfer—if you happen to be into the kind of guy who lives out of his van and chases waves for a living. If I'd lived a different life, maybe. But, as it is, I'm a million miles from this guy's wavelength.

He's still grinning, waiting for me to answer his question.

I finally relent. "No. Never."

"Where are you from?"

"Texas."

"I tried surfing in Galveston once. Wouldn't recommend it."

"Yeah, it's not really known for its surf."

"I'm Lucas." He holds out his sandy hand.

I take it lightly. It would feel rude not to at this point. "Dusty."

"You here on vacation?"

"Conference." I give a little nod toward the hotel, where the party at the bar is gaining momentum.

"You look too young to be at a work conference," he comments. "Is this your first time in Hawaii?"

"Yes."

"How come you're not hanging out with the stiffs?" His question is ironic, like he already knows the answer to that question.

"I wasn't really feeling the whole getting-hit-on-by-Brad vibe."

He laughs. "Fair enough. Just to be clear, *I'm* not hitting on you. I'm only offering to give you a free surfing lesson."

"Thank you, but no. I'm just enjoying the beach."

"You'd enjoy it a lot more if you were out there catching your first wave. It's absolutely required as part of the full Hawaii experience."

"Honestly, I'm not…dressed for it." This bikini really is sort of skimpy.

"You're in *Waikiki* now, Dusty. Skin is good. Trust me, you won't regret your first feel of the power of the ocean underneath you. It's a religious experience. Seriously."

I bite my lip.

"Come on, Dust. You know you want to. It'll change your life."

Am I considering doing this? "I'd fall off."

"Luckily, if you do, you'll land in warm, tropical water that's only around four feet deep until way, way out. Can you swim?"

"Yes."

"Good. Let's go."

"You must have other customers."

"Nope." Lucas jumps up and goes over to his surfboard, placing it on the sand in front of me. "Your life is never the same again after you catch a wave. It changes *everything*. Your Karma, the way you manifest the rest of your future, your entire path."

Damn it, he really is sort of convincing. I *have* always wondered what surfing would feel like. And when he puts it like that, how can I not? "Are you sure you don't mind? You don't have other appointments?"

"I'm done for the day."

He's still smiling. Maybe surfing makes a person blindly happy. I have the sudden urge to find out.

"Okay," I finally say. I climb to my feet, following him to his surfboard. "I'll pay you. You don't have to do it for free."

"The hotel employs me. I could sit on my ass all day and not take a single lesson and still get paid. This will be purely for my own enjoyment." He seems harmless, and he's persuasive. "I love helping people get their first surfing rush. Watching people's lives changing right in front of your eyes is about as real as it gets." I can see why the hotel pays him without worrying about a schedule. I can't imagine he's ever short of customers. "And I promise not to hit on you like Brad," he adds.

"I could do without that, thanks."

"This is a spiritual lesson and nothing more."

"Thank you."

"You're welcome. Now that we've gotten that out of the way, come over here and stand on this board."

"I've never even been near a surfboard before, so you might need to lower your expectations."

"I don't have any expectations, but if I did, you've already exceeded them. You're by far the most beautiful girl on this beach." More grinning. "Oh, shit, did I just break our rule?"

"I think you might have, yeah."

He shakes his head and his long dreadlocks swing. There are little beads on the ends of a few of them. "Okay. Sorry. Forget I said that. Now, watch me. Stand like this, in the middle, arms out but not too far. Feet like this. Get your balance. Everyone has the urge to lean back but I want you to do the opposite. Lean into it."

I spend the next hour learning how to get my balance. And then I follow Lucas out, paddling like he does. And then I proceed to spectacularly fail to stand on a live, moving surfboard as it jettisons me at what feels like a hundred miles an hour over open water.

I try a dozen times but it's much harder than it looks.

"One more," Lucas hollers from where he's sitting on his own surfboard. "You almost had it that time. Do it again."

"Maybe I'm not cut out for this!" I holler back at him.

"You are! You almost had it. Get your footing. Lean into it. Here comes a good one. Go!"

I paddle as the wave approaches me and, just as it starts to crest underneath me, I stand up. I lean into it, getting my balance.

And just like that, I'm surfing.

I'm standing on top of the wave as it carries me along its rolling surge and Lucas was right. It's the best feeling I've ever had in my goddamn life. In this moment, I feel like the most powerful person in the world.

I can hear Lucas cheering as he surfs in behind me.

I lose my balance and fall off.

But as I climb onto my surfboard and let the waves take me back to shore, that taste of magic has transformed me. My limits have been obliterated. I'm as invincible as the forces of nature.

Whoa. Would you listen to yourself?

Lucas follows me back onto the beach and sets his surfboard on the sand next to mine. "That was awesome, Dusty. You're a natural."

I'm still buzzing and breathless. "You were right."

"Surfing's the source," he says simply, and I can't help sort of agreeing with him. "And now you can watch your life explode with good energy. I'd offer you another lesson tomorrow but I'm headed up to the North Shore tonight to see some friends. Want to come?"

I laugh. "No. Thanks. I've got the conference tomorrow."

"Ditch the conference."

I wrap my towel around myself. Lucas watches me do this. For a split second, still riding my high, the thought flickers through my mind: I could cash in my way overdue V-card with a random surfer while on a work trip in Hawaii. I could attend my last day of the conference as a newly-experienced, take-life-by-the-(literal)-balls sex goddess, with adrenaline still spiking through my veins from both joyrides.

And never see him again.

Objectively, he's a good-looking guy—all dimples and bright eyes.

But there's no part of me that wants to jump the conference ship and sail away with Mr. Waikiki. If anything, catching that wave only ramped up my ambition. *I can surf.* Which means I can do anything.

I decide I won't ask Lucas to do me the honors. As nice as he is, I'm not feeling any real chemistry. Besides, I don't do casual relationships—which is part of the reason I'm still a virgin at the advanced age of twenty-three.

I had plenty of attention from guys in college. But most of them were only interested in partying non-stop and talking endlessly about beer and football.

My roommate Emma told me the first time is always terrible anyway. Emma's advice was to rip off the band-aid with any random stranger and then find someone you're crazy about to help you get good at it.

But to me that sounded like terrible advice. I could never quite bring myself to follow it. I always felt like there should be something more to that first time than mechanics and just getting it "out of the way."

Or maybe I'm an idiot for making it into a big deal when it isn't. It's just sex, according to Emma.

The fact that it's been so hard to find any kind of genuine connection with a guy has made me wonder if something's wrong with me. Maybe I'm just too picky. There doesn't need to be fireworks and instant electricity, does there? I guess that's what Emma meant. A spark could turn into a bonfire, given long enough.

But I've never felt more than a flicker for anyone. Not even once.

Even now. "I can't ditch the conference, Lucas. But thanks for the lesson. Really."

"You'll remember me for the rest of your life. This is the day everything started to change for you. You'll see."

"I hope you're right," I laugh. "Have fun on the North Shore."

"You sure you don't want to come?"

"I'm sure. Enjoy those waves." He makes a sort of sad face and I smile at him, turning to make my way back to the hotel. "Bye, Lucas."

"See you around, Dust." He wanders up the beach to where his van is parked.

You should have gone with it. He was cute.

No.

I want to *feel* it. *All* of it.

I want to get totally freaking swept away.

Maybe it doesn't happen that way. Maybe you never will.

I guess I need to come to terms with the fact that it'll probably never happen like that for me. Maybe I'm just too focused on my career for any kind of relationship at all.

I head back up the beach toward the hotel's patio. As I get closer, I feel the heat of someone's gaze and I glance up at the raised table with the best view.

A man is sitting there. He's wearing a suit, and sunglasses. His tie is loosened and the top button of his shirt is undone. It's immediately obvious that his suit is expensive and beautifully cut. A far cry from the polyester Brad and his cronies favor. This guy's probably wearing Armani and it fits him in a way you can't help but stare at. There's something ideal about it.

There's something ideal about *him.*

My stomach does a funny little flip.

An iPad is in front of him on the table but its screen isn't lit up. His eyes are on me.

As I walk past him, he slides his glasses up, as though to get a better look.

"Impressive," he drawls.

At first I'm not entirely sure he's talking to me. I glance behind me and a smile quirks at the corner of his mouth. "Sorry?" I finally say.

"The surfing. Not bad for a first try."

"How did you know it was my first try?"

"Just a guess."

Was he watching the whole time?

"You didn't click with Surfer Boy?" His voice is deep

and has a smoky husk to it that causes the tiny hairs on my arms to rise.

Wow.

He's all swagger. He has thick dark hair and eyes that match the color of the ocean water. His lashes are too long for a man, especially one that's so…*male.* They give him an almost romantic appeal.

He's sexy without even trying. He's got the cool, animal confidence of a lion surveying its territory. Big and cocky and fully comfortable in his own skin.

But I'm in too good a mood to be intimidated by him. "Oh, I clicked with Surfer Boy. He gave me the best ride of my life."

His low laugh does things to the low pit of my stomach…fluttery things that send little currents of warmth… lower.

I bet he smells good. I bet he's rough.

His handsomeness is rugged and seasoned. He might be in his late twenties or close to thirty. Compared to Lucas, this guy oozes *alpha*-ness on a level that's almost absurd. "I could give you better," he replies casually, his blue eyes dancing.

This makes me smile. "You think so?"

"I'm free tonight if you want me to prove it."

I laugh before I can hold it back. Talk about arrogant. "Thanks for the offer, but I'm busy tonight."

"Doing what?" His mouth is made for the kind of sin I haven't yet managed to get up close and personal with. I don't know how I know this, but I do.

"I'm afraid that's none of your business." *Cuddling up with Colleen Hoover in my California-king-sized helping of Egyptian cotton, thank you very much.*

"Have a drink with me."

I keep walking, flustered by the sheer magnetism radiating off the man. Something about the look of him, the slow smile, the Rolex—ugh, he's obviously loaded—are freaking me out. I know for a fact he's right. He *could* give me better. I don't know much about anything but even *I* know that. "Maybe another time."

My pulse flutters. A low heat simmers. Some sixth sense whispers: *him. He's the kind of guy you want to cash in your V-card with. Right there.*

I keep walking.

The last thing I need right now is a one-night stand with a smug, bossy ego-maniac who's probably got a wife and kids back in Connecticut.

I try to silence the voice of my inner sex goddess— who doesn't get the opportunity to make appearances very often but here she suddenly freaking is—and right now she's insisting: *what you need is to get thoroughly laid by that big, sexy tomcat.*

Shit. I'm getting…*hot.* Just from the heated gaze of a total stranger.

I feel…tingly and…*wet.*

Before I do something I'll wildly regret, I head toward the lobby, glancing back at him once more.

He's still watching me and he has a sort of dejected

look on his face. Mixed with all that alpha gorgeousness, his disappointment is almost…cute.

I hurry inside to the elevator, pressing the fourth floor button.

I get to my room and order room service and a glass of champagne because I feel reckless and it's a better option than jumping into bed with the loaded Casanova downstairs.

Is it?

Yes.

I have a lot to celebrate.

I surfed today. I learned things.

I saw a real live alpha male in the wild.

I congratulate myself on my restraint. Of course I'd regret a one-night stand with a random stranger. Even if it was the first time in my life my body has *reacted* to a man like that, that doesn't mean I'm cut out for sex without strings. I'm a girl on a mission. I need to keep my eye on the ball.

I've made the right decision.

No, you haven't! He would have been an absolute BEAST in bed. How often do you come across men who have I WILL GIVE YOU LOTS OF ORGASMS practically tattooed across their forehead?

By the time I mentally shoo my inner sex goddess away and sit out on my balcony, glass in hand as I peek down at the table at the far end of the patio, Mr. Swagger is gone.

ALSO BY JULIE CAPULET

I Love You Series

The Obsession Begins (free)

XOXO I Love You

XOXX I Love You More

Love You the Most (free)

Sexy Standalones

Max

Cowboy

McCabe Brothers Series

Hopeless Romantic

My Hero

Arrogant Player

Music City Lovers Series

Nashville Days

Nashville Nights

Nashville Dreams

Nashville Lights

Hawthorne U Series

Lovestruck

Paradise Series

Devil's Angel

Wild Hearts

New York Billionaires Series

Billionaire Boss

Billionaire Grump

Billionaire Devil

Billionaire Romantic

Standalone Rom-com

Beautiful Savages

ABOUT THE AUTHOR

Julie Capulet is an Amazon top 20 bestselling author of contemporary romance. She writes steamy he-falls-first romance with heart, heat and fairy tale HEAs. Her stories are inspired by true love and she's married to her own real life hero. When she's not writing, she's reading, traveling, walking on the beach and watching rom-coms.

www.juliecapulet.com

www.ingramcontent.com/pod-product-compliance
Lightning Source LLC
Chambersburg PA
CBHW022014300726

48970CB00003B/881